my mind has been the most discontented
and restless one that was ever
put into a body too small for it

—john keats

how do I know?
because my little man tells me.
… the little man in here

—barton keyes, *double indemnity*

ADJUSTMENTS

a novel

will willingham

T. S. Poetry Press • New York

T. S. Poetry Press
Ossining, New York
Tspoetry.com
© 2019, Will Willingham

Cover image by Linda Tanner.
http://www.flickriver.com/photos/goingslo/popular-
interesting/

ISBN 978-1-943120-37-6

Library of Congress Cataloging-in-Publication Data:
Willingham, Will
        [Fiction. Midwest stories. Insurance stories. Manhood.
            Romance. Friendship.]
        Adjustments: A Novel/Will Willingham
        ISBN 978-1-943120-37-6
        Library of Congress Control Number: 2019914699

to will, who let me tell his story before I knew I shared his name

to laura, who seemed to know everything before I did

1

What does an old man need with a pair of roller skates?

Like a lot of things, this was something Will would trouble over, but never know. Yet there they were, scuffed gray leather, hanging by frayed laces on a dusty walnut church kneeler just inside the front door.

The old man was on the phone, and Will noticed that he favored his left side when he walked away after letting Will in the door. Will knew the old man didn't use the skates. He could see Joe praying, yes. (Standing up.) Skating, no.

Joe Murphy had called twice to reschedule their appointment after all, saying he'd thrown his back out a couple of weeks ago and was laid up so he hadn't been able to do any housekeeping. Will appreciated his good intentions. Most folks don't see the need to tidy up for a claim adjuster. Isn't that the whole point—that a house would be a mess after a sudden brush with fire or water? He hardly even noticed anymore, cutting through cobwebs or stepping over underpants lying on the floor, legs open, right where someone had walked out of them on the way to the shower or bed.

But then again, he thought, maybe Joe *did* roller skate. Maybe that's how he'd hurt himself, practicing some sort of spin move on inline poly wheels on the narrow paved road crossing in front of his faded green bungalow, like it was perfectly normal for seventy-five-year-old men to do this in a quiet farming town. He probably even had a widowed neighbor named Midge who practiced her belly dancing behind a walker on the front lawn.

Not much surprised Will anymore. "Leaky roof, single story," the dispatch note from Mad Dog had said. "Keep it simple. You'll be back by noon."

"Right," he typed back. "Noon next Friday."

The only predictable thing about working claims with Mike "Mad Dog" Delaney was that Will could predict *nothing*. Odds were, Hurricane Camille herself had resurrected after all these years and was coming his way, all dressed up in the straight line skirt of a supposed open and shut case.

He remembered the day Mad Dog said, "Leaky drain pipe. How hard can it be?" The next thing he knew, he was suited up in his coveralls crawling in the mud under the double-wide through spider webs thick enough to hide your grandmother, with the angry homeowner standing outside wielding a hammer, threatening to nail the skirting shut and leave him inside with the snakes and rats.

When a guy's day could start with a man falling asleep with a cigarette watching Colbert and starting his bed on fire, or a woman having a heart attack behind the wheel and crashing her car into the side of the local hunting lodge, her last breath exploding through safety glass and into a brick wall, the element of surprise got harder and harder to come by.

~

Will Phillips had been an adjuster for as long as he could remember. And before that, he'd dreamed of it. Saturday afternoons when his friends were playing tackle football in the vacant lot, he was watching *Double Indemnity* in black and white. When no one was home he'd sneak into a three-piece suit and tie from his father's closet and lean across the kitchen table like it was a big wooden desk, making believe he was his hero Barton Keyes lecturing Sam Garlopis about insurance fraud. He'd tousle his hair and hold a Tootsie Roll between his fingers, punching it into the air like Keyes' stubby cigar. *Every month hundreds of claims come to this desk. Some of them are phony. And I know which ones,* he'd say, staring at Garlopis until he squirmed. *How do I know? Because my little man tells me. … The little man in here.* He'd turn his thumbs to point to his chest and then slip them into the vest behind the gray pinstripe lapels before he turned to look out the window, pausing to put a little more heat on his imaginary Garlopis.

Will wanted to be an adjuster someday, a job no one else he knew had ever sought on purpose. He would learn to listen to his own little man.

He interned with La Salle Mutual in Chicago during college, and by his 25th birthday had a desk of his own downtown, smoked three packs a day and kept a fifth of bourbon in his bottom right desk drawer which he never drank before 2:45 in the afternoon.

Images of that gray cityscape out his 16th story window filled his mind when Joe Murphy had said he retired early from the Chicago fire department with a herniated disc. Will considered the coincidence, that they both left the city for these flatlands where every distance is measured by how many miles it is from the old Johnson place that burned down back in 1978. He decided it was just that: a coincidence.

The old man ended his call and slipped his phone into his pocket, apologizing again for the mess. "I'm working on an addition to the house so I have a place to put all this stuff."

He waved his arms as though to take all of it in.

Joe Murphy shuffled through the dining room to the living room, and a puff of dust hung low to the ground with each movement. Will suspected he left a trail too, but didn't turn to look. His nostrils burned with the ammonia of cat urine and he nearly stumbled over the calico that wove between his feet while he walked. Murphy dropped himself into an easy chair, the nubby boucle pattern worn bare on the arms and seat. Will looked around for another place to sit. A large golden retriever lolled across the davenport, layers of fur covering the back and arms and piled on the floor in front making clear that it was a davenport for one. He decided to stand where he was, which might mean not having to brew himself a flea dip when he got home.

That the old firefighter was well groomed seemed out of place. His polo shirt and Wrangler jeans were clean and pressed, his hair combed, his white sneakers laced and tied. He had a manicured green lawn and clean-swept sidewalks. A polished black Silverado pickup sat in the driveway. But every visible inch of space inside the house was covered with thick gray dust and stack upon stack of collected miscellany. The dining room table was piled with unopened packages of lightbulbs, a dozen boxes of golf balls, books, cartons of paper cups. Most of the packaging was hard to make out because of the dust film.

With his throat tightening against competing odors, Will reached for his work gloves in his back Levis pocket, wishing to add one more layer of separation between himself and the space he'd entered.

To his left he noted a Hammond organ. Its keys were littered with greasy brown *x*'s and *o*'s, morsels spilled from the cat dish next to the music rack on top. The organ was the same as he remembered from the den in his childhood home on Dupont Street. He reluctantly stuffed the gloves back into his pocket and stepped to the side of the organ, leaning his hip against it. He crossed his feet in front of him. With his open, ungloved palm pressed against the frame next to the keys, he turned to look at Murphy, who was petting a gray cat in his lap, just behind the ears.

~

Why would a guy like Murphy suddenly decide to call in a claim? His house—piled high with collected junk, cat litter, and dog hair—was slowly eating itself from the inside, its habitable space growing a tiny bit smaller every day. He said he'd peeled the carpet out ten years ago, but never got around to replacing it. Putty colored wallpaper was blistered and cracked on two walls and stripped to the wainscot on another, leaving the plaster exposed. From the looks of the kitchen, he hadn't fixed a meal in his house since the 1990s.

An ice dam built up on his roof last winter, and Joe Murphy ended up with a small leak in his living room. The faint line of brownish discoloration, not even three feet long, would be barely noticeable under the most meticulous housekeeping. But six months later, Murphy said, he's leaning back in his chair petting the cat and sees it. A glaring eyesore, he called it, and it kept him up at night.

The old man eased the cat to the floor and got up from his chair.

"Hey, come over here and help me, would you?"

Will followed him to the built-in oak cabinet next to the fireplace. A painted ceramic Madonna, supported by cobwebs strung between the wall and her baby-blue shoulders, stared down at them from the mantle while Murphy leaned into the cabinet. He pulled out a leather case and set it on a chair. A cloud went up from the orange velour seat cushion, like a giant smoke ring.

He fingered the latches but didn't open them. "I've been worried all that water got in back here. You're going to love this little girl."

Will cursed himself under his breath. He should never have let the old man sit down. He would pay for his split-second lapse of sociability with Murphy on stage for an afternoon of show and tell.

The old man exhaled and flipped the latches with his thumbs, in perfectly timed unison. He lifted the top and stared inside, then slowly ran his rough hands along the red crushed velveteen.

"I haven't played her in ten years," he said, as he lifted a white squeeze box from the case. "She's a hundred years old. I've got two others, but she's the most beautiful of the lot."

He shuffled back across the room, cradling the German concertina in his arms. Then he dropped himself into his chair and touched each of the pearl inlaid keys. "You know the old carousel horses?" he asked.

"I do," Will said.

"Then listen."

Damn, Will thought. He looked at his watch.

Murphy closed his eyes and started playing. Will turned

toward the kitchen, certain that polka dancers were just waiting to spin out in a row of rounded skirts and beehive hairdos.

The dancers didn't come, but the old man kept playing.
He opened his eyes. "I don't read music, you know."

"What then," Will asked. "I suppose you just feel it?"

"Something like that," Murphy said and closed his eyes
again, smiling like a man who had never smiled before.

Will took his phone from his pocket and tapped a quick
text to Mad Dog.

*Job bigger than you thought. Reschedule afternoon calls. Damn fool
will take all day.*

He wondered if Murphy was one of those lonely folks
who concocted reasons for someone to visit. One day it was
the plumber, the next day the electrician. Today was Wednes-
day, a perfect day for the claims guy, just to have someone in
the house. It was like those widows who lived in his granddad's apartment building and always had some complaint
about a small appliance gone haywire and called Clarence to
fix it. He was famous for his handyman skills, and ever since
Grandma had passed on, a half dozen or so women set their
sights on Tucson's oldest most eligible bachelor. Usually it was
a matter of tightening a light bulb or just plugging in the "broken" appliance while the damsel in a fancy new dress and fresh
coat of "Besos Red" lipstick batted her eyelashes and said,
"Oh, silly me." He saw the ruse, but wasn't above enjoying a
slice of pound cake and coffee in exchange.

But the old man? It was hard to see where anybody besides
Murphy had been in this house in years. Even a plumber or
electrician.

Will unclipped his tape from his belt. He fiddled with the

tab absentmindedly, pulling out a few inches and letting it spin back into the case with a small thwack. He tried to match it to the old man's rhythm, failing every few times. Will had no good sense of rhythm. In his junior high marching band days, he was given a pair of cymbals to carry, one tucked ceremoniously under each arm. *Whatever you do,* his band director had told him, *don't let the plates touch each other.*

Cymbals were meant to crash, but for the privilege of wearing the uniform, Will fought against the magnetic force that seemed determined to pull the two together. In truth, it was really the hat. He liked the mystery of the tall furry hat sitting just above his eyes, obscuring them slightly. And he liked the spats over his shiny black shoes, for no real reason at all.

During the homecoming parade in 8th grade, Will lost the battle with magnetism and allowed the very top gold edges of the plates to skim each other. He hoped no one heard it, but then felt the thump of Randy Dalbright's trombone slide on the back of his head. It hit just right to open the spit valve, and he felt Randy's cold saliva run down his neck.

"Left! Left!" Randy hissed. "Your other left, Loser." He bumped Will's hat with the slide on every downbeat. Will had gone out of step and never could tell his right from his left under pressure, so he hop-skip-stumbled through the rest of *Hit the Road Jack,* trying to regain his stride while his left shoulder rolled forward and back resisting the trickle of spit now making its way down his spine. He tried not to let the cymbals touch when he raised his right hand to move his hat out of his eyes.

After the parade, Will hid in a practice room until everyone had gone, then folded up his uniform and set it on Mr. Reeve's desk. He wrote a note in red pen on the back of a hall pass and set it under the hat, polishing a smudge off the onyx brim with the cuff of his shirt:

> *I never did like music anyway.*
> *William Phillips*

~

Murphy stopped playing and Will let go about six inches of tape into the case with a loud snap. Something about wearing a tape on his belt made him feel stronger, more rugged. Some guys used a laser measuring device, but Will always figured those pansy-asses just wanted to take the easy way. Anybody could point and click at the red dot on the wall. Will used a Mighty Max, heavy duty, and replaced it every six months to keep it tight. On quiet afternoons in the office he'd lean back in his chair with his feet crossed on top of his desk and ease the tape inch by inch into the air to see how far he could stretch before it collapsed. His record with the Mighty Max was 13′ 2″ even though the tape was only rated to twelve feet. It took patience and a steady hand to push it along another foot. He was sure he could get another two inches out of it but every time he tried lately, Mad Dog hollered something from across the hall and startled him, so the tape would collapse.

Will went to the corner where Murphy's water stain was and moved a small stack of boxes to the side to get within reach, then extended his tape above the built-in bookcase. He rounded up to four feet and shook his head at the idea of patching and painting this tiny corner space, considering the rest of the room looked like it had already had that encounter with Hurricane Camille back from the dead. He scratched the numbers onto a sheet of quadrille paper on his clipboard and flicked his pencil back into his shirt pocket.

This would be a good time to shake Murphy's hand and say, "I've got to do my paperwork. I'll be in touch."

But the old man was way ahead of him.

"I've got a real mess in my garage."

"Your garage?"

"Don't know what happened there, maybe there's a hole in the roof. Come on," Murphy said. He waved Will toward the back door. "Let's have a look."

Will glanced at his watch again. It didn't make a difference now, but maybe the old man would get the hint. He clipped his tape back on his belt and stuck his clipboard back in his bag, then picked up his gear and followed.

Murphy had a small breezeway between the kitchen and the garage. Inside, the sheetrock was falling off the outside wall, and square acoustic tiles had fallen one by one from the ceiling and littered the floor. Will ran a finger along the drywall as he stepped down the short set of stairs. It was soft, damp. A speckled black pattern had made its way along all of the edges and matched the strong moldy smell when Murphy opened the door.

"When did this happen?" Will asked.

"Gosh, I don't know. I never go back here, it's such a mess. Probably November. Maybe December. But there was too much snow on the roof to check it out."

"That's six months ago. Did you call your insurance guy?"

"Well, no. I didn't think much of it. Forgot all about it until you came. I was just so worried about all that water in my living room."

"Worried." Will nodded. "Yeah, sure."

He wondered about Murphy's sense of perspective. A barely visible water stain kept him up at night. Walls and ceilings collapsing were entirely forgettable. And they weren't even to the garage yet.

Will pulled out his tablet and penciled a quick sketch, then took his tape and measured up the walls.

The old man pushed past him and opened the door. The garage space had finished walls and a high ceiling, large enough to hold two vehicles, but his Silverado pickup sat outside in the driveway, subjected to harsh prairie elements while cases of diapers and deodorant and boxes of old clothes and dishes sat protected under the roof. The graying walls were stained brown from water running behind the sheetrock, the oval and horseshoe-shaped discoloration looking almost like the plain surface was morphing into wood grain. The drywall on the ceiling sagged over half the space, weight of water-soaked insulation pressing down and wishing to be set free. Piles of Murphy's accumulated wealth in irresistible flea market grabs left once-stiff cardboard caving under water's softening effects. Joe didn't seem to notice.

"Look over here," he said. "I bought these shelves to put my books in but they're ruined."

Will turned around. The old man had a half dozen sets of bookcases from KMART, unassembled and still in the packaging. He was right. They would be useless after sitting wet for six months, pressed wood soaking up moisture like a sponge.

"I haven't even moved my full library from Chicago yet.

I'm going to build an addition to hold it. My brother will help me."

So the old man had family. A brother, at least. This was good. Will wondered when was the last time this brother came to visit.

He took a few pictures of the walls, ceilings, boxes. He eyeballed the length of the garage but didn't bother to get out his tape. Most times, he used it for show. He could estimate visually within six inches. Will was tired.

"Do you know Ivan Rebroff?" the old man asked.

"Rebroff? Haven't heard of him. Is he your contractor?"

"No, no. Rebroff. *R-e-b-r-o-f-f.* Write it down. You'll want to look him up later."

The old man's eyes flickered brighter than the twitchy garage fluorescents should have allowed. Will smiled from one side of his face. "Let me guess. He sings or something."

"He sings? Oh, he sings! In a four-octave range. Are you done in there? Let's go listen."

Murphy was already in the breezeway waving his arms and remembering the night he heard Rebroff live in Paris.

Will wiped a hand down his face and let out a deep sigh. He looked up at the ceiling and let his shoulders sag. He patted the wall as he trudged past. "You're here every day, huh?"

He found the old man in the living room rummaging through a pile of CDs, where he finally pulled the one he was after and pushed it into his player.

Ivan Rebroff's bass reverberated off dingy walls while Will let the old man go on about the singer's history as though they had studied voice together in the day. As the song reached its end, Murphy put a finger to his lips to hush himself midsentence and pointed the other hand toward the sound of Rebroff's aria. He tipped back his head, stretched out his arms and directed the final measures.

The old man stood frozen in time as he and Rebroff held the last clear note. Will knew he had slipped away to the opera house of his mind.

He walked quietly to the kitchen to see if Murphy had any coffee and two clean cups.

2

Will stopped at the kitchen entrance, hands on his hips, and stared. Newspapers stood stacked on one counter, from the gold-flecked Formica top to the overhead cabinet. On the other, a half dozen boxes of heavy duty trash bags, a Hamilton Beach Blend-Pro still in the box, empty Kool Whip containers with a random assortment of screws and wing nuts and a tangle of wire. The rest of the space and the double sink were filled with leaning piles of plates, cups, and saucepans, coated with a rough black film, making it impossible to guess the last meal eaten from any of them.

He opened a cupboard. Empty. He opened another. Two flowered melamine plates and an empty sugar jar. He opened a third and found seven cans of chicken and rice soup with red and white labels, lined in a row. Will picked one up and turned it over. "Sell by Aug 2006." He put it back and closed the door. He wouldn't open the refrigerator.

Will walked instead back through the dining room and saw Joe in his shabby chair, hands folded across his belly, leaning his head back with a peaceful smile.

"I'll be right back," he said, and stepped out the front door.

Eight years ago, Will traded his white Toyota truck for his blue Ford F350 pickup. He'd been partial to the old Toyota, but out here a guy was frowned upon for driving an import. He'd had too many grinning farmers tip back their feed store caps and twirl toothpicks with their tongues threatening to send the dogs after him if he drove that un-American piece of shit onto their property. He decided it was bad for business. Maybe even bad for his health.

Oh, those guys looked genial enough in their brown Carhartt coveralls and flannel shirts while they meandered out to show Will the grain bin where that wind last July tore the metal clean off. But he'd seen enough of those same mild mannered fellas take pokes at each other after a couple of drinks at Marvelle's Bar downtown because one of them drove a red tractor instead of the most high and holy green. He decided it wasn't worth the risk, and let the old girl go.

He wasn't fond of Ford anymore than Chevy or Dodge, a distinction these farmers made nearly as strongly as between John Deere and International. But Will liked that the trucks were numbered, not named. It was simple, orderly. And made sense. An F350 is bigger than an F150. Nothing like misappropriated names of places or cultures like Tahoe or Dakota. The names didn't mean anything about a truck, but marketers with whopping Superbowl ad budgets pretended they did.

Will kept his truck equipped like his office. Even like a small house on the road. Once he left the office, he never knew when he'd get back. He had his computer and a portable printer/scanner so he could upload from the field if he had to. He carried audio and video recording equipment in case he had to conduct an interview or stage impromptu surveillance. He always tossed a gym bag with a change of clothes in the back, and carried his old red and white cooler full of sandwiches, chips and Twinkies.

He reached into the cooler and grabbed a bag of chocolate chip cookies his landlady had given him the day before, then reached for his thermos on the passenger seat. He shook it.

"Hmm. Might be two cups left."

Back inside, he found Joe just as he left him, still lost in Rebroff's faded echo. Will pulled a wooden chair from the dining room table and swatted it a couple of times with his gloves to clear the seat. He carried it to the living room and set it next to Joe's chair, then set the cookies and thermos on the side table and grabbed a package of Styrofoam cups he'd seen earlier.

"Hope you like your coffee dark, Joe," he held out a cup. "I brew it a little stiffer than the girls down at the café."

The old man opened his eyes. Something crossed Joe's face. Will wasn't sure what, and wondered if the color of the old man's eyes had shifted just a little, from the green that twinkled over Rebroff to something more like the gray dust of the room. Joe glanced at the floor, and then popped up his head and took the cup with a playful grin.

"I don't suppose you brought along any cream?" He winked, and put the cup to his lips.

~

Will took the long way home. The day was already shot anyway. And after an afternoon of entertainment by the old man and his musical stylings, Will was shot too. He wouldn't go back to the office. He could file Joe's report early enough in the morning.

The GPS on his dash erupted in digitized vocal panic when Will drove past the on-ramp for the interstate highway and its straight line home. Taking the old highway would add 45 minutes to the drive, meandering through every tiny town in the valley.

"Make a U-turn!" the little box harped.

"No, thank you" Will said softly, looking out the side window toward the purplish Coteau hills lining the horizon.

"Make a U-turn!" It seemed more emphatic this time.

"Make your own damn U-turn, Barbara." He yanked the cord from the socket and flung it against the passenger seat. "I'm taking the scenic route."

Will couldn't go anywhere without the GPS. He didn't even know his left from right without thinking of which hand he put on his heart. Back in junior high Home Ec class he had to write the letters *L* and *R* on the back of his hands to make sure he didn't serve from the wrong side of the table. Old Mrs. Waverley would make him stay after for reaching in from the right. Figuring directions that didn't correspond to a side of his body was impossible. He couldn't choose east from west without a compass.

He and the directional gadget spent so much time together on the road he had named her Barbara. He needed her, but their relationship was full of rancor. She was always telling him what to do, and he was always not doing it.

"You're just here for backup," he would say to her. "The farmer gave me good directions this time." He knew, though, that there wasn't a farmer in six counties who could give directions a city boy could follow. Barbara had saved him more than once on an old dirt road late at night. He'd taken to always asking the farmer for a landmark to tell him he'd gone too far. Even so, he was regularly driving past the old school house or fireworks stand or electrical substation anyway, or when a guy told him to go south "another four or five miles after that big curve by the stock pond," always going ten miles or so, never quite sure which curve was the big one.

He drove past the green highway sign announcing that he was entering Erin Springs, pop. 99. He'd worked in this town a few months ago. A customer had cleaned out his truck one Sunday afternoon and left the doors open to air out. He came back out after dark and shut the doors for the night. In the morning, turned out, he'd trapped a raccoon in the cab. Turns out a raccoon can do an awful lot of damage to a pickup cab overnight.

The man had called him when he was a couple of miles from town, saying he'd meet him because the best roads to his place were washed out from the heavy rains.

"Sounds great," Will said. "Where should I meet you?"

"Oh, don't you worry," the farmer said. "I'll see you when you come to town."

Will had turned left between the Prairie Dog Supply store and the grain elevator, the only road into town. Main Street looked to be about two blocks. He saw a half dozen pickups but none with drivers. A couple of guys in faded coveralls and feed store caps leaned on the rail outside the Old Timers Café. He drove slowly along the street, feeling like there may as well have been a sniper on the water tower with binoculars. He finally pulled up in front of the Farmers and Merchants Bank and parked. As he took his phone out of the holster and pulled up his contacts, he felt a shadow crawl up on his left side. He turned and saw a man outside his window, grinning ear to ear under his camouflage Ranger cap. Jimmy was friendly enough, but Will couldn't shake the creepy feeling of having driven into a *Twilight Zone* episode, 99 sets of eyes peering on him that he couldn't see.

Erin Springs now in his rearview mirror, he shook it off and kept driving. Soon, Vendry Tower stood out his side window. He'd always wanted to climb it one day but never seemed to have the time when he came by. He'd heard a guy could see three states from the top.

Will parked in the gravel lot, unplugged his phone from the charger and slipped it into the holster. He locked his car and dropped the keys in his pocket, a habit he kept even here where there wasn't another living soul for twenty miles. He skipped over the murals on the wall and readings in the interpretive center. He didn't care much for interpretive nonsense, just wanted to get on with whatever he was doing, not listen to someone else's explanation of a thing. Passing through the commons, he went on to climb the stairs.

Three flights in, he was breathing hard and his legs felt like jelly. *Come on, old man. You can do this.* He fought an urge to turn back and stood by the rail, looking out at the prairie sprawling. *Nope, you're going all the way up so I don't have trees in my view.* Will wished for a cigarette and a drink and felt older than he thought a forty-five-year-old ought to. Taking a long break after flights four and five, he told himself the view would be spectacular. Something in him kept pushing, though he was wheezing now, struggling to lift a foot as high as the next step.

He made it to the sixth level and slumped to the ground, his back to the rail and his butt on the rough wood. It felt cool through his jeans. He hung his hands over his bent knees and rasped out short hard breaths, feeling as though his chest might break open and his heart spring out like a jack-in-the-box.

Will needed to cut back on the cigarettes. Barbara had told him that. The real Barbara, not the black box that perched on his dashboard. He only smoked a pack a day when she told him to cut back. At her prompting to smoke less, he upped his consumption to two packs a day.

He desperately yearned to spite Barbara. But he only had to see her shiny blonde hair, soft curls falling onto her shoulder or look into her deep sea blue eyes. Just get a glimpse of her shapely legs under a short black skirt and he did every last thing her never-stopping, sing-songing voice recited on the list of all the things she might like him to do for her.

Latent resentment can look like a lot of other things. When he started tearing the cellophane off a third pack every day, he knew Barbara was slowly killing him.

Will's phone buzzed softly against his hip. He ignored it, hoping it was a ghost buzz. Sometimes he felt the vibration in his joint even when his phone was sitting on his dresser.

It buzzed again. He pulled it up and propped it against his thigh, squinting against the setting sun to read the screen.

Mad Dog. Of course.

"You coming back in tonight? I have a new house fire in Fergus. I know it's late, but I could use a hand if you have one."

Adjusting was a solo operation. That's the way God made it, Will used to say. Long hours alone on the road, picking fights with talk radio hosts or joking with cows that made their way past the electric fence, just to get somewhere and spend thirty minutes and a few megabytes of memory card storage on a claim. Sure, there might be small talk with the widow watching *The Price Is Right*, or a good laugh with the farmer who figures the best negotiating position he can have is grinning behind the controls of his front-end loader while he had a guy ten feet in the air in the bucket. But to Will's mind, adjusters worked in closely guarded solitude, behind walls erected by silence. Anything a guy would say on a job would surely be twisted into a hangman's noose to use against him. One couldn't risk getting emotionally involved and God forbid a policyholder mistook an adjuster for a friend, only to be deeply betrayed when he had to point a nail-bitten finger to the finer points of a policy contract.

On this, he and Mad Dog were agreed. One's best work was done alone and a claims guy had to be able to face an angry farm wife and her drooling Dobermans on his own. But they were also agreed that from time to time there was a certain usefulness to having a partner. On a large fire, they could sweep through a house in half the time, one jawing with an anxious homeowner and holding her at bay while the other made his way through the wreckage without Chatty Cathy at his elbow.

Will didn't know how he'd even make it back down the tower steps, and hated the idea of working all night, but he figured he owed Mad Dog a favor or two. He typed back: "No sweat. I'm a half hour out from town. Pack your gear; I'll pick you up."

He hit send and let the phone drop to his lap. He took it back and tapped, "Oh, and can you make me a sandwich?"

One foot already in the cab, he was about to pull himself up into the seat when he saw the Barbie doll head below his door, on the gravel next to his front tire. He slowed up and cocked his head, staring at hers. Will stepped back down, leaned and picked it up by the matted blond hair. He dangled the head in front of his face and murmured, "What the hell happened to you, little girl?"

For Will, everyone and everything had a back story, the things no one knew, no one saw, sometimes no one would even guess. He thought about Mrs. Owens. A nice lady by all reports. Never said a cross word to anyone, had no real problems, was in perfect health. One day, she's driving down the highway at 65 mph and her heart stops. Just quits. Right there in the car. She careens off the road, through the ditch, across a parking lot and rams into the cinder block wall of an out-of-the-way hunting lodge that was just getting ready for the lunch rush. The impact knocked a wall off center and jammed up a video poker machine inside. Mrs. Owens was pronounced dead at the scene.

Will had flipped through the pages of the autopsy, something he hated to do. It always felt like peering in at someone who can't tell you they don't prefer to be peered in at. He didn't wish to know that her body was opened in the usual manner and found to be without abnormality. He didn't wish to know that she had four dollar bills and twenty-six cents in change in her purse along with a tube of lipstick ("Pink Possibilities" shade), a grocery list (she was out of milk) and pictures of her grandkids (she had seven—four girls and three boys). He concluded that there was likely no known preexisting condition that gave rise to the heart attack and was satisfied it couldn't be determined if the cause of death were cardiac arrest or blunt force trauma, though the coroner seemed comfortable enough saying it was the blunt force trauma like the chicken and egg question had a valid answer. Either way, Mrs. Owens was dead and a guy wanted his building paid for. What Will couldn't shake was her shoe. She arrived at the morgue in a long-sleeved T-shirt, blue jeans and one black shoe. What on earth had happened to her other shoe?

It was most likely hidden in the grass, knocked off during the crash or when she was extricated from the LeSabre, front end crumpled into the back seat. One day, he supposed, someone on a road cleanup crew would find the shoe and drop it into a black Hefty trash bag without another thought to Mrs. Owens, her story long since forgotten. That one shoe would take its storied memory with it to the bottom of the landfill to decompose alongside Eggo Waffle packages and Fisher-Price high chairs.

"Look, Doll," Will said, picking a pebble out of her hair. "Heads don't just go missing in parking lots. Especially with such a clean neck cut. Your story is safe with me." He climbed into the truck and dropped the head into the glove box, then started the engine and pulled back onto the highway.

3

Mad Dog was waiting at the curb in front of the office when Will drove up. They had a small office space on Main Street. Will had worked out of his apartment for years, but eventually tired of policyholders knowing where he lived and dropping by unannounced with paperwork or puncturing his tires at night. He and Mad Dog took advantage of the low price of real estate when business after business closed its doors when the supercenter box store arrived the next town over. There was an attorney a few doors down, and a dentist across the hall. It was sort of a one-stop shopping experience, Will thought. Everybody's least favorite people under one professional roof.

With a flip of his wrist, Mad Dog tossed his gear in the back and climbed into the passenger seat. "What happened to you today, Phillips? Thought you'd be back by noon."

"That's what I thought too," Will said with a slight smile. "That old guy you gave me — he's a real piece of work."

"Ha! You'll never learn. Get in, get done, get out. Just the facts, I keep telling you. Just the facts and you're done in no time."

"Yeah, yeah. I know. I'm a sucker for a lonely old man with an accordion." He yanked the GPS loose from the windshield and tossed it at Mad Dog. "Tell Barbara to set us up for Fergus, would you?"

Mad Dog opened a manila file jacket and tapped an address onto the screen while Will pulled back onto the highway. "What do we know about this one, Mike?"

He rattled off loss facts in his best *Dragnet* voice, something that both amused Will and made him embarrassed for his longtime partner. Mad Dog always wanted to bust someone, finding something suspicious under every charred throw pillow, but he wouldn't likely find his unsolvable mystery in this fire. The way it sounded, somebody just didn't put out a cigarette. Half the house was incinerated before a neighbor noticed and called 911.

"I brought you a sandwich." He handed Will a thick ham and Swiss on rye.

"Thanks. Mustard?"

"It's in there," Mad Dog was grinning as Will bit into the sandwich and squirted mustard onto his shirt.

"Dammit. Grab me a napkin from the glove box, would you?"

Mad Dog opened the compartment and pulled out a wad of napkins, and the Barbie doll head fell onto the floor. He whistled, then reached to pick up the head. "Who's the babe?"

"Leave her alone. Put her back with the rest of the napkins."

"Just wait till I tell the guys at United Casualty about this. They already thought you were just the sweetest thing after that Dixon fire you worked together."

"Listen. They were total jerks. All I did was ask that punk Kramer to stop spitting on the floor like he was in a Little League dugout. It was somebody's living room. These companies don't teach their young guys any respect at all anymore."

"Easy there, Phillips. The house was a total loss. It was coming down the next week. Nobody cared about the carpet."

"Doesn't matter. It's the principle of the thing. Guys should be taught to treat every house like it belongs to their grandmother. I would never spit on the floor. Ever."

"Oh, and I suppose you'd never put your big dirty boots on a precious little Barbie dress either?" Mad Dog was laughing now, and unscrewed the cap from a water bottle. "Yeah. They told me about that too. What's with you? You've been doing this work for too long to be getting all sentimental about a kids' toy."

"Look. I asked Kramer to lift his foot so I could pick up the dress. I put it on a shelf so it didn't get stepped on again. That's it. Think if that little girl came in and saw it getting trampled."

"You're getting soft, my friend."

"Soft. Sure."

Will had always had to be the redhead—the one with the bangs cut so short they looked like a scrub brush sticking out of the doll's forehead. His sister and her friends chose all the pretty dolls, then gave him the redhead and said, "This one looks the most like a boy. You take it. You be the bad guy."

"What do they need a bad guy for anyway?" he'd ask himself as he stuffed the doll into his pocket and rode his bike down the hill to the woods. He would climb his favorite tree, away from everyone and everything and forget all about the dolls until one of the girls would come, sent as the messenger, to complain he wasn't playing it right. "You're supposed to capture us! Come on!"

He'd climb down from the tree with a grunt and walk his bike up the hill to find the girls, who would scream and run away. He had to chase some of them until he caught them and took their dolls, then he'd go back to the woods and hang the dolls from a low branch so they could be rescued easily enough when the girls came looking.

He could hear as they ran back up the hill, giggling and squealing, telling each other that Will Phillips didn't even know how to be a good bad guy.

Will looked at his partner from the corner of his eye. When Mad Dog lifted the bottle to his lips, Will turned the wheel toward the shoulder just far enough to hit the rumble strips. Water splattered out of the bottle into Mad Dog's face.

"Shut up, Mike."

He flipped on the radio hoping to divert Mad Dog's attention to something besides the Barbie head now suffering the indignity of bouncing in the glove box with napkins, a flashlight and a bag of throat lozenges. Remembering the Tuesday night Cubs game, he clicked to ESPN, patting himself on the back that he sprung for the satellite radio subscription. He was a lifelong Cubs fan but out here it was hard to catch a Chicago game even with cable.

Until the day his father had showed up unexpectedly at his kindergarten classroom and took him out early to go to Wrigley Field for his first game, Will didn't know anything about baseball. His ears and yellow-white hair, in need of a trim, stuck out from under a blue and red cap while he sat straight in his seat, feet dangling and not reaching the ground. He felt small in all the noise and colors of the vast stadium and tried not to let his feet kick the seat ahead of him, where a man with a cigar was talking loudly with his friend about the Cub's chances. The man turned around and patted Will on his knee. "Whaddya think, kid? We got a winning season going.

They gonna break the Curse of the Billy Goat this year?"

Curses and billy goats were news to him, so he just shrugged and looked at his father to answer, but his father was busy reading the program. The man blew smoke into his face and put his hand on his knee again, squeezing it this time. "Well, kid? Whatsamatter? They gonna do it?" Will held his breath and wriggled his knee, but the man's hand was too heavy. He pulled the brim of his cap down just over his eyes, hoping if he couldn't see the man, then the man couldn't see him.

It seemed to work. The man turned back to his friend and jabbed him with his elbow. "What kind of kid doesn't want to talk about his team winning a pennant?" Will tugged at his cap again but it wouldn't come any further over his face.

Until that day, baseball was what his brother Tom played on Saturday mornings. Tom played on the local Little League team and got to wear a gray flannel uniform with cobalt trim and lettering across the front. He had a matching baseball cap with a cursive white S on the front, and even though flannel seemed warm for the summer, Will wished he had a uniform like Tom's. Each game day, Will's mother gave him a dime which he used to buy a grape Bubs Daddy from the green and white painted concession stand, and he and his sister Molly walked around the ball field all through the game, nibbling pieces off the foot-long tube of bubble gum until he hardly had any more room in his mouth for it, listening to fans taunt the other team with calls like "We want a pitcher, not a belly-itcher" and "Batter-ay, batter-ay," neither of which made any sense to him.

Will and his father sat just a few rows up from first base.

His father turned to him and pointed at the man standing at the base. "That's Ernie Banks. Best player the Cubs have ever had. Pay attention; he's a legend." Will watched Ernie Banks like he was told. He watched him play the base, he watched him when he batted, he watched him as he sat in the dugout. There may as well have been no other players on the field; he only watched Ernie Banks. He studied the way he kept just one toe on the bag while he stretched his other leg and arm out as far as he could to nab a ball on a line drive down the first base line. Will only stopped watching Ernie Banks when a vendor walked by calling "Peanuts! Get your peanuts!" He looked at his father then, with wide green eyes that always seemed to serve him well with his dad.

"You won't like them. You have to open them. And they have little skins on the inside that will make you squirmy. You want Cracker Jacks instead."

Will said nothing, but held his gaze. Finally his father waved the peanut vendor over and passed a quarter down the row. The vendor threw a bag of peanuts back, which his father picked out of the air like he'd seen Ernie Banks do. He opened the package, took out two peanuts, one of which he handed to Will and the other he held the long way between his thumb and index finger. "Watch what I do now." He gave the peanut a quick squeeze and it split clean down the middle. He turned the shell over, dropping two well-dressed peanuts into his palm, then gave each one another little pinch between his fingers, sliding them out of the brown skins. He popped them into his mouth and smiled at Will.

"Now you try. I'm not opening them for you."

Will positioned the peanut the way he'd seen his father do,

then squeezed. The peanut did not budge. He squeezed again, feeling his small muscles tighten up and down his arm but still the shell did not crack. He glanced at his father, who was watching Ernie Banks. He put his two hands together, thumb over thumb and index over index and squeezed one more time until his hands shook, hoping his father wouldn't see it took both hands. The peanut cracked down the seam and Will was so surprised when the shell gave way he nearly dropped it on the ground. He held it open in his palm, studying the round peanuts inside, thinking they looked like stowaways hiding under brown blankets in a small boat. He picked one out of the shell and gently squeezed it out of its skin. His father was right: he didn't like the feel of the thin skin between his fingers, and shook it off his hand quickly. He wiggled in his seat but he needed his father to be wrong about this. Will spent the rest of the game squeezing peanut shells until his hands hurt, slipping each out of its skin and eating every last one until his belly ached, but not saying a word to his father.

Now the nearest ball park was a good four hours away, but sometimes he drove to the city just to watch a game no matter who was playing. He always sat up from first base, and always bought a bag of peanuts, crushing each one between his index and thumb with a single crisp snap. Only rarely did he squirm when he slid the peanuts out of their skins.

The phone in his holster buzzed and he tapped his earpiece to answer the call.

"Claims, Will Phillips."

"Hello? Can I talk to Will Phillips?"

"This is Phillips."

"This is Joe Murphy. Do you remember me?"

"Sure, Joe. Of course I remember." He looked at Mad Dog and rolled his eyes. "Is everything okay? It's not raining there, is it?"

"No, no. It's not raining. Listen, I was just tidying things up after you left today."

"Is that right? You were tidying things up, huh?" Will smiled.

"Yeah. I like to keep things from getting out of hand. Say, I found your thermos jug on my coffee table. What do you think I should do with it? I could bring it to your office tomorrow."

The last thing Will needed was Joe showing up at the office. He'd have no way to get him to leave.

"No, it's okay. I have another," he lied. "I come out your way pretty often. How about if I stop by the next time and pick it up?"

"Oh, sure. That would work. When do you think that will be? Tomorrow? I'll be gone for doctor's appointments on Friday."

"Not this week, I'm sure. But I'll let you know when I'm coming, Joe."

"I'll just rinse it out and have it waiting for you here then."

"Perfect, Joe. Thanks for letting me know. I'll be in touch, alright?

Will tapped his earpiece to end the call and rubbed the back of his neck. Mad Dog slapped himself on the leg and laughed out loud. "Oh, little Willy-boy. You got yourself a grandpa. I'll betcha a dime and a donut he hid your thermos when you got ready to leave so you'd forget it. He's got you made."

"I thought I told you to shut up."

4

Barbara broke a long silence from the dashboard, ordering Will to take a left in .6 miles. He considered taking a right to spite her—and Mad Dog—but thought how far he was already from his warm bed. He slowed and took his left off the highway, dutifully following Barbara's guidance to their destination.

Will parked his truck at the curb and got out. He spread the paperwork on the hood to brief himself on the details, then looked up at the house. Story and a half, 1930s construction. White paint peeled off aged wood slat siding. Black window trim, mostly chipped away. The downspouts were unhooked from the gutter and from the ground he could see vegetation peeking up over the top of the eaves troughs. Unless a house burned down entirely, it wasn't always noticeable from the street that anything at all had happened, and this house, in the waning sunlight, just looked tired, not burned out. Will walked around to the right and saw the back end of the house, an addition, was blackened. A hole gaped in the roof where firefighters broke through to extinguish the flames. Smoke still curled out from the smoldering attic, barely visible against the dusk sky.

Then he heard the growl.

"Mongrel at 11 o'clock, Phillips." Mad Dog issued a quiet warning from the cab in code, as though otherwise the brown and black boxer would comprehend. Will stood still, looking from the corner of his eye. A dog charged off the front porch from his left, barking and snarling. By now he should know better, but in all his years of onsite visits, he rarely remembered to check for dogs before exiting his vehicle. Will kept his face toward the back of the house. This was his way. If a dog approached friendly, he sweet-talked and crouched down to pet it. If it came aggressive, he ignored it. Or at least he wanted the dog to believe it was being ignored. But he was always ready to move.

The dog did not slow and from his sideways glance Will could see the scruff on its neck up and angry slobber hanging from its loose mouth. He was about to jump to the side when the dog jerked back with a yelp, reaching the end of a rope tethering it to the porch and sprawling onto its back; then it jumped back up and strained at the end of the rope, barking and showing yellow teeth.

Will relaxed. "You're fine, old fella. Settle down. I'm one of the good guys."

He stepped back off the curb and onto the street in a good-faith show for the dog. A woman came from behind the house, brushing uncombed blonde hair from her face.

"Mitzi! Quiet!" She yanked the rope and kicked the dog lightly in the backside to send it back to the house. "Get on out of here." She looked at Will, then Mad Dog. "Damned dog is just a cupcake, really. But she puts on a pretty good show. I'm Nina. This is my boyfriend's house, but he's working."

Mad Dog stuck his hand out the pickup window to shake the woman's hand. Her eyes were puffy under narrow glasses with green frames, her stained V-neck cotton shirt not quite enough to contain all of her. An ample behind slipped out from under her cut-off denim shorts. Will noticed her hands were blackened and her cheeks lined. She'd been in the house looking for her valuables, with mixed success, no doubt.

"I'm Mike," Mad Dog said. "You'd better put your dog away while we're here, Ma'am. My friend Willy is afraid of dogs. Probably wet himself already." He grinned and winked at Will from his seat behind the car door.

Will had a rule about never arguing with his partner in front of a customer, but Mike Delaney had no qualms about saying whatever crossed his mind, and so he often found himself at the wrong end of Mad Dog's jokes. He looked at his feet and clenched his jaw, then stepped up on the curb, strutted over to Nina and introduced himself.

He shook her hand and gave her his business card, taking over the conversation even though this job was Mad Dog's and Will was only along as the extra hand this time.

"Don't mind my assistant," he shook her hand and gave her his business card. "He's just going to tag along to see if he can learn a thing or two. Listen, I'm sorry for the situation here. I know it's hard. Let's go around back and get a look at things so we can get you back on your feet."

Will followed Nina around the house, but not without a quick turn and grin at Mad Dog, still eyeing Nina's Boxer on the front porch from his seat in the cab. He got out and jogged a few steps to keep up.

The yard was short, narrow. An alley cut across the back. There was no car. The grass had been cut, but from the looks of the weeds along the fence line the trimming was rarely done. Three children—one boy, two girls, probably between four and eight—sat in webbed lawn chairs in a row along the garage by the alley. Three pairs of bright colored Crocs hung from their feet, dangling above the ground. They wore stained T-shirts, dirty faces, and up-from-bed lopsided hair. Each had a slice of pizza from a box in front of them on the ground and traded sips from a single plastic bottle of Pepsi they passed between them. None of them spoke, even to each other. Will smiled in their direction. They looked down at their Crocs in unison.

Will turned back to Nina. "Do you have a place to stay?"

"The Red Cross is putting us up at the Super 8 tonight. After that I just don't know. My mom will take the older two kids to their dad's in the morning. But I don't have anywhere to send Lucy Mae. She'll have to stay with me and Justin."

Nina looked toward the children along the garage and pulled at the elastic of her watchband, twisting it around her index finger.

"Is Justin going to meet us?" Will asked. "And what about Pamela? The policy is issued to Justin and Pamela."

"Pamela is Justin's ex. The divorce isn't final but she's long gone. Justin works long hours. He won't be here until late."

"How long have you been with him?"

Nina pushed her hands through her hair from her temples to the back, holding the tangled mess of blonde into a makeshift ponytail.

"Five months. Maybe four."

"Alright," he said, writing in a small black notebook he'd pulled from his pocket. "Let's get to work. Tell me what happened."

"What happened? What the hell kind of question is that? My effing house burned down is what happened."

Will looked up from his notebook. Nina was staring up at

the charred rafters exposed in the open roof, hands on her hips, defiance set in her clenched jaw. He knew without knowing that the dark shadows under her eyes didn't come from a house fire on a clear afternoon in May. He wanted to brush her blonde tangles away from her cheek.

He pushed his right hand into the pocket of his khakis and took two steps toward the house, away from Nina.

"Let's try this a different way," he said. "Why don't you just tell me about your day."

Nina laced her fingers behind her neck. "I'm sorry," she said. "You probably see this all the time. I'm still in a little shock, I guess." She picked up a lawn chair from the ground and opened it, offering it to Will. "Do you want to sit down?"

"No, I'm fine. But maybe you could use a break."

"Hey, you kids!" she shouted, turning suddenly toward the garage. "Get off those chairs and bring them here for the insurance guys. Right now!"

"Nina. Really, I'm fine. I move around a lot anyway."

The two older children sat still in their chairs. The smallest, with soft red curls, got up and dragged her chair across the lawn, stumbling once. She stopped in front of Mad Dog, let go of the chair, and scampered behind Nina, peeking out from around her leg. Mad Dog opened the chair and sat.

Will leaned against a section of the deck that was not burned, legs stretched out in front of him. He slipped his pencil behind his ear and closed his notebook, putting it into his shirt pocket.

"Okay then? I'm not even taking notes. Just tell me about your day. Start with breakfast."

Nina sat down hard on her chair. The webbing was broken

in spots, and her fleshy legs pushed out through the bottom. Lucy Mae crawled into her lap.

"Well, I got up at 7. Justin was already gone for work. He works a lot." She rubbed her eye, smearing more soot on her cheek. "I came downstairs and started the coffeemaker, then went out to the deck for a cigarette. Justin doesn't like me to smoke in the house, you know? I use that coffee can in the corner for the butts so they don't make a mess." She waved a hand toward the deck. Will spotted a black can in the corner, tipped on its side. If he had to guess, he'd say the fire started in that corner. The burn damage seemed to be the worst there, siding burned off and stud walls exposed and charred in both directions. The deck floor and rails were burned away in that corner and the windows were shattered.

"Okay. What did you do with your cigarette before you went into the house?"

"I put it out in the can. Like I always do."

"Then what?"

"I went inside. Had coffee. Brushed my teeth. Got dressed."

"And then?"

Nina pulled at her watchband again. "Then I watched TV until the kids got up. Then I fixed them lunch."

"Did you use the stove?"

"No. They ate peanut butter sandwiches and potato chips."

"Okay. After lunch?"

"After lunch I cleared the dishes and sent the kids outside. I sat on the deck and had another cigarette. They started begging me to take them to the park and they were making me nuts. So I put my cigarette in the can and told Lucy Mae to get me Mitzi's leash. I hooked up the dog and we walked to the park. We were there for an hour, maybe, and then came back. The house was on fire when we got here. I screamed and told the kids to go to the neighbor's. I called 911 on my phone, and then Justin." Nina was crying now. "I tried to get in but there was too much smoke. There was just too much god-damned smoke."

Will didn't speak. He took out his notebook and started writing, letting Nina gather herself.

Mad Dog broke the silence. "Your cigarette, Ma'am. Do you remember if you put it out?"

This was the thing about Mad Dog. The question surely had to be asked. But not yet. Another 30 seconds or so would not derail the investigation. But nuance was a quality Mad Dog had in short supply. Will shot a glare at him sitting imperiously in Lucy Mae's lawn chair and returned to writing, to distance himself from his partner's poor sense of timing.

Nina sniffled and wiped her eyes with the back of her hand. Will pulled a clean handkerchief from his pocket and held it out to her.

"Thanks," Nina said, and dabbed at her eyes with the blue and red plaid cotton square. "I don't know. That's the thing. I thought I put it out in the can. But maybe I didn't? Maybe I hurried too much and missed the can and didn't notice. The kids were making me crazy. Maybe… Maybe."

"Where was Justin?" Mad Dog asked.

"He was at work," Nina said. "He works a lot."

Mad Dog leaned back in his chair, arms folded over his chest, and looked from Nina to the house and back again.

"I know what you're thinking," Nina said, her voice suddenly high. "Fat lazy bitch burned her house down. It wasn't like that. It wasn't."

Mad Dog got up and stepped toward Nina. "No, no. I wasn't thinking that at all."

Will needed a diversion. He'd seen Mad Dog try to talk his way out of holes like this before. He didn't know how to talk to women, always handling them like they were only good in the kitchen or his bed.

"Hey Mike," he said. "Run to the truck and grab the gear. Let's go ahead and get the damages scoped."

"Sure thing, Phillips." Mad Dog jogged toward the front of the house. He was crass, yes. But he wasn't stupid.

"Listen, Nina," Will said. "If you want to take the kids to the hotel, maybe they could play in the pool a while and you can relax. I'll call you when we get what we need here and we can go over a few things. Do you want me to drive you?"

Nina wiped a hand across her forehead. "No, it's just a couple of blocks past the park. We'll walk. You'll call me, right?" She was used to this, guys like Mad Dog thinking they knew all about her life, seeing her in the most stark, simplistic terms.

"Yes. I'll call you. Promise."

She yelled for her kids, with a tired voice, and walked down the alley as Mad Dog came back around the house. "Thanks for getting her to move along, Phillips. Thought she was coming for me," he said. "It's so much easier to work without the homeowner underfoot anyway."

He handed Will his phone. "Your phone was ringing when I got to the cab. Looks like you missed a call from your Grandpa Joe."

5

Will stood back and looked at the house, hands on his hips. *You started the fire alright, Nina. But not the way Mad Dog thinks.*

Three kids. A dog. No paying job. Nowhere to go. Will would pull Justin's financial records and give them a good going-over, but Nina had nothing to gain from starting the fire. The insurance company wouldn't be paying her a dime for her clothes, the kids' toys, even a meal while they were out of the home. She ran the household. Cooked, cleaned, serviced Justin-who-works-a-lot when he made his way home some nights. But Nina just lived there, wasn't a "resident family member" according to a carefully worded insurance policy. The company wouldn't give a damn about her. There was no reason at all for a woman like Nina to burn down a house, but from the looks of things, with one bad flip of a cigarette she unwittingly did.

"Phillips!" Mad Dog was shouting from the front of the house. "You planning on moving in with her? Grab the end of the tape and let's get going while we can still see anything at all."

Will looked at Mad Dog and dropped his head.

"Phillips!"

"Yeah, yeah. I'm going," Will said. He jogged up to the front, picked up the end of the tape from the ground at Mad Dog's feet, and walked it to the back of the house.

"Twenty-seven and a half," he called out, and started walking to the next corner.

~

It was 11:00 when they pulled up next to Mad Dog's Ranger pickup back at the office. Will left his truck running.

"You want me to unload?" Mad Dog asked.

"No, I'll get it tomorrow. I'm beat." Will turned the steering wheel. "Oh. And I'll be late in the morning."

"Alright. Goodnight, Willy." Mad Dog took his coffee mug and tool bag and left. Will leaned his head against the headrest, eyes closed, until he heard Mad Dog's truck start, back up and pull away. Then he drove the few blocks to his house.

The enormous residence where he rented a room was built at the turn of the last century. It had lost a bit of its luster, but in its original splendor, it was really something. Unique woodwork in every room, stained glass throughout—including a full-length window at the landing of the grand staircase between the first and second floors—fireplaces, a back stairway for the hired help. There was an elaborate configuration of dumbwaiters and pipes built in the wall as an early low-tech intercom and delivery system. He'd even heard the third floor had been a ballroom once, complete with oak parquet flooring. Now it was sectioned off into apartments, the only way the builder's granddaughter could afford to keep the house in the family.

Pearl Jenkins was in her late seventies. She rented the top floor to two young women who worked nights at the warehouse, and she gave Will a bedroom on the second floor in exchange for $200 a month and a few odd jobs. She let him use the bathroom and an efficiency kitchen and made a frequent point of reminding him not to leave his towel on the floor and to put his dishes away.

When he first moved in five years ago, Pearl often came up to check on him and managed to challenge him to a game at the pool table her father had left in the study. It always went the same way. "My father said pool was no game for a lady," Pearl would say. "He never taught me to play."

She'd ask Will for a few pointers, cajoling him into helping her hold the cue stick correctly. "How do I hold this silly thing?" She'd wave the stick around in the air, nearly swiping Will on the head, until he obliged. Then he'd stand behind her, reaching around to help her position the cue. When he gently lifted her hand off the table, she'd accuse him of being fresh.

"Oh, Mrs. Jenkins. You've caught me at it again," Will would say. "Your charm is irresistible." Then he would kiss her lightly on the cheek and step back.

With a twinkle in her eye, Pearl would say, "Listen here, Mr. Phillips. To make up for it, I insist on a game. But I always shoot so badly I end up with an itch."

"Scratch," Will would say with a wink. "But just one round. Pool is no game for a lady."

"Oh, yes. Of course. Scratch. I can never remember the terms in these silly billiard games." Will mouthed the words along with Pearl, he'd heard them so many times.

"Bet me twenty dollars. I'm sure you could use the easy cash," she'd say.

"I sure could, Mrs. Jenkins. You're on."

Pearl beat him every time, until eventually he knew every time he heard the stairs creak it would cost him another twenty bucks.

Blue and red light from the window rested on the green felt table top as he walked past the study on the way to his room. He couldn't remember the last time he'd paid his pool hustling landlady twenty dollars. The arthritis in her knees made stairs untenable and she hadn't been up to nag him about his housekeeping in months.

He stood in the doorway a little longer, smiling at Pearl in the dark, then walked to his room and flipped on the light. Will's room was drab. Beige wallpaper from around 1950 peeled off the walls. A single dim light bulb hung from the electric cord out of the ceiling, which was exposed plaster and lathe. Despite the glorious woodwork in the rest of the house, the windows and door frames in Will's room were painted white. He had a single bed, his grandmother's blue quilt wadded on top of wrinkled striped sheets that should have been changed two months ago.

His keys dropped with a clank on the small mahogany dresser as he unbuckled his belt and let his jeans fall to the floor, forgetting to take off his boots first. He stumbled to the bed, pants around his ankles, and sat down in his boxers to loosen his boots. He pulled his phone from the holster, stripped off his Levis and threw them into the corner, missing the laundry hamper by two feet. Will toppled onto a flat, bumpy pillow without a pillowcase and lit up his phone to turn it off for the night. He saw the missed call alert from Joe Murphy, a blinking green light for a voice message.

"It's almost midnight," he said aloud. "If that's not after hours, I don't know what is. Tomorrow, Joe. Surely my thermos can wait until tomorrow."

Will slipped the phone under his pillow and rolled onto his side, pulling the quilt up to his chin. He jockeyed around the bed for a comfortable position, changing from his left to his right a dozen times. Finally he lay on his back staring at the lathe on the ceiling, following the pattern of the shadows from the outside light. Despite Pearl's frequent fussing about it, he'd never gotten around to putting shades up on his windows. It wasn't a busy street, and if any dead bodies left in the vacant funeral parlor across the way wanted a look at anything, he and his boxers were happy to oblige.

He counted wood strips from the window to the light bulb, never getting past thirteen before he lost his place.

"Damn it." He reached for his phone, then pressed the dial button and let out a long sigh.

The old man answered, and Will could hear opera music in the background. He hesitated. "Joe? Hey, I know it's late. I just got in and saw I missed your call."

"No problem, Will!" Joe sounded delighted. "I'm a night owl anyway. I'm up listening to La Bohème. You've heard it?

"Uh, not sure." Will looked at the lathe. "Wait. Is that the one Cher and Nicholas Cage go to see in *Moonstruck*?"

"So you know it then. Exquisite. Anyway, you're calling about your thermos, not the opera, I suppose. It's all cleaned up and waiting for you in the kitchen."

"Well, um, yeah. My thermos." Will paused. What did he call Joe for in the middle of the night? He just extended himself and now the old man would think they were friends and call him every day. He set the phone on his chest and closed his eyes.

Joe's voice crackled through the tiny speaker. "Will? Are you still there?"

He picked up the phone and sighed. "Yeah, sure. I'm here. Sorry about that. Phone cuts out sometimes, you know? So, right. My thermos. I have an appointment at a horse ranch north of you the day after tomorrow. Think maybe I could swing by on my way back and grab it? I hate to think it's cluttering your place up."

"That would be great. What time should I expect you?"

"It's hard to pin down a time, Joe." Will searched his mind for an escape hatch. "You could just leave it on your back step. I don't want you waiting around for me if you've got things you could be doing."

"Where've I got to go, Will? I don't have any doctor's appointments that day. I'll just be here. Early or late afternoon?"

"Late. Late afternoon." This way, Will figured, he'd be needing to get home and couldn't be cajoled into more exploration of Joe's junk and cultural artifacts. "Listen, sorry again for calling so late. I'll see you Thursday, late afternoon, okay?"

"Okey doke, Will. See you then."

"Goodnight, Joe." Will clicked his phone off.

Goodnight, Joe? Goodnight? *Mental note: Never talk to clients after 8:00 at night, and never, ever from bed.* Mad Dog would never let him live this one down.

Of course, Mad Dog would never know about it.

Goodnight, Joe.

6

The phone fell to the floor as Will turned onto his side and pulled the quilt over his chest. He faded off to sleep in his red plaid boxers, black socks, and graying white T-shirt. Even by himself, Will hated to be uncovered. He only took his shoes off for bed, and left his socks on except in the shower. A guy never knew when he might have to move fast, and there wouldn't always be time to bother with shoes and socks when needing to run for one's life. He didn't mind wearing a T-shirt when he was alone, but kept to long sleeves when he left the house.

Barbara claimed not to mind, but there always seemed to be a flicker of something when she eyed other guys, tan and shirtless, at the beach. Will had shaded himself under a large umbrella, SPF 75 slathered over whatever small bit of skin was exposed.

The beach held a certain aura of terror. It didn't help that he grew up in the decade of the disaster movies—*The Towering Inferno*, the *Airport* series, *The Poseidon Adventure*, *Jaws*. When his family visited the beach during spring break when he was 10, he was warned about jellyfish and how they could sting him. What was worse, he was told, they were not easy to spot, so a guy could easily step on one and be stung in the foot and injected with venom, and it would feel like being electrocuted. Maybe a guy would even die. When they got to the beach, Will's father practically had to push him out of the car. Will stood barefoot, frozen on the sand, socks and shoes in his hands, well back from the tide and unable to appreciate the vastness or wonder of the ocean, overcome by his fear of death at the slimy tentacles of an unseen jellyfish.

He was grateful for the frigid temperatures on the Florida coast that day so that no one felt like staying very long in the cold wind. He always figured he only narrowly escaped a stealth jellyfish that had fixed its twenty-four eyes on his ten little toes. He wiped the sand quickly from his soles and pulled on damp socks and shoes, retreating to the old blue Chrysler and the safety of the back seat. Tom and Molly clambered in after him, chattering about cold water and soft sand and arguing over who picked up the biggest shells. Will hadn't picked up any shells at the beach. He had no reason to remember having been there.

Now, in the big old house, it was a night of fitful sleep, with Will frequently half-awakening to images of drowning and electrocution and the feeling of slime and sand between his toes.

The night sweats had been waking him for months now but he was afraid to think too hard about the cause. When he woke early, he cursed and threw the blanket off, welcoming the rush of cool air against his wet skin. His T-shirt was soaked through. *You're like a woman in midlife, Phillips*, he said to himself, lying on his back with his arms out, knees bent up, trying to keep skin from touching skin until he cooled down. A near-full moon flooded through the trees into his room casting light strips across his legs and chest.

"How long is it going to be tonight?" he said aloud, to no one in particular. Most nights he lay awake an hour or two. Sometimes he fell back to sleep just before his alarm. Will never used to set an alarm, believing the jarring from sleep was so unsettling it put him in a foul mood all day. When he stopped sleeping through the night, he started looking for tricks to sleep better and read somewhere that not having an alarm kept a person from sleeping soundly because he couldn't stop always up looking at the clock. So he started setting an alarm, but still hated the jarring so much that he was always up looking at the clock anyway, hoping to wake before it went off. Either way, it left him in a foul mood all day.

As the perspiration wicked away, his skin began to feel chilled. He got up and plodded down the dark hallway, felt along the wall in the bathroom, not wanting to turn on the light, and sat down on the toilet. Mad Dog would say only a woman sits down but it was the middle of the night and Mad Dog was an ass. What did he know about women? Besides, Mad Dog wasn't here. Will sat with his head in his hands, wondering how much coffee he'd had and if the stream would ever end.

The stream did end, after what seemed like half an hour. He didn't flush. It would upset Pearl to know this, but it would also upset Pearl to wake to the sound of his flushing as it went through the old house's pipes. He walked back into the dark hallway and into his room.

Will punched his pillow a few times to fluff it up, pulled the blankets back over himself and closed his eyes, even as he knew he wouldn't be sleeping. It just felt like one of those nights, no matter how tired he was. He looked at the clock: 3:22.

Rolling over, he reached under the bed and pulled out a *Sports Illustrated* magazine. He had other magazines, but they were in one of the small closets in his room. He kept his work clothes and an old stereo setup in one of his closets, and the other had some of Pearl's old things and he never used it. He found the magazines stacked in a corner behind her wedding dress and some long tablecloths one day, and guessed a former tenant must have left them behind.

At least he assumed the magazines belonged to the former tenant and that they weren't Pearl's. Of course, one never really knew. People so often thought they knew things about other people that simply aren't knowable. Maybe Pearl had secret trysts with Dottie, the retired auto mechanic who could swap out a catalytic converter faster and cheaper than any of the guys coming out of trade school waving their fancy diplomas around. Will missed the days when Dottie was still working and he could take her out for a piece of pie and coffee to work out the kinks of an auto repair he was writing up. She wore crisp khaki work shirts and chinos, slicked her thick brown hair back with Brylcreem like Ronald Reagan in *Bedtime For Bonzo*, and had a voice that dropped a full two octaves lower than Will's.

The thought of Pearl, the fancy lumberman's grand-daughter, cavorting with Dottie on the sly made him chuckle softly to himself. *They'd look pretty sweet together, actually,* Will thought, fumbling on the floor for his keys.

He squeezed the little flashlight on the ring so he could read the latest news about the Cubs. Baseball was still the only sport he cared about. Football and basketball had too much contact, too much stimulation. Baseball was sedate, more cere-bral. A guy had time to think as the game dragged on.

By four o'clock Will was antsy, but it felt too early to get up. He'd tried to sleep again after realizing the magazine didn't have a single story on the Cubs. And he didn't want to read about the Yankees. He stared at the moon until he lost track of time. Knowing he wouldn't sleep again, he got up and opened his window. The screen was missing already so he crawled out through the small opening onto the wood shakes of the porch roof below his room. It was brightly lit by the moon, and there, in a spot where the moss growth on the shingles was less, he sat down. The night air was cool and damp. A blanket would have been nice, but it seemed too elaborate, so he just sat, knees pulled up to his chest, listening to the quiet of a small town just before dawn, silent save for the occasional 18-wheeler that passed through on the three-lane highway that cut the town in two. The birds weren't even up yet, and the slight breeze made the leaves rustle like they were whispering secrets to each other about the guy in his underwear on the roof. It'd probably be in the weekly newspaper along with who poured coffee and "a good time was had by all."

There in the moonlit silence, Will found himself wanting. Lacking, yes. He always found himself lacking. But tonight he also found himself wanting something he couldn't quite put his finger on. A wishing he felt in his chest and as the silence grew more quiet, the wanting grew more noisy.

"Cigarette," he said aloud. "That must be it." He crept back to the window and crawled in, grabbed a flannel shirt from the floor and his cigarettes and lighter from his Levis pocket. He thought about taking his phone so he could check the time, but remembered he'd told Mad Dog he'd be in late, for no real reason at all.

He went clumsily back out the window, rapping his shin on the sill on the way out and muffling a cry of "Ouch!" into a low grunt, then sat down and leaned back against the house and rubbed his leg. He lit up and pulled in deeply, holding it a few moments before letting out nice and slow. The light breeze carried the smoke toward the open window.

"Pearl," he said. "Dammit."

All he needed was for Pearl to smell smoke in the house and she'd be calling 911. When all his buddies on the volunteer fire department showed up, it'd be more than the trees gossiping about the guy on the roof. He knelt in front of the window and closed it to just an inch, so he could get back in, then held his cigarette away from the window and rested his head against the chipped asbestos siding, closing his eyes to listen to what was left of the night sounds.

I should go camping sometime. Maybe I could sleep like this.

He took a few more drags of his cigarette, then ground it into the shingles and dropped the stub into his shirt pocket. There was enough left worth keeping for another time. With his hands resting atop his bare knees, Will dozed off with his head against the wall.

When the birds woke him, he found the morning light working its way across the wood shakes. Traffic was picking up on the highway and it was best to get off the roof before the neighbors spotted him. He slid his fingers into the open crevice in the window and pushed up. The window wouldn't budge. He shifted, getting on his knees in front of the window and sliding both hands in and pushing again. Again it wouldn't budge.

Will placed his palms against the sash and pressed up. The humidity had tightened the window just enough that he couldn't open it back up. There he was, squatting on the front porch roof in his boxers and socks, stranded. He didn't have his phone. He didn't have his shoes.

This is why a guy always, always has his shoes. Damn.

He got up and walked the perimeter of the roof, looking for his best way out of the situation. The downspouts were loose and wouldn't hold him. But the front porch had a waist high rail. If he could reach that with his feet, he'd be home free. Will got backward on his knees and eased himself over the edge. Once before on a windy day when his ladder blew away from the house, this had worked. Maneuvering his way down in the corner where there was an ornamental column supporting the roof, he managed to wrap his legs around the column and held onto the gutter tray with one hand while he grabbed one of the flourishes at the top of the column with the other. It was good, actually, that he didn't have his jeans on, because his clammy bare legs held the column while the denim would have slid. He shimmied down the column until his foot reached the railing and was so proud of getting off the roof that he forgot his age. He turned toward the yard, planted his feet and squatted, leaping to the ground, then landed on his right foot, turning his ankle and crumpling to the ground behind the hedges.

Holding his leg, Will curled up and clenched his jaw to keep from crying out in pain. The door across the street creaked open and slammed shut and the neighbor's dog started to snort and sputter. The dog knew Will was there, but his neighbor did not, and walked down the sidewalk with her dog straining backwards against the leash.

Will stood, stayed hunched behind the bushes, and held himself up on the fence as he hobbled to the back where there was an outside stairway accessing the second story of the house. He'd pulled himself halfway up the stairs when he heard the door open below him and Pearl's footsteps patter across the back porch. He stopped and stood still. Pearl walked out into the yard and shook out a rug from her kitchen.

Who shakes their rugs at 6:00 in the morning?

Pearl turned to go back and paused to look up at the trees shading the back yard. Will watched her, silently, hoping. As her eyes came back down, she caught his gaze and dropped her rug on the ground.

Will looked at his feet and sighed.

With her hands on her hips, she shouted up to him. "Mr. Phillips! Are you just getting in for the night? And Lord, have mercy! Where are your pants?"

"Mrs. Jenkins, you might be the most observant person I know. You remind me of a man in a short story I read once, this guy that noticed things that people would rather were left unnoticed. You might enjoy it."

Will had to think fast. He concluded his best approach would be to answer the way one must answer children's questions about delicate subjects: Answer only, and precisely, the question asked.

"My pants are right where I left them. On the bedroom floor."

Pearl's mouth opened. Then it closed, as though she had something to say, but didn't. Will moved in swiftly with a diversion.

"I think I'll go put them on. It's chilly out here. Maybe you should pick up that rug off the ground before it gets dirty, and then maybe you'll pour me a cup of your fresh-brewed coffee."

"Oh," Pearl managed, looking at her rug in the grass. She picked it up, gathering herself. "And have you had your breakfast? I'll make you some toast with jam."

"Perfect," Will said. "I'll be right down." He pretended to tip his hat, nodded, and went quickly up the stairs.

"Oh, and Mr. Phillips," Pearl said as he opened the door. "Come down through the servants' entrance straight into the kitchen, please. My living room is a fright and I don't want you to see it."

The old Jenkins house had, in fact, actual servants' quarters on the second floor—now his kitchenette—with a separate enclosed staircase into the main floor kitchen. Pearl's living room was undoubtedly spotless as usual, but she often made a point of telling him to come through the servants' entrance as though to remind Will of her status. He always obliged. It was a small thing, and it seemed to make her happy.

Well played, Phillips, he muttered to himself as he walked into the bathroom. *Today it's Pearl. Tomorrow it's Joe. You may as well quit adjusting and open up a senior daycare.*

7

Will leaned over the sink and splashed water on his face, then looked up into the mirror and sighed at his reflection. His eyes were red and underlined with dark half moons. His graying blond hair was tousled. He cupped his hand against his face. At least he didn't have much of a five o'clock shadow. His facial hair was light and he'd never been able to grow a respectable beard. Pearl would know he'd been up all night for sure. She might be polite enough to avoid asking, but she might not be.

Pulling on his jeans and pushing his feet into his boots gave him a sense of relief at the feel of laces wrapped tight around his ankles, happy for the simple security of proper footwear. He ran his hands through his hair a few times and headed for the staircase, the smell coffee enlivening him.

Pearl made coffee the old fashioned way. At least it was old fashioned to Will, though not as old fashioned as brewing it in a kettle on the stove with an egg to collect the loose grounds. She brewed coffee in a tall silver General Electric percolator, nothing like the acrid, anemic dribble he made in his drip machine. What Will really needed was a French press to brew himself a stiff cup every morning. He could sit on the porch roof and drink it slowly, savoring the earthy notes while he hoped for a glimpse of his neighbor when she came out to walk her Jack Russell terrier. But it would take forever to fill his thermos with a French press, and he'd probably have a heart attack before the day was up taking in that much caffeine. No, he was doomed to be an all-day tepid coffee slurper and miss the charm of a proper morning coffee ritual.

Will walked down the old wooden stairs to the servants' entrance, making an extra effort to clomp loudly on the bottom few steps. Pearl lost track of the outside world when she worked in her kitchen, and he'd startled her before, barging into her kitchen unexpectedly when she hadn't noticed him on the stairs. He rapped on the door before he opened it, then stuck his head out and said, "Good morning to the most beautiful woman in town," before coming all the way into the kitchen.

Pearl bustled around the spacious, immaculate room. She'd set two small plates, cups and saucers on the breakfast nook table. A tray of pastries sat on the center island. Pearl picked up a towel from the counter and wiped her hands. "Don't just stand there with your hands in your pockets." She nodded toward the tray. "You did come in through the servants' entrance, didn't you? Take that tray to the table."

He smiled and picked up the tray and teased. "Mrs. Jenkins, I thought you said toast. I feel like I just stumbled into a tea party for your little lady friends."

"I was going to give you toast and coffee and send you on your way, but it's been so long since you've come by, and I had these goodies from the bakery I bought yesterday on the day-old shelf. I warmed them while you were...getting dressed."

Pearl wouldn't ask again about his pants. If she hadn't been caught by surprise outside, she wouldn't have asked at all. She was too proper for such things. But that didn't mean she wouldn't leave openings for him to fill in the blanks if he chose. And if he didn't choose, well, then she would just let her imagination fill in the blanks and enjoy herself along the way. Will decided to let her imagination have this one. She'd no doubt enjoy the tale of his getting caught out on the roof, but would be terrified knowing how he'd crawled down. He didn't think it was right to worry people more than was absolutely necessary.

"What do you hear from your grandchildren?" Will slid into a seat at the table, his back to the wall so he could face his landlady.

"Oh, they're just precious, you know. Growing up so fast. My first grandson just graduated from high school and my last one just finished Kindergarten. So there you go. They're all too busy to come and see me very often, but they send me pictures and newspaper clippings. And they call on the phone now and then. I suppose I'll have weddings to go to before long. And maybe great grandchildren. Though I don't know that anyone's quite ready for that just yet."

Pearl tipped the silver percolator and filled Will's cup. "Tell me something about you, Mr. Phillips. Your work is always so interesting. Don't you have a story for me today?"

"Well, we've had more than a few fires lately."

"Oh, I don't want to hear about fires. They scare me. I don't know how I'd get out of this house in one piece. And all the heirlooms. I think I'd just hold on to my mama's china doll in the living room and let the flames take me."

"Don't worry about a fire in this house. I just checked your smoke detectors last week. All the batteries are good. And you know I don't smoke in the house." He put a hand on his chest and felt the cigarette stub in his shirt pocket. Poor Mrs. Jenkins. How would he explain burning her front porch right off the house?

"Say, did I ever tell you about the time that old Doctor Runyan faked the theft of his truck?"

"Dr. Runyan," Pearl said, letting her lips play with the "R," forming a tiny round opening like a camera opening from a pinhole to a wide angle. "Sounds like a poet I once read. Or a lumberjack. No, I don't think I've heard that one."

"He was a wily character, Mrs. Jenkins. The kind of fella I'd like you to avoid when you go on those dating sites on the library computer looking for a man to warm your feet at night."

Will winked at Pearl, and she tipped her head shyly, looking at him over her glasses in a way that didn't confirm or deny his allegation. "Why, I didn't know a person could find a man on a computer."

There was something in her dark eyes he hadn't noticed before, a curious mix of affection and mischief, with a tint of loneliness around the edges. "I did take a class at the library one time. I was trying to figure out how to run that beast of a machine the kids set up for me. Oh, it's all so confusing. I'm supposed to use that Skeep thing. Or maybe it's Skape. I don't know. It's like the video telephone from an old James Bond movie. But it never works for me. They say I should be able to see the grandkids, but it all looks like a cartoonish Monet painting. Computers must be faster in California, I think."

She went on. "The kids say they can only see the top of my head, that I don't have my camera adjusted right. But I don't see any camera. And my hair must look a fright then." She smoothed her hand through her hair at the back, combing it against her neck with her fingers. "So what about this Bunyan character?"

"Well, Mrs. Jenkins. Like I said, Dr. Runyan is a wily fellow. He reports that someone stole his pickup near Williston. This is before the big oil drilling started up there, so you know how desolate it could be between there and Dickinson. It's January, a day when it it's only going to get up to 10 below. The good doctor tells me that he's on an old township road on the way to a little farm place he keeps on the side. I know something is a little fishy right off, because he can't remember the township road number."

Pearl poured more coffee in Will's cup. "Now, Mr. Phillips. Don't be so hasty. Do you know I got turned around on my way to play bridge at Waterville the other day? I drive there once a week and know the way by heart. But I ended up going south instead of north. Maybe the doctor was just having a bad day."

"You could be right, Mrs. Jenkins. But if that's all it was, the doctor was having the worst day in history. You know how it is when you're talking to someone and you realize he's making it all up as he goes along?"

"I think I've noticed that some time before. Say, for instance, when you ask a fellow on a staircase where his pants might have gone." Pearl lifted her cup to her lips, curled on one side into a very slight smirk.

"Yes. Something like that." Will smiled at Pearl and shook his head. "Anyway. This Runyan fella tells me that he stopped to pick up a young couple hitchhiking on this little township road that doesn't have a name but leads to his farm in the middle of backwater North Dakota in January when it's ten below. And I say, 'Excuse me, Dr. Runyan, but I think I'm going to need to get you on record about this. Do you mind if I turn on my tape recorder?' Well, he doesn't like it very much, but he's smart enough to know he doesn't have a choice, so he agrees. And so I tell him, once the tape is running, that what he says to me can be used in a court of law (even if it probably never would be) and he says he understands."

Will stopped for a sip of coffee. Pearl rested her chin in her hand and ran her index finger along the rim of her cup.

"He goes on and tells me that this couple needed a ride, that they were on their way to New Orleans. Mind you, this was not long after Hurricane Katrina, so God only knows what they were headed to Louisiana for when people were tearing out of there like schoolkids after the last bell. He says he'll take them to the next town but first he's got to stop at his farm place and hook up his tractor. He has some snow to move out of the parking lot at his office. The young guy, he gets in the front, and the girl gets in the back of the cab, right behind the doctor. He says the girl's wearing a red wool coat, pea coat style, and the fella's wearing an oversized army jacket. They aren't wearing gloves or caps."

"No gloves or caps!" Pearl put her hand over her mouth. "Goodness! They must have been frostbitten. The poor dears. This doctor fellow couldn't have been too terrible. He picked up a couple of freezing teenagers and got them out of the cold, after all."

"No, Mrs. Jenkins. They weren't frostbitten," Will smiled. "This is the thing about made up stories. The young couple wasn't real, so they couldn't have been frostbitten."

"You're making this story up? Shame on you, Mr. Phillips. I wanted a real story about your real work."

Pearl reached for her cup and Will put his hand gently

over hers. "I'm not making the story up, Mrs. Jenkins," he said softly, holding her gaze and seeing she was upset. "I'm telling you a true story about a story Dr. Runyan made up."

She puzzled for a moment, then turned her head toward the window, as if looking into a camera, and smiled and cocked her head. "Oh. That's different. Never mind."

Will laughed out loud and picked up his cup, gesturing an accolade toward Pearl with it and said, "Mrs. Jenkins, I may never tire of your Emily Litella."

"I'm sorry for the disruption, Mr. Phillips. Please go on."

"So he drives them to his farm and hooks up a flatbed with a late model John Deere loader and off they go. About five miles from Dickinson, he says the fella in the front seat tells him to pull over. 'You want out here?' he asks, and the guy says, 'No, I want you out here.' The young fella pulls out a Swiss Army knife, opens to a small blade and jabs it at the good doctor who of course pulls obediently to the side of the road."

"That's terrible," Pearl said. "I remember when my daddy was robbed at knife point in Chicago. He made like he was going for his wallet, then knocked the knife loose with one hand and decked the man with the other, just like that." She slapped her hands together to suggest a job well done. "Your Dr. Runyan sounds like a coward."

"Well, I'm not sure what all he was, but it sounds like your father was a brave man."

"He was," Pearl said, her face softening. "He was."

"So, Runyan says the kids take his wallet, throw him out of the truck and drive off toward the north, and he has to walk to town. Remember how far I said they were from Dickinson?"

"Five miles."

"Yep. And remember how cold I said it was?"

"Ten below."

"Yep. Ten below. He tries to hitchhike, but no one comes by because it's such a remote stretch of highway. I ask him, 'Don't you have a cell phone, Dr. Runyan?' Yes, he says, of course he has a cell phone in his pocket. But he doesn't think to call for help because his service provider is notorious for terrible coverage outside of town. So he drags himself, half dressed (they don't let him take his coat or gloves, which for some reason he left in the back seat even while he was hooking up the trailer). He goes into Denny's which, he says, is the first restaurant he saw when he got to town. Never mind that Denny's is a mile into town, and a guy passes no less than twenty other businesses of various types that would have gladly taken in a bedraggled, half frozen victim of a carjacking without question. But he goes to Denny's, and the waitress won't let him use the phone (his cell must still not be working) because it's for customers only so he takes a table and orders a BLT and a coffee. Then she lets him use the phone so he can call the police. An officer shows up minutes later, but he doesn't want to go to the station to file his report because he just ordered."

"He's a sensible man, this Dr. Runyan." Pearl smiled.

"Sensible? Yeah. Okay. Sensible. Frugal too, I suppose. Criminal. Call him what you like," Will answered. "The officer takes his report there in the Denny's booth and then the doctor asks him to call an ambulance. 'What do you need an ambulance for?' the officer asks. 'Well,' Runyan spits out. 'The guy cut me, of course. I need wound care.'"

"My heavens! When did the man cut him? He never mentioned that."

"Exactly, Mrs. Jenkins. He never mentioned it. The officer tells him he doesn't seem to be bleeding so he'd be glad to just drive him to the clinic where his family can meet him, but Runyan is insistent on at least going to the emergency room. He gets the check and pays his bill—"

"Wait a second. I thought they took his wallet."

"I did too. So Runyan says they let him keep his driver's license and a ten dollar bill for his trouble."

"Well, that was nice of them."

"Yes. Nice. Runyan created characters with a conscience of sorts, perhaps in an effort to compensate for the failings of his own."

"Well, I do hope when he went to the doctor they checked him for frostbite. He must have been a popsicle."

"Funny you should mention that. I pulled his records from the ER. He was noted to be in excellent health, a physically fit man in no obvious distress. He presented with a one-inch cat scratch on his upper left thigh. The physician noted there was no blood on his slacks, and they were without cut or tear."

"Left side?" Pearl mused, sliding her thumb and index along the handle of her cup. "Interesting."

"You're catching on, Mrs. Jenkins," Will smiled. "And the record was silent as to frostbite. Not a word. This guy's story was so half-baked he had the sheriff investigating and the state's attorney ready to file fraud charges if we could just find something solid to pin on him. We couldn't, and ended up buying him a new pickup, flatbed and tractor. This is the way it is in the insurance business. You have to set aside truth in favor of what you can prove."

"I don't know how you sleep at night, Mr. Phillips."

"You don't know the half of it." Will thought of his early morning meditation on Pearl's porch roof. "Would you believe I got a call from the sheriff in the spring? They found the pickup. Care to guess where?"

"I would have no idea, and you know how I hate guessing games."

"The truck was parked in the back lot of a convenience store directly across the street from Denny's. The plates were taken off and the store owner didn't notice it there until he was doing his lot cleanup after the snow melted. Figure that one out."

"What in the world?" Pearl said.

"We took the truck to sell it, and found it had over 150,000 miles on it, even though it was only a few years old. Tranny was about to blow. Tires were bald. Odds are he didn't want to fix it and couldn't sell it, so decided to abandon it and make a little easy money on the way. Probably sold the tractor and flatbed for cash. They were never recovered."

"My stars. Now I'm going to wonder about my own doctor. What do you suppose he's up to?"

"You don't have to worry about Doc Wilson. What you see is what you get with him. Want to hear the best part of the story?"

Pearl nodded with a smile and finished her coffee. "There's more?"

"Yep. About six months after the whole thing went down, Runyan called me and demanded to know when I was going to pay his dental bill."

"Dental bill?" Pearl's eyes widened.

"Yes, dental bill. I figured he just had his insurance companies mixed up and told him he should call his medical or dental company. But he said, 'No, you have to pay it. It's from that carjacking incident in January. My teeth are all loose.'"

"'What?' I asked. 'Your teeth are loose?' I couldn't figure his angle on this one. 'Well, yes,' he said, and he seemed awfully upset about it. 'How did your teeth get loose, Dr. Runyan? And maybe before you answer I should turn on the recorder again. I think there's going to be some interest in your answer.'"

"I turned the recorder on and asked him again. 'My teeth were loosened during the carjacking when I was struck in the mouth with a lead pipe.' I tried to mask my shock. 'A lead pipe? And who struck you in the mouth with a lead pipe?' I asked. 'The girl in the red coat,' he said. 'Because I didn't get out of the car fast enough.'"

"The girl hit him?" Pearl asked. "Golly, I think I might have too. You know, if I had a lead pipe handy." She giggled softly.

"I'd like to see that, Mrs. Jenkins." Will smiled. "So I said, 'Listen, Dr. Runyan. I'm curious about this. Why is it that we've talked more than a dozen times, I have over 90 minutes of a recorded interview with you, you've been examined by a physician, you've been interviewed repeatedly by law enforcement, and yet, somehow, after six months, this is the first time we're hearing about a girl hitting you in the mouth with a lead pipe?'"

"'Well,' said the doctor, 'No one ever bothered to ask me that.'"

Pearl laughed out loud, a full, spirited laugh that seemed much larger than her, the kind of laugh Will had once heard someone say "contained a whole universe." She gracefully tossed her head back, and as she did, a single silver lock slipped loose from her French twist and tumbled onto her shoulder. Will couldn't help but join Pearl's mirth, finding her delight utterly irresistible.

"Oh, Mr. Phillips," she said, as both their laughter began to subside. "I don't know how you do it. I'd have been ready to strangle that scheming doctor."

"It's part of what keeps me coming back. Seems like every day turns up a new character, never a single one like the last."

Will looked over his coffee at Pearl, who had quieted and was absentmindedly staring into her cup, again running her finger along the rim. The silver tress now hung across her front, nearly into her lap, its soft variegated waves catching bits of the sun. He hadn't realized how long her hair was, never seeing it apart from her classic updo.

With a quick tip of his cup he drank down the last of his coffee and got up from the table. "I'd best be moving along or Mad Dog Delaney will chew on me for his midmorning snack."

"You'll come again, Mr. Phillips? It's really been too long," Pearl said, as Will carried his dishes to the sink.

"There's nothing quite like your coffee and day-old pastries. Of course I'll come again soon." He lifted her hand and gave it a light kiss and bowed. Pearl smiled in a way a person smiles without realizing, staring over Will's shoulder out the window at some other someone far off somewhere. Will reached and gently tucked the loose lock of hair behind Pearl's ear. "You're doing alright, Mrs. Jenkins?"

Pearl started, shook her head just slightly. She combed her fingers behind her ears and said, "Yes, yes, of course, Mr. Phillips. I'm just fine. You get off to work now. And let's keep our pants on today."

Will tipped his invisible fedora and disappeared behind the door to the back stairs, leaving Pearl to gaze out the window a little longer.

8

By the time he'd showered, brushed his teeth and thrown on some aftershave, it was still only 8:30. Mad Dog expected him to be late, but here he was right on time. He couldn't go in yet or his partner would indeed chew him, for snack and then for lunch. Will could just hear it.

"What're you doing here, Willy? Couldn't wait to get to work? There ain't no teacher here—don't know whose pet you're trying to be. But hey, if you're looking for something to do, I have a sports coat in the closet. You could pretend to be your daddy, and I'll go play football with the real neighborhood boys. I even have a cigar you could pretend to light. Unless you'd prefer a Tootsie Roll, I mean."

Why he'd ever confided that story to the likes of Mike Delaney he'd never understand. Delaney carted it out every chance he got.

A light breeze brushed across Will's arm, the window open the crack he'd left it during his early morning escapade. "There we go," he said aloud, and crouched down to open it the rest of the way. It slid right up, as though to spite him, and he cursed it. He propped a tall textbook on its edge to keep the window from avenging itself, then looked back for a book to take out with him. Dozens of unfinished and unstarted books piled up in an uneven stack on the floor beside the dresser. He ran his finger down the spines and stopped at a thick aged slate-colored volume with the old Random House Olympic torch runner emblazoned on the side. He imagined the runner was gold once, but was now worn to a dirty beige against the black oval. *The Complete Poems of Keats and Shelley*. Will smiled. Brother Benjamin had given it to him. He loved the old volume but hadn't touched it in months.

He harbored a hidden inclination toward poetry but in the hard boiled world of adjusting, reading a sonnet seemed like something that could get a guy killed. It was perfect, Ben had told him. Like a book with a compartment cut out of the pages to hide a flask of whiskey, this one also let a guy hide a secret vice: the cover was bound upside down. So he could read the book, and if anyone saw him, it would look like he was posing.

Plausible deniability.

The stack nearly toppled when he slid the book out. He pushed the rest against the wall and crawled out the window onto the porch roof. The crisp yellowed pages—warped and curled together from moisture—let out a musty odor when they opened. Random House hadn't had the foresight to print a publication date, so its age would be forever a secret. The first half of the book contained John Keats. The latter half was Percy Bysshe Shelley, with explanatory notes from Mary Shelley. He'd managed to avoid reading Mary Shelley's *Frankenstein* in high school, not wanting to mar the joy of watching Gene Wilder in the classic Mel Brooks *Young Frankenstein* film with images from its namesake.

The aged paper crackled as he flipped pages, searching out his favorite passage.

> *Oh for ten years that I might overwhelm*
> *myself in poesy; so I may do the deed*
> *that my own soul to itself decreed.*

Then I will pass the countries that I see
In long perspective, and continually
Taste of their pure fountains.

"Ten years, Keats?" Will muttered out loud. "Ten years is a hell of a long time to wait to do something your soul already decreed. What's the deal, man? What are you waiting for?"

Will asked the same questions as many times as he'd read the verse. What did Keats want to do, why would it take so many years, and what the hell ever got done just because a guy decided to overwhelm himself in poetry called by an old fashioned word?

Then again, maybe that's why it would take so long, Will thought. Poetry could surely slow a guy down.

"Well, Phillips," Will said, "at least Keats' soul had decreed to do something. That's more than you've got."

It was true. As best as he could tell, Will's soul had decreed no deed to itself to do.

He set the book beside himself on the shingles and rested his head against the house with a sigh.

"Your soul, Phillips. I wonder if you even have one."

Of course he had a soul. It might have been shriveled and dried up like the few apples that hung stubbornly on Pearl's apple tree through the winter, but he had one. Will worked in extremes. Black and white. On or off, hot or cold. Barbara used to say he'd go from zero to sixty in no time, never able to pace himself between two points. He didn't have room in his head for a shriveled soul in need of attention—only good souls and no souls. And since he couldn't see a good soul, he saw soul-less.

Did Joe Murphy read Keats? For all the books he had in his house, surely he read a few poets. He could probably tell Will about the taste of pure fountains, Joe could. When he saw Joe the next day, he'd bring the Keats along. The old man would like that. He reached for the book at his side, but bumped it, sending it skittering down the slope of the roof. He half dove for it, trying not to slide off himself, but it was too late. The corner of the thick gray volume hit the edge of the gutter, flipped up and toppled right over the edge of the roof.

"Damn," Will muttered, then heard the startled gasp of his landlady below.

"Damn again," he said, crawling on his knees to the edge of the roof.

He peered over and found Pearl on the sidewalk with a watering can in one hand and the other on her hip staring at the book splayed open in the grass. She followed its path up to the roof and stared at Will, blinking behind her glasses against the sun.

"Mrs. Jenkins, I am so, so sorry. It didn't hit you, did it?"

"For the love. What are you doing on my roof?" Pearl demanded.

"I was out here to read in the fresh air, and the book slipped, and, well…this." He opened his hands.

Pearl bent over and picked up the book. "And Keats, Mr. Phillips? Am I to believe you were on my roof reading John Keats?"

"Well, umm, yes," Will said, figuring there was no better story than that.

"I have never heard of anything so ridiculous in all my

life." Pearl tucked the book under her arm and strutted away. She stopped after just a few steps, turned back and looked up at Will, who was still peering over the edge of the eave. Something flashed across her jet black eyes. Maybe anger. Maybe mischief. Will wasn't sure.

"I'll have you know, William Phillips, that when I was a girl, I only read Emily Dickinson on that roof. It's no place for John Keats."

Until just now, he hadn't connected silver-haired Pearl Jenkins and the legendary Butler kids, of which she was surely one, as lumberman Pete Butler's granddaughter. There were stories around town about how the Butler children used to climb out their bedroom windows and jump from one ledge to the other. He watched Pearl walk away, smiling at the eye-twinkling smirk he knew she must be sporting.

Young Pearl Butler must have scared her mother half to death, all for a little Emily Dickinson on a mossy cedar-shake roof.

Will stood and put his hands in his pockets, surveying his neighborhood in the cool morning breeze. An old church stood on the corner of the next block. The stone bricks were blond, almost golden in a way that looked warm, belying that they were still cold as stones can be, holding up the framework of a massive oak door twice Will's height and probably as thick as his middle. The finish was peeling off the wood doors and window frames. A few pieces of color were broken out of the stained glass designs along the side of the building. Churches were built like fortresses, meaning to call to the downtrodden, if one could just pry open the six-ton door with fingers that splintered and bled. This one had closed down a couple of years ago when they were down to a half dozen parishioners, too few to bring in an offering sufficient to keep the lights on. They deeded the building over to the historical society for a dollar and let them pay the bills. Now they just turned the lights on for tours, by appointment only.

The mortuary across the street had been shuttered for years too. They'd been bought up along with other smaller family funeral homes in the region by a one-stop-shopping death and dying conglomerate out of Nebraska that built a new funeral home mini-mall south of town. But of course no one wanted to buy the old house, considering all the dead people that had been in it over the last hundred years. Will sat with a whiskey and the realtor at the Prairie Schooner Grill one night and told him, "Nobody should be afraid of the old Thomas house. Nobody's actually ever died in a funeral home. They show up already dead."

Next to the abandoned Thomas Funeral Home was a brown three-story rental with overgrown junipers ready to blockade the front door. When Will first moved to town, the Downing sisters still lived there. Butler built the house for their father, who had been the mayor (to hear them tell it, for about a hundred years) in the 1920s. Frances and Jenny never married and were never seen apart. Will saw them in the supermarket on hot July days, dressed as they were all year long, in elegant hats they bought in 1950-something and full length gloves, playing the part of some nonexistent aristocracy in their heads. They stayed in the brown house from the day they were born until the day they died. Well, until the two days that they died. Jenny, three years younger, died the day after Frances, on her 73rd birthday.

The Downing house had held his interest since he noticed the new renter. Cameron Julian moved in from Minneapolis three months ago as the new head of the telecommunications company. She kept to herself, a trait Will found appealing, and she went away almost every weekend, a habit he found quietly intriguing. He'd only seen her a few times. Once, when he went to pay his overdue wireless bill and she happened to be walking through the office. Another time when he pulled into Pearl's driveway, she was just getting out of her Toyota hybrid. And then one day she was walking her dog.

Now, the door of the old brown house popped open while he was still staring and Cameron walked out. She wore a navy suit and carried a thin black briefcase over her shoulder. Her long, honey hair was tied up in the back and bounced like a schoolkid skipping on the playground as she took the steps down to the sidewalk, smiling into the air as she walked.

Here was an unobstructed view of a beautiful woman who didn't know she was being watched. He looked down at his wrist, studying the time, which he had no need to know, until he heard the car door slam. He looked up again when she was shielded from his clear view by the reflection of trees against the side glass.

Cameron drove away and Will walked to the edge of the roof as if he'd follow her right off the edge, stopping instinctively as he reached the eave.

9

It would be a couple of hours before Mad Dog would expect him in the office. Will stood at the edge of the eave looking down the street where Cameron's car was no longer visible. He fumbled his shirt pocket for cigarettes. As he flicked his lighter, he remembered.

"Nina! Damn."

He'd forgotten to call her last night as he'd promised. Odds were good she'd forgotten too, given the chaos with the kids and her exhaustion. At least he hoped she had.

"She'll understand," he said out loud. "Can't imagine she hasn't dropped the ball a few times herself. Besides, it was late. She probably fell asleep as soon as the kids dozed."

Will pulled out his phone and called Mad Dog.

"Hey little Willy sleepyhead. Did you have a nice rest at Grandma Pearl's?" It irritated Will the way Mad Dog answered his calls without saying hello. It was a power move he made unconsciously, designed to throw the caller, who normally had the upper hand at the start of a call, off guard. Will hated caller ID for this reason alone.

"Fine. Great night. Listen, we forgot to call Nina. Can you check her file and give me her number?"

"Sure, Phillips. I'll give you your girlfriends' number. But why are you calling? The Schmidt claim is mine."

"Well, it was yours. Until you pissed off the customer. Think she's going to work with you now? I practically had to throw myself on top of you to keep her from scratching your eyes out. Reassign the case to me. You go off to coffee with

Stu and Charlie. You can have the next one."

"I could win her back, Phillips. I have a smooth side, you know."

"Sure, yeah. I've seen your smooth side. So have a dozen women in town who call it something else. Forget it. I'm not risking a complaint from the insurance company because you forgot how not to be an ass. Give me her phone number."

Mad Dog had no shame. He wanted coffee with his buddies Stu and Charlie more than he wanted to work his way through a house fire case that belonged to him, with a lonely, oversensitive woman and her histrionics, as he saw them. He told Will the number, laughed and hung up. Will imagined him doing an exaggerated fist pump in the air and shouting "Yesss!" while he spun a circle in his desk chair.

The breeze tickled Will's neck and he brushed his fingers through his hair, thinking it was time to see Stella for a haircut. His normally-straight hair would curl around his ears when it got too long and Will found combing it every morning to be a significant commitment. He turned his face into the breeze and wondered how much of his workday he could spend up here on the roof, then punched Nina's number into the phone. She picked up on the first ring and had not forgotten as he'd hoped; she was waiting for his call.

"Nina, hi, it's Will Phillips. Really sorry I didn't call last night. It was so late when we wrapped up, I think my brain just shut off."

Nina was quiet, gracious. She said she was tired too, and thanked him for calling.

"Here's my plan," Will said. "I'm going to send an initial report to your insurance company this afternoon. I'll ask them to send Justin an advance, probably a couple of grand, to take care of your living expenses while we work out the damages. I'll call a guy I like to work with who does good restoration, to get with you to sort out your contents—what can be salvaged and what can't. And I'll need you to get a contractor lined up who can do the structural repairs. When you find a guy, have him call me so we can crunch numbers."

Nina sniffled into the phone but didn't answer.

"Nina?" Will said softly. "Still with me?"

After a pause, Nina answered. "It's too much, Will. I don't know where to start."

"You said the kids were going away, right?"

"My mom is taking the older two."

"Okay then. After they go, you and Lucy Mae get some lunch. Then make a few phone calls—I'll text you the numbers of a couple of contractors I know in Fergus. Ask them to come bid the job and call me. And when my friend Steve calls, tell him you need help with your personal stuff. He'll set you up good. I promise these guys won't jack you around. Does that seem doable for today?"

Nina sniffled again. "I think so."

"Good. Once you have everybody lined up—probably next week—I'll come back and we'll all meet at the house and hammer out a game plan. One step at a time, Nina. That's all you have to do."

"Oh," Will added, "and cry if you feel like it. I hear it helps."

Nina laughed softly. "Okay." Will pictured her pulling her curls away and pinching up her face trying not to cry, which he figured was far less attractive than just crying, but he knew women did this anyway and wondered if they realized.

"You have my number," he said. "Call me if you think of anything."

"Thanks."

"You bet."

Will disconnected the call and put his phone back into its holster. He finished his cigarette on the roof, then crawled back through the window, gathered his keys and wallet and left by the back stairway.

He drove past the telecommunications office on Main Street on his way to the office and turned the corner, circling back around the block while he debated whether to stop. It would be pretty nice to be able to watch a Cubs game any night he wanted. He heard there was a channel that played all major league games. He pulled into a parking space and checked himself in the rearview mirror, fiddling uselessly with a stubborn curl behind his right ear. Definitely needed to call Stella for an appointment.

He got out of the truck, tucked his shirt into his jeans and walked inside. A young woman sat behind the front counter at her desk and looked up when Will came in. He scanned the large open office space looking for his neighbor, in case she happened to walk by. Her office was toward the back, flanked with full-length windows. Her desk was empty.

"What can I do for you today, Mr. Phillips?" asked the girl at the desk.

"I'm thinking of getting cable."

"Oh, do you have satellite now? We can switch you out."

"No, I don't have satellite."

"Are you switching carriers then? We can do that too.

Easy, since the house would already be wired."

"No," Will said. "I don't have any service. Actually, I don't have a television."

"You don't have a TV?" The girl's eyes grew wide. Apparently she'd never heard of anyone who didn't have cable, let alone a television.

"No. I should get one?" Will tried to prolong the conversation, looking behind the girl to see if Cameron would appear while they talked.

"Well, I've just never known anyone to order cable service without a TV. Why do you want it?"

Will smiled. "Well, I've been thinking of getting one. I figured maybe if I got cable hooked up, then I'd have more reason to get a television. You know, get my money's worth."

The girl hesitated, not sure whether to take him seriously or not.

"Which do you recommend getting first—cable or a television?"

"Ah, can you hold on just a second, Mr. Phillips?" She stepped back from the counter, not taking her eyes off Will. He folded his hands and rested them on the counter, amused with himself and looking winsome. The girl ducked her head into an open door and spoke to someone Will couldn't see. "Ms. Julian, could you come out here for a moment, please?"

Will tried not to smile any more than he already was. The girl had played right into his hand, as he knew she would. She was wired the way the young adjusters were, at the big insurance companies he'd worked for. They knew their scripts, everything in an "if-then" cadence, and performed brilliantly as long as nothing came along that didn't fit their carefully defined parameters. Like a guy who wanted cable but didn't own a TV.

She was lost.

Cameron Julian came out of the side office and stepped confidently toward the counter. "What can I help you with, Ashley?"

"Well, Mr. Phillips here wants to order cable service."

"Yes?"

"But he doesn't have a TV."

"Oh?" Cameron looked at Will, and Will looked back with a distinctively boyish grin.

"I know," he said. "I'm probably the only guy in town who doesn't have a television. But I'd kind of like to be able to watch the Cubbies and I heard I could get that major league channel."

"Cubs fan, eh?" Cameron said with a smile. "Twins fan, myself." She put out her hand and introduced herself. "Nice to meet you Mr. Phillips. I'm Cameron Julian."

"I know," Will said, then caught himself. "I mean, I'm an investigator. I guess I know a lot of things."

Cameron raised her eyebrows slightly and tipped her head.

Will blushed. "I mean, not that I know a lot of things like I'm a genius or something. I just ... collect information. Yeah. That's it. Not that I'm collecting information about you. In particular."

A smirk crossed Cameron's face and she shifted her weight.

"Look, never mind that, okay? Call me Will." He looked at his feet, wishing he'd gone straight to the office. "If I promise to get a television, can I get cable for it please?"

"Well, you'll have to provide verification of ownership within 24 hours of installation."

"Are you kidding me?" Will looked up at Cameron, who was grinning at him. "I'm sorry. I think I got this started all wrong. Umm. I rent a room from Pearl Jenkins in the old gray house on 7th Street. Do you know it?"

Of course Cameron would know it, but he didn't want to reveal he knew where she lived.

"Oh, of course! Pearl Jenkins is a real gem. I live right across the street."

"Seriously? In the old Downing place? What a coincidence."

"You're not the Mr. Phillips she keeps telling me I need to meet, are you?"

Will smiled. He shifted mentally between irritation at Pearl for not letting him make his own first impression on Cameron and relief that he did not have to make his own first impression on Cameron. He decided it was probably for the best, assuming Pearl had talked to her on a good day, when she hadn't found him pantsless or on her roof. "She's been telling you that, eh? I hope she's said good things."

"Well, she said you're a lousy pool player, you leave your towels on the floor, and you smoke too much. But also that you are a marvelous storyteller and that your crankiness is just for show because of your work."

Will put his hands in his pockets and looked at the floor. "She didn't say much then, hmm?" A moment later, he was pulling at the curl behind his ear, wrapping it around his index finger.

"Oh, and she said you need a haircut."

Will laughed. "Well, she's nothing if not thorough. I guess you know all you need to know about me then."

Cameron turned to the computer on the counter and tapped a few keys. "So. Are you really going to buy a television to use your cable, or are you just here to meet me on a Pearl's errand?" She smiled.

Damn, he thought. *This is a bold woman.*

Of course, he knew how it looked. And she was mostly right, except that Pearl hadn't sent him. She hadn't even mentioned Cameron, or her clandestine operation, which seemed curious. A good Yente usually worked both sides of the matchmaking equation. Unless, of course, she was trying to protect Will, didn't want him falling for some beautiful woman who would never be interested in someone like him.

That was it: Pearl wasn't sure Will could win someone like Cameron.

But then, Pearl had never seen Barbara.

Will straightened, smiled. "I want cable. Really. I'm stopping by Pete's this afternoon to buy a television. Promise."

"Very well then. Let's get your account set up. Looks like Pearl already has cable to the house, so we just need to split it out and run it up to your apartment. One of the guys will be over later this week. And I'll be sure to tell Pearl we met."

"No, don't," Will said. "Don't tell her. Let's just play along, our own way." He winked.

Cameron frowned for a moment, then smiled. "You're on, Mr. Phillips."

10

Will spent the afternoon in the office. He put his camera card into his laptop and downloaded the pictures from Nina's fire. He uploaded them, one by painstaking one, into his reporting interface, describing the detail of each shot with phrases like "northeast corner of kitchen burned to studs" and "smoke damage to siding on rear elevation." At one point during the afternoon he picked up a roll of tape and threw it across the hall, hoping to clip Mad Dog in the head and disrupt his whistling in the office across from his, while he photocopied a new lawsuit.

Somehow Will never seemed able to fully enjoy both parts of his work at the same time. There were days he wanted to do nothing but the paperwork. Compiling estimates in the solitude of his office, not having to go out, not having to deal with customers. Other times he despised the tedium of the desk.

It occurred to him that Barton Keyes had a secretary in *Double Indemnity*. Someone to take dictation, fill out his forms, assemble his reports into something coherent. Will grew weary of pricing sheetrock, deciding whether to allow for one coat of paint or two, and longed for the road, drifting from farm place to farm place, from one small adventure to the next.

The people fascinated him. From scheming Dr. Runyans to sweet little ladies like Pearl to that wild-eyed woman who threatened to trap Will under her doublewide. He chuckled. That woman, with unruly red hair that looked like she combed it with a rake, was the only customer who'd ever really terrified him. Most of the time the threats made him laugh quietly inside his head, but this woman seemed to be part wolf, and when she bared her teeth a guy had to stand back.

Will worked a short stint as a supervisor for Universal Indemnity's national claim office. The gig turned out to be a lot of adult day care and taking complaints, trying to persuade customers that even if they didn't get what they thought they deserved, their adjusters were honestly more than 12 years old and really were knowledgeable professionals. When a customer complained about too much depreciation taken off their settlement, Will loved to say, "Well, I see Bruce only took 30 percent. If I were handling this claim, I'd have taken 50. Looks like you got a good deal. And now I'll probably have to write Bruce up." Of course, he wouldn't be writing Bruce up. But more often than not, the customer would all of a sudden be eager to work with Bruce again.

One afternoon a young woman from New Jersey called, livid because her adjuster had written to put a used bumper on her twenty-two-year-old Honda Civic POS (the informal industry term for a Piece of Shit, an older, high-mileage vehicle that was not much more than a rolling total loss). She told Will she was sending her boyfriend down there to beat the shit out of his sorry ass.

Will had taken one too many cranky phone calls that day, and had no time for someone threatening bodily harm, especially over a few dollars and a repair that probably would improve her car. These were the times he relished putting the small town's remote location to good use.

"I understand you're upset, Ma'am," he said, following the script for empathy. "I would be too. Listen. If you're wanting to come to the office to beat up my sorry ass (and believe me, it couldn't be sorrier), here's what you'll need to do. You're in Newark, right? That's handy, since you have an airport there. Get your boyfriend a flight to Minneapolis. It's lovely this time of year, so you should think about coming along. Oh, and make sure you have a rental car reserved. (I can get you a discount with Hertz, if you'd like.) Just take I-494 out of the airport to the west, then pick up US Highway 12. If he drives straight through, he'll be at the office in just under half a day. Now, we close at 4:30, so if he gets in late, just have him check in to the Motel 6 on South Elm Street. I'll be at my desk by 8:00 in the morning."

The girl hung up around the time he said "rental car," but Will kept on for the sake of his office mates who needed a late Friday afternoon laugh.

Sometimes he missed those days, working with people from all over the country. But then he was confined to a desk in a tall brick building and had no windows. Now at least he was on the open road a few times a week. His farmers with their slower and gentler ways were good company, and only one had ever threatened to put the dogs on him that wasn't in jest. Even then, it wasn't that the dog was so mean, but he'd been in a recent tussle with a skunk. The farmer made his point.

Will finished his narrative report detailing the likely cause of the fire and apparent damage, stacked the documents into a single digital file and emailed it to the insurance company's inside claim rep, a short, wiry twenty-something named Christopher Davis, who had trouble growing sideburns

He looked at the clock. 4:28. It felt like he'd been working on the Schmidt case for days. He popped open CNN on his desktop computer. He'd been a news junkie once, from the time CNN changed the news world with the opening explosions of the first Gulf War, covering the conflict 24 hours a day. America got to know Bernie Grace and Wolf Blitzer as they reported from under the furniture in their hotel, having no idea how the news cycle would turn on its ear and begin to dominate American life. Will stayed up until 4:00 in the morning during the 2000 election, anxiously waiting for the Miami-Dade returns to decide the Bush-Gore contest, not realizing it would take weeks and a handful of court decisions to decide how to count all those hanging chads. He thrived on the news then, as it seemed to feed an insatiable hunger for knowledge. No, it was not for knowledge. It was for information. There was a difference.

After another election cycle he'd been done and barely kept up. Most weeks now he only checked in on Saturdays over breakfast, figuring that any event that had staying power would still be active in the headlines by then. But this week the government had run itself out of money and shut itself down for the first time since the Clinton administration, and he wanted to know if anything had changed.

It hadn't.

He opened his desk drawer and pulled out a bottle of bourbon and a highball glass. Just then, Mad Dog stuck his head in the door.

"I'm checking out for the night, Phillips." He shook his keys. "You closing up soon?"

Will leaned back in his chair and put his feet up on the desk, crossing them at the ankles. His boots were still marked with soot from Nina's fire.

"Come on in, Mike. I'm just winding down for the day." He held the bottle toward his partner. "Drink?"

Will slid the glass across the desk. Mad Dog caught it as he sat down in the side chair, then sighed and slicked his hand down his face, fingering his neatly trimmed goatee. Will was always a little jealous of his partner's salt and pepper beard. "Glad today is over." Mad Dog tilted the bottle.

"Long one, eh? What're you working on?"

"That Edith Landberg burn case for Alliance Mutual. She's got Parkinson's. Shakes like a leaf. She had to go and overfill her coffee mug on a day when the regulator was out on the Mini Mart's coffee machine. So she spills the coffee all over her hand, burns it right up."

"How bad?"

"Third degree. It's nasty. 'Course, all these places are run by teenagers now. Nobody can find me the paperwork to say when the machine was serviced last. I'd like to put it on the maintenance company. Alliance wants me to put it on Edith, like people with Parkinson's should ever only drink iced tea."

"Who are you working with there? Alliance is usually pretty reasonable."

"Cindy Greenfield."

Will whistled and shook his head. "Except Cindy Greenfield." He tipped back the last of his drink and set the glass on the desk for emphasis. Cindy Greenfield was a tough sell. Will had managed to persuade her to see things his way on a couple of cases over the years but most of the time, when they disagreed, she came out on top. Mad Dog tended to agree with her more often than not, cynically believing everyone was out to make their retirement bucks on his dime. It was unusual to see him siding with a claimant.

"'Course, it's not like I care about the lady, or anything," Mad Dog continued, knowing what Will was thinking. "I'm trying to protect the company. She could have a pretty solid case and we could settle it before it gets out of control, but Cindy's having none of it."

Will screwed the cap back on the bottle and set it in the drawer. "Good luck with that."

Mad Dog set down his glass and pushed back his chair. "You playing poker tonight, Phillips?"

"Nah, not tonight. Have some things I need to take care of." He picked up his keys and phone and slapped Mad Dog on the back on his way out the door. "Try not to lose all of it tonight, eh Mike?"

Will walked down Main Street to the flower shop and picked out a small bouquet for Pearl. He didn't know what kind they were—Pearl surely would—but he liked that they looked a little wild, not like flower shop flowers. Then he crossed the street to Pete's TV and Appliance to see about a television.

Pete Carlson came up from the back room when Will walked in and set off the bell. Most stores on Main Street installed motion sensors in the front, not having enough foot traffic any more to justify a full time person on the sales floor. Staff could be working in the back room and still know when a customer came in.

"Hey, Phillips. You didn't have to bring me flowers." Pete smiled and reached for the bouquet. Will slipped the flowers behind his back and reached to shake Pete's hand in a single motion.

"These flowers aren't for you, but I'm sure there's a gorgeous fella out there who would love to bring you flowers if you didn't live out here in the middle of nowhere. How's a guy supposed to know where to look for you?" Will brought the flowers back out in front of him. "These are for Pearl Jenkins. Need to make up for almost knocking her out this morning."

"Oh?" Pete's eyebrows arched.

"Long story, but it involves John Keats and Emily Dickinson. You'd enjoy it—over a beer sometime. Listen, I need a TV. Finally going to get cable in my room."

"Geez, Phillips. You get cable and you'll never come out again."

"Nah, just want to be able to watch the Cubbies."

"You want something big? I can give you a great deal on a 55-inch plasma screen. Mount it on the wall, pivots to any angle. You'll love it."

"Hell, Pete. I don't think my little room has a wall big enough for a 55-inch television. How about something compact, like I can set on my dresser. Maybe 21 inches."

"Tell me you at least want high def. There's no other way to watch baseball."

"Whatever you say I want, Pete, I want. Make it high def."

Will picked out the TV Pete told him to pick out, paid for it, and carried it out of the store and back down the street to his truck. He parked behind the house and knocked on Pearl's back door. She answered drying her hands on a blue and white checked apron. Will bowed and held the flowers out.

"Indulgences, Mrs. Jenkins. I am so sorry for nearly letting John Keats split your skull this morning."

Pearl laughed and took the flowers with a little curtsy. "Come in, Mr. Phillips, before all the flies in the county find my kitchen. I need to put these in water."

She rummaged through a dark oak cupboard under the sink for a vase, then rearranged the flowers in it until she was satisfied. "I'm glad to see you've the good sense to bring a lady flowers, Mr. Phillips. You never know when you might meet someone you take a fancy to."

11

Will rose early the next day after an uneventful night's sleep, the first in months without an episode of night sweats. He showered, dressed and brewed a pot of Folgers, as black as he could persuade Mr. Coffee to drip it. With Keats in hand and a tall mug of coffee on the windowsill, he crawled gingerly through the window and onto the roof, congratulating himself on his quiet morning discovery.

The sun was up and making its way through the flowering-whatever tree, which he'd never taken the time to learn the real name of, in Pearl's front yard. The light glinted playfully off the top of tiny red berries that had replaced the blossoms of a few weeks ago. Will noticed for the first time that the berries were born red—they weren't formed green so they could redden as they ripened.

"Huh," he said aloud. "They come that way."

He slid his thumb into the yellowed pages of his book and opened to "Endymion," a work John Keats was clearly not happy with before he published it. He prefaced it with an apology of sorts in which he conceded it wasn't fit to print but he had given up improving upon it. There was nothing more he could do, he said, and while he saw that he should be punished for it, no one would actually do so. "No feeling man will be forward to inflict it: he will leave me alone, with the conviction that there is not a fiercer hell than the failure in a great object. This is not written to forestall criticism, of course..."

Well played, John. And I'd thought that technique was the handmaiden of the modern Internet writer.

Will used to peruse a lot of writers online to occupy him-self between appointments but grew weary of reading work that was prefaced by the author's preemptive comment, "I probably shouldn't hit publish..." which was probably true, but it always managed to get the writer a shopping cart full of affirmations like, "No, really, this is great," and "Don't be so hard on yourself," when clearly the writer should have been a little harder.

Of course, Will was no literary critic. He didn't know enough to say whether "Endymion" was poetic brilliance or if Keats should have given it "another year's castigation." But he was happy enough to have it published, if only for the poet's anterior lament.

> *The imagination of a boy is healthy, and the mature imag-ination of a man is healthy; but there is a space of life between in which the soul is in a ferment, the character undecided, the way of life uncertain, the ambition thick-sighted: thence proceeds mawkishness, and all the thousand bitters which those men I speak of must necessarily taste in going over the following pages.*

Will closed the book on his finger without reading a word of "Endymion" and held it in his lap, rested his head against the cool asphalt siding and closed his eyes.

> *...a space of life between in which the soul is in a ferment, the character undecided, the way of life uncertain...*

The creak of the screen door across the street in the early

morning quiet startled him at the same time as his phone rang. He jerked upright from his slouch and fished his phone from his shirt pocket.

"Phillips."

He paused. "Oh, good morning, Joe. You're up awfully early."

He stood to his feet in time to see Cameron Julian going down the front steps of her house.

"You bet, Joe. I have business at a ranch a couple of hours north. Figured I'd stop by your place on my way back."

Will looked away from Cameron and toward the old church, while she walked to her car.

"It'll be late afternoon so no need to sit around the house waiting for me. I'll call you when I leave the ranch, give you an ETA. How would that be?"

A door slammed shut and he looked down into the street as he bid Joe goodbye. Cameron stood next to her car, hands on her hips, looking up at Will on the roof.

"Good morning, Mr. Phillips."

Will reached to put his phone in his pocket but missed, letting it fall to the cedar shakes. It slid down the slope of the roof just as the Keats book had done the day before. This time it dropped into the gutter. Will hadn't moved.

"Mr. Phillips?"

He closed his mouth, which he had opened just before dropping his phone, in hopes of an answer which didn't come. He opened it again.

"Umm. Good morning, Ms. Julian." He collected himself, put his hands in his pockets and puffed out his chest, taking a deep breath and looking into the sky. "Beautiful morning, don't you think?"

"What are you doing up there, Mr. Phillips? And does Mrs. Jenkins know you're there?"

"Well, John Keats and I sort of dropped in on her yesterday. But listen, would you mind just calling me Will? Feels awfully formal to be talking to a guy on a roof that way."

"Cameron, then, to you. I need to get to work. You'd better get down before she catches you up there again."

"Right. I'm off to interview a ranch hand. Have a nice day, Cameron."

"Same to you."

Cameron opened her door. "Hey Will. Don't forget your phone."

12

Will loved trips out into the Coteau. He lived in the bottom of a bowl, in the Arbon Valley. But once he got out onto the highway, he could see the blue-purple Coteau ringing the lip. Today, he would drive right into it and with any luck (and Barbara's snippy cooperation), he'd not get lost in the hills.

He took the interstate part way, then defied Barbara's histrionics just for the fun of it and exited to take a county road to the north. After three or four minutes she stopped recalculating and conceded to the new route. Will mused over the dilapidated farm buildings that cropped up in fields near the highway, one of his favorite parts of being on the road. He wondered when a certain swayback barn had last held livestock, or what year a granary with half a roof was last stocked. He always saw an old farmer in his mind, blue and white striped Dickey overalls buckled over a belly grown round on a certain farm wife's meat and potatoes at every meal. He pictured him there touching the splintered boards starting to give way on the old building, thinking about just one more harvest before moving to town.

Entering the hills was like driving off the map into an other-world with all the spaciousness of the prairie but with the rich contours of softly rounded peaks and deep bottomed gullies, dotted with tree groves filling out with the green of spring.

After a couple of hours following Barbara from one lonesome, winding gravel road to another, Will arrived at Northwind Pastures, a horse ranch and supper club a good hour's drive from anywhere else. It was the kind of place a guy could take his wife because she thought the Death by Chocolate dessert really was to die for. Only the early reservations could get a seat by the window of Northwind's log cabin lodge, where he could watch the chef grill him a 20 ounce steak at the end of a pitchfork over the nightly bonfire, in some sort of primal tradition.

He parked in the gravel lot between the lodge and the horse arena and walked around to the entrance. Waiting at the counter, he felt the stares of five junior high girls wearing bed head and their nighties in the dining room, looking at him over bowls of oatmeal and blueberries. Will fidgeted at the counter, rolling the round knob on the silver toothpick dispenser until he had discharged the makings of a doll-sized raft, if he only had a length of dental floss to lash the toothpicks together. He'd learned years ago never to turn around but it did not stop him from feeling the stares keenly.

After a minute that felt like twenty, a short, rotund woman came out of the kitchen in Roper boots, dark blue jeans and a white apron. The food service head covering made her look like she was on her way to surgery.

"Can I help you?" she extended a plastic-gloved hand with bits of ring macaroni stuck to the fingers.

Will hesitated, then pulled a business card from his briefcase and slipped it between two of her fingers in place of a pasta-laden handshake.

"Will Phillips. I'm here to see Amos Bruner on an insurance matter."

"Oh, right. Amos said you'd be coming. Have a chair by the bar, and I'll let him know you're here. Can I get you something? Coffee? Water?"

"A cup of coffee would be great, thanks." Will sat down at the bar, positioning himself so the girls were in his line of sight. If they could sense the awkwardness of their continued staring they might go back to their oatmeal.

The cook returned with a cup of tepid coffee. "Amos will be right out. Cream?"

Will looked into his cup. "No need, thank you though."

He pulled his phone from the holster. None of the messages required his attention but he flipped through them a few times to appear busy and important for the sake of the pre-teens. Reprieve came in the hard footsteps against the wood floor. Amos Bruner, owner of Northwind Pastures, was a tall, slender man in his late 60s. He wore thick-heeled Durango boots with a sharp pointed toe and weathered Levi 501s. A leather holster hung off his western belt, holding a black handled pair of pliers, standard issue for any respectable cowboy. He tipped his hat toward the back of his head and clapped a hand on Will's shoulder.

"Mr. Phillips? Sorry to make you wait."

Will put out a hand. "Mr. Bruner? Nice to meet you. And no problem. I think I'm a little early. I didn't get lost."

Amos chuckled. "Let me show you around and then we can go talk in my office."

Will closed his briefcase and tucked it under one arm, following Amos into the dining room.

"You met our campers? It's our girls intermediate week. Cassandra was here two weeks ago for our advanced camp."

Will smiled at the girls as he walked past, which they took to mean they should resume staring. Amos pointed to the loft, accessed by a rough-hewn wooden staircase. "We've got bunks up there for about twenty. House campers in the spring and summer, hunters in the fall and winter. Serve 'em meals in the dining room and then open the supper club to the public on the weekends."

He stopped by the door to the kitchen and waved a thumb. "You already met Darla, our cook. At night she supervises the campers. And down the hall here is my office. Let's go sit."

Amos eased behind his enormous pine desk while Will took a seat opposite and opened his briefcase. "Mr. Bruner, what I need to do is photograph the grounds and in particular where Cassandra fell. I'll need to meet the horse she was riding and interview any of your staff who were present. I'll also need any paperwork you have on the horse. Registration, purchase records, vet records, you name it."

"Well, she was riding Pharaoh. Bought him about a year ago; never had a problem."

Amos picked up his phone and dialed. "Cade, I need you to come to the office and talk to the insurance guy about Cassandra Mills."

He opened a drawer and pulled out a stack of yellow and blue papers, rifled through and pulled out Pharaoh's paperwork. "I'll go make a copy of this for you. Cade will be in here any minute to talk. He's my ranch hand and runs the riding camps."

Will sat back and looked at the photographs framed all over Amos's walls—cowboys and ranch hands and horses at shows and rodeos. Amos came back in with a young cowboy.

Caden Carson stood nearly six feet tall. He took off his

Stetson and shook his blond hair that was tousled in an intentional way. If he lived in California instead of the Dakotas, the muscular young man would surely be a surfer, not a ranch hand. A silver belt buckle as large as a tea saucer—not one earned at a rodeo but designed to look like one—held the ends of his embossed leather belt together, clearly not needed to hold up a starched, tight pair of dark Carhartt jeans that could stand up in the corner on their own.

He put his hat on the desk. "I'm Cade, the head wrangler. Amos said you needed to talk to me?"

"I do, yes." Will motioned to a chair. "I need to interview you about the facts related to the Cassandra Mills matter."

Cade blinked. "Am I being sued?"

Will smiled at Cade, who couldn't have been much more than twenty, leastwise far too young to be facing a lawsuit for doing his job. He should be sued for flashing that sparkly white grin and winking those deep blue eyes in a room full of young girls, though.

"Not that I know of, Cade. As best as I can tell, she was treated and released from the ER with a mild concussion and has recovered nicely. I'm here because the insurance company is taking precautions. You never know which way the wind might decide to blow."

Will set his digital recorder between them and questioned Cade Carson, verifying that he took all the usual precautions when Cassandra Mills rode Pharaoh. He confirmed that Cade was standing nearby, as he always did, and that it appeared she had pulled the rein too tight on one side when she mounted, so that Pharaoh began to spin, as he was trained to do, when the rein was pulled. Rather than loosen her grip, Cassandra reached for the other rein, and Pharaoh reared up, throwing Cassandra to the ground and then falling back on top of her. According to Cade, it all happened too fast for him to intervene.

The ranch hand took Will out to the barn and arena where the incident occurred so he could photograph the scene. Pharaoh wandered up to the fence and aside of sneezing on his hand when Will reached to pat his nose, he seemed to be a gentle horse that got pulled the wrong way.

Will was pleased to see a bright yellow sign on the fence advising patrons of South Dakota Codified Law 42-11-2 that exempted equine professionals from liability for injuries or death due to inherent risks of equine activities. Meaning, the horse owner or trainer isn't going to be responsible for things that horses do in the course of being horses. Will snapped a photo of the sign for his file.

After a couple of hours at the ranch, Will had gathered the information he needed. He couldn't help thinking, though he had no idea why he thought it, that Joe Murphy would enjoy this place. He packed his gear and the file away and stopped back at Amos's office to tell him he was finished.

"Feel free to call me if anything comes up. And if the family contacts you, best to refer them to me for any questions. That way you can keep running your business and be well thought of, and I can be the bad guy if anyone needs to be."

"Thanks for everything, Mr. Phillips. Stop by some weekend for a steak."

"I might just do that, Mr. Bruner." Will smiled and shook the rancher's hand. "Have a great afternoon."

He passed through the dining room on his way out, happy to see the girls had dressed and gone to the barn for a grooming lesson. He went out to his truck and drove off the ranch in a direction that felt like south but without plugging Barbara in to be sure.

13

Will checked the clock. If he'd grown up a Boy Scout, he would have been able to tell by the sun's position, nearly straight overhead, that it was just after 1:00. *Damn.* If he didn't get lost, he'd be at Joe Murphy's by 3:00. Joe could have him captive for hours before he could make a polite excuse to be on his way.

"What's your problem, Phillips?" he asked aloud. "You stop, exchange a few niceties with the old man, pick up your thermos, and say goodbye. How hard is that?"

Seemed not hard at all. Will wasn't looking for new friends, after all, certainly not customers who'd become friends.

Margery Burnette was determined to be his friend. He'd been called to her house near the lake last winter. Margery was a snowbird, spent the cold months in a retirement villa in New Mexico. She came back early when her neighbor called last February.

"Margery," she said, "your ruby chenille lamp shade is hanging in your apple tree. Did you come home and not tell me?"

No, Margery had not come home. She was still lying poolside under a floppy cotton hat on a chaise lounge at the villa in Santa Fe, reading the latest Oprah book club title, sipping sweet tea through a straw and humming the notes of the big country hit single she was going to write. She caught the next flight home to find her house turned upside down by a handful of truants who'd gotten bored on just the second day they skipped out of school.

Will spent two hours with Margery going room by room through her stately three-story summer home, taking notes as she listed what was missing from each. Drawers had been dumped out, beds stripped, furniture broken and slashed with a box cutter they didn't think to take with them. They had kicked the back door in, but closed it securely, propping a patio chair against it from the outside when they were done, as though to keep out other delinquents like themselves.

In the master bedroom, Will knelt amidst pink and purple nighties strewn across the floor. He picked up an overturned drawer from Margery's vanity table and slid it into its slot. Margery rummaged in the closet, looking one last time for a ring she insisted had been in her jewelry box. Will looked up to see her bury her face in a full length mink coat and let out a single low, muffled moan. She held herself there a moment, then pulled back and wiped her face on a bright orange and purple scarf she picked up from the floor.

"I said I wasn't going to cry, Mr. Phillips. Now look at me."

Will picked up a nightie, folded it and set it into the drawer before pushing it closed. He stood up.

"If you needed to cry, Miss Burnette, it would be understood. By now you've earned it."

"They stuffed steel wool into my garbage disposal and ran it until the motor burned out. Who does that?" she asked, looking at Will as though this sort of question had an actual answer.

"And they carried my boudoir lamp shade out into the yard and left it there to hang in the snow. Why, Mr. Phillips?

Why?"

"I don't know, Miss Burnette. If we knew the answers we could probably solve the problem, and then guys like me would be out of work."

Margery looked at Will, who was pulling blankets up to the bed.

"I write songs, you know. Famous ones." She paused. "I shouldn't tell you that. It's a big secret."

"A secret, eh?" Will smiled and picked up two oversized pillows and tossed them gently onto the bed.

"Yes, a secret." Margery picked up a turquoise necklace from the floor and reached behind her neck to hook the clasp. She slid her hands behind her salon-dyed big Nashville platinum hair to lift it out from behind the necklace. "You watch the big awards show? That song that won song of the year a few years ago—I wrote it."

"Is that right? I have to admit I don't listen to a lot of country music, but maybe I know it, if it was a big hit. What song?"

"Oh, I can't tell you which one," Margery said, wagging her finger at Will. "Part of my contract. I've probably said too much already."

"Well, of course I don't want to get you into any trouble," Will said. "I'll pretend this conversation never happened." He winked.

Margery played with the large turquoise pendant hanging over her ample bosom. "Oh, you're impossible. So easy to talk to, it seems like I'd tell you anything. I only write songs for one artist—he's won a lot of awards. He pays me $50,000 for a song, and neither of us tells anyone. He makes like he writes them himself, but he doesn't. That's our deal. But trust me, you've heard all kinds of my songs without knowing it. And he looks after me pretty good. He was livid when he heard what happened at the house. Wanted to fly right out here and I had to tell him that was nonsense. Besides, how could he show up in this little town without bringing on all the paparazzi?"

Will nodded. "You sure don't need a bunch of Nashville reporters in your front yard."

"He sent me that big bouquet of flowers in the living room though. Did you seem them?"

"Shoot. I must have missed them on the way in, but I'll be sure to take a look and appreciate them right before I go."

"I want to take you to lunch."

"Oh, that's very kind of you Miss Burnette, but I can't let you do that."

"But I want to." She leaned onto one foot in such a way that Will almost felt she'd stomped it, without lifting it from the floor.

"I have this big long code of ethics I have to follow. Even have to sit through classes on it every year to keep my license. I just can't accept gifts from people. It's a rule. You don't want me to have to sit through more boring lectures, do you?" Will smiled.

"So I can't send flowers to your office, either?"

"Well, folks don't usually send flowers to guys like me anyway. But no."

"And if I did send them you'd refuse them? You would send the florist away with them?"

"Well, no, I'd probably take them if they showed up at the door. But I'd give them to my landlady."

Margery Burnette crossed her arms over her chest and tapped her foot, squinting her eyes at Will.

"How long then?"

"How long?"

"Yes. How long do we have to wait? If I called you in six months, then could we be friends?"

Will chuckled at the memory and reached to turn on the radio, which happened to be tuned to the country station and happened to be playing a very popular song by a former vocalist of the year, which may have been written by a woman sipping sweet tea through a straw poolside under a floppy hat at a retirement villa in Santa Fe.

Barton Keyes never had this problem. He waved his big cigar in the air from behind his big wooden desk and scared people who hadn't even done anything wrong into thinking they were guilty. He could make anyone sweat. And nobody ever begged to be his friend. Will needed a big cigar. Or a big desk. Instead he got lonely retirees and overwrought single mothers who wanted to be his soul mate.

His phone rang. He didn't recognize the number. Will punched the radio off with two fingers and clicked his headset on.

"Claims, Phillips."

"Hello, I'm looking for a Ray Johnson." He didn't recognize the voice.

"Sorry, You must have the wrong number. There's no Johnson here."

Will disconnected the call and reached absentmindedly to his lap, taking the loose fold of his Levis in his hand.

Around mile marker 56, Will realized he was on Highway

10 traveling east, not south. Highway 10, apparently, didn't run north and south. He wondered how far he was from Colbyville but refused to ask Barbara for help.

"I'll work it out, Barbara," he said, glaring at the closed glove box. "I'll work it out."

~

Will looked ahead and saw a sign for Country Road 14 and slowed. When he reached the intersection, he turned left. He didn't know where County Road 14 would lead, but the dashboard compass said he was pointed south, and the road was paved. That was good enough for today.

About a mile down the road, he crested a hill and saw he was at the top of the Coteau. He pulled to the side of the road, almost into the ditch because there was no shoulder, something Barbara would surely chastise him for, had she'd been turned on. There was no traffic on the narrow two-lane road, but he flipped on his hazards just in case, grabbed his cigarettes and phone and pulled the keys from the ignition. Across the highway, he stood above the valley and followed the ribbon of light-gray asphalt in varying degrees of disrepair as it wove down the side of the bowl through prairie and pasture, dotted with an occasional clump of trees or scattering of cattle. Spring greens were beginning to streak through the amber and brown fields, tall grasses laid flat by wind and the weight of snow, now melted off. *When people talk about the landscapes that seem to go on forever, they're talking about this place,* Will thought. Mixes of every color on the palette, but muted into the shades of the Dakotas' open prairies, finally met at the far reaching horizon by an even vaster, empty blue sky.

"Was it worth leaving your skyline office?" Tom had asked one Christmas when Will had gone home to Chicago.

Will hadn't known how to answer his brother then. The move was complicated, not made with a single rationale or objective. He put his hands in his pockets and filled his lungs with a long, deep inhale of fresh country air. Surveying the endless valley he said aloud, "Yes, Tom. It was worth it."

He lit a cigarette and stepped down into the ditch to walk the barbed wire fence line. A small flock of sheep was grazing a thousand feet or so ahead but somehow hadn't picked up on his presence. He leaned a shoulder on a utility pole and watched them, occasionally letting out a low sound mimicking their staccatoed bleats.

A woolly brown sheep with black around the eyes and ears stopped munching grass at its feet and looked up at Will, catching his eye. They stood in a faceoff, staring each other down for a good two minutes before the sheep turned and ran, its companions chasing after, though clueless as to what they were running to or from.

Will laughed, then checked his phone for the time.

2:00. He should call Joe.

Joe answered on the first ring, as though waiting for the call.

"Joe, it's Will."

"Hello Will. You're still coming today, right? I have your thermos all ready for you."

"Yeah, you bet. I actually got done a little ahead of schedule. Hope you don't mind if I show up early."

"Oh, it's fine. I was going over to ogle antiques at the auction barn this afternoon but if you're coming early I'll stay home. When will you get here?"

"That's a good question, Joe. I'm not completely sure where I am. I should plug in the GPS and see what she says." He started toward the truck. "Listen, I'm on Culver County 14 just south of Highway 10. Any idea where that puts me?"

Joe laughed. "Directions really aren't your very best thing, are they?"

"I've been told that a few times."

"You're about an hour away. You could go back to Highway 10 and go east about 20 miles, then drop south on County 23. It'll take you straight into town. Call me if you get off track."

"Hey thanks, Joe. See you in a bit."

Will got in the truck and opened the glove box, pulling Barbara out for good measure. He plugged the cord into the socket, and lied, pressing "Okay" to confirm he wouldn't try to operate the GPS while driving. Then he yanked the cord back out and put it back into the glove box.

"Forget it, Barbara. I don't need you for this one. I've got it."

He slammed the door shut and started the truck.

~

Joe was standing outside his front door when Will arrived. His golden retriever was lying on the concrete stoop at his feet, front paws and head lolling off the top step. Joe waved with both arms when he saw the truck come around the corner. Will wasn't sure if it was Joe's delight at his coming, or if he was afraid he'd miss the house and drive on by. He hoped it was the latter.

Parking at the curb, he sat for a minute, bracing himself for what surely would not be a quick in-and-out to pick up his thermos. He knew without fully admitting it to himself that if he stayed the rest of the day, he would be partly to blame. It would surprise no one that a lonely old man would welcome the company of a virtual stranger, even the claims guy. But Will couldn't sort what it was that *he* wanted from the old man, and clearly, he wanted something.

He got out of the truck, walked to the passenger side and leaned his back against the bed. "I made it in a single day, Joe. What do you think of that?" Will grinned at the old man.

"I was starting to worry a little about you," Joe smiled. "I've heard they make a device now that talks to satellites or some remarkable thing, and it can guide you to your destination with laser-sharp precision. Maybe you should look into one."

Will laughed and shook his head. "Don't get me started, Joe."

The dog got up and plodded down the three steps to the sidewalk. At the bottom, he stretched, then trotted toward Will.

"Archie! Come back here," Joe scolded.

Will crouched and put a hand out toward the dog, palm up. "Hey, old fella."

The dog ignored Joe and kept coming. Will scratched him behind an ear.

"Archie! Come!"

"He's fine, Joe." Will riffled the softness. "Archie, eh? Great name for a dog."

"For Archibald MacLeish. The poet."

Will looked up at the old man, who was still standing on the steps, and smiled. "Why doesn't it surprise me that your dog is named for a poet, Joe?"

"Heh. I suppose it's not surprising at all. Do you know him?" Joe recited from memory:

> *Listeners of thousands of years and still no answers—*
> *Writers at night to Miss Lonely Hearts: awkward spellers—*
> *Open your eyes! here is only ear and the man!*

"Know of him, yes. Read him, no," Will said.

"Then listen up, Will. You need some MacLeish in your life."

> *There is only you: there is no one else on the telephone:*
> *No one else is on the air to whisper:*
> *No one else but you will push the bell.*
> *No one knows if you don't; neither ships*
> *Nor landing-fields decode the dark between:*
> *You have your eyes and what you see is.*
> *The earth you see …*

Joe looked into the sun. *The earth you see …*

"Oh, fiddle. I can't remember the rest. He says women and their soft breasts are as beautiful as they appear to be." Joe looked toward Will, still petting Archie on the sidewalk. "Do you know anything about a woman's breasts, Will?"

"More than a guy ought to, I suppose, Joe."

"Then a guy like you would like the piece, I should think."

A guy like me? Will thought. *What the hell does a guy like Joe Murphy know about a guy like me?*

"Oh, wait! There's this." Joe kept reciting.

> *Write it yourselves! Write to yourselves if you need to!*
> *Tell yourselves there is sun and the sun will rise:*

"Yes, I think a guy like you will like it, Will. Be sure to look it up when you get home and tell me what you think."

Will stood to his feet, debating whether to pull his Keats volume from his briefcase and ask Joe what *he* knew. He voted in favor of getting home sometime before next week and left it be.

"My town's library is pretty small, and the poetry section could fit in a shoebox. But I'll see if they can't order me in something from Mr. MacLeish from the state."

"Wonderful. And I suppose you'd like your thermos?"

"That would be great, Joe. And then I'll get out of your hair."

"Come on inside and I'll get it for you."

Come on inside. Will leaned to give Archie a final pat on the head. *That's the beginning of the end right there, and Joe knows it or he would have brought the thermos out to me. Damn, damn, damn.*

Against his better judgment, or perhaps in precise keeping with it, Will followed the old man into the dusty foyer, wondering if déjà vu counts when it is self-inflicted and foreknown.

"It's on the coffee table in the living room. Really, come on in."

Will felt something move between his feet and jumped back, then realized it was a charcoal gray cat pressing against his ankle. "Geez, Joe. I'd forgotten all about your cats," he lied.

Joe turned around. "Oh, that's just Emily. You must have made quite an impression on her last time you were here. Usually she doesn't come out of the bedroom."

Will held up in the dining room, now with two cats weaving in and out of his ankles, rubbing their fur against his pant legs. He pretended not to notice they covered his blue jeans with softly shed fur and bent down to pet them but pulled back quickly when Emily hissed. "Hey, what's the skinny little orange one's name?"

"The orange one? Eliot, of course," Joe called from the living room. "Say, I figured you probably missed your coffee today, since I still had your thermos. Can I get you a cup?"

Coffin nailed. Joe had planned to get him into the house for coffee. Will pulled his phone from his pocket to check the time, though it didn't matter since he'd kept his calendar open for the afternoon. *Get out of here now, Phillips, or plan to spend the rest of the day. You decide.*

"Well, I did have a cup before I left the ranch," Will said, and walked forward into the living room. Joe stood by his tattered rocker. He had swept the living room floor clean of Archie's gold fur piles and wiped down a wooden dining room chair, which he'd set next to the coffee table. The table was covered with a wrinkled lace tablecloth. There were two tall foam cups with plastic covers from the gas station two blocks away on the table, along with six Oreo cookies arranged in a circle on a paper plate.

Will paused. Joe smiled.

"But you know, the ranch's coffee was pretty terrible. I could use a decent cup."

14

The old man motioned to the wooden chair and Will sat down. Joe dropped into his rocker and picked up a cookie. "Used to keep these around for the neighbor kids," he said, twisting the dark wafers apart. The frosting stayed on one side. "When they used to stop and see the Missus."

"Oh yeah? When was that?"

Joe looked down into his lap. "Ten years."

"I'm sorry."

"Three months. Six days."

Will took a cookie and broke it in half with his thumbs. He took a bite.

"What was her name, Joe?"

"Millie."

The two sat in silence. Archie walked to the side of Joe's chair and rested his head on his knee.

"When I was a young man, I checked a poetry anthology out of the library to impress her so she'd go out with me. Had to read the thing to keep up the ruse, and before I knew it, I was hooked. 'Course, by then, so was she. Every day for thirty-seven years, Millie read me a poem over breakfast. "

Joe winked at Will. He took the top off his coffee and dipped his cookie in halfway. Will considered the soggy crumbs collecting at the bottom of the cup and shifted in his seat.

"Poetry can be a peculiar gateway, Will. It can be a way into all kinds of things that don't seem to have a way in, or that we don't even know we *want* in."

"I do read a little, Joe. I suspect you may be right. Especially about taking a guy into places he didn't know he wanted to go."

"Who do you read?"

"Well, the other morning I was reading Keats, at least until the book slid off the roof and nearly took out my landlady."

"I never knew Keats to be a violent sort. He must have been provoked somehow. He made it up to her, I hope?"

"Flowers go a long way, Joe."

"Who else?"

"Oh, I don't know. I'm not so well read. Billy Collins, Tony Hoagland. A little William Stafford, some Adrienne Rich. I read Neruda to practice my Spanish."

"Ah, Neruda, I knew it. " Joe nodded and smiled. "You are a man who can appreciate what a poet has to say about a woman's breasts."

Will pulled his shoulders in, feeling mildly exposed amidst the old man's clutter.

"You tidied up a bit, Joe."

"You noticed! Yes, I told you. I don't like for things to get out of hand." Joe looked around the living room, his face brightening at his accomplishment. "Say! Remember when I played the concertina for you?"

"Yes, of course. Very nice."

Joe got up and walked to the bookcase. "Well, I kept it out. I've been playing every day. Feels so good to have her under my fingers again."

He lifted the squeezebox out of the case and carried it to his chair. He began to play a tune and Will absentmindedly tapped his foot against the bare wood floor.

"Do you play an instrument, Will?"

"I don't. Used to play in the band in Junior High, but it didn't work out. Turns out I had a little trouble with rhythm."

The old man held the concertina out to Will. "Here. Come on, you should have a try."

Will waved his hands in front of him. "No, Joe. Really. That would be an awful thing for you to have to listen to. Your neighbors will probably call the police."

"My neighbors? Nah. Midge wouldn't mind."

"Wait. You have a neighbor named Midge?"

"She's a dancer. She's used to loud music."

Will laughed out loud. "Really, Joe. No. I don't think so."

Joe got up from his chair and stood in front of Will. "Put your coffee down, young man. You're going to give this a try." He set the concertina in Will's lap, then took his hands and fed them through the end straps. "Like that. Now, just press your hands together and pull them back apart."

Will was right. It sounded terrible. But Joe ignored the noise and Will's protests. "Just keep going. In and out, in and out. You'll get it."

He heard Randy Dalbright's voice hissing in his ear and cold spit running down his neck. But Joe was relentless. Will pulled and pressed, producing mournful, wailing sounds. "It's no wonder they call them bellows, Joe," Will shouted over the racket coming from his midsection.

Joe waved him off. "You're like a seventeen-year-old his first time in the back seat. Nobody's going to mistake you for Rudy Valentino. Let her show you where to put your hands."

"The buttons will give you a different note when you push or draw. Let me show you." Joe walked back to the book shelves and opened a second black leather case. "I told you I have three of these, right? They never get any attention anymore." He pulled an ivory instrument from the blue velveteen and sat back down in his chair with it. "Watch me."

Will stopped.

"And keep playing."

Joe started playing what sounded like a polka. Will didn't know any polkas but he'd seen enough of the dancers at the county fair to believe they all sounded like the same song with different titles. Beer Barrel Polka. Pennsylvania Polka. Blue Skirt Polka. Then there were the polkas that were called waltzes but were still just plain old blue skirt polka-dotted polkas.

He watched Joe and tried to mimic his pushes and draws until they were almost in synch. Then he tried to match his fingering on the buttons to create different notes. He stretched out his fingers and felt along the tops of the smooth, rounded buttons on each end of the bellows. He was unsure about pressing them just yet, but traced his middle finger along the top of each, trying to settle into Joe's pattern.

Will finally gave it a try, pressing his finger onto a button, then his thumb onto another, while he continued with the pushing and drawing with his hands. He winced at the sound but Joe hollered to him to keep playing, so he did, awkwardly.

Resigned that Joe would not let him stop, he leaned back in his chair and stretched his legs out in front of him. With his eyes closed, he walked his fingers from one button to the next, sometimes pressing down, sometimes enjoying the smooth feel under his fingertips. He began to relax.

Will didn't realize Joe had stopped, lost in the movement

of his fingers as he felt his way along the buttons.

"Will," Joe said. "Hey, Will."

Will opened his eyes.

"Song's over," Joe grinned.

"Oh yeah?" Will asked, holding his last draw. "Well. How'd we do?"

Joe laughed. "We did great, Will. You're a natural. You should really think about getting yourself one of these. I could watch for one at auction. You could learn to play."

"Oh, I'm not so sure about that. I think Pearl Jenkins might just throw me out of her house if I started wailing with this thing every night after dinner."

"Is your Mrs. Jenkins so sorry as all of that? She can't appreciate the sound of a gifted musician on his way to greatness?"

"No, no," said Will. "You're right. She'd probably pick up marimba mallets or something and join me. I'm not sure which I'd feel worse about."

Joe took a drink of his coffee and carried his concertina back to its case. Will leaned back in his chair, tipping the front legs off the ground. He laced his fingers behind his head, leaving the instrument resting quietly in his lap.

A tuft of padding fiber stuck up through a small tear in the upholstery as Joe eased himself back into his chair, bracing himself on the worn brown arms. He pointed at Will's feet.

"All four wheels on the floor there, fella. Tip too far and you'll be all over the floor."

Will grinned and brought his chair forward. "My mom used to use that exact line. 'All four wheels on the floor. You'll fall and crack your head wide open.'"

"There's that, too," Joe said. "Cracking your head on my floor would be an inconvenience to be sure. But I was more interested that you not break my chair. And my concertina would be smashed to bits."

Will got up to put the instrument away.

"Your mother was unsuccessful in breaking you of the habit, though, I see." Joe smiled.

"Well, I didn't actually have the habit. Not then, anyway. She was always scolding my brother for it. Tom was the one always stretching the boundaries from the outside, seeing how far he could move them."

"And you were sitting quiet and proper at the table, one hand in your lap, shoulders straight, and the pinkie of your other hand out while you sipped hot chocolate from a tea cup, rolling your eyes at such nonsense, I suppose?"

"Worse than that." Will set the concertina into its case and snapped the latches shut with two loud clicks. "I'd most likely have been under the table, trying to make myself disappear behind one of the legs."

"Is that so?" Joe said. He didn't ask another question, or disagree, or change the subject. He just left "Is that so?" hanging in the air in such a way that Will felt he had no choice but to continue talking, and in such a way that he didn't really mind at all.

"That is so, Joe." He sat back down in his chair, all four legs on the floor. "I was one of those kids born with a guilty conscience. Didn't matter who was in trouble, or with whom, or for what. I always figured it was me they were really after. Sometimes the anticipation was too much and I fessed up to things someone else had done, just to end the suspense."

Will rubbed his hands together, alternating one after the other, and studied a knot in a wood plank on the floor. It looked like an eyeball staring back at him, the darkest part of the center like a dilated pupil, knowing, boring into his soul. Any moment he expected to hear a telltale tick-tocking from under the floor.

He looked at Joe. His eyes were much kinder than the floorboard. "Well now. I'm not quite sure at all how we got here. I'm not one to go opening my coat and exposing myself to innocent bystanders."

Joe smiled. "I don't mind, Will. I think you could say we're friends. I'm happy for conversation between friends. Tell me. When did you finally decide it was okay to...tip your chair back?"

Will combed his fingers through the hair at the back of his neck. "Much later, Joe. Some days I'm still not sure it's even okay to *sit* in the chair."

He picked up his cup and put it to his mouth, tipping his head back to finish off the cup, even though he'd emptied it ten minutes ago. "It's been a good afternoon, Joe, but I should be probably get moving along." He stood and put his hands in his pockets.

Joe looked up from his chair, something in his eyes Will couldn't identify. Sadness? Understanding? Curiosity? He got up and rested a hand on Will's shoulder. "Sure you can't stay a little longer? I know the coffee is gone, but I do have more cookies."

"I really should get going, Joe. My partner is back at the office probably thinking I got trampled by a horse at the ranch."

"Alright. Maybe you could let me know if you ever come through this way again? By now you should be able to find the place pretty easily." He grinned.

Will laughed. "I *should* be. Doesn't mean I *would* be." He gripped Joe's strong, rough hand. "But I'll definitely call if I can sneak in a quick visit."

The two walked out of the house together. Will went to his truck and waved to Joe, who stood smiling on the doorstep, as he drove off.

15

Will drove through town looking to find his way back to the highway. "Phillips," he said, "how hard can it be to find your way out of a town ten blocks wide?"

He'd driven past the small supermarket three times before he recognized the circle he was traveling. The clock on the dash said 4:50. With a sigh at the realization he wasn't going to get back to the office today anyway, he pulled into a parking space at the front of the store and went in. The teenager at the front till had straight brown hair parted at the side and combed to partially cover one side of her face. She hadn't quite mastered the seductive "smoky eye" with her eye shadow, though clearly it wasn't for lack of trying. Even so, keeping just one garish eye out in the open was probably to her credit. Her blue smock hung loosely over a tight T-shirt, pulled over a slight bulge at her waist pushed up by too-tight jeans. Will silently wished this period in teenage fashion would fade quietly away.

"Excuse me," he said. "Can you tell me how to get to the Interstate?"

She blinked at Will and chewed her gum a little slower, tilting her head to the side. "The Interstate?"

"Yes."

"The Interstate." The girl drew out each syllable as though it would conjure some knowledge she clearly did not possess. "That's the big one? I think we take that up to Fargo." She brushed the hair away from her covered eye.

Will focused on the sign above her head and bit the inside of his cheek to keep from a sharp answer. Why was he not just asking Barbara? She was no more pleasant to talk to but at least she gave him straight answers. He'd never once heard her ask about "the big one."

"Yes. The big highway that goes to Fargo. Can you tell me how to get to it?" He shifted on his feet. "Please?"

The girl twisted her long hair around a finger and blew a large purple bubble that burst softly across her nose. *It's okay, Phillips,* he told himself. *She's a person, not a caricature. But she does do a damn fine impersonation of a caricature. You have to give her that.*

"Umm." She turned to face the door, "That's north, right? Then you would go left past the elevator and drive for a while. And then you would turn. But I'm not sure where."

"You're not sure where? But you do know you turn."

"I think so. Yeah. You definitely turn. Does that help?" She smiled.

"Immensely. Thank you." Will looked toward the back of the store. "I don't suppose there is anyone else here?"

"Bob, I think. You want to talk to him?"

"Sure." Will pointed toward the meat department. "That way?"

"Yeah. Just walk down Aisle 2. You shouldn't have any trouble finding him."

The sound of a bubble popped lightly into the air as he walked away. *Shouldn't have any trouble. I get that a lot.*

He walked past the peanut butter and salad dressings in Aisle 2 and found a man in a white apron leaning over the meat counter refilling the flat iron steaks from a stainless steel cart.

Will cleared his throat. "Excuse me, are you Bob?"

The man stood upright and turned, wiping his hands on

his apron. He stood a good six inches taller than Will, broad shoulders stretching the sleeves on a black T-shirt. His blond hair was shaved close to his head and he sported a trim reddish soul patch under his bottom lip.

"That's me. What can I help you find?"

"The Interstate, actually."

"The Interstate? Is that all?"

"Yes, sorry. That's it. Just needing to get back to Dennison. I understand from your girl out front that I should go left, drive a ways and turn. Think you could fill in the blanks for me?"

Bob laughed and put out his hand. Will studied it a moment and looked at the packs of red meat he'd been handling. He swallowed and shook Bob's hand, then stuffed his own in a fist into his pocket.

"Brittany. There are things she's good at; we're pretty sure of it. We're still waiting to discover them. Guess we can rule out directions as one."

"I know the feeling."

"Listen. Main Street runs in front of the store. Go east all the way out of town and for another two miles. It'll take you right to the highway."

"I shouldn't turn?" Will asked. "Are you sure?"

"Don't turn. Not until you get to the on-ramp."

Bob moved a few more steak packages from the cart and Will imagined a nice ribeye sizzling on the grill. Maybe he would treat Pearl to dinner.

"Have any specials today, Bob?"

"T-bones. Best price of the season. I can wrap them up good for you so they stay cold all the way back to Dennison if you want."

"No ribeye?"

"Better price on the T-bones, but I've got 'em, sure."

"Wrap me up a couple. Not much fat, mind you."

Will took the steaks, wrapped in white butcher paper under newspapers for insulation and headed to the front, hopeful that running the cash register was one of Brittany's things. He passed the cooler on the way and saw Bob stocked Sam Adams, a lager the stores didn't carry at home. Pearl was the type who would prefer a nice Riesling, but she'd probably already have one in her cabinet. He reached into the cooler and pulled out a case.

He couldn't show up with steaks and beer and nothing else. Pearl would insist on cooking something or pulling leftovers from her fridge. Other people's leftovers made Will terribly nervous. He detoured to the deli and picked up a small container of a Mediterranean pasta salad with black olives and tiny pepperonis. Pearl would think they were cute. He tucked the steaks under one arm and carried the beer in one hand and the salad in the other.

Bread. I should get bread, he thought, as he veered toward the bakery. He picked up a crusty baguette and slid it under his arm above the meat.

Phillips, enough, he muttered under his breath. *You came here for directions and look at yourself. You're a grocery-shopping happy little homemaker. Check out. Now.*

He started for the front of the store again when remembered dessert. *You don't need dessert. Check. Out.*

Will decided he was right. If Pearl thought she needed dessert, she'd probably already have a pie baked. And if not, he could always take her for a walk downtown for ice cream. He carried his items to the cashier, almost dropping the meat when he pulled the bread from under his arm to set it on the conveyor.

"Did you find everything okay?" Brittany asked. "And Bob?"

"Yep," Will said, "I found Bob and all these things I wasn't really looking for."

She ran each across the scanner and Will bagged his own groceries, a habit he'd picked up since stores started staffing almost exclusively with teenagers who got too caught up in talking about their next break than getting any work done.

He swiped his debit card through the machine and took his receipt. As he drove off to the west he imagined surprising Pearl and firing up her grill. Noticing 3rd Street out his window, he realized he'd driven away from the store in the wrong direction. He turned to go around the block and approached Joe's house, slowing. Archie was in the front yard chasing a tennis ball that kept bouncing away from him and Joe was sitting on the stoop reading the newspaper under the porch light.

Will pulled up to the curb. Joe looked up and smiled. "You still in town, Will?"

"A bit embarrassed to admit it, Joe. But yeah."

"Got lost, did you." Joe shook his head. It wasn't even a question.

"A little," Will chuckled. "Even after I got directions at your grocery store, I still turned wrong."

He looked at the grocery sack on the passenger seat. He'd seen a gas grill around the back of Joe's garage when he'd been there the first time to scope the water damage. Pearl wasn't actually expecting him, and by the time he got home she'd likely have had her dinner.

"Hey, Joe. Does your grill still work?"

"Gosh, I have no idea. Haven't touched it since…well, a long time."

"Want to try it out?" Will held up the grocery sack and Sam Adams and grinned like a little boy who'd just found his Christmas presents under his parents' bed.

Joe jumped off the front steps like that little boy's brother and ambled down the sidewalk. "A splendid idea, Will. Come on inside."

Will opened the door and got out, reaching back in for his groceries. As he turned to close the door with his shoe, he stopped and set the beer down on the seat and opened his briefcase. He pulled out the gray Keats volume and tucked it under his arm.

Groceries in one hand and the beer in the other, he pushed the cab door shut with his hip. His phone started to buzz in its holster as he crossed the street. He hesitated, then let it go and kept walking.

Joe was already back at the door, holding it open as he waited for Will. He beamed. "I was going to head down to the senior center for congregate supper, but I can do that any day. I don't remember the last time I had someone in for a meal."

"First things first, Joe. Let's check out the grill. Matches?"

Joe waved Will into the house and followed him to the kitchen. He rummaged through a drawer but found nothing.

"Never mind, Joe," Will said. "We'll use my lighter."

"Your lighter? When are you going to give that up, Will? You know it'll kill you one day."

Will's phone buzzed again. "Nah, pretty sure whoever is calling me will do me in first." He looked around for a place to set his groceries. "Hey, Joe, clear me a space on the counter, would you?"

Joe closed the drawer and stared at the counter top, bewildered as though seeing the stacks of paper towel rolls, unopened jars of peanut butter and cans of Folgers coffee piled as high as the cupboards for the first time. "Oh. Gosh. The kitchen has really gotten away from me this week."

He picked up two jars of pickles and pushed the piles apart to make room for Will's sack of groceries. "Here. Set your stuff down right here." He tapped the open space with one of the jars, then turned away to find a place for his pickles, turning in a circle three times like a dog looking for the spot he'd marked the day before, and finally opened the refrigerator, which was completely empty, and set them on the top shelf.

Will set his things in the cleared space. "Joe," he asked, slipping his hands into his pockets and leaning back against the counter. "When's the last time you used the kitchen?" Joe's face lit up to answer. "I mean, really used it. For more than piling stuff you're not going to eat?"

Joe looked at the floor, and when he looked up Will was sure his eyes were a shade more gray than they had been.

"I don't know, Will. Long enough that it probably doesn't matter anymore how long."

The two held each other's gaze for what felt to Will like an hour, and then Joe's eyes suddenly sparkled green again. He clapped his hands together. "Your lighter, Will. Let's go see if we can blow up the grill."

He smiled and pulled a red Bic lighter from his shirt

pocket. Then he tossed it straight up into the air and caught it with a backhanded flip of his wrist. "Here you go, Joe. Let's get something started."

The phone buzzed again, now the third time in less than ten minutes. Will pulled it from its holster and sighed when he lit up the display. He tapped the "Ignore" button. "Mrs. Decker," he mumbled.

"Do you need to take that, Will? I don't mind."

"No, Joe. I don't need to take it. It's after business hours. I would lose my mind if I took every call. That's why the good Lord invented voice mail. After she wears herself out calling, she'll leave a message. Bet you a quarter it'll take another four times."

"You're on," Joe said. "But I might point out that you took my calls after hours. Even placed one to me pretty late in the evening once."

Will rolled his eyes and grinned sideways at Joe. "Yeah, well, that was different. I'm not sure how, but it was different."

Mrs. Decker wouldn't need to leave a message. Will already knew what she wanted.

"One more day," she'd ask. "Give me just one more day."

She'd beg for more time and Will would feel like a Chicago mobster about to break some poor sap's leg over a gambling debt. The truth was, no matter how many times a guy gives a lady like this "one more day," it's never enough days to do what needs to be done. That one more day is burned up, every time, like the fuse on a stick of dynamite and *Boom!* The one more day's gone and all that's left to show for it is a bigger mess.

He'd been giving Mrs. Decker "one more day" for over

two years now and the statute of limitations was about to run on her case. If he gave her one more day, it would cost him with the insurance company. So that was it. No more days. No more time. No more extensions. He was done.

His old boss Jimmy Martin had once called him *Mrs. Claus* when he went soft on a claimant and gave him an extra day in a rental car. One more day and $52.78 gets you *Mrs. Claus.* Jimmy always knew how to hurt a guy. Any adjuster worth his salt was no Santa Claus with a big bag of goodies over his shoulder. But *Mrs.* Claus? The little woman who stays home and packs a nice lunch and stirs little marshmallows into hot cocoa for her Santa? No. Will would learn to be less like Mrs. St. Nick and more like Ebenezer Scrooge on a cold winter night. He would say to his spindly Bob Cratchett of a Mrs. Decker, "No."

"No more days," he said aloud.

Joe raised his eyebrows.

Will knew, of course, that he would give Mrs. Decker one more day. And he would be haunted late into the night by the ghost of Jimmy Martin, rattling heavy chains and moaning, "Mrs. Claus. Missssus Claaaaus."

"It's different, eh?" Joe said. He winked. "For starters, I'm sure I'm much more charming than your Mrs. Decker."

"You're absolutely right about that, Joe." Will walked down the five steps to the back door and held it open with a slight bow, waving the old man through. "Why don't you and your charm go see if you can't get a little something going on the grill."

Joe chuckled. "I'll have you know, Will Phillips, that I've lit a few fires in my day." He pressed a hand against the wall to steady himself as he walked down the steps. "'Course, I extinguished a few, too."

16

Will followed Joe out the door, clapping a hand on his shoulder as he passed.

"Careful on the sidewalk, Will," Joe called back. "Been meaning to have someone take a look at that."

Will walked behind Joe, stepping around the large pieces of concrete that had been broken away.

"Heaved and broke the winter after I poured that cement." Joe tapped a smaller chunk with his toe. "Sometimes I think we should just all stay indoors in the winter. Learn to live like bears. Sleep from December to March."

"Sounds like a great idea to me, Joe. But, umm, I think the sidewalks are still going to heave when it gets cold, even if we're all sleeping."

"You know what?" Joe asked, not waiting for an answer. "It's guys like you who kill good ideas. It's like you crouch in the bushes with a bayonet, just waiting for some poor sucker with a spark of an idea who's foolish enough to say it out loud, and then you lunge out and impale it with your superior insight." Joe was behind the garage now, Will a few steps behind. "You cut right through me, Phillips. It's a good thing the fellow who invented the wrist watch didn't know you. Or Marie Curie. Or Al Gore for heaven's sake."

"Alright, alright Joe. Point taken. But remember, I get paid to poke holes in things. It's what I do. Sometimes I forget I'm off the clock." Will came around the corner of the garage to find Joe next to a Weber grill leaning against the wall with one wheel missing.

"Gotcha," he said, grinning.

Will shook his head. "This is it?" He squinted at the rusted cover of the small grill and thought of all the reasons the grill would never light, but thought better of naming them off to his optimistic friend. "Well, let's see what we can make of it."

He brushed the leaves off the cover and leaned into the handle to lift it. The cover fought back, hinges whining. He raised his eyebrows at Joe.

"Nothing a little WD-40 can't fix," he smiled.

"Right."

Will crouched to turn the valve on the gas tank and hesitated with his hand on the knob.

"Rightie-tightie, Will," Joe said. "Leftie-loosie."

"Never has a more useful rhyme been written," Will said, "assuming a guy knows which is his left and right." He struggled against the knob. "Hmm. Won't budge. Have a vise grips in your garage?"

Joe cupped his hand over his chin and cocked his head. Will waved him off. "Never mind. I have one in my bag. Be right back."

As he rounded the corner and walked quickly back to the road, his boot caught the lip of one of the sidewalk cracks and he stumbled forward, catching his balance just before he would have tumbled onto the ground. *This is an idea you could have stood to poke a hole in, Phillips,* he said to himself. *You're never going to get supper. And you're never going to get home.*

"Yeah, yeah," he answered himself back. "But I'm here now. Nothing much to be done about it but enjoy myself and do a good thing for the old man."

At times like these, Will felt like Fred Flintstone, caught

between a small figure on each shoulder shouting in his ears, like the universal balance between good and evil was about to be tipped on his one small act. The Fred-devil stood on one side, jabbing at him with his pitchfork and appealing to his baser instincts while the Fred-angel glistened in white on the other, imploring him to do good.

How did Flintstone manage the voices? Will wondered. How did he reconcile these competing parts of himself—clearly they weren't external forces but fragments of his own self that cajoled him—each convinced he was independent of the other, wholly separate and able to survive on his own.

Kids in front of the television had no clear understanding of Flintstone's struggle to survive the competition. As a boy, Will sat for hours and watched the cartoon, never knowing it wasn't written for children. Hell, it was hardly written for adults. Polarized voices plunged through his ears and into his brain, vying for domination of a man's psyche, neither willing to give ground to find a common space between them. Flintstone labored in ways a cartoon audience would never appreciate, a man's man, doing a man's work in the quarries, wearing a rough-hewn blue necktie and a dress. The man who sported a five o'clock shadow from dawn to dusk wore a *dress*.

Keats said it. Perhaps it is the thing that pins all men in some way to the mat: "My mind has been the most discontented and restless one that was ever put into a body too small for it."

"No, John Keats," Will said aloud. "You don't get that medal. You were not the most restless and discontented one. Believe me. There were others. Still are others."

Will was at his truck now. He grabbed his tool bag from

the cab and jogged back to the garage.

"Keats, Joe," he said as he got down on one knee next to the grill. "If I ever get this thing going, we need to talk about Keats."

"I am certain of nothing but the holiness of the Heart's affections and the truth of the Imagination," Joe said, eyes closed. He opened them. "That Keats?"

"Yes, yes. That one." Will clamped his pliers onto the valve and gave it a hard crank. "There you go, Leftie-loosie. Got it." The knob turned freely. He pulled off the grips and stood up. He punched the ignition button twice with his thumb. "Let's see what this old baby can do."

Joe looked inside the grill. "Hmm. Looks like nothing. Push it again, Will?"

Will pushed it again with no response. He pulled his lighter out of his pocket and flicked it, reaching his hand into the grill hoping to catch the stream of gas with his flame.

"Nothing," Joe said.

Will got down on the ground and lay on his back, his head next to the tank on the cart. He pushed and pulled on the hose, checking the connections between the tank and the grill.

"I'll just stay over here by your feet, Will. That way if it blows up I can drag you away from the conflagration by your boots."

Will lifted his head to look at Joe. Joe smiled.

"Old firefighter tricks. You know."

"It's not going to blow up, Joe. There's no gas coming out."

"Oh, gosh. And I was just getting in the mood for heroics."

"I might still need you to drag me out of here, even if I'm not on fire." Will pulled his head out of the cart, rolled onto his side and pushed up to his knees.

"Aw, you're still pretty spry. You'll be fine." Joe put out a hand to help Will to his feet.

"I don't know if the line is plugged or if the tank is empty, but it's not going to go. How long did you say since you used it last?"

"Probably last summer, maybe the summer before," Joe said.

Will studied the grill, all of the black paint replaced by rust. He looked back at Joe and wiped his hand across his mouth.

"Oh, who am I kidding? I have no idea. It's been years. You know that."

"I'm about hungry enough to eat the steaks raw, Joe. What's our next step?"

Joe paused. "Charcoal."

"Charcoal? That'll take an hour. And do you even have any?"

"Nope. But the store is still open. Get in my truck."

"You're kidding, right?" Will asked. "Listen, why don't we just grab something at the Main Street Café and call it a night?"

"No, I'm not kidding. I eat four meals a week at that café and I'll be damned if I'm going to eat one there when I could be grilling steaks. Besides, they don't serve past lunch."

Joe dangled his keys in front of Will's nose. "Just get in. Let's go."

Will shook his head and looked at the ground while Joe

half skipped to his Silverado in the driveway. It was as though Joe's body was restoring itself in front of him. *You started this, Phillips,* he thought to himself. *You can't walk away from the old man now.*

He smiled at Joe, who was grinning behind the wheel like a teenager ready to go pick up his girl.

"You win." He climbed in and pulled the door shut. "Let's go."

When they got to the grocery store, Joe went in by himself. "I've been there once today already," Will said. "I think I'll wait for you here."

~

The two men returned to Joe's house with a bag of self-lighting charcoal.

"Do you have a Little Smoky or something, Joe? Or are you thinking we just pile the briquettes in the driveway?"

"Hmm. Forgot about that part now, didn't I?" Joe took off his cap and ran his fingers through his white hair. "Let me think."

Joe opened the door to his garage and disappeared inside. Will waited in the driveway, knowing Joe would come out empty handed.

"Too much junk in there," he said when he came out. "If I have one, we won't find it tonight. Just dump them in the gas grill."

Will stared at Joe for a long minute, then shrugged and said, "What the hell. You're the firefighter."

The two tinkered with the grill until long orange fingers

curled around the briquettes. Will stood back with his hands in his pockets admiring their work. "Well, Joe, I think we got her."

Joe smiled, arms folded across his chest. "Been a while since I actually accomplished something around here, Will. Even if it took some improvising, this is really something."

"My granddad was an improviser," Will said, poking at the charcoal with his wrench. "Used to stay at the lake with him and my grandma when I was a kid. I remember introducing him to s'mores one day after he'd grilled burgers for supper. Told him all about how I'd learned to make them in my camping class at school. He thought they sounded great and wanted to try them out but didn't have any of the right supplies."

Will folded the empty charcoal bag in two and dropped it into one of Joe's silver trash cans. "So we rummaged through the cupboards and found some of the tiny marshmallows and a box of stale vanilla wafers. When my grandma wasn't looking, he showed us her secret stash of chocolate stars."

"Every grandma has a secret stash of something, don't you think?" Joe said. "My grandma used to hide walnuts. Grandpa used to say she was part squirrel."

Will laughed. "Well, by the time we had it all figured out, the coals had grown cold outside, so we put our makeshift s'mores in the broiler. Burned 'em to a righteous crisp. They were terrible and wonderful at the same time."

"There's much to be said for the circumstances of our experience, Will. The most simple and mundane things can take on deep and memorable dimensions depending on where we are, or with whom, or any number of things."

"What do you mean, Joe?" Will leaned his back against

the garage.

"Well, if I were to serve you charred mounds of cookies and chocolate and marshmallows after dinner tonight, I'd bet you would eat one to be polite, because you're that well-mannered, but then you'd excuse yourself from any more, probably quip about wanting to keep your girlish figure. The burned treat had meaning that day because your grandfather served them, not some nutty old man you barely know."

"Probably true, Joe. Though I have to say no one has tried to serve them to me since." Will smiled.

"But I'll venture to guess you have a fondness for chocolate stars. And you never indulge in them even so."

Will raised his eyebrows. "You're good, Joe. Very good. I've never thought about it before but yes. I'm fond of chocolate stars but I never eat them."

"'Touch has a memory,' Will. Your man Keats said that."

"Did he, now?" Will looked up.

"He did. If it had fit into his poem, I think he would have said taste and smell and sound have a memory too."

"Say more."

"What more is there to say? He said what I've been saying. Aesthetics matter. Place matters. Our senses remember and replay these things back to us, to our fingers, or our nostrils, or our tongues."

Joe looked at Will. Will said nothing.

"Let me give you an example," Joe said. "When I was a young man I spent some time in South America. There was a customary tea, a ritual really, the *mate*. It was served in a communal cup and shared among friends. Nasty stuff. It tasted like burnt pumpkin and was taken boiling hot through a metal straw. Eventually, I acquired a taste for it and brought some home with me. I brewed it in my apartment in Chicago just as I had been taught to do, but it was back to tasting like burnt pumpkin. Well, I'm not the kind of fella who gives up easily, so I tried it again. But this time, I held the *mate* under my nose and breathed in the steam. As I did, I remembered the steam rising from the tea pot as the cup was refilled. When I ran my finger along the lip of the wooden cup, I felt the brush of a friend's hand against mine as she passed me the cup. I began to hear the laughter and storytelling from a cold night around a fire next to the Rio Parana, and all of a sudden the tea tasted like *mate*, not like burnt pumpkin, enough so that I refilled the cup again and again and was transported to that riverbank."

Joe held out his hand and rubbed his thumb against his fingertips. "Our senses have memory, Will. Memory is physical. It's embedded into our cells."

Will stared silently at Joe's hand, rubbing his own thumb against his fingers with his hand in his pocket, feeling skin against skin. He felt Barbara's finger across the back of his neck and despite the smell of charcoal and lighter fluid six feet away, was sure he smelled Chanel N° 5. *Could you have been any more of a cliché, Barbara?* he thought.

"Tell you what, Joe," Will said. "I want to test this theory of yours and Mr. Keats. Let's go in and see if we can't find a bottle opener. I'd like to see what my tongue remembers about Sam Adams."

Joe clapped his hands together and smiled. "Yes! Let's go do that." He started walking up the sidewalk to the house. Will hesitated a moment, watching his happy friend approach the back door, then shook his head lightly and followed.

17

Joe was waiting for him in the kitchen with a cold bottle in each hand. "Here you go, my friend."

"Any idea where we'll find an opener? I'm not tough enough to do two of them with my teeth."

"Don't waste your teeth on them," Joe laughed. "You still need them for a few years yet." He pointed his bottle toward the cabinet. "There you go. Once upon a time I had the sense to bolt it in."

Will tipped the top of his bottle into the opener and pried off the cap. He took Joe's bottle and did the same, handing it back to him with froth edging its way up the neck and out the rim of the bottle. He held his bottle out toward Joe's. "To memory, Joe," he said. He put the bottle to his mouth and took a long drink, wishing Sam Adams could wash the taste of Barbara off his tongue.

Joe took a sip from his bottle and smiled. "To memory," he said, motioning toward the kitchen entrance. "Let's go sit. The coals will be a while yet."

Will nodded. "I just need to wash this grease off my hands. I'll be right there."

He turned on the faucet and held his hands under the stream until it warmed, feeling clear water run through his fingers. He looked on the countertop for soap. There was none. *Really?* he thought, looking over his shoulder and all around the kitchen. *They make TV shows about guys who live in houses like this. He has to have a crate of soap stashed somewhere that he picked up on some 'don't miss this' sale.* Will kept his hands under the water and opened the cupboard below the sink with the toe of his boot. Half-used bottles of kitchen cleaner lay on their sides, but no hand soap.

Damn. He held his hands under the water another 30 seconds, the only part of him that felt remotely clean, then turned it off and picked up one of a dozen rolls of paper towels piled on the counter to his right. He looked as he wiped his hands. No wastebasket. He saw a small pile of wadded paper towels and crumpled newspapers on the floor beside a cabinet and shook his head.

"Geez, Joe. What have you become?" he said softly. He smoothed the two used paper towels against his leg, then folded them twice into a small square and pushed them into his back pocket. "Sorry, man," he said, looking at Joe's trash pile on the floor. "Can't do it."

Joe was bent over his stereo in the living room. "You're going to love this one."

"Yeah? Who do we have today? Renfro? Chekhov? Crap. What was that one guy's name?"

"I don't know any Renfro," Joe smiled. "And Chekhov wrote short stories, not music. I see you didn't look up Ivan Rebroff like I told you."

"Well, you know. Things come up." Will tipped back his bottle. "A busy adjuster only has time for so many opera singers."

"Choose the right ones, and you don't need that many. Anyway, no. This is The Doors."

"The Doors?" Will cocked his head.

"You've heard of them, I hope?" Joe dropped the needle lightly onto the turntable. "My tastes are more varied than you might have thought. Now, sit."

Will looked around. He wouldn't take Joe's chair. That left the couch. Archie sprawled across two of the three cushions and he wouldn't fight him for it. Besides, sometimes, if he looked at it in just the right way, he could swear he saw the upholstery moving. He looked over his shoulder and saw Emily tiptoeing along the organ keys. He slid the bench out and carried it over by Joe's chair, set his book on the end table between them and sat down.

Joe picked up the book. His face lit up. "Say, where did you get this?"

"A friend gave it to me."

Joe ran his finger along the bent spine, rubbing the smooth Scotch tape across the top with his thumb. The warped pages stuck together and he flipped through them. The monastery's library must have had a leak at one time.

"Wait here." Joe got up and left the room, returning a few minutes later with a second book, one in each hand. They were identical, except there was no tape on Joe's and the cover was a deep slate blue with no scuffs. The edges of the pages were a lighter shade of the cover, and not speckled with water droplets like Will's.

"Of course, mine is bound right side up," Joe said with a laugh, holding his copy out to Will.

He took both volumes in his hands. "No kidding? The same one?"

Joe's book was pristine. Not a bent corner or torn page, and not even a smudged finger print or speck of dust. It may have been the first thing Will touched in Joe's entire house that did not make him flinch inside.

"Where'd you get yours, Joe?"

"Picked it up at an estate sale years ago." He dropped into his chair. "Go ahead. Read something."

"Oh, I've read lots of it already, Joe. But I'm a guest in your home. I'm not going to sit here and read a book. I can do that at my house."

"Out loud, Will. Read something to me."

"Oh." Will looked down at his hands. "I, ah—I see." He flipped through the pages of Joe's book, his eyes going out of focus. "I'm really not much of an out-loud reader, Joe."

He closed the book and set it on his thigh, resting his hand on the cover. "It's really beautiful next to mine."

Joe picked up Will's copy and thumbed the pages. "They're the same. Open it. Look inside. Read something."

~

Will had discovered the sound of his own voice one day when he and Tom were playing with his dad's old reel-to-reel tape recorder from the radio station where he worked. After Tom had recorded a brilliant spoof commercial for McDonald's, Will recorded a hilarious news report about a large Collie named Houdini that had recently escaped his owners by opening a basement window with his teeth, running across the fenced yard, crawling through the doggy door into the garage and jumping through a broken window. After an extensive dog-hunt was called throughout the city, as Will's story went, the dog was found sitting at the end of its owner's driveway waiting for his children to come home from school and play. It was a story based on the antics of Will's own dog, Rascal, who they always thought they should have named Houdini because he escaped from every form of confinement they tried with him, just to show off to the other neighborhood pets.

When Tom rewound the tape and played it back, he laughed and laughed at the story. Will's cheeks flushed and he ran to his bedroom and hid in the small space between his bed and the wall, sobbing until he fell asleep. He'd never known the voice that other people heard. It wasn't the thick, steady voice he heard inside his head when he spoke. The voice on the tape was awful. High pitched, weak. Soft. Will wanted never to speak again, never wanted anyone to hear that voice coming out of him. That was the year his report cards started coming home with comments like "Doesn't participate in class discussions" and "Needs to speak up more." That was also the year he learned the word "enunciate" because he heard it used so often.

~

Joe stopped thumbing and opened the book. "The sonnets start on page 28, Will. Let's each do one. I'll go first."

> *Many the wonders I this day have seen:*
> *The sun, when he first kist away the tears,*
> *That fill'd the eyes of morn; —the alurell'd peers*
> *Who form the feathery gold of evening lean;—*

Will listened as Joe read aloud, finishing with the final couplet:

> *But what, without the social thought of thee,*

Would be the wonders of the sky and sea?

Joe's voice was deep and seemed to inhabit Keats' words, giving them a vitality he'd not heard in them before.

"Reading poetry on the page is nice, Will. But it's not all it could be. Reading it aloud—or hearing it read—gives it another dimension. It's as though vocalizing the words completes the poem. Try the next one?"

He stared at the page, hardly seeing the words. "It's a little—You're kind of putting me on the spot, Joe." Even as he was trying to tell Joe how he couldn't, he found Joe's asking very hard to resist, as though Joe knew things Will wanted that Will did not yet know.

"Give it a try. I don't have any scorecards. And then we need to check the coals. I'm getting hungry."

Will ran his index finger along the words, stopping under the Roman numeral marking off the poem. "To a bunch of asterisks," he said. He looked up. "Who was the asterisk?"

"I don't know. Could have been his girl Fanny, I suppose. He sometimes put marks instead of her name."

Will looked back at the page and opened his mouth, which felt very dry. Joe already knew the faults of his voice by now anyway. He read.

Had I a man's fair form...

He stopped. *How the hell did I draw this poem, of all poems? I should have read first*, Will thought. *There's something about this old man.*

Will knew there was an intimacy that accompanied being read to. He sensed it here in Joe's living room as much as he'd sensed the difference as a small child between listening to stories on his record player and sitting on his mother's lap while she read to him. A human voice attaches to flesh and blood, and to warmth. Joe knew this, surely. There was a reason he was insistent.

He started again.

> Had I a man's fair form, then might my sighs
> Be echoed swiftly through that ivory shell
> Thine ear, and find thy gentle heart; so well
> Would passion arm me for the enterprise:
> But ah! I am no knight whose foeman dies;
> No cuirass glistens on my bosom's swell;
> I am no happy shepherd of the dell
> Whose lips have trembled with a maiden's eyes.
> Yet must I doat upon thee, —call thee sweet,
> Sweeter by far than Hybla's honey'd roses
> When steep'd in dew rich to intoxication.
> Ah! I will taste that dew, for me 'tis meet,
> And when the moon her pallid face discloses,
> I'll gather some by spells, and incantation.

"Joe, is that really a sonnet? Keats had a helluva rhyme scheme going on there."

"Well, Shakespeare didn't write them all, Will. Don't believe everything you heard in high school English."

"I'm not sure what I heard in high school English. It wasn't my best subject."

Will didn't hear much that Evangeline Foster said in English class, except maybe that he didn't have enough note cards to construct a proper bibliography for his term paper. He did have vague memories of Miss Foster typing wildly with two fingers on an ancient manual typewriter at her desk. He recalled she had a deeper voice than any woman deserved and it would randomly drop another octave midsentence when she read *Macbeth* to the class. And he remembered the way she would push out her lips and scrunch up her cheeks, rotating her contorted face in a circle to move her glasses up when they slipped down her nose.

But Will's memories of Barbara in English class were clearer. She sat in the front row opposite Miss Foster's desk. Light danced off her silky blonde hair, always tied up with a ribbon that matched her sweater, whenever she raised her hand to answer a question, which frequency was always in direct proportion to the frequency with which Miss Foster asked questions. Barbara always had an answer. He remembered the curve of her small teenage ass, fit snugly behind the pockets of her stonewashed Guess jeans when she stood at the board to diagram a sentence. She always smirked at Will, slouched in a desk at the back of the room, when she turned to go back to her seat. Every day she would rush out of class, only to wait outside the door for Will, hugging her books to her chest even as she would wave him in close, knowing he would have to dip his head down toward her cleavage to listen to whatever new thing she wanted to whisper in his ear.

He followed Barbara around like a doper would follow a guy carrying a dime bag with a hole in it. He never asked another girl out in high school; Barbara wouldn't stand for it. But then, he never went out with Barbara in high school. She wouldn't stand for that either.

"Never mind high school," Joe said. "Tell me about the sonnet you read. What did you hear Keats say?"

"Don't ask me that, Joe. I just read the things. I don't pretend to know what they mean."

"Not asking you to. Just asking what you heard. If you and I go to the lake, will we hear the same things?"

"Sure. We'll hear the waves lapping at the shore," Will replied.

"Well, maybe you will. But I'll hear the gulls yapping at each other. My neighbor Midge will hear two fishermen talking softly in a little boat." Joe smiled. "She has a thing for men with big nets. Point is, there's no one thing for everyone to hear, no one meaning everyone has to understand and agree on. So. What did you hear?"

Will looked at his boots, noticing a little mud by the outside right heel. He'd need to clean that up when he got home.

"Tension," he said. "I heard tension."

"Tension? What kind of tension?"

"Oh, don't ask me to explain, now. I can't put my finger on it," Will said. "But it seems like Keats lives with some kind of tension. Between what he is and ought to be, or maybe between who he is and wants to be. Listen to the guy: 'Had I a man's fair form,' 'I am no knight,' 'I am no happy shepherd.' He wants something he doesn't have. A certain kind of man he seems convinced doesn't reside in him." He looked at Joe. "Or maybe he does but is somehow tethered to a different sort of existence that's somehow really apart from himself."

"There. You see? You heard Keats say something in that poem."

"So you heard it too, Joe? The tension?" Will's eyes

widened.

"Actually, no. I didn't hear that." Joe smiled. "It's like the waves and the gulls, Will. I was rather set adrift by the 'honied roses.' Keats had quite a way with images, you know? I don't think he really meant literal roses and dew in that poem, if you get my meaning. Do you?"

Will scowled and looked down at the poem. He looked at Joe, an eyebrow up. "Going to 'taste that dew,' eh Joe?"

"Only in poetry these days. There comes a time in a man's life when he takes his rich intoxication wherever he can find it."

Will laughed. "But no tension. You don't hear a tension at all."

"Tenacious, you are," Joe said. He took a drink. "Yes, there's tension. Keats spent a good deal of time living with yearnings he could not seem to satisfy. He could not save his brother from his illness, could not support himself, could not be with his beloved, could not appease the critics, could not stave off death himself."

"A tension between soul and body, do you think?"

"That, my friend, I don't know. His letters suggest that he seemed to come to some sort of peace with the mystery in which he found himself, whatever it was."

Will closed the book and held it in his lap, not saying a word.

"Read more of his poems, Will. Take your time. They'll tell you what you want to know."

"Yes?" Will asked, looking up.

"Well, that or you'll get tired of it and decide you don't care anymore."

Will laughed.

"Steaks, Joe. Let's go put them on."

18

Will drove home late, his belly full from the grill and his head full from Joe. Together they seemed to devise a sort of deep satisfaction he only partially recognized, as though he'd touched it somewhere before, or perhaps seen it, but never fully possessed it. He couldn't wait to get home to his bed in his sparse little room in Pearl Jenkins' sprawling house. He sensed somehow that if he could settle his mind enough to fall asleep in the first place, he would sleep through until morning for the first time since he could remember.

He drove faster, not wanting to squander such an opportunity and knowing the sheriff wouldn't be patrolling at such a late hour on a weeknight. The Vendry Tower approached on his left and he lifted his foot off the accelerator slightly. *No, Phillips,* he said to himself. He pressed against his knee with his hand to put his foot back into the gas. *I don't care how good you feel. You're not climbing tonight.*

His tires crunched on the gravel parking pad behind the house around 1:30. He went softly up the back stairs so he didn't wake Pearl. In his bedroom, Will loosened his belt and unzipped his jeans, plopping down on the bed to take off his boots. He set them on the floor and dropped backwards onto the pillow, his eyes already closed.

Moments later, he fought to open his eyes against the morning sun streaming across his bed. He slapped at his hip and shouted in what was really a low mumble, his mouth barely moving, "Shit. Mad Dog, I thought you put out traps. Damn mouse crawled up my pants." He struck his hip again.

"Don't just stand there laughing. Give me the hammer."

Will swung his free arm, empty-handed, and rolled off the bed, landing on his hands and knees. He forced his eyes open now and saw the oak floor. He grabbed at his hip, still tingling, and realized his phone was ringing in his pocket. He dug it out and looked at the caller id. Cameron Julian. Cameron? Calling? In the middle of the night?

He pressed his thumb against the phone to answer and put it to his ear. He rasped a garbled "Phillips," his tongue dry and swollen to the roof of his mouth.

Cameron sounded unsure. "Is this...Will?"

Will cleared his throat and rolled his tongue around his mouth. "Yesh. Yes. Will. Sorry, haven't talked yet this morning."

The staircase creaked and Pearl's voice floated up the steps. "Mr. Phillips, is everything alright up here? I heard a crash."

"Hold on a sec, Cameron," he said, and held the phone against his stomach. "Yes, Mrs. Jenkins. Everything is fine. I, ah…" He looked around the room. "I, ah, just tripped over my boots."

"Who are you talking to up there? You didn't bring a girl home last night now did you?"

"No, no, Mrs. Jenkins," Will tried to smile, hoping it would make his voice sound more convincing and his situation less ridiculous. "I didn't bring a girl home. I'm on the phone and I'm really just fine. I'll come down in a minute to see you. And prove it."

"I'll be waiting, Mr. Phillips."

Will listened. There was no more creaking, so she had

stopped coming up the stairs. But she was also not going down the stairs.

He put the phone back to his ear. "Okay, sorry about that. I'm back."

"Listen," Cameron said. "I just wanted to check with you on the cable installation. I guess my crew came over to set you up yesterday but you were out."

"Oh, umm, right." Will rubbed the back of his neck. "I ended up working late last night. Can they try again today? I should be home around 4. And they can always talk to Mrs. Jenkins. She'd show them in."

"Well, she sent them away yesterday. Told them they were at the wrong house because everyone knows Will Phillips doesn't have a television set."

"Oh, whoops." Will chuckled. "I'll have to make sure to let her know things are changing."

"Alright then. I'll send them this afternoon. Have a nice day."

"Thanks for the follow-up, Cameron. And you too." Will put his phone in his pocket, wondering why the regional manager would be following on installation no-shows. He listened for Pearl. She was silent. He walked into the hall and peered over the rail. She stood on the third step up, her head cocked toward the upstairs, one hand on the banister and the other on her hip.

"Good morning, Mrs. Jenkins," Will called down the stairs, smiling. "I'm off the phone now."

Pearl looked up at him and scowled. "You scared me half to death with all that ruckus. Are you sure you are by your-self?"

"I'm really sorry about all the noise. I should have known to put my boots under the bed. And I was talking to Cameron Julian."

"Cameron Julian is up there with you? Mr. Phillips! I will not have that sort of thing in my house. You two have barely met."

"Now, Mrs. Jenkins. Do I detect a hint of jealousy?" Will started down the stairs. "Cameron called me." He held out his phone. "Do you want to see the call log?"

He lit the display on his phone and saw seven missed texts from Mad Dog. "Good grief. What time is it, anyway?"

"It's 10:00, Mr. Phillips. I wondered if you were ever getting up today." Pearl scowled again as she stepped back down. "What's this about you getting cable, anyway?"

"I bought a TV. So I can watch the Cubs play."

"Sure you did." Pearl shook her head.

"It's in the truck. I need to bring it in so I can set it up. If the guys come back today, would you please let them in?"

"Oh, very well." Pearl turned to look at Will when she reached the landing. "You could always watch your hockey games with me, you know. I have a television in the sitting room."

"That's very kind of you, Mrs. Jenkins. Sometimes a man wants to do things by himself. Listen, I should be getting to work." He smiled. "By the way, it's baseball."

"Is that right?" Pearl crossed her arms. "Good to know. By the way, a new television is a pretty expensive way to meet a girl who lives across the street. But then, I suppose, sometimes a man wants to do things by himself."

Will's smile went flat. Pearl turned away from him and

walked toward the kitchen.

He stood for a moment, then opened the texts on his phone while he walked upstairs. Mad Dog had been texting him since 8:30. The first was a new assignment for a crash scene investigation in Longville. The next six were the same, Mad Dog's supposed heartfelt default when Will didn't check in as expected: "u ok?"

"Note to self," Will said. "Don't count on Mad Dog to actually come find me if I'm in trouble."

He texted back. "Thanks for your concern. I'm fine. Assignment received."

Will stood in his room, looking from the blankets tangled on the floor to the bed to his boots to the closet, needing to get ready for work but unable to orient. With half the day spent (and a night of dead-sleep he'd not yet been able to appreciate) he needed to move fast. He grabbed a clean pair of Levis and a shirt from his closet, nearly identical to what he was wearing except the shirt was blue checked, not red. He pulled a matching pair of boxers and a white T-shirt from the drawer and went down the hall for a quick shower.

He wiped the shower steam off the mirror with the outside of his sleeve and ran his fingers through his hair. He brushed his teeth and took another look, realizing he hadn't shaved. *No matter,* he said to the mirror. *Your five o'clock shadow doesn't show up until midnight a week later.* He hung his towel, smiling in his head at Pearl, and left for the office.

~

"Where the hell have you been?" Mad Dog demanded when

he walked in. "I've been taking your calls all morning."

"Yeah? Sorry. Who called?"

"Well, that Nina babe called about her fire."

"What did she want?"

Mad Dog picked up a tablet from his desk. "I don't know. She didn't want to talk to me."

"Anybody else call?" Will asked.

"Nope. Just your girlfriend Nina."

"How many times?"

"Just that once." Will raised an eyebrow. "Come on, Phillips. You know how it is with a girl like that. Just that one time feels like twenty when it's over." Mad Dog laughed.

Will picked up the newspaper from the desk and walked across the hall to his office. Mad Dog called after him. "Hey, I need you to do that accident scene. My hip's been acting up and I shouldn't be out playing in traffic. You don't mind, do you?"

"No, no. Of course I don't mind." He saw the stack of pending cases on his desk and sighed. "I'll call Nina from the road."

A green tennis ball bounced across the hall and rested against Will's boot.

"Hey, throw that back, would you?" Mad Dog held up both hands, another ball in one and the other open to catch the toss. Will bent to pick up the ball.

"What are you working on today, Mike?"

"Well, I'm meeting Stu and Charlie in a few minutes for coffee."

"Another full day, I see." Will threw the ball, spinning it just enough to skip off a sheaf of loose papers on his partner's desk. Mad Dog lunged from his chair to catch them as the pages fluttered to the floor.

"Oops. My bad."

Will sat down at his desk. His pencil cup—a plastic mug with a large red C that he'd gotten at a Cubs game as a boy—was to the left of the desk phone, not where he kept it on the right. A yellow legal pad in the middle of his desk was flipped to a blank page, and the previous page had been torn out. A small torn piece was still attached at the top, left behind like a hanging chad. The hangers-on made Will uncomfortable, disordered. He always folded them over and neatly finished the tear-off. He did the same this time, rolling the small corner of the page between his fingers and then dropping it into his waste basket.

"Been in my office lately, Mike?" he called across the hall.

There was no need to ask. He could feel when someone had been in his space, even before he could see it.

"Oh, yeah. This morning. Took a call in there."

Will shifted in his chair.

"And why was that?"

"The phone rang while I was at your desk."

Will closed his eyes.

"Right."

"Well, why would I come back here to answer it?"

Will rubbed his palm up and down along the top of his thigh.

"What were you in here for, Mike?"

"Oh, no reason, really." Mad Dog stuck his head into Will's doorway and grinned. "I'm heading out. I'll tell Stu and Charlie you said Hello."

"I didn't say Hello." Will scowled.

"I know. But I like people to think I work with a friendly guy. Someone not so afraid of people."

Mad Dog flipped his keys into the air and caught them with his hand behind him as he walked away. Will saw another green tennis ball on the floor to the right of his chair. He reached for it and wound up to throw it.

"I'm not afraid of people!" he called as the door slammed.

He opened his hand and let the ball drop to the floor. It bounced under his chair and then rolled against the wall.

"I just don't always know what to do with them," he said softly, his shoulders slumping.

Will scanned his desk and credenza for anything else Mad Dog may have touched. He had a way of putting his fingers on Will's things whenever he came into his office. No matter what it was, he just always needed to pick something up. Rarely did he put it back in the same place.

There was something about the way Mad Dog held Will's things that seemed to make their value dissipate into nothingness. A book, a photograph, a round stone or a shell from the lake. These were the things Will surrounded himself with at work, making the place he worked safely his own in ways he didn't do in his room at home. Though he wouldn't mean it as such, Mad Dog's very presence in Will's office could feel like a threat to his safety. Certainly to his sanity.

Except for the tablet and pencil cup, the desktop appeared otherwise untouched. His laptop was in his briefcase, the monitor on the desk used only as an extension.

He opened the top drawer.

It looked orderly enough. He picked up a pack of spearmint

gum, left from the last time he thought he would stop smoking. The pack still had five pieces. He'd only chewed two before he lit up.

"Mad Dog," he hissed.

The fifth stick was an empty foil wrapper folded neatly and slid back into the pack.

There were things Mad Dog did for no real reason except that he could. He took a peculiar delight in working Will into an unwinnable corner: put up with his ways and endure the petty invasions, or resist them and be understood as a territorial fool. How Mad Dog ever settled a claim was a mystery when he was so adept at creating losing propositions.

Will slipped his laptop out of its black padded case and opened it to his email. He located the new assignment and printed it. A double-fatality motor vehicle accident. He was to get photos of the scene and diagram the accident, and also stop for a copy of the crash report from the courthouse. He put fresh batteries in his camera, dropped the printout into an empty manila folder and loaded his briefcase.

Halfway to the door he stopped and went back, opening the bottom drawer of his desk. He rummaged around for the key to the drawer and found a small plastic dome that looked like a tiny gray igloo. Inside the chute was a glass eye. He chuckled, remembering when his nephew had given him the portable motion sensor he'd found in a gadget shop. Alex had set it in the bathroom one night when Will was visiting Tom's family, hoping to scare him with the alarm when he got up in the morning. It went off screeching in the middle of the night instead when Will got up to use the bathroom. Alex forgot setting it up by then and was as startled by it as anyone in the house.

Will turned on the switch and set the device in the corner between the credenza and his file cabinet, aimed so that as soon as Mad Dog would reach the desk, it would activate and hopefully his partner would need to change his shorts before his next coffee with Stu and Charlie.

Then he took his shells and stones, the two books and photograph of a blue sunset on Lake Michigan and slid them into the top drawer. He put the gold key in the lock and clicked it.

"This is what happens when you only give people shitty choices, Mike." He dropped the key in his pocket, picked up his briefcase and walked out the door.

19

Once he got on the highway, Will called Nina back. She had only been checking in, letting him know they'd found a house to rent that would have room for all the kids and let them keep the dogs. He felt relief that he would not be asked to approve a hotel room with a pool and fine dining at the local Country Kitchen for the next three months. Justin was sleeping at the shop most nights, she said, only coming home "when he wanted some." She laughed when she said it, but not in a way that sounded like she was amused.

Will wanted to ask why she stayed, but he didn't. He knew why and didn't want to put on her the humiliation of saying it out loud or creating a story he would never believe. He agreed to stop back next week and see how the contractors were coming along. Their conversation ended abruptly when Will drove into the hills, notorious for their poor cell coverage.

He reached to turn on the stereo, selecting the first disk in the changer, a Yiruma piano collection. The irony of being soothed by the very music Mad Dog would mock him for was not lost on him. He turned up the volume and imagined returning to the office. In his fantasy, Mad Dog would growl, "What the hell did you put that motion alarm out for?"

And Will would answer. "No reason, really."

An hour north of Langford, Will pulled to the shoulder and opened the file. He dialed the phone.

"Clay County Sheriff's office. Dispatch." It sounded like a woman's voice.

"Good afternoon. This is Will Phillips. I'm handling a

claim for Western Insurance for an MVA that happened outside Longville Friday night. Wondering if the crash report is finished yet and if I can stop and pick it up?"

"Driver's name?"

Will looked at his notes. "Wilkins. Mary Wilkins."

"Oh, yeah. That was an awful one. Two dead. Mary Wilkins was my piano teacher when I was a little girl."

"I'm sorry."

"Oh, I hadn't seen her in twenty years. It's not like we were close. Anyway, Deputy Martin has that one." Keys clacked in the background as the dispatcher looked up the case. "Yep. The report is ready. You can stop at the courthouse and get it. Fee is $4.00. Cash only."

"Thank you, Ma'am."

"Yep," she said. "You betcha."

The accident happened east of Longville. He would stop in town first and get the report so he'd have the deputy's description of the crash. He pulled Barbara from the glove box and plugged her in, programming the GPS to find the courthouse before he got back on the highway.

"Drive to highlighted route," she said.

"Barbara, sweetheart, I'm on the shoulder. That is the highlighted route. I think I can manage this part."

Will drove past the Rolphs County courthouse and found a parking space at the curb a half block away. He dug a handful of change from the center console and dropped two quarters in the meter. "Half hour should do it," he said, patting the meter on the head. He stood with his face tipped to the sun, twisting at the waist to stretch his back from the drive.

Inside the courthouse, he winced at what his tranquil

world on the remote Dakota prairie had become. An armed security guard greeted him with a nod motioning to the conveyor to run his briefcase through the scanner. The hum of the belt, turning all day in its perpetual loop was the only sound in the vast marbled chamber of the vestibule. Odds were good the belt had carried nothing in the last hour.

"What do you have in the bag?" asked the officer, his voice cracking like a pubescent boy, which, with his pimply cheeks and thin blond flattop, he could easily have been.

"Files, camera, recorder. A few tools," Will answered.

"Can't take the camera in. What sort of tools?"

"Tire gauge. Screwdriver. Pocket knife."

"God. A pocket knife? What are you thinking? You can't bring that kind of stuff in here."

"Well, I'm not thinking at all, apparently. Look, I just need to pick up a crash report." He held out his business card between two fingers. The young man took it, looked indifferently at both sides and handed it back. "How 'bout I just leave the bag here with you?"

"No sir!" Will jumped at the voice that barked from behind a black partition at the end of the scanner, half expecting a Rottweiler baring its teeth. Instead, another officer, a squat woman with black hair pulled back tight to her scalp stepped out.

"You cannot leave your belongings here." She pressed her closed fist into the open palm of her other hand in front of her chest. Her biceps flexed as she rotated her hand back and forth, pulling the crease of her starched black sleeve flat across the bulge. Will involuntarily took a step backwards. "Could have explosives and such, and then what would we have? The case stays with you."

"Right." Will forced a smile and swallowed. "Look, today's not the best day for me to become a threat to national security. Let's say I just take the bag back to my truck."

The boy guard folded his arms across his chest and the woman put her hands on her hips. Both glared at Will. He held the briefcase in front of his chest and backed toward the door.

"Damn," he said as he jogged down the stone steps. "I wonder what she did to get those pipes."

At his truck, he pulled the Wilkins file and left the bag on the seat. He dropped another quarter in the meter to make up for the time lost to his imposition of a severe threat to the security of Langford County.

When he walked back in the door, it was as though he'd never been there before. The skinny guard pointed to the conveyor without speaking. Will set the file on the black mat and watched it rattle along toward the scanner.

"What's in the file?" the guard asked, frowning as he forced his voice lower.

"In the file? Geez. Eight pages. Two staples. One paper clip," Will smiled. "Sir."

The file disappeared behind the flaps and the other guard ordered him through the metal detector. Will noticed her nametag. Phyllis Edwards. The machine beeped as soon as he reached the threshold.

"Step out," she ordered. "Take off your jacket."

Will complied, slipped off his jacket and laid it on the conveyor. He stepped back into the machine and set off the alarm again.

"Shit," he muttered, hoping she didn't hear him.

"Step over here please, Sir." She pointed to a pair of yellow shoe prints painted on the floor. "Extend your arms."

Will aligned his work boots into the yellow shapes, put out his arms and leaned his head back, staring at the copper dome three stories up, debating mentally whether his position felt more crucifix or centerfold. When he felt Officer Edwall's wand against the inside of his leg, he decided centerfold.

His leg twitched; he clenched his jaw.

"Just be still, Sir. I thought you left your implements outside."

"I thought so too," Will said. "Sorry for the hassle."

She ran the wand across his chest and along his arms, then down his front. The unit beeped just below his navel. She moved the wand back and forth, eliciting the incriminating beep each time she passed over his fly.

"I assure you," he said softly. "There is nothing in there."

The woman looked up at Will, spread-eagle in the yellow footprints and held the beeping wand in front of his midsection.

"Belt buckle," she said. Will met her stare. "You should have taken that off. Give it to me and walk through once more."

He pulled his belt loose and stepped back into scanner, which finally stood silent in seeming acknowledgement of his lack of mettle.

Officer Edwards picked up the file from the conveyor. "Three staples, by the way." She patted Will on the arm with the file. "Now where is it you need to go?"

"Records," Will said, buckling his belt.

"Up one flight and to the left."

"Well, this has been very ... special," he said. "Thank you."

The corner of Phyllis Edward's lip curved ever so slightly and she tipped her head, almost imperceptibly. Will walked away and started up the winding staircase to the second floor. "Don't cause any trouble while you're up there."

The Public Records Office was a wide open layout of a dozen or so desks adorned with family photographs, flower vases, stuffed animals and candy jars. All but two, whose monitors were dark, were staffed by women of various ages, from the twenty-something pregnant brunette in the corner by the window to the wispy sixty-something, silver hair pulled up in a ponytail wearing yoga pants and looking as though her next stop was the gym to train for her half marathon. Three women stood at their workstations nearest the long counter separating their space from Will's, discussing a new craft project one had discovered on Pinterest.

Will looked down the counter to the end of the room. Every few feet, an overhead sign designated a particular class of record that could be secured. Nearest him was the line for birth and death certificates, followed by marriage records. Further down, court records, real estate transfers and so on. He didn't see a station for motor vehicles so he walked down to the court records line and approached the counter. He smiled to himself that with such a well-organized floor plan, designed to manage substantial traffic, he was still the only patron in the room.

A woman two desks down looked up at him, then at the COURT RECORDS sign above his head. She went back to work at her computer screen. The remaining women continued their activity, oblivious to his arrival.

A letter-sized notice was taped to the counter, typed in all caps in Comic Sans font:

RING BELL

FOR

SERVICE

A red arrow drawn with a Sharpie pen indicated a silver call bell to the top left of the paper.

He looked toward the woman two desks down, hoping to catch her eye. She continued typing. He shifted a step to his right, thinking to insert himself in her line of sight. She turned to the other side of her desk and rummaged in the bottom drawer.

Don't make me ring the bell, Lady. He stared at the back of her head, willing her to turn. She did not.

Will held his hand over the bell, looking at her once more, hoping. She was motionless now, still hunched over the drawer as though daring him. He tapped the plunger once, lightly, with his index finger, then quickly put his fingertips to the side of the bell to silence the reverberation.

The room went silent. Typing and conversation stopped midsentence and every head turned to look at Will standing alone, stupidly, under the COURT RECORDS sign at the counter. The woman two desks down shut the drawer and spun her chair. She stood and walked to the counter.

"Can I help you?" she asked, as the rest of the room resumed its earlier activity. She smiled in the way a woman can only do when her hair is pulled too tight back into its bun.

"Um, yes," Will said, placing his hands on the counter. "I am looking for a crash report."

The woman sighed, then pointed to the sign over Will's head. "You're in the Court Records line." She motioned to her right with her thumb. "You need Public Safety."

"Oh, right. Sorry about that." The woman turned and walked back to her desk. "You can't help me?"

"You're in the wrong line." She sat down.

Will looked at the sign to his left and back to the woman at her desk. He walked a few steps to his left and stood silently under the PUBLIC SAFETY sign.

The women in the office continued with their activity, and after a few moments Will had learned no less than seven things he could do to repurpose an old pair of jeans. There was an identical notice at this line, only the tape at the corners of the paper had been outlined in black ink by another patron forced to wait there. He wondered if the doodler had stood in the right line to begin with. He studied the bell, alternating looks to the woman at the desk, now with her back to him.

"Don't make me ring the bell again." This time he said it aloud, though no more than a whisper. A woman at the first desk looked up. "Excuse me, sir?"

"Oh, sorry. I was just hoping not to have to ring the bell again. You're all sitting right here, after all. Can you help me?" Will ran a hand through his hair and shifted his weight.

"Oh, sure. I'll get someone." She turned. "Barbara, someone's at the Public Safety line."

Barbara? Will thought. *Figures.*

The woman two desks down got up and walked to the counter. "Wait," Will said. He pointed at the court records line. "Why couldn't you help me when we were over there?"

"I did help you. I sent you to the correct line." She shook

her head at him as if to say that even a small child could understand the simplicity of her bureaucratic operation. She reached under the counter and pulled out a packet of forms. "Fill it out completely and bring it back. Fee is four dollars."

Will took a pen from his pocket and began to fill out the request form.

"Sir, you can't stand there and complete the form. You'll be in the way. Take a seat by the window please and get back in line when you're finished."

Will looked around. There was still no one else anywhere in the room waiting for service.

"Ma'am," he said.

Barbara the courthouse worker pointed sharply to the chair against the wall. "Have a seat by the window, Sir."

Will squinted at the woman, then picked up the file and papers and sat down. She walked back to her desk.

He sat in the gray upholstered office chair with his head resting against the wall for two full minutes before he leaned forward, balancing the file folder on his knee as a flimsy writing support while he completed eight pages of extraneous information Barbara would neither need nor care about just so he could obtain the report. He wondered what sort of life winds itself up in this sort of maze, imposing rigid structures indiscriminately in contexts where they served to preserve order and others where they created meaningless chaos. Could this Barbara distinguish the two? Or was she fully able but unwilling, gaining something that felt like living while she siphoned the same sensation from another for no reason but that she could?

As he turned to page 5, he imagined what it might be like

for her to loosen her hair, pulling against her face as tightly as she pulled against others. Would she feel a wave of freedom or would she feel as though she were coming apart, like her whole being might fall out the back of her head if she relinquished this one bit of control.

Will finished the form and put his pen back in his shirt pocket. He braced himself and stepped back up to the counter, rustling the papers to attract her attention. Barbara did not look up. The woman at the desk next to her did. Will motioned toward Barbara, but the woman shook her head and pointed at the bell. She shrugged.

He stood quietly for a moment, then reached for the bell. He held a finger on the side to muffle the sound, then tapped the plunger. Metal clacked against metal and Barbara looked up, scowling at his subversion. The woman who shrugged smirked at Will, then busied herself with paperwork at her desk. Barbara pushed back her chair and walked to the counter.

"Can I help you, Sir?"

Will slid the forms across to her. "I think these are complete."

She flipped through the pages and tapped them on the counter to order the stack.

"Four dollars."

Will pulled a ten from his wallet.

"I don't make change."

"Excuse me," Will asked.

"I don't make change. You should pay in ones."

"I don't have anything smaller."

"Then you can pay ten, or you can come back when you have correct change."

"Do you take debit cards?" Will tried.

"Yes. A twenty dollar minimum."

"And you don't give change."

"Right."

His meter was about to run out. "Two women are dead. I guess I'll pay the ten to find out what happened to them."

Barbara blinked, then snatched the ten from Will's fingers. "It'll be about 15 minutes. You can have a seat—"

"By the window. Yes, I know."

Will sat down to wait. He closed his eyes and leaned his head against the wall. He began to think of all the others who had been sat down by Barbara in the same chair, resting their heads against the same spot on the same faded brown houndstooth wallpaper. He eased his head slightly forward, off of the wall, and held it steady, still looking relaxed to anyone who cared to notice but keeping clear of the space where someone else rested his head. It felt important that Barbara not see his agitation at her hoops, even as he twisted and turned to get through them.

His neck muscles tensed as he held his head still. He began to tap his hands on his knees in time with the background music sifting out of the speakers in the ceiling. He opened his eyes just in time to see Barbara return to her desk.

She was back. Even so, Will didn't move. He would wait her out, fake-relaxing in the uncomfortable chair with his head not against the wall, tapping his hands to Bureaucratic Barbara's brainwashing beat as an act of solidarity with every other man she'd tried to enervate with her bell and refusal to offer change. He would sit and wait without flinching, without checking his watch, without looking in her direction.

Barbara, apparently, could sense a good challenge. She sat down and began typing at her computer. Will convinced himself from the rhythm of the keys that she was not typing real words, just clicking aimlessly to make herself appear busy and make him wait. Didn't matter. He would wait. Mary Wilkins wasn't going anywhere today anyway. When his right shoulder began to twitch from his motionless position, Will began to count the suspended ceiling panels in the large office. He marked each by pressing a finger against his knee. He'd counted twenty-four across and was on his third time through his ten fingers for the length of the room when Barbara cleared her throat. He sat upright.

"Mr., umm, Phillips, is it? I have your report here." She set the papers on the counter and turned to walk away. She stopped and looked back with a sigh. "Oh, and course we're so interested in how we're doing so please rate my service with our brief survey online." She rolled her eyes and walked back to her desk without another word.

Will let out a laugh, which he quickly diverted into a cough when Barbara glared at him. He stood and picked up the report. "Thank you so much. You fine ladies have a wonderful rest of the day. And you, too, Barbara."

He left the office, flipping through the pages as he walked. Four-lane highway, Wilkins was eastbound in a LeSabre, crossed the line into the path of a semi going westbound. Struck head-on. Both left the road. Wilkins rolled. She and her passenger were dead at the scene. No injury to the trucker. One witness.

Mary Wilkins and her passenger were in their late seventies, right about the same as Pearl Jenkins—a thought Will decided right then not to entertain again.

20

The trucker involved in the accident that killed Mary Wilkins was out of Oregon. He'd be long gone and Will would have to track him down by phone. The witness was local. Will called and arranged to meet at the scene.

Walking back through the courthouse vestibule, he nodded silently to the security guards who stood with their arms crossed over their chests looking as bored as they deserved to be. They nodded back.

According to the report, the crash occurred east of town, at around mile marker 169. He drove back and forth on the highway until he found the mile marker, next to a sign advertising free ice water at Wall Drug, just 251 miles away, reminding him to wonder again, as he sometimes did, how he ended up here, in a place as homogenous as whole milk, known best for its red state politics, giant presidential heads carved (by which he meant blown up with sticks of dynamite) into the side of an otherwise beautiful mountainside, and a massive building decorated in corn cobs.

He pulled to the shoulder and stopped, setting his hazard lights before he got out. He reached into the back seat from the passenger side for his camera and measuring wheel, though from the sound of things he doubted there would be any skid marks to measure. Neither driver had time to brake. Swerve, crash, done.

The reflective lime green highway worker's vest he wore for highway work made him feel like a kid playing dress-up, but gave him a better chance of not being run down himself while he got closer to traffic than most people would prefer. He walked along the shoulder, looking for debris—a piece of a grille or broken headlight glass—that might mark where the crash took place. About a thousand feet ahead of the truck, he got his answer: tire tracks going off the shoulder and partway down the ditch. He stopped. He'd stood in a similar place a hundred times before, but it never seemed to get easier. He followed the tracks to where they stopped partway down the slope, and photographed the spot where they ended and the car flipped, sunfish-style.

At the bottom of the slope, the grass was trampled by emergency vehicles and personnel who'd worked frantically, he imagined, to save two women for whom it was already too late. Mary Wilkins had been crushed into the dash on impact with the semi. Her passenger, unrestrained, flew through the glass without so much as a fare thee well when the car rolled in the ditch. The two women, perhaps best friends, died at the same moment, in the same place, but alone, thirty feet and a mass of twisted steel between them.

Will crouched at the grassy ditch bottom where two bright bouquets, wrapped in shiny cellophane, sat atop broken glass fragments, leaning against a headlamp housing. Soon enough, the highway department would plant a "Why Die" marker on the shoulder, the ominous red X marking the spot where the crash victims had passed on, the rhetorical question more a chilling cautionary tale posted on a stick than a dignified memorial of a life lost.

A shout from the road broke Will's contemplation. "Hey! Are you Philip?"

He looked up. A green and white Volkswagen bus was

parked on the shoulder and a bearded man in a blue Mets cap and faded jeans stood in front of it.

"Phillips." He held a hand to his eyes to shield the sun. "Will Phillips. Are you Derek?"

"Sure am," the man said as he walked down the slope. "So sad. Just can't get it out of my head."

Derek Jeffers made a reasonably credible witness. He ran a local bar and grill that broke even most years, was married with one child on the way. His beard was close-trimmed and he was clean-cut. His jeans were faded but, if Will was not mistaken, had a faint crease down the front suggesting they'd been lightly pressed or at least neatly folded before they were put away. He spoke with a firm voice—strong but not loud—despite a mild stutter. He looked a guy in the eye both when he spoke and when he listened, a trait Will found remarkable even as it made him uncomfortable. Jeffers had worked hard to carry himself this way, likely over many years.

"Give me a quick rundown of how the scene played out so I have a good sense of it, and then we can sit in my truck and I'll get you on record."

Jeffers took off his cap and ran a hand through curly black hair. "Well, I was driving right behind Miss Wilkins's car, headed toward Longville," he said. "She was in the inside lane, going slower than she should have been, maybe 50 or so. She should've been in the slow lane, so I was getting ready to pass her on the other side. The tractor-trailer was coming the other way." He pointed to the west with his cap. "The guy was pretty close, maybe just back to the other side of the mile marker." Will looked down the highway. "I don't know what happened, but all of a sudden she went across the line into his path. The trucker tried to swerve, but it was too late, man. He couldn't do anything. I took the ditch on the north side to get out of the way, and he ended up in the ditch right in front of me. Just missed. Miss Wilkins flipped into the ditch over here, and, well. You know."

He looked away from Will for the first time since he'd started talking, staring at the ground. "I don't know what happened. But there wasn't a damn thing he could do. Boom."

"Did you know either of them well?"

"The passenger—Miss Weber—she used to come in to the café with a group of women on Tuesdays when I had the senior discount on lunches. Her bridge club, I think." He smiled wryly. "If I had to guess, she and Miss Wilkins were probably arguing over points when it happened. Lucille Weber had a reputation for cheating."

"Alright. Listen, let's head up to my truck and I can get a quick formal statement from you, and then you can get back to work. I hate to take any more of your day."

"It's fine, really. Anything I can do to help."

Derek Jeffers twisted the cover off a can of Red Man. Will hadn't seen his back to notice the faded ring on his back pocket. Jeffers took a pinch of dark leaves in his fingers and wedged it inside his lower lip.

The first—and only—time Will had chewed tobacco was at summer camp in 8th grade. He'd skipped the leather-working course and gone down to the dock with Kelly Bidwell one afternoon. Kelly was a rugged cowgirl twice his size. She pulled a can of Copenhagen from her pocket and a flask of peppermint schnapps from the waistband of her pants, hidden from the counselor by the blousy front of her strapless cotton sun top.

Kelly had made it her personal mission for the week to toughen Will up. She'd made him ride a horse the day before, and when the horse tossed him off, she picked him up off the ground like a rag doll and heaved him back into the saddle, insisting it wasn't just an expression old farmers use. She taught him a couple of good punches he could use in a fight, and said that a guy like him needed to be able to defend himself. Now she was showing him how to pinch the leaves, pull back his lip and push in the stash. She told him not to swallow, but just spit to the side.

Will's mouth filled with Copenhagen-infused saliva until a thin brown trickle rolled out the corner of his mouth. He wiped it with the back of his hand, feeling his cheeks fill with the putrid mix. He wouldn't spit. Tom had tried to teach him to spit like the baseball players, quick, small, clean. But he always ended up with spittle on his chin or a slimy string hanging. He couldn't do that with Kelly, so when she looked away, he swallowed. A whole mouthful of nasty brown spit-juice. He gagged.

Kelly laughed.

"I told you not to swallow it, you damned city fool! You spit it out, like this." Kelly aimed at a small clam shell, hitting the top with a brown splotch. She laughed so hard she fell backwards onto the beach. In his panic, Will swallowed again, this time taking the tobacco with him. He gagged and coughed, spitting the remaining leaves out of his mouth and into the lake.

Kelly tossed him the flask. "Take a drink," she said. Will caught it and threw the flask back onto the sand.

"What the hell is wrong with you? Paid good money for that, plus had to put out for the guy who bought it for me." Kelly bent over and picked up the flask, brushing off the side. She opened it and took a drink. All her considerable strength seemed to concentrate in holding her lips together as it went down. Then she opened her mouth in an O shape and let out a slow breath of icy peppermint. Will thought her eyes might have watered just barely and he wondered if she were really such the roughneck she liked people to think.

She screwed the cap back on with a thick sandy hand and threw it to Will again. He held it between his thumb and middle finger, slightly away from his body.

"Drink," Kelly said.

"It's just—"

Kelly cut him off. "It's just that you've never had a sip of liquor? Worried about what your mommy might say? 'Bout time you got started. Life's too short."

"It's not that. You...You already drank out of it." The lake seemed larger than when he'd first gotten to camp. "Backwash, you know?"

"Spit? You're afraid of a little cowgirl spit?"

"Well, there's sand, too. And I already have this weird feeling in my mouth from the chew." He spit to the side. A small spot of brown floated on the surface, bobbing with the waves next to his shoe. He took a step to the side. "Look. Just...no. Not today."

"My god. Wipe the damned thing off and take a drink. You'll feel better. Promise."

Will looked at the flask, still extended away from his middle between two fingers. His neck felt hot.

"Don't make me come over there."

Will looked at Kelly. He looked back at the flask.

Water crossed over his feet, soaking his sneakers and wicking up his pant legs. He tried to lift his foot but the wet sand sucked back at the rubber sole and held him in place. Goosebumps prickled against his Levis. He noticed how skinny his arm looked in a T-shirt.

Just then he heard splashing and felt his head jerk back. He stumbled into the water, skinny arms and legs flailing. Kelly yanked the flask out of his hand and dragged him out into the water with a grip on the hair at the back of his head. He should have had it cut before camp. She unscrewed the cap with one hand and forced the bottle to Will's lips, holding his head back to receive the icy drink. He clamped his mouth closed tight, feeling the grit of sand against his skin and the crushing of his lips between the hard glass and his teeth. Kelly pushed a finger between his lips and howled "Yee haw!" as she emptied the bottle, part into Will's mouth and part into the lake, excess running down his chin and neck into the water.

"Never said No to rodeo, Willie Phillie." Kelly pulled her leg behind Will, taking his legs out from under him before she let go of his hair, dropping him into as sputtering heap of arms and legs in knee-deep water.

She splashed back to shore, guffawing the whole way, and sat down on the beach. Will coughed and spit, falling back into the water as he tried to get to his feet. He reached for the dock to steady himself. Before the rising heat reached his ears, he doubled over in the water and vomited.

Kelly stood, polishing the mouth of the bottle with the front of her blouse.

"You are such a girl," she said as she walked away, leaving Will standing in the lake amidst algae, Copenhagen leaves and the morning's oatmeal.

Will smoked his first cigarette because of Kelly Bidwell. He traded Jed Smith KP duty for two cigarettes. One, he smoked alone in the woods for practice, knowing from watching television he would choke and cough his lungs out the first time. He couldn't have a repeat of the scene at the lake when he was trying to reassert his clearly absent virility. The second he kept in his Levis pocket waiting for the right moment.

His moment came the fourth night of camp. He'd walked out of Movie Night, a western. Clint Eastwood irritated Will, always surrounded by helpless women who lost their clothes for all the wrong reasons. He was rough with them and a terrible conversationalist, and still they swooned over him, even before he actually did anything heroic, which usually wouldn't even have been necessary if Eastwood's women had been written with any intelligence at all. He leaned a shoulder against a tree and put his hand in his pocket, rolling the cigarette between his fingers. He tried to curl his lip like Eastwood. That's what it was, he decided. Women loved the way he curled his lip. And he had a really big gun.

The lodge door slammed shut and Will looked up to see Kelly's silhouette against the glowing doorway. She must not like Eastwood either, he thought.

He quickly stood upright and pulled out the cigarette and Jed's lighter from his pocket. It lit up on the first try—he'd practiced that too—and then leaned back against the tree, stretching his legs out in front of him and appearing fully at ease. He pretended to look at the stars while he waited for

Kelly to approach. "There you are, little Willie," she called ahead. "I was just telling the girls about you and your first chew. I wondered where you ran off to."

Will turned. "Oh, hey." He blew a lungful of smoke toward her. "Eastwood is such a bore. Good showman but he's got nothing under his script. I decided to go for a walk and have a smoke." He swallowed a small cough as it crept up his throat.

"Willie Phillips smokes. Well, I'll be damned. And here I thought you were as pure as the driven snow." Kelly stood with her hands on her hips, looking Will up and down. "Maybe I was wrong about you. Gimme one."

Shit. He didn't see that move coming. He should have traded Jed for three. His dad always told him he was better at tennis than chess. *Think fast, Phillips.*

"Oh, umm. Sorry. Was just enjoying my last one." He took a long drag on the cigarette and let it out slowly. "But here." He held it out to Kelly.

She hesitated. "It's your last one, Cowboy. We still have two days of camp."

"Half a cigarette won't make much difference then, will it," Will said. "Really, take it. It's fine. I know a guy I can bum off of."

Kelly took what was left of the cigarette and a long pull. She held it in while she handed the cigarette back. Will waved it off. "No, no. Finish it."

"You sure?"

"Yep, sure. You've seen what happens to me when something's already been in your mouth."

Kelly chuckled and blew a line of smoke into the night

sky. "You're okay, Phillips. I think I know a girl you might like."

In that moment, Will felt as though he'd crossed some imaginary but before now impassable threshold, carried over on a magic carpet that floated along a thin trail of nicotine and other deadly chemicals into a room of rough-shaven and ripped men, where testosterone surged through the air shafts alongside oxygen. It didn't matter to Will who this girl was or even if he ever met her. He suddenly knew he needed the air in that room to survive, and Kelly Bidwell, by virtue of a slender white cylinder just three inches long, had deemed him worthy to breathe it.

It cost him cleaning the latrine, but Will managed to broker himself a deal with Jed for another half dozen cigarettes. He didn't mind latrine duty; it was the only time he could lock the door and use the shower, which he was now even more in need of. Kelly made good on her offer, and for the rest of the week, Will held the soft, warm hand of a petite girl from Skokie with amber curls and a sweet smile that may have rivaled that of Neruda's beloved Matilda. She laughed at all his jokes, even the ones others didn't understand, and when she asked him not to smoke, he put the last of his cigarettes in his suitcase and didn't touch them again. Of course, later there would be Barbara, and he would find a reason to take them out another day.

Derek Jeffers opened the passenger door and leaned out to spit on the gravel shoulder, coughing a little for having left the chew in his mouth too long. "Excuse me," he said as he closed the door and wiped his mouth. "Sorry 'bout that. Guess I shoulda waited until we were done." He pointed to the digital recorder sitting on the center console between them in

Will's truck.

"No problem," Will said, silently agreeing with Derek that it would have been better to wait to chew until he was out of a stranger's truck. Probably nerves, he figured, as he absent-mindedly turned a box of menthols over against his knee with his left hand.

"Anything else you can think of?" Will asked.

"Nope, that's pretty much how it happened."

"And were your answers true and correct to the best of your knowledge?" Will tried to inject a somber tone as though he were actually in court.

"Oh, yessir," Derek answered. "Honest to god truth."

Will turned off the recorder and played back a few seconds to ensure the recording was successful.

"Listen," he said, extending a hand to Derek, "thanks for meeting me out here. Really appreciate it. I think that's all I need."

"Happy to help," Derek replied as he shook Will's hand. "If you need anything else, you know where you can find me."

He got out of the truck and jogged across the highway to his VW van and drove off while Will pulled out his phone to check for new messages. He played back a voice message.

"Mr. Phillips? Are you there?" Will chuckled. Pearl hated voice mail, but he had to give her credit for using it anyway. "I want you to come to dinner tonight. That nice Ms. Julian is coming and the two of us won't have enough to talk about alone. There should be someone closer to her age, don't you think? Even though I do think she's much younger than you. Anyway. You'll come at 6:30."

Will checked his watch. It was 3:00. He'd have time to get

home and clean up.

"You could come down earlier of course and help me cut vegetables but you are so busy all the time you will probably just blow in here with the tumbleweeds at 6:45. Don't do that. Try to be on time, alright? 6:30, I said. Okay. See you. Pearl."

She always added her name at the end like she was writing a note and not recording a message. Will smiled, thinking he couldn't love Pearl Jenkins any more if he tried. He pressed the Callback button. She would want to hear his promises to arrive on time.

"Hello?" Pearl answered on the second ring.

"Mrs. Jenkins. It's Will. I got your message."

"You'll come then, of course."

"Yes, I'd love to join you and—what's that girl's name again?"

"Her name is Cameron. You'll be on time? I told her 6:30 and I really want you here by then. Show her how prompt you can be. Girls like that."

"I'm pretty sure that timeliness is not the top quality women are looking for in a good man. But let's be clear about this: I am coming to dinner with you because you are the best cook in the county. Not because you invited you invited whatshername."

"Cameron Julian, Mr. Phillips. Girls also like men who can remember their names."

"Okay, okay. I'll write her name on my hand so I don't embarrass you. And I have an idea," he said, with the slightest hint of mischief. "You don't mind if I bring along a friend, do you?"

"A friend? Whom do you have in mind, Mr. Phillips? It's

a bit forward to ask the host if you can bring someone else, don't you think? Tacking someone onto a dinner invitation?"

"You know my manners, Mrs. Jenkins. Sometimes I make you think I was raised by savages. You've said that. Look, you'll want to play cards after dinner, and threesomes are impossible. Last time you played with a dummy hand I'm sure you were cheating."

"I just don't want someone getting between you and Ms. Julian. Erm, I mean, I don't want someone she doesn't know, that she'd be uncomfortable with."

"Promise you. My friend will make everyone comfortable. And besides. Cameron is a big girl. She can handle meeting new people. Let me bring a friend, please? I promise it will do nothing but fan the flame of your little Yente dinner. Okay?"

"Well. Why do you always get your way with me?"

"Because you think I'm cute, Mrs. Jenkins. I'll see you at 6:30. Or before, if your vegetables need cutting."

"Hmph."

Will disconnected and pulled up Joe Murphy's number in his phone. Joe also answered on the second ring.

Two peas, Will thought. *Match made.*

21

Pearl had not told Will to come down the back stairs, but he did anyway, knowing she'd be in the kitchen frantically bustling around with her final dinner preparations. While he was in the shower, he decided what he had done to Pearl bordered on cruelty, if cruelty could be a little sweet. She would be frazzled enough wanting everything to be just right so she could later say her dinner was his and Cameron's first date. But introducing a mystery character into her carefully-crafted plot line would be nearly too much for his tightly-wound landlady-turned-matchmaker.

He should tell her Joe was coming, he thought as he slid the offset triangle of his four-in-hand knot on his narrow plaid tie under the points of a blue Oxford shirt. Pearl also hadn't told him to wear a tie, but he'd made the mistake of showing up for dinner once before with an open-collared shirt. There are some things a guy only has to learn once.

It would at least be a small relief to her to know he wasn't bringing himself a date, which would be humiliating for Cameron and in turn for Pearl, and ultimately for his date who would be smart enough to see what had just happened.

He buckled his belt over the button of his brown corduroys and slipped on his shoes. No, he must not tell her about Joe. That small sense of relief would make just enough space for her to stop worrying about Cameron and start worrying about herself, and it would be like a cold front meeting a warm front and a tornadic funnel cloud the likes of which had never been seen on the Dakota plains would tear through

Pearl's kitchen. No, he would say nothing. Joe would have to be a surprise. He would simply continue to assure her that it was a good thing, that when dinner was over she'd be glad he'd invited his friend.

Will would, however, tell Cameron. He needed her help in case things backfired, to ensure Pearl did not direct her straight-line winds of fury against Joe. Cameron would need to be prepared to shove Will out in front of the bus while she grabbed Joe out of the street. Joe, of course, was good-natured enough to be able to handle anything Pearl dished out. But Pearl would hate herself in the morning.

He made his usual exaggerated stomps down the back stairs to alert Pearl of his arrival.

"My heavens, Mr. Phillips. Must you sound like an entire pack of horses got loose and are galloping around on my servants' stairs?"

"Wolves travel in packs, Mrs. Jenkins. Not horses." He gave her a light kiss on the cheek. "And they are very quiet."

"Except for the snarling right before they devour you," she said. Pearl slammed the knife hard through the carrot lying innocently on her wooden cutting board and a slice shot off the edge and into the sink. Will picked it up popped it into his mouth.

"Oh, Mrs. Jenkins," he said as he moved beside her. "You are very anxious about what I've done." He put his hand over hers on the knife handle. "Please don't worry. I wouldn't do anything to ruin your evening. Promise." Her hand loosened under Will's. "Let's cut the rest of the carrots, shall we?"

Pearl sighed. "Well, yes. But only because they need to be cut. Not because I'm not still upset with you. You're on very thin ice with me, Mr. Phillips. If you make a fool of me or that nice Miss Julian, you can count on your rent going up."

Will took his hand off Pearl's. She kept chopping calmly away, seemingly content at her newfound tactic to keep Will in tow.

"You're going to fine me?"

"Yes," she said. "Twenty-five dollars a month for each time you slip up. Now stop flirting with me and go put on an apron."

"An apron?"

"My, but you seem the poor listener tonight. Must I repeat everything? Yes, an apron. In the pantry. I want you to mix up the gravy and I'd hate for you to splatter it all over your fancy pants."

"An apron. I don't need an apron."

Pearl turned from the counter and looked at Will, one eyebrow raised and the other pressed into a scowl. She pointed the long chef's knife toward the pantry. "Apron, Mr. Phillips, or get out of my kitchen."

Will put his hands up in front of his chest and made his way to the pantry with his back to the wall. "Of course, Mrs. Jenkins. An apron." He ducked inside the pantry door.

Pearl happily chopped her way through another carrot. Will called out, "Are these the only ones you have? Perhaps there's an apron Mr. Jenkins used to wear?"

"Mr. Jenkins didn't come into my kitchen very often. They're one size fits all. Just pick one."

Will looked at the three aprons hanging on hooks inside the pantry. Flowered. Ruffled. Each one. "Sure you don't have one that's less…festive?" He wondered how much he could talk his rent down if Mrs. Jenkins made *him* look foolish.

"It's a festive occasion, young man. Come on now, gravy is waiting."

Will pulled an apron off the hook, bright red begonias trimmed with white eyelet lace. He came around the corner and put the top loop over his head. Pearl turned and wiped her hands on her own bright flowery apron and said, "You look dashingly domestic, Mr. Phillips. Turn around and I'll tie you."

"Domestic wasn't quite the look I was going for. How about I just strap on my tool belt? It'd catch the splatters and keep my fancy pants nice and neat without making me look like the florist shop blew up on me."

"I like you in begonias. Oh, that reminds me. Did you bring flowers tonight?"

"Umm, no. Was I supposed to?"

"Oh, Mr. Phillips. You are incorrigible. There's a bouquet in the refrigerator. I thought you might forget. We'll act like you brought them. Now take the beef roast from the oven and get to work on the gravy."

Will opened a drawer and pulled out two green oven mitts, then took the roaster from the oven. He turned and closed the oven door with his foot. He transferred the roast to a large cutting board Pearl had set out and was picking up the roaster to drain the drippings when the doorbell rang.

"Oh, dear," Pearl said, looking at the clock. "One of them is early."

"You just keep working. I'll get it. It's probably Cameron."

Will needed to get to Cameron first. And if it were Joe, well, he needed to get to him first too. He bolted for the pantry and into the dining room, too fast to hear Pearl call out after him.

"Mr. Phillips, you might want to take off that pretty apron!"

Will saw Cameron, split into a dozen tiny images through the beveled glass of the entry. He reached for the doorknob, not taking his eyes off the intelligent, savvy young woman standing on Pearl's wide porch. It took longer than it should have to realize he still had an oven mitt—and the begonia covered apron—on. He yanked off the mitt and pulled open the door, greeting Cameron with a sheepish grin.

"Come in, come in." He motioned with the mitt toward his apron. "I'm sorry, Pearl has me helping in the kitchen. I'm hoping she'll take it off my rent."

"Anyway, come in. Come in." He gestured to the parlor and giant staircase, evening sun streaming through the vast stained glass on the landing in a colorful array. "Be it ever so humble, there's no place like Pearl Jenkins' home."

Cameron stepped in and looked around. "What lovely woodwork."

"Yes, it is. As local legend has it, Pearl's granddaddy was a lumber man and built the house to showcase his wares. The birds-eye maple in the dining room is stunning. We should go there before Pearl decides you and I ran off together before we even enjoyed her wonderful cooking."

Cameron tipped her head. "So you're okay with her matchmaking, even though you know nothing will come of it?"

Will swallowed at her certainty. "Well, yes. It's not the first time Pearl has had me down to dinner, you know. I've learned to moderate my expectations. She, on the other hand, keeps turning them up." He put the oven mitt under his arm and slid his hands into his pockets, rocking forward and back on the balls of his feet.

"I didn't," Cameron started. "I didn't mean—"

"I know," Will said, and smiled. "Look, before we go in there, I need to tell you I invited a friend."

"Oh?" Will thought he saw Cameron's eyes darken, her pupils widening impossibly across the deep pools. She shifted her weight and brushed a hand across her bangs in what seemed an effort to appear nonchalant.

"Yes, and Pearl is incensed. I didn't tell her who it was, and if it goes badly, I'm looking at a spike in my cost of living that even Congress couldn't achieve."

There was a tap at the glass behind them. Will rushed past Cameron to the door. "Joe! Come in," Will said, shaking Joe's hand and clapping him on the back with the oven mitt.

"Why, you're looking quite lovely tonight, Will. Is the apron new?" Joe laughed. "Now I feel underdressed."

"Consider me the baseline control, Joe. Pearl Jenkins thinks I was born underdressed, so everyone looks dashing next to me." He put a finger under his collar to adjust it. "The bow tie is a nice touch. You look downright professorial."

Cameron cleared her throat. Joe pressed Will out of the way with a sweep of his arm. Cameron stood facing the two men, arms crossed over her chest, a smirk planted on her face.

Joe stepped forward and extended his hand. "You must be the fair Ms. Julian I've been hearing about."

"Hearing about?" Will said. "I mentioned her once, today, when I invited you to dinner."

"Ah, Will likes to be coy."

"Call me Cameron, please."

"If you will call me Joe." He lifted Cameron's hand and

dipped his head to lightly kiss the back of her hand.

"Oh, good grief," Will said.

Joe pointed his index finger back and forth between them. "So this is the match your landlady is working up?" He let out a soft whistle. "She's no slouch, I guess, your Mrs. Jenkins."

Will scowled. "What is that supposed to mean?"

"Well, she's got her work cut out for her, is all. You were right, Will. You're terrifically outclassed here. Not going to be an easy sell." He smirked at Cameron, who laughed and bit her lip.

Will rubbed the back of his neck. "Thanks for the vote of confidence, Murphy. Listen, that's why you're here. Cameron and I already know, I mean, we'll humor Pearl for tonight. But if you play your cards right—and I mean literally, there'll be a game after dinner—-then you can redirect her efforts… elsewhere."

"Mr. Phillips!" Pearl's heels clicked against the oak floor of the dining room. "Where have you gone to? And thank you so much for not making the gravy like I asked you." She appeared around the corner drying her hands on her apron.

"Oh! I didn't know our guests had arrived, since you haven't let them in yet." She squeezed Cameron's forearm and smiled. "Welcome, Miss Julian. So happy you could come."

Pearl turned toward Will and glared before reaching a hand toward Joe. "And welcome to you as well, Mr. ah—"

"Murphy," Will said as Joe took Pearl's hand in both of his. "Mrs. Jenkins, meet my good friend Joe Murphy."

"Enchanted," Joe said, bowing lightly.

Pearl waved her guests toward the dining room. "Please, come in, have a seat. I'm delighted to have you both here."

She turned to Will, narrowing her eyes. Smiling through clenched teeth, she said, "Mr. Phillips, I wonder if I could see you in the kitchen please?"

Will folded his hands behind his back and clapped his ankles together. "Of course." The four walked single file to the dining room, then Will followed Pearl into the kitchen.

In one single, fluid motion, Pearl snatched a white dish towel off the counter, twirled it into a rope, then turned and snapped it at Will's knees. He jumped back and Pearl continued to advance, chasing him with the towel around the kitchen until she had him cornered between the wall and the trash compactor by the stairway door.

Will threw up his hands, hoping his lack of protection would cause Pearl to stop snapping the towel. She took one more shot, slapping at his abdomen, which stung through his thin cotton shirt. He rubbed his belly with one hand and put the other out toward Pearl.

"Okay, Mrs. Jenkins. I think that's enough now."

She put her hands on her hips and let the towel hang down at her side. "What were you thinking? Why on earth did you invite a man my age to dinner?"

"I'm sorry. I know how you prefer your men to be younger."

Pearl snapped the towel again, catching his bicep. Will rubbed his arm. "This is not a double date, Mr. Phillips. I won't have it. It's humiliating for me. And for that innocent man out there. What's your pawn's name again?"

"Joe Murphy," Will said. "And he's not a pawn. This should be no more humiliating for you than it is for me when you parade me past your long line of hopefuls. Maybe if it's good for the gander it can also go good for the goose. Not that I think you're a goose, of course. Anyway. At least I brought you a date you have a chance with."

Pearl stepped backward and leaned against the sink. "Is that what this is? Payback?" she said softly. "I work hard to bring nice girls I think you would like. Is it my fault you don't hit it off? I can't do everything for you, Mr. Phillips. And I can't imagine you'd set me up this way just to even a score."

"You're right about that. I wouldn't." Will stepped out of the corner and leaned on the counter next to Pearl. "Look. I appreciate all the dinners. The way you are always on the lookout for someone for me. But it doesn't work that way. I'm just not the kind of guy that—" Will looked down at the linoleum floor tiles. "Cameron's great, you know? I think we'll be good friends. But Joe, Mrs. Jenkins. I've never met anyone like him. He lives alone in a shambles. His life sort of imploded on him somehow. But he knows things. Deep things. The world needs him to come out of his house. I thought maybe the two of you could be friends."

"I am not taking on a charity case, Mr. Phillips. I have my hands full with you."

"He is not a charity case. I promise."

"This is not a double date."

"No, it's not."

"I have more towels in the drawer."

"I know you do. And you are skilled with them." Will brushed the back of Pearl's hand with his own as they stood side by side at the sink. "Please? Let's have a nice dinner. Get to know Joe Murphy. And then let's play some cards. I didn't tell him how you cheat."

"I don't cheat," Pearl bit her lip. "But all the same, it's best not to let on to him."

"Of course not."

"I do get lonely, Will," Pearl said softly.

"I know. So do I." Will laced his fingers between Pearl's and they stood quietly.

"Now take off that apron and put the gravy on the table. You look ridiculous, like my little sister."

"Thank you." Will pulled the apron off over his head and made as though he was checking his reflection in the polished shine of the refrigerator, tipping his head to the left, then the right.

"Am I bleeding anywhere?"

He felt a thwack to the small of his back as Pearl snapped the towel lightly one last time. "Oh, don't be such a sissy. A little blood never hurt anybody."

"Actually, I was hoping for a little. You know, to show Cameron I'm tough like that."

"Of course. I should have thought of that a long time ago. What girl wouldn't want a fella who would fight a little old lady in her kitchen, and be the one who came out with battle wounds?"

"Good point." He straightened his tie and turned to face Pearl. "So am I? Bleeding, I mean."

"Lord, have mercy." She threw the towel at Will's chest and picked up the meat platter. "Bring the gravy you didn't make. And fix your hair. You look like the Wreck of the Hesperus."

Will hung the towel and combed his fingers through his hair. He picked up the gravy boat and followed Pearl to the dining room.

"Everything okay in there?" Joe smiled as he stood up from the table.

"Yes, everything is just fine. Thank you for asking, Mr. Murphy, and please, sit down." She set the platter on the table and wiped her hands together. "Mr. Phillips here is a little late on his rent, again, and I wanted to talk to him about some chores he'll be doing for me as a service charge."

Will slid Pearl's high back wooden chair out and she sat down. "Careful not to scratch my oak floor, now." As he took his seat, he asked, "So what did you kids find to talk about while Mrs. Jenkins was extracting payment from me?"

"Ms. Julian was just telling me about her move from Minneapolis and the adjustment to small town life."

"Please," Cameron interjected. "It's Cameron. I'm not one of your mother's friends, so there's no need for titles."

He laughed. "That's a hard lesson for some of us to put aside, you know. But very well. And there will be no Mr. Murphy from you then, either. It's Joe."

"Well, where does that leave *us*, Mr. Phillips?" Pearl unfolded a yellow linen from her red plate and smoothed it onto her lap. If there was something Will loved about dinner at Pearl's, besides her fine cooking, it was the way she set a table. For all her formalities, Pearl did not like to use her wedding china, and laid out her mother's Fiestaware instead. Each place setting was a different combination of bright colors. It didn't matter the occasion. Dinner at Pearl's colorful table always felt like he thought a birthday party was supposed to feel.

He shook out the faded cobalt napkin from his coral plate and started to tuck it under his chin. Pearl narrowed her eyes and he gently pulled on the bottom corner and lowered it onto his lap.

"Well," he said. "Seems to me that a few minutes ago in the kitchen you called me 'Will' for the first time in the twelve years I've known you. So maybe it's time for us to join our friends on a first name basis."

Pearl pointed the carving knife at Will. "You notice every-thing." She turned it so the handle faced him. "Slice the roast, Mr. Phillips."

"Or," Will said, reaching gingerly for the knife, "you know, just for tonight. We could try it. If you can't sleep tonight, I'll personally walk to you to church tomorrow so Father John can hear your confession."

Pearl put up her hands. "Oh, I certainly don't want to be the odd man out here. I'll try it. For tonight. Don't get any ideas, Mr. Phil—Oh, dear. Will." She shook her head. "Just don't get any ideas."

"Pearl hates when I get ideas," Will smiled. "I think I have some pretty good ones, too." He cut through the roast, serving a thick slice onto Joe's plate, steam rising and thin dark juices running across his plate. "Cameron? Let's have your plate."

Cameron looked hard into Will's eyes from across the table. He knew she was saying something but hadn't any idea what. "No, thanks, Will. Why don't you take that piece, and give the next one to Pearl."

"Oh, umm. Okay." Will returned the look, trying to grasp what Cameron was not saying.

"Cameron, dear. Did he slice off too much for you? He thinks everyone eats like a man. Or maybe you wanted a piece from closer to the center? It's not quite as well done."

Cameron was still holding Will's eyes and he suddenly understood. Or thought he did.

"Joe," he said. "Pass that salad to Cameron. From what I've heard, Pearl's three-bean salad is the biggest hit at the church potlucks. At least until you get to the dessert table. I understand she rules there, too."

Pearl waved him off. "Oh, you exaggerate, Will."

"I'd be happy to," Joe said, "though I should serve myself some before I let the lovely lady have it." He scooped a large helping of beans on to his plate. "A plant-eater, then?" He smiled at Cameron as he passed the large green bowl.

"Yes, I'm vegetarian, Joe." She set the bowl beside her plate and reached in with the antique sterling spoon. "It's like we were talking about before. I think it's not very common out here, so I try not to make much of it."

"You're a vegetarian?" Pearl asked. "Oh, I do wish you'd said something. Here I've gone and killed the fatted calf."

"Oh, Pearl, I wouldn't have wanted you to go to any trouble. The bean salad really is perfect. And the potatoes."

"Well, of course they are. But if I had known, I could have made chicken."

Will put a hand over his mouth and leaned over the side of his chair, pretending to pick up his napkin.

"Pearl, you are very sweet," Cameron said. "But truly. The meal is perfect, just as it is."

Will felt a kick to his ankle and saw Pearl's shiny black pump retreat under her chair. He jumped and knocked his head against the underside of the table leaf.

"Mr. Phillips, what is it you are doing down there that is so important? I assure you, I vacuumed earlier today."

"The floor is spotless, as always. I don't know why we're

even eating at the table. We should be picnicking on the oak tongue-in-groove." He sat up and wiped his mouth with his napkin. "Found it." He tapped his knife on the table. "You are supposed to be calling me Will, by the way. It really does make me feel more like myself."

"I have half a mind to show you what I can do with a couple of board feet of tongue-in-groove. And you stay up in your chair now or I'll call you worse than that."

"Now, Pearl. We're all happy here. Pour some of my delicious gravy on your roast and tell me what you think of it."

Pearl took a bite of her food. "Needs salt."

"I knew it. I never put enough salt in." Will snapped his fingers.

"You didn't make the gravy, Will."

"Oh, right. I owe you one." He grinned at Pearl and ladled gravy onto his potatoes. "Can we talk about something else now?"

Pearl sipped her ice water and scowled at Will over the top of the glass. She turned to Cameron and smiled.

Will looked away. "Believe it or not, Joe is from Chicago too, isn't that right Joe?"

"But you're not from Chicago, Mr. Phillips," Pearl corrected him before Joe could answer. "You're from Naperville. That's 30 miles away. You don't hear people from Longville saying they are from Dennison."

"True, but Naperville is pretty much Chicago. Same difference," Will said. "And, it's Will."

"Same difference, Mr. Phillips," Pearl said, raising an eyebrow. "And what a ridiculous expression. Mr. Murphy, are you actually from Chicago, or do you just go around saying you are to show off, like Mr. Phillips here?"

Joe laughed and set down his fork. "You have a delightfully sharp wit, Pearl. I imagine not everyone can stay ahead of our friend Will." He clapped Will on the shoulder. "I'm from actual Chicago. The real deal. My parents and my brother and I lived with their parents and my mother's brother in a walk-up flat in Logan Square—that's a neighborhood, not another city like Naperville—between Logan and Diversey. Married my high school sweetheart and we lived six blocks from my parents. Stayed there until I retired."

"And what work did you retire from, Mr. Murphy?" Pearl's expression softened and she set her glass down.

"Please, I don't want to add to the fun between you and Will, but it's Joe. I'd sure love it if that's what you called me." He smiled at Pearl, then looked at his lap and fingered the stitching along the edge of the sunset linen napkin. "I was a firefighter. Thirty-seven years."

"You must have seen a lot of excitement serving on the Chicago fire department," Cameron said. "What made you move out here?"

"My wife." Joe looked up. "Her grandparents lived here and she loved to visit when she was a girl. She was enamored with Main Streets and county fairs. She'd lived her whole life in the city, but she wasn't built for it. Before she'd agree to marry me, I had to promise one day we'd live here."

Joe looked over at Will and his eyes filled. Will nodded almost imperceptibly. "Hey, old man. If you're done with the mashed potatoes, why don't you pass them over here."

"It's possible I'm just not done with them." Joe winked.

"Goodnight nurse!" Pearl kicked Will under the table

again, hard. He stifled a groan and shifted in his seat, reaching a hand down to rub his shin. "I am so sorry, Mr. Murph— Joe. I have been trying for years to teach Mr. Phillips some semblance of good manners. I've decided tonight it is beyond hope. From now on, I'm going to set him a place in the kitchen while the grownups dine in peace out here."

Pearl glared at Will and snatched the gravy boat from his hands. He shrugged. Cameron held back a smile and reached for the salad.

"Oh dear. It's not as bad as all that," Joe said, chuckling. "He does mean well."

"Really, Pearl. Joe's right. It's part of why you find me so charming."

"It shouldn't surprise me at all that the two of you would stick together." Pearl pushed her chair back from the table and picked up the water pitcher, which was nearly full. "I'm going to get some water."

Will looked at Cameron and nodded slightly toward Pearl. Cameron slid her chair out and stood. "I'll help you."

Joe and Will half stood as the women got up, then settled back into their chairs.

~

Pearl set the pitcher down hard on the counter.

"Is everything okay?"

"Oh, this dinner is just not going right at all. Between Will inviting his friend and not telling me you'd rather have chicken, and now his dreadful table manners. I don't understand how it is I haven't already strangled him. It's probably good I can't make it up the stairs to his bedroom anymore. He is incorrigible."

Cameron put an arm on Pearl's shoulder. "He means well, Pearl."

"Why does everyone say that about him? And why can't someone who means so well not ever get it right?"

"They're boys. Sure, they look like men. They're old enough to be men. But look hard at them, Pearl. They're boys, through and through. Look, I think Will really likes Joe, and I think he really wants you to like him too. He's just trying too hard."

"Well, he could have at least told me about his cockamamie scheme before the man showed up at my door. I planned this dinner to help him out and this is how he thanks me."

Cameron smoothed the front of her sweater. "If I could say so, Pearl, I think you might be trying a little too hard too."

Pearl looked up. "What?"

"You want him on his best behavior so he'll make a good impression on me. But it won't matter. Will on his best behavior won't impress me."

"Oh, I see." Pearl looked at the floor and her shoulders drooped. "I'm very sorry to have put you through this dinner tonight if you already knew you didn't care for him. How very awkward for you. He'll be humiliated, of course. And angry at me for it."

"Pearl, stop. That's not what I meant. I enjoy Will's company just fine. He's funny, smart. And he covers it pretty well, but he has a sensitivity that intrigues me. I just mean that I'd rather he wasn't on his best behavior. I think we'd all enjoy the night more if he could just act like himself."

Pearl smiled and grabbed Cameron's hand. "You like Will. You'll go out with him." Pearl did a spin on one foot and had to catch the counter to get her balance. "This is so exciting.

I've never gotten this far with Will before."

"You are very sweet, Pearl," Cameron said. "But let's not get ahead of ourselves. I don't need Will to impress me, but that doesn't mean I'm ready to date him. Or that he's ready to date me."

Pearl stood still and smiled. "Good enough for me, Dear." She picked up the water pitcher and handed it to Cameron. "Here. Pretend to fill it for a minute. I'm going back in."

There was a new bounce in Pearl's step as she walked toward the butler's pantry. "I finally picked a good one," she said, rubbing her hands together, then pushed the door open and walked through with her head held high.

Cameron leaned against the counter and sighed. "It doesn't mean I'm ready to date *anyone,* Pearl."

~

"I'm so sorry about that," Pearl said as she took her seat at the table. She smiled wide. "We were out of water. Cameron's bringing it. What else can I get you, Joe?"

"I'm just fine, Pearl," Joe said, placing a hand on his round middle. "Can't tell you how long it's been since I've had true home cooking. I'm stuffed."

"You left room for pie, didn't you, Joe?" Cameron set the pitcher on the table and sat down. "I saw a gorgeous apple pie on the counter. I think it's still warm."

"My grandmother's recipe," Pearl beamed. "And yes, it's still warm."

"I'll make room," Joe laughed. "It's not right for a man to turn down a still-warm apple pie from a beautiful woman."

Will looked at Joe and cocked his head.

"That's right, Will," Pearl said. "You better have saved room too. You heard what Joe said about the pie baked by a beautiful woman." She tucked a curl behind her ear.

Will moved his legs to the other side of his chair, just in case. "Of course I have room. You took the potatoes and gravy away from me."

Pearl smiled and said nothing. Will turned to Cameron and Joe. "It's because of the pie, you know. A lot of guys think I live here because of the rent, but I could find cheaper rooms. It's really just the pie. Warm from the oven, melting ice cream slowly trickling down the sides. You will never—"

"Oh!"

"Pearl?" Will asked. "I didn't mean anything about the cheap room. It was a joke."

"No," Pearl said, putting her face in her hands. "It's not your dumb joke." She looked up at Will. "Though, thank you for what you said about my pie." She put her face back into her hands. "I forgot the ice cream. As good as my pie is, it's not the same without."

Joe scooted his chair back. "I'd be happy to run out for some. It'd only take a minute."

"Great idea, but I'll go," Will said. "You are our guest. Look, you kids all stay here and psychoanalyze me. I'll be back before you have the coffee ready."

"This is so embarrassing," Pearl stood at the table. "Let me get my purse."

"Sit, Pearl," Will said. Pearl glared. "Sorry. Sit please. Let me do this. I want to." Will smiled and walked out.

She picked up the mashed potato bowl. "I may as well

clear dishes while we wait."

"I'll help you," Cameron said, getting up.

"Oh, no dear," Pearl said, waving her off. "Wait. I have a better idea. Run out the back and go with Mr. Phillips."

Cameron shook her head. "Oh, he'll be fine. He can manage ice cream, I'm sure. Let me help you with the table."

"No, really. Go with him. No doubt he'll do fine with the ice cream but I'd just like you to go along." Pearl bumped the pantry door open with her hip and hurried into the kitchen to the back door. She stood on the porch and waved to Will, who was backing out of the gravel driveway into the alley. He rolled down his window.

"What is it, Pearl? You want Rocky Road instead of vanilla?"

"Wait a minute, Cameron would like to go with you." She turned back to open the porch door. "Come on, Dear. He's waiting for you."

Cameron stepped outside. Pearl gave her a light push on the backside, but Cameron didn't miss a beat. "We'll be right back now," she said. "You and Mr. Murphy had better be on your best behavior."

"Oh, heavens, Cameron. I hardly know the man. Now get going before the pie cools."

22

Cameron got in Will's truck and buckled her seatbelt. Will turned and grinned.

"I wasn't asking to come along, you know," said Cameron. "She practically dragged me out the door and pushed me off the porch."

"I know. It's her way."

"Just so we're clear. It was Pearl's idea. She's so flustered tonight, I didn't want her to be any more upset."

"I understand. She told you to come along. She does that when she senses a person wants to do something and isn't saying so."

"Oh, no, Mister. It wasn't like that. I was going to stay and help be a buffer between her and Joe. If anything, I'd have sent Joe along. It was Pearl's idea all the way through."

"Okay. Pearl's idea. That's the story we'll go with."

Cameron shot a look at Will. He smiled and turned into the grocery store lot.

"She called you incorrigible tonight. I defended you, but she's probably right."

Will parked and turned off the truck. "She's called me worse. And she's usually right." He reached behind to his back pocket. "Damn. I left my wallet upstairs."

"Oh, no. And I didn't bring my purse."

"She'll flip if we come back without the ice cream. The pie's going to be cold as it is," Will said, rubbing the back of his neck. "Oh, hey. Pop the glove box open. Sometimes I have a few ones in there."

Cameron opened the glove box. Two black pens fell out, along with the head of a Barbie doll. Cameron picked up the head and brushed the long, blonde hair off its face.

"What's this doing here?"

"It's a doll head. Barbie, I think. I mean, it's not Barbie. It's a Barbie doll. Head. Yeah. Barbie doll head. I think it's Francie. Her sister. No, wait. Francie was her cousin and was never blonde. Skipper, I think. Right. Skipper. She was blonde once. Not now, of course. Her hair now is black and purple. But it used to be blonde once." Will reached across the seat and rifled through the glove box while he talked. "Okay, here we go." He waved a five dollar bill in the air. "Always keep a little cash in the glove box. Never know when you might need some ice cream."

Will closed the cab door and waited for Cameron to come around the truck. "Stacie," he said, snapping his fingers.

"What?" Cameron asked.

"Barbie's other sister was Stacie. Younger. Twin to her brother Todd." He turned to Cameron as they walked through the automatic doors into the store and smiled, pleased with himself for being able to talk his way to the bit of trivia he sought.

Cameron tilted her head, then shook it. "Of course the doll is Skipper, Will. I could have told you that. Anyone who's ever been a little girl could tell you that."

"But…" Will said, brow furrowed. "You asked what it was. And that's what I answered, even it if took me a little while."

"Ah, I see. You're one of those guys."

"And which guys are those?"

"The 'asked and answered' guys. I apologize for leaving the excruciating but apparently necessary specificity out of my question."

Will pulled out a cart and started walking. He motioned with his head to the right. "Freezer section is this way."

"Will." Cameron stood by the cart rows.

He looked back. "Hmm?"

"You can't buy enough ice cream with five dollars to require a cart."

"I know." He kept walking. Cameron stood and watched him a moment longer, then hurried to catch up.

"Will."

He scanned the freezer case.

"You should know something," Cameron said.

Will turned and met her stare. "What's that?"

"You just used up your one time on a Barbie—no, wait, on a Skipper—doll and vanilla ice cream."

"My 'one time.'" He leaned a shoulder lightly against the freezer and folded his arms across his chest. "Maybe you should tell me about that."

"Look. I'm not the kind of girl who runs after a guy. You get one time, and that's just so I can tell you it won't happen again, since you didn't figure it out on your own."

Will straightened and pushed his hands into his pockets. "And you running to me in the grocery store was my 'one time.'"

"Yes." Cameron looked behind her and waited for a woman with a full cart to pass. She lowered her voice. "You just spent it on a stupid little doll head."

Will stood still a moment, then opened the freezer door

and pulled out a quart gallon of vanilla bean. He set it in the cart. He waved Cameron forward. "After you," he said.

Cameron paused, then turned and walked toward the registers, Will following behind without a word. She lifted a copy of *National Enquirer* from the rack while they waited their turn behind an elderly man buying a half gallon of milk, a box of Lucky Charms and three scratch-off tickets.

She turned to Will. "Let's try this again. What I wanted to know back there was why is the severed head of a Barbie doll in your glove box?"

Will smiled. "That's what you wanted to know? You get that it's a different question completely, right?"

"Right. Only you knew I wasn't asking you to tell me which Barbie character the head belonged to, right? Are you going to start another diversion or just solve the mystery for me?"

"I don't need a diversion. Nothing to hide. I'm sure you'll find it all very uninteresting, in fact. I—"

"Evening, Mr. Phillips." The cashier motioned to him. "You find everything okay?"

"I did, thanks. Every one thing on my list." He touched Cameron's arm lightly. "Give me a second, okay? This is not a diversion, it's keeping the line moving."

"Cigarettes tonight, Mr. Phillips?" The tall cashier tossed his head to the left to shake his brown bangs out of his eyes. "I can call the manager up."

"Nah, not tonight Eric," Will said, gesturing with his eyes toward Cameron.

"Oh, uh, right. Umm…I heard you…quit."

"No, you didn't hear that. Because I didn't. Haven't found a good enough reason yet."

"Maybe you will soon, Sir." Eric glanced at Cameron, who was still flipping through the *Enquirer* pages pretending to care which aging former Hollywood starlet's Botox injections went awry.

Will smiled at him. "Maybe. Never know."

The cashier picked up the ice cream and reached for a plastic sack. "Never mind, Eric," Will said, waving him off. "I don't need a bag." He took the ice cream and turned to Cameron. "You all done reading over there?"

Cameron closed the magazine and slipped it back into the rack. "Brad and Angie split up." She pushed the cart through the checkout aisle and they walked together to the exit.

"Now, about the doll head," Cameron said as they approached the truck. "You were saying?"

Will opened the cab door on Cameron's side. "Yes, I was saying. It's going to turn out to be pretty anticlimactic after all this drama, I'm afraid." Cameron got in and Will closed her door and walked to the other side. When he climbed into his seat, Cameron was holding the head, twisting the long blonde hair into a bun and holding it to Skipper's small head with her index finger. "I loved to do their hair," she said.

"I found it."

"You found it?"

"Yes, I found it. In a parking lot. All by itself. Nobody else. No body, in fact, which is a shame because as I recall, Barbie's body was, well…" Cameron lifted her finger from the doll's head and the hair popped out of its bun and tumbled down her invisible back.

"Right," Will continued. "Never mind her body. Barbie has really taken a lot of flack for that."

"You found it in a parking lot. Okay." Cameron's eyes narrowed and she thought a moment. "But what happened between the head lying on the pavement and the head bouncing around in your glove box?"

"I don't know."

"You don't know?"

"Have you noticed how you repeat me a lot?" Will half-smiled.

"Have you noticed how you express incomplete thoughts a lot?"

"If they're so incomplete, I don't know that I'd go around repeating them."

"Whatever." Cameron frowned. "Why'd you pick it up?"

"It felt important."

"It felt important?"

Will started the truck. "You're doing it again."

Cameron laughed softly. "I know. I'm sorry. What seemed important about it?"

"I have no idea," Will said. "I mean, I'm sure I probably do have an idea. But I don't know it yet." He slowed for the four-way stop a block from Pearl's house. "Do you ever have that?"

"Do I ever know something I don't know?"

"No, do you ever not know something you do?"

"Sounds like the same thing to me." Cameron shook her head.

Will laughed. "I suppose it does. Probably is." He turned onto Pearl's gravel and shut off the truck, then shifted in his seat to face Cameron. "Have you ever discovered something one day, only to realize later that maybe, somehow, something in you knew it all along and was silently, stealthily moving you toward that discovery?"

"Sounds a little determinist to me."

"Nah." Will shook his head. "I think I'm just not explaining it very well."

"Why did you keep the doll head, Will?" Cameron wrapped the doll's hair around her little finger. "It's sweet, you know. But I just really wonder why."

"I do too. But I just don't know yet. All I know is I have this same feeling about lost things."

"Lost things?"

"Things that are missing. That head. It's missing its body. 'Course, somewhere in a little girl's closet is a body that's missing its head."

"She's probably already thrown it away."

"Maybe. Maybe not. Maybe she keeps it as a spare. I used to change the heads on my dolls all the time. Sometimes it was really hard to get the neck plug-thingy into the hole under her chin. It was a super tight fit." He put his fists together to demonstrate.

"You used to?"

Will paused and looked at his hands. "Yeah, well, you're repeating me again."

"I am. I'm sorry."

"Anyway." He opened the cab door. "Lost things. I once investigated a claim where a woman had a heart attack going 65 mph on the highway. Lost consciousness and drove the car off the road and into a building. Tragic. Never knew whether the heart attack killed her or if it was the impact. Either way, she was dead at the scene."

"That's terrible."

"Yeah, I know. But there was this thing in the autopsy that haunted me for weeks. She was missing a shoe. I mean, they inventory all her personals—the color shirt and pants she had on, her necklace, a ring, the lipstick in her purse, even the 63 cents in change. But she had only one shoe. Two feet. One shoe. Where the hell was the other one? Was it still in the car somewhere? Did it fall out when they extricated her from the vehicle? Did she know something that morning that she didn't really know and for some reason leave home with only one shoe? If I'd have read the autopsy before I investigated the scene I'd have spent the day combing the ditches for it."

"Ever get an answer?"

"Nah. There was no answer. Everybody was doing their jobs—report the facts. No reason to speculate on something that had nothing to do with the accident or cause of death."

"She didn't need the shoe anymore, Will," Cameron said softly.

"Maybe not. Tell that to the brown slip-on in the road ditch somewhere that hasn't seen a good foot in years. That shoe has a good story. I'm sure of it."

"I love a cute pair of shoes as much as the next girl. Actually, from the look of my closet, maybe even more. But shoes don't tell stories. They're just shoes."

"The hell they don't. Listen, when they bury me, make sure I have shoes on both feet. I don't want the left one talking." Will winked at Cameron. She smiled.

"Hey, were you really running to catch me in the grocery store?" Will asked.

"Ice cream is melting, Will. We'd better get inside."

23

"Rebroff. *R-e-b-r-o-f-f.* I'm sure our boy Will can help you look him up on the Internet."

Will could hear Joe as he followed Cameron through the back door into the kitchen. "You'll love him, Pearl," he called out. "Quite the voice." He set the ice cream on the counter and opened a drawer to find Pearl's scoop. "Sometime, you'll have to ask Joe to play his concertina for you."

"You don't have to shout, Will. Good heavens. I'm right behind you."

Will jumped, startled at Pearl's silent arrival behind him. "Sorry, Pearl. Didn't hear your usual bustle when you came in." Pearl did not return his smile, but reached for a dish towel.

"Easy, now." Will put his back to the counter and his hands in front of him as he moved to the other side of the sink. "Let me get the pie, okay? I couldn't find the knife and ice cream scoop, so maybe you could grab them."

Pearl let the towel dangle past her knee and twirled it slowly in the air forming a thick, white cotton rope. He questioned to himself the wisdom of putting a knife in her hand at just this moment.

"Cameron, Dear," she said without taking her eyes off Will. "Take some dessert plates from the cupboard behind you. Mr. Phillips and I will be along momentarily with the pie."

Will looked over Pearl's shoulder toward Cameron, pleading with his eyes and a smirk that curled into a curious mix of playfulness and fear. Cameron turned and opened the cupboard, lifted out four plates and closed the door softly. Then she turned to Will and smiled. She raised her free hand near her cheek, waved twice, and slipped out of the kitchen. "Was that Ivan Rebroff you and Pearl were talking about, Joe?" Her voice trailed off as the door to the butler's pantry swung closed.

Will smiled his most boyish smile. "Now, Pearl. Let's be reasonable. *Bustle* is such a lovely word, really. Chock full of energy and excitement." He turned the corner at the end of the counter and sidestepped to the wall. Pearl swung the free end of the towel up, catching it in her left hand, and stepped toward him.

"Yes, I'm familiar with all the energetic fuss and rumpus, Mr. Phillips."

"We agreed you would call me Will, remember?" he blurted as he grabbed the handle of the door to the back staircase, spun, and hopped up on the step.

Pearl rushed to the door and closed it on him. "I'm serving warm pie and ice cream in two minutes, Mr. Phillips. Don't come back to the table without your manners. They've been absent all night." She turned the lock and gave a firm nod of her head into the air, quietly amused at herself. Then she shook out the towel and wiped her hands on it, pulled a knife from the wood block with a flourish, and picked up the pie. She walked out of the kitchen, pushing the pantry door open with her hip and leaving Will stranded on the back servant's stairs.

"Where's Will?" Pearl asked as she set the pie on the table. "I thought he came ahead of me with the ice cream."

Cameron stifled a snicker. Pearl raised an eyebrow in her direction.

"That man," Pearl said. "I imagine you are a good help in the kitchen, aren't you Joe?"

"Millie and I used to cook together all the time," Joe said. "I don't care so much for the kitchen these days."

"We were talking about Ivan Rebroff, right?" Will walked briskly into the dining room from the hall, straightening his tie. He ran a hand through his hair. "Sorry about that. I just had to run upstairs and use the little boy's room." He looked around the table. "After all that bust—commotion—and we still don't have ice cream?" He pointed to the kitchen. "I'll get it."

Pearl stood at the end of the table, hands on her hips and eyes following him to the door. "He's a handful, Cameron," she said, almost, but not quite, under her breath. "I wonder if you're up to it."

"Excuse me?" Cameron said.

"Oh, nothing, Dear. Just thinking through my mouth."

Will came back with the ice cream and a scoop and set them on the table. "Joe, Cameron, prepare yourselves." He smiled at Pearl, showing all of his teeth. "Apple pie is Pearl's true calling. What you're about to experience is her labor of love, a deeply heartfelt gift to the world. When we're done here, you'll look at the few perfectly flaky crumbs left in this silver tin and be torn between the great tragedy of its emptiness and the deepest satisfaction your stomach—and heart—have ever known. I promise you: It will have you believing in the goodness of the world once again."

He held out a hand toward Pearl. "May I?"

Pearl was blushing now, and tucked her chin toward her chest. She laid the knife across Will's palm resting her own hand for the briefest moment on top of his. "Oh, Will. How you do redeem yourself, time and time again."

"I am powerless against your apple pie, Milady." He dipped his head.

Joe began to clap. Laughing, he said, "You two should take your show on the road. You're really delightful together."

Cameron raised her water glass into the air. "Agreed!" Then her face turned serious. "But could we please have pie first?"

Will cut the pie into eight pieces and dished it onto the four plates, leaving exactly half the pie in the pan. Once, during the Belinda Markway episode of Pearl's "Match Made in Heaven Dinners," he'd cut only six pieces. Pearl was more patient, more hopeful in his future prospects in those days, and waited until after her guests had gone to explain the pie should be cut into eighths. "A proper young lady will think the slice is too large, and that you'd think of her as a horse for eating it all, so she will pick at it and not finish. An eighth, on the other hand, feels like just a sliver—in fact, that's what she'll often ask for—and then she'll likely even take you up on seconds if you offer."

Will had protested, saying that two-eighths was clearly more pie than one-sixth, but Pearl shushed him. "It's pie math. Pie math is different. Look, if we're going to get you hooked up with the girl of my dreams, you're going to have to just trust me sometimes."

Belinda Markway had tried to decline the pie, saying it was too much, but Will served it to her anyway, telling her to just eat a little if that's all she wanted. She relented after the third time, but insisted on only a half scoop of ice cream. She poked at the pie with her fork, taking just a nibble here and a nibble there so that Pearl began to fret that her pie had somehow failed and asked Belinda no less than six times if there wasn't something wrong with the pie, or if she could get her something else, anything, like an Oreo cookie since she didn't happen to have any other desserts on hand. In time, Belinda ate the pie, and the ice cream, but never did return Will's calls after that, which Pearl blamed to this day on the over-sized dessert and Will's inability to do pie math.

He then discovered the added benefit of eight slices being that he might be called to Pearl's kitchen later in the week for a leftover piece, warmed in the oven with a slightly melted scoop of vanilla ice cream dripping down the side. Of course, that was not bound to happen this week even if there were leftovers, if he couldn't sufficiently make amends for his transgressions tonight.

Pearl placed a scoop of ice cream next to a slice of pie and passed the plate to Joe. "Thank you, Pearl. I've been looking forward to this all evening." He set the plate in front of him and picked up his fork. "Now, were you all really wanting to hear about Rebroff's music, or were we just using him to give my friend Will some cover?"

Cameron laughed. "It might have just been cover, Joe. But good cover it was." She put her hand up as Pearl reached to set a plate in front of her. "No, really. Why don't you let me have that next one. It looks smaller and I just want a sliver."

Pearl turned to Will and smiled her best "See what I told you" smile, the one where she always kept her lips tightly closed, where her eyes sparkled and where she lifted her shoulders back. She set the plate in front of Will's seat and pulled the sides of her sweater together in front of her chest, making a small, triumphant "Hmmph" sound. When she turned back to Cameron, Will rolled his eyes. He'd learned the lesson early enough with Belinda Markway, but Pearl found it necessary to remind him of it each and every time a woman wanted a small slice of pie. *Just a sliver.*

"It is a damned complicated thing, being a woman," he said, not realizing he'd said it aloud.

The others stopped what they were doing, Joe with a fork halfway to his mouth. Pearl lifted her own plate from the table. "Mr." She paused. "Phillips."

"I … umm …"

Joe set down his fork and put his hands together, index fingers touching and pointing together at Will. "As I was saying," he said. "Ivan Rebroff."

Will put his hands in his pockets and turned around in a circle. "I'm afraid we might just have to call tonight a wash, Pearl. I'm sorry."

She wiped her hands on her napkin and sat down, waving Will into his chair. She began to laugh with Cameron until Will and Joe joined in.

"I never know what's going to happen when I have Mr. Phillips down for dinner. Maybe one of these days he'll pick a girl and we can stop having these first encounters."

Will shifted in his chair. "And on that encouraging note for Cameron, maybe Joe could tell us a little more about this Rebroff fella."

Joe smiled. "Well, of course I could. But I'm not sure we're all equally interested."

"Say," Pearl said, pointing in the air at Joe with her fork. "While you kids were at the store, Mr. Murphy and I found a family connection. It's really wonderful. Tell them, Joe."

"Oh, yes. Wonderful." Joe wiped his mouth and then folded his napkin and set it beside his plate. "Yes. Millie's grandparents—on her mother's side—had a farm near Graughton. That's why this is the area she always wanted us to retire to. As a girl she visited twice a year, and stayed on the farm for two weeks every summer."

Pearl chimed in. "And would you believe my Grandpa Tate had the grocery in Graughton? I used to spend a month there in the summers, and Grandpa always gave me little chores to do. I'm betting Millie came into the store when I was there."

"That's fantastic," Will said. "You two are connected from way back and had no clue. Did you ever come out this way with Millie, Joe?"

"Years ago. Before her grandparents sold the farm and moved to town. We'd been married just a couple of years then."

"What was the family name again?" Pearl asked.

"Hafer," Joe said. "Millie's granddad was named Jacob Hafer."

"Hafer." Will's brow furrowed lightly. "Had a claim for a Hafer out that way once. Bet you still have family there, Joe."

24

Will laced his fingers behind his head and let his bent arms rest like wings against the pillow. How in the world did the conversation tonight make it all the way to Hafers in Graughton? He sighed, half smiling, half frowning, in his bed as he thought back through the unexpected path of the night at Pearl's, from her angry towel-whipping to Joe's surprise harmonica solo as the four of them stood on the porch saying their goodnights. "Easier to carry with me than a concertina," he'd said, only partially joking. And somewhere in between, there was Cameron.

He realized that at some point during the evening, Pearl's interest in Will impressing Cameron shifted in favor of making her own impression on Joe, and he understood her ire toward him and its peculiar intensity, had something to do with this. Most nights, Pearl reveled in Will's missteps—sometimes he suspected she even orchestrated them. She would chide him, throw up her hands in playful resignation for his date in a "Boys will be boys; Will will be Will" sort of a way. It was possible Pearl had not yet realized this about herself, but Will had seen it last year when she invited Ginger Rollins, the red haired hygienist from Dr. Mohler's office. Will thought they were hitting it off nicely. She was laughing at his jokes, even setting him up for a good line here and there. When Ginger started feeling around at the possibility of seeing Will another time, Pearl caught on.

"Help me clear the dishes for dessert, Mr. Phillips," she said, then waved him off as he stood up from the table. "Oh, never mind. I forgot how you go all to pieces when you get a little something on your hands, and I'm fresh out of latex gloves. Maybe Miss Rollins could help me instead." Will sat back down and the two went into the kitchen together. He heard Pearl talking and the two of them laughing, but couldn't quite make out what was being said. When they came back, Pearl had a smug grin on her face and Ginger wouldn't look at him the rest of the night.

Pearl worked her role as hard as any matchmaker ever had, but always managed to sabotage her own best work. If Will met someone, her job would be done. And worse, Will might one day move out. It was true: Pearl, in her charming and innocent style, humiliated Will time and time again in order to maintain their well-crafted way.

If Joe hadn't been at the table tonight, she'd have been more attentive and seen what was happening between Will and Cameron—the sideways glances, the inside jokes, the way his eyes occasionally took their time around the soft curves of her tailored white blouse when she reached across to refill his water glass, and the way she thought to refill the glass as often as she did. If she'd have noticed, she would never have sent them to the store together. But she hadn't seen. Joe was blocking her view of anyone else in the room.

Instead of the usual mischief-making over Will's idiosyncrasies, Pearl had been genuinely embarrassed by Will, and fearful it would reflect poorly on her in Joe's eyes. He'd never seen her like this, never been tapped and pinched under her table so many times. Will put up with the chiding in front of the candidates Pearl brought in, let her make a cartoon of him before women he didn't really want to date anyway, because it was part of the fun he had with Pearl, sort of the Jenkins &

Phillips show they'd grown comfortable with. He endured it because it was Pearl, and Will loved Pearl, and Pearl made the world's finest apple pie.

But this felt different. Pearl was not teasing him. Will had, somehow, maybe just by showing up, humiliated her. Of course, what she was missing the whole time is that there were folks who liked Will just fine without her help. Two of them had been sitting right at the table all night long. Joe didn't see Pearl through a filter of Will. He just saw Pearl. And from what Will gathered, Joe liked what he saw.

Will had no idea how he was going to fix this.

He stared at the ceiling some more.

"What would Barton Keyes do?" he asked himself aloud.

He thought a while, half dozing on his bed.

Barton Keyes would have done something long before he got himself into this predicament. He'd have put Pearl in her place years ago, wouldn't be taking orders from an old widow living on Social Security and a measly rent check from a miserable boarder who didn't know how to be a real man. Barton Keyes would lay it out for Pearl, let her know who was in charge, and never take another kick under the table again.

Will got up and put his shoes on. He ran his hands through his hair and tucked in the tails of his shirt. Pearl would pay no attention to him if he looked like he'd been in bed with his clothes on.

He tiptoed out to the hall, trying not to make the old floor joists creak, and stood at the top of the stairs. He leaned over the rail to listen for signs that Pearl was still up. The lights were off downstairs, a blueish glow on the staircase cast from a streetlight through the stained glass.

Pearl Jenkins was in bed. It wouldn't do to wake her for loud declarations of The Way It's Going to Be Now. And who was he kidding anyway? He was no Barton Keyes. He wouldn't stand up to Pearl. He had no stomach for such confrontations. Anyway, he knew how it would go. He'd gather the balls to speak his mind, tell her he wanted her to start treating him like a man and stop making a fool of him in front of her guests. She would be crestfallen, probably even tear up, and tell him how sorry she was, that she didn't know, and call herself a silly old fool. Will would feel terrible and tell her to never mind, that she was right to do it, and of course he'd just been having a bad day. Even as he'd ask Pearl to stop making him her whipping boy, he'd beat himself back into submission so she didn't have to.

Will made a dozen such refusals of himself every day. It was simpler to have these conversations with himself than with others who only thought they understood him and what he wanted.

He walked quietly back to his room and turned off the light. *When will you learn, Phillips?* He took off his shoes and dropped over on the bed. *You don't have it in you to be that kind of man. You're still the rosy-cheeked boy with green eyes and blue eye shadow.* He pulled a pillow over his face.

~

"Come on, please? Mom said I could only go if you came with." Molly had been cajoling Will for an hour to go to Allison Ludwig's house for facials with her friends. Allison's mother was a beauty consultant with a cosmetic company and was doing makeovers on Allison's friends for her birthday. Molly had been talking about nothing else for a week.

"No," Will said. "Makeup is stupid. What do I want to do with a bunch of girls and lipstick all afternoon?"

Molly smiled and poked him in the arm. "Barbara Roberts will be there. She's Allison's best friend. I know you have a thing for her."

"Shut up."

It was true. Will had had a crush on Barbara since he was twelve.

"Allison's mom makes the best snacks. You can just sit and watch TV. No one will even care. Come on. I'll owe you one."

Molly owed Will about 952 ones by now. She rarely paid her debts and when she did, it was usually in foreign currency. "I won't tell Mom you're the one who left the freezer door open," she'd say, even when Will hadn't been the one that did. "We're even!"

Will gave in that afternoon and went with Molly to Allison's. Before he could slip away to find the television, Mrs. Ludwig had cornered him and walked him to the dining room table where Molly, Allison, Barbara and three other girls were each sitting opposite a small vanity mirror and a spread of sample cosmetics in little black trays and white tubes. "You can take the seat next to Barbara," Mrs. Ludwig said, and gave him a light push to his back between his shoulder blades.

"Oh, it's okay. I was, umm, just going to watch—"

"No, no. You're not going to watch everyone else get beautiful." She pulled his blond hair, which had grown past his collar over the winter, into a short ponytail with her hand, and put an arm across his shoulder. "Don't be shy. We'll make you beautiful too."

The girls around the table snickered and looked down at their makeup trays.

"But I'm not—"

"Go sit now. You wait and see what we can do to you."

Will shook his hair loose from her grip and trudged to the open chair, hanging his head. He sat down and kept his eyes in his lap, refusing to look when Mrs. Ludwig instructed the girls on the proper way to wash for a deep skin cleanse, how to apply a foundation base, and how to brighten their cheeks with a subtle rosy blush. He was fidgeting with an eye shadow brush, mixing the blue and green on his tray absentmindedly when Mrs. Ludwig decided she'd help get him out of his shell by using him as her model for all the techniques she was demonstrating. She had him move his chair to the head of the table and by the end of the afternoon, they all agreed that he was the most amazing transformation of the day. "Trade that grubby yellow T-shirt for a pink halter top with a scoop neck-line, and you'll have to beat the boys off with a stick," she said as he and Molly left the party.

Barbara followed them out the door as Will tore the plastic headband from his hair and flung it into a bush. He shook his head and roughly tousled his hair with his fingers, which now hurt from being pulled from its natural part and cowlick. He pulled his shirt up to his face to wipe it clean.

"I didn't know you could look so pretty, Phillips," Barbara said.

Will looked at his sister. "Why didn't you help me?"

Molly shrugged. "I don't know. Maybe because you're so cute."

"Simply gorgeous," Barbara agreed with a laugh. "Don't know how Miss Wickham will keep her hands off you in class."

Will clenched his jaw.

"I think Mrs. Ludwig was right, by the way. I have just the halter top, if you want to borrow it," Molly said.

He shoved Molly from behind with both hands to her shoulders. She stumbled a few steps, then began to laugh. "Oh, geez. Come on. So you're a girl. You're not going to die from it."

Will's eyes blurred. He turned and ran, wind pulling his tears straight back from the corners of his eyes into his hair. He ran four blocks before he stopped beside a tree, leaned over with his hands on his knees, panting for breath and feeling certain that he would, indeed, die from it.

There was no telling people things, he decided. They would believe what they wanted to believe, just like Mrs. Ludwig, and saying something wouldn't matter. Best to put the energy into getting through the day—or the year—with as little eye shadow as a guy could.

~

Will picked up his phone and dialed Joe's number. After a few rings, it switched to a message. "The Northeast Telecom customer you are calling has a voice mailbox that has not been set up. Please try your call again later. Goodbye." He never understood why that robotic message said "Goodbye" at the end, as though the string of sounds digitally cobbled together was supposed to sound sincere. "I can't do a thing for you.

Have a nice life."

Where was Joe? Will wondered. *He should have been getting home about right now. Maybe he switched his phone off for the night.*

He set his phone on his chest and folded his hands across his middle. Staring into blackness, he pondered calling Barbara.

Barbara had never needed a real man. She needed a man devoted to *proving himself* because a man who needed to prove himself would do anything for her—anything to be seen with her. Being seen beside Barbara's beauty was all the proof such a man would think he needed.

There was nothing in the world Barbara would love more, he imagined, than a call from Will "just needing to talk." His had been an intricately woven dependency and in the years they'd been apart he had come to think less about the sexy pair of legs that promised to open a way under her short black skirt and more about where she must have hid the other six.

Especially in the summer, he shared his space in Pearl's house with a handful of spiders who found their way in and plenty of room to work. One often greeted him in the shower early in the morning, blinking her eight eyes from the corner in sweet unison, awaiting some unsuspecting insect to fall into her handiwork and die. Not that the fly she hoped to entangle and sip on for breakfast was so innocent. No, the fly could outwit cats and the morning's rolled up *Tribune*, but turn around and tumble blindly into her lacy bed sheets and die an intoxicating, asphyxiating death—pursed spider lips running the length of him and he not apprehending his doom until that final slurping sound like when a straw reaches the end of a rootbeer float.

Did the flies know that's how it worked, he wondered. Did they not see the web and fly into it like a dog crashed into a clear glass patio door? Did they see it and think that only the careless flies get caught, tempt fate by diving and buzzing the strands, now and then get snagged? Or did the spider smile her sexy smile, turn back the sheets and lay out a foil-wrapped mint and handwritten poem, the fly just playing his part, let his hind wings do all his thinking and fall right into her bed?

Will wasn't sure he knew which it was for him. Of course it was easy enough for a guy to do his thinking from a zippered tent. But for him, that was always more like whispering in an echo chamber, partial sounds drifting and hoping for something to bounce off. Barbara never turned down the sheets for him. He just walked in and laid down on top of the bed covering, wishing against all he possessed for her to take him, knowing all the while she never would.

There was no final slurp of the straw at Barbara's soda fountain. She took her sips from Will's soul slowly, left time in between for him to replenish, think he had fortified himself, never quite finishing him off. It seemed to suit her more to keep him around.

He hadn't spoken to Barbara in twelve years, not since he left Chicago, which was far more about leaving Barbara than leaving the city. Joe moved to the Dakotas to keep a promise to his wife. But Will came to the Dakotas as much as anything because it was a place Barbara had promised never to come to. She gave him a list one day of all the places she would never live. At the top of the list was the Midwest. The rest were named by city, but the Midwest was erased from possibility with a single motion, an entire region Barbara seated herself high above as though she were not, at that very moment, actually living in it.

Too folksy, too backwater, too earthy, she said. She could never live in a place so close to the source of her food.

When Will left Chicago, he knew he might also hate South Dakota, that he could also be miserable here. But Barbara was slowly draining away his life, and perhaps on the plains it would be a sort of misery he could grow to love.

He opened his phone and clicked on R in his contacts. Barbara Roberts stared back at him from the screen, her blue eyes daring him to step back into the web, tangle his hands and feet in her sticky mesh once again. He traced a finger along her cheek, then let it travel to the green phone icon and pressed Call.

May as well fluff the pillows, Phillips. You just took her up on an offer she hadn't even made yet, he muttered, shaking a fist toward his own face. He quickly slid his finger to the End Call button, but not without hearing her sultry voice. "Sorry I can't take your call right now—"

Fool! Every damn time, you do this. She'll see the missed call. She'll know she still has you. You might not think you're set up that way, but you do still do your thinking from behind a zipper. Will took his hair in both fists and pulled his head from side to side. *When are you going to learn?*

He reached for the pack of Camels on the nightstand and got up. "Damn you, Barbara." He walked out of his room and down the hall to the back exit, lighting a cigarette before he was even out the door. He sat on the top step in the cool night, head in his hands, and letting the cigarette hang from his lips and smoke drift back into his face until his eyes watered. When he was done, he ground out the butt on the wood step and flicked it over the railing. Pearl would find it in the morning and be incensed. *Too bad, Pearl. You won't let me have a coffee can up here. One's bound to land in your flowers now and then.*

He was still holding his phone, as though there was a chance Barbara would call back. She never did, except for the first time, five months after Will left. He was missing his old life and called her. He hung up as soon as she answered. She called him back, scolding him for interrupting her dinner with Nick Sartell, the young and handsome CEO of Simplify, a tech startup, as though he were somehow supposed to know where she was or who she was with. Will said something lame and transparent about not calling her, that it was a butt-dial. She knew it wasn't true and made some condescending remark.

"Nick Sartell is gay, Barbara," Will had said. "Should work out swimmingly for you."

He had no idea why he said it. He didn't even know for sure whether Sartell was gay, but he had a sense about these things and was usually right. Barbara hung up on him and never called again the eight times since then that he had reached such a point of despair as would compel him to dial her number.

The smart man would delete her number from his phone, he told himself. Will was clearly not that man. *Never again,* he told himself each time. *I'll never do it again.*

Will looked at his phone, turned it in his hand. He stood to his feet, leaned against the railing and threw the phone into the bushes separating Pearl's house from the historic schoolhouse next door.

"Screw you, Barbara."

Will walked back inside the house. As he closed the door, a bluish glow flickered in the grass along the hedges. After a few moments, the light went out. He was already down the hall.

25

Will woke early but stayed in bed much longer than usual the next morning. Most Saturdays he went to the bakery with the guys and played dice over a fried cinnamon twist and a cup of coffee. His whole body ached in what he liked to call a "Barbara Hangover" and he didn't want to see or talk to anyone. Around 9:00 he heard Pearl downstairs and remembered the cigarette in the flowers. He rethought his cavalier ideas about upsetting her and got out of bed, pulled on his jeans and hustled out the back way. He dug around in the peony bush under the stairs and found the cigarette butt. Glancing up at the kitchen window to make sure Pearl wasn't standing at the sink, he then went to the bushes to find his phone. The low battery light was flashing. When he lit up the home screen, he saw a missed call.

"Uhhn, Barbara!" He jerked his hand to get away from the phone, tossing it back into the shrubbery.

Will took a step back. "No way. She didn't call back. She wouldn't. Ever." He put his hands in his pockets and stood facing the bushes, then contemplated walking away and leaving the phone, chalking it up to a "mysterious disappearance" and getting a replacement through his phone's insurance plan.

"Mr. Phillips!"

Why in the name of all that's holy does that woman have to shake her rugs every single morning? Will did not turn around.

"Tell me you are not relieving yourself into my boxwood." Pearl's heels clomped down the cedar porch steps.

He shrugged his shoulders.

"Mr. Phillips!"

Will turned. "For heaven's sake, Pearl. I know you think I am a complete savage after last night, but please. I would never do that. Not in town."

"I am sorry, Mr. Phillips. It just looked like— Oh, never mind. Do you want to come in for coffee? I have fresh danishes from the bakery."

"I don't think I do," Will said, surprising himself and Pearl with his quick certitude. "Thank you, though. There's something I need to accomplish. Maybe I'll stop later this afternoon."

"Alright then," Pearl said softly. She picked up her rugs and went back inside.

Will turned back to the bushes and reached in for his phone. He pushed it into his back pocket and returned to the stairs, walking quickly on his toes, stray bits of gravel in the grass poking into his bare feet.

He stopped in the small kitchenette upstairs for a glass of water and took three ibuprofen tablets before he went back to his room to lie down. He pulled the phone from his jeans and held it upright on his chest. The small blue alert flashed on and off above the darkened screen, like Barbara's eye winking, teasing, inviting, mocking, first alternating and then at once, all of them together until finally he had to know. He wouldn't call her back, no. Of course not. He just wanted to know how long she waited to call him back. He opened the home screen. One missed call. No voice message. He held his finger over the call log icon. *You are not calling her back, Phillips. Not.*

At last he pressed the little picture of a clipboard and brought up his call log. He blinked and swallowed hard.

There it was.

11:23 p.m. JOE MURPHY

"Joe?"

Will sat up and rested on his elbow as though it would help him see his phone more clearly. "What the hell."

He released a sigh of relief that Barbara hadn't called, but then felt his ears heat up because Barbara hadn't called. How could she be so small? He felt relief that Joe must be okay, then shook his head in irritation that Joe had called so late.

"Pick one, Phillips. Pick one feeling and just go with it for five minutes. Otherwise, let the whole thing go." Will plugged the phone in and set it on the nightstand. "I don't really want any of them, thanks."

He pulled the blanket to his chin, turned to his side and fell asleep.

About an hour later, his phone jarred him from deep sleep. He rolled over and grabbed it without opening his eyes. "Look, Barbara, I didn't call. Not really. My phone butt-dialed. It does that. I need a new phone. I promise, it won't happen..."

"Will? Is everything okay?" Joe interrupted Will's sleep-addled Barbara raving.

"Huh, wha-? Joe? Geez. Sorry, man. I was asleep."

"Oh, I'm so sorry. I didn't mean to wake you."

"You didn't. I was sleeping. Yesterday, I mean. Today I was awake. Already." He rubbed a hand across his face and sat up. "Joe? Did I call you?"

"Last night, Will." Joe chuckled. "I called you back, but you didn't pick up. Probably sleeping already."

"Or in the bushes."

"Excuse me?"

"Nothing. Never mind. Everything okay with you, Joe? You didn't answer when I called last night and I thought you'd have been home."

"The craziest thing happened. Freakish. If I were a betting man, I couldn't get these odds."

"Tell me."

"You're not going to believe this. I got out of my car last night, turned to close the door, and got nailed right in the middle of the face with a baseball."

"Holy shit, Joe! Are you okay?"

"Fine, I'm fine. There's a baseball diamond to the west of my place. You know it? Of course you do. You've been here. The American Legion team was having batting practice when I got home, and one of those kids hit the most beautiful line drive—well, I'm told it was beautiful. I guess I can't really say for sure. Ball came over the fence and *Boom!* Dropped me straight to my knees."

"What did you do?"

"Well, fortunately, Midge was out. You know, my neighbor. The dancer, remember? She was working out some new moves on her porch (you must see her sometime) and she saw the whole thing. She rushed over (I think she has a thing for me) and took me to the emergency room. There was a lot of blood. I almost fainted. But it's all pretty good now. My glasses are bent sideways and I have a fantastic shiner. Slightly displaced fracture of the nose, they say, so I guess I'll be smelling sideways for a while."

"Damn. I'm really sorry to hear that."

"Oh, it's fine. Could have been much worse. Figure there's not much margin for error when you're talking about a head, so an inch or two to the right or left and I've got a fractured orbit or fall down dead."

"Guess we should've let you play that last verse on the harmonica like you wanted. Could have missed the whole thing."

"Nah. Consider myself lucky. Going to buy a lottery ticket today, see if I can't milk this good fortune a little longer."

"Buy me one too. I could use a change of luck today."

"Will do, Will. Say, did you need something when you called?"

"I called?"

"Last night. I tried to answer from the ER but Midge took my phone away and made me lie down on the exam table. 'I used to be a nurse,' she kept telling me. She just wanted me lying down, I think."

"Oh, right. Yeah. I called last night." Will laid back down on his pillow and rested his arm across his eyes. "Nothing, Joe. Just wanted to make sure you got home alright."

"Sure that's all it was?" Joe asked. "You don't seem like the kind of guy that's always checking after things."

"Heh. You're right about that. Figure most things will tell you if they need something. You just have to be paying attention to catch it." Will looked out the window. "Archie tells you things without saying them, right?"

"Oh, sure. He scratches at the front door with his left paw when he has to go. But—you'll like this—when he wants to go check for squirrels," Joe said, "he scratches with his right."

"Somehow that doesn't surprise me."

"So then, Will. What were you calling about last night? Were you scratching with your left paw or your right?"

"Ah," Will chuckled, his voice flat. "You're good at this."

"Nah, just a lucky guess. What's a guy who spends most days in his house with a dog, a handful of cats and a lot of dust know about how people think?"

"I don't know what I wanted, Joe." Will closed his eyes and pinched the bridge of his nose between the index and thumb of his right hand. He knew Joe would believe that he *did* know, and Will suspected he would be right. But there are things a guy can know, and then there are the things a guy can name. He figured Joe would understand this as well.

"You don't know, Will?" Joe asked. "Or you can't name it yet?"

Will smiled a half smile. He was right about Joe. "*Yet*," he said. "You're a hopeful guy."

"The naming will come. That's why you need to keep reading the poets. For centuries they've been the ones finding names for things that have none."

"You sound a little like Salman Rushdie, my friend."

"Keep reading, Will. Maybe you'll even write some of those names down yourself."

Will laughed. "I've never had a customer quite like you, you know?"

"Notice how you didn't tell me *No?*"

"You're a hard man to say *No* to."

"I wonder if you know why you came out here."

"I came out to handle your claim, Joe."

"No, not to my house, though you did a fine job with that. I got a check from the insurance company this morning," Joe said. "I'm talking about coming out here to the Dakotas. I came for my wife, too late for her to fully appreciate it. Been here ever since to make it up to her. I wonder if you know why you came. And why you stay."

Will sighed.

"Why'd you leave Chicago, Will?"

"Damn, Joe. Don't beat around the bush. Just go ahead and ask me what you want to know."

"You don't have to answer, Will. I don't actually need to know. I have this hunch, though, that you do."

Will sighed again and ran his hands through his hair. He needed a haircut. Something shorter. More definitive.

"Let me ask it a different way. Did you *leave* Chicago, or *come* to Dennison?"

"You're going to play semantics now?" Will's tone tightened, a mild irritation evident that he hadn't felt before toward his friend. "I did both, obviously. I am not there; I am here."

Joe chuckled. "Easy, boy. Like I said, I don't need an answer, but I think you need the question. Seems to me most times when folks get a new place to live they are either moving toward something or away from something else. And it also seems to me that more often than not, it's the escape that is the bigger draw than the new opportunity. You see what I'm saying?"

"Yeah."

"So which was it for you? Did you leave Chicago, or did you come to South Dakota?"

26

Joe's answer was wrong, Will thought as he drove toward the mill that afternoon. He had to measure the width of the road and then go see a farmer to measure the width of his tractor, to prove what he and everyone else involved in the accident already knew: that the tractor wheels were over the yellow line because the tractor was wider than its lane.

Not hard to figure, really. Tractors aren't designed for the road. They're made for the field. Problem is that fields and machine sheds are connected to one another by roads and sometimes a guy has to drive his tractor on the highway to get to where he needs to work. And it would be nice if other guys driving their four-wheel drive pickups or low-rider coupes with subwoofers pounding all the way to Winnipeg would see them and take a little special care. But often enough, they don't, and they charge up on those big boys lumbering down the highway and get so busy laying on the horn and brandishing their middle fingers that they don't slow themselves down. And then their fancy wheels hit the soft shoulder too hard so they go tumbling into the ditch, screaming not for their lives but for the end of the farmer who took up too much of their side of the road.

If a guy could make himself slow down just a little, Will believed, just long enough to see who he's sharing the road with, maybe see why he's in your lane sometimes, maybe a guy'd be willing to give somebody else a little more room to get by.

His thoughts went back to Joe as he passed the Legion

post over the bridge on the left. Joe was no doubt partly right, that he came to South Dakota for his wife, to make good on his promise to her. But Joe was forgetting his own lesson about how things can be more than one thing at a time. Will believed Joe didn't just *come*, but also *left*. He'd been in Chicago his whole life. *Leaving your supposedly happy family to keep a high school promise wasn't enough to move out here,* he thought. No, Joe left Chicago as much as he came to South Dakota.

But why? Was there a family feud? Or could he just not bear to wake up without a place to go after thirty-seven years of fighting fires? Was it regret? Some kind of penance for a disappointment he'd brought upon Millie?

Maybe Joe was a fugitive from justice! He'd moved here in '85, not so long after the big Franco heist in Chicago. Maybe Joe was involved and figured no one would ever look for him in the middle of nowhere, like the Nazis who hid out in Argentina and Chile after the war, thinking it was the last place anybody would look for them. Hiding in plain sight on the open prairie.

Will laughed at himself as he pulled his truck onto the shoulder and stopped. "You're reaching pretty hard, Phillips," he said. "You don't want to answer Joe's question so you just made him into a criminal."

"It could happen," he answered himself, as he pulled his measuring wheel from the back of his truck. "It could happen."

His mind kept churning as he walked to the edge of the road. *And what about Cameron? Why isn't Joe probing her about why she came out here? If there's anybody who must have a story, it's Cameron. Young, urban professional, promising career ahead, comes out to the friggin' boondocks to manage a no-name telecom just begging to be eaten by one of the big three if they just knew it—and the state—existed. She's all but thrown herself on a shiny, silver career-sword coming out here.* Will rolled the wheel across the narrow tarred road, jotted measurements into a small notebook and snapped a photograph in either direction.

"So ask Cameron what she is running away from, Joe," Will said, throwing his wheel into the truck and snapping the bed cover back down hard. "Quit nagging me about Barbara and ask Cameron her story, you goddamned old bank robber."

Will climbed up into the cab and slammed the door. He started the truck and jabbed at the vent button with his index finger but missed and turned on the radio instead. He pulled his black and white striped cap down over his ears, almost covering his eyes, crossed his arms over his chest and slumped down in his seat.

"Stupid, stupid old man. Think you can throw around some fancy talk and all the books you've read and then I'm just going to believe you know what you're talking about. You don't know me, Joe. You don't know anything about me."

Will didn't hear the tires on gravel behind his truck and jumped when he heard a tap on his side glass. He fumbled for the window switch, locking and unlocking the doors before he got the window to roll down.

"Jeremy," he said, sitting up. "Uh, hey. What's up?"

Deputy Roundleg leaned down to see into the cab. "Everything okay, Phillips?"

Will pushed his cap back on his head. "Oh, yeah. Sure," he said. "Just came out to get some scene photos from an accident."

The deputy glanced around the cab.

"Hey," Will said. "You didn't happen to be the guy who responded to that deal here last month where the Grand Prix swerved to miss a tractor and rolled into the ditch?"

Roundleg stood upright and laughed, his belly shaking over his belt. He pointed to the intersection. "Sure did. Ron Miller's guys are hauling liquid manure and this joker is late for work and runs right up on the honey wagon before he decides to veer to the right to avoid hitting the wheel. It'd been raining and the roads were slick as hell. Jackass is lucky he didn't end up covered in shit."

"Can I quote you on that?" Will chuckled.

"Sure can. I don't give a crap about these guys who come in here to work crews building the new mill. They act like they own the town and everybody needs to treat 'em special." He put his hands in his pockets. "They don't vote in this county and hopefully they'll finish work and get the hell out of here in a few months. I might actually get a day off then."

Will laughed and wrote a note on the file.

"You done here?" Roundleg asked.

"Yeah, just finishing up my notes."

"Best get going then. Shift's about to end over there and you don't want to be on the road when these guys all break for Happy Hour."

"Point taken," Will said. "Thanks for the info."

"See you later, Will." Deputy Roundleg walked back to his Durango.

Will signaled, looked behind and pulled out onto the highway. "I could use a Happy Hour," he mumbled as he drove toward town.

Mad Dog was putting on his jacket when Will walked into the office. "Hey, little buddy. I'm just heading out for a beer with Stu and Charlie. You going to come?"

"I'd love to. But I need to catch up on some paperwork before I go home," Will said. "Thanks though."

"You bet. I left some phone messages on your desk. That Nina woman called and chewed my ass again."

"Why can't you just be nice to her, Mike?"

"I am pretty nice to her. She just doesn't recognize it because she'd been getting dragged around by Justin and guys like him for so long she doesn't know what a nice guy looks like."

"Oh, right. I forgot. You are Mr. Virtuous."

Mad Dog tossed his tennis ball and bounced it off Will's head. "Listen, plenty of women think I'm a nice guy. In fact, I'm going to go see if any of them are at Marvelle's right now. Later, sucker."

Will bent to pick up the tennis ball and walked into his office. As usual, his phone had been moved and his papers shuffled.

"Dammit, Mad Dog. Why can't you —" He stopped and threw up his hands. "Forget it. What difference does it make?"

"What's that, Willie?" Mad Dog stood in Will's doorway.

"Nothing. Never mind." He sat down.

"Alright then, I'm out." Mad Dog zipped his jacket and turned to go. "See you tomorrow, Willie Boy."

Will leaned back in stared at the ceiling. "Hey, Mike?"

"Yeah?"

"How'd you end up here?"

"This is where I work, duh."

Will rolled his eyes. "No, here. Dennison. You didn't grow up here. How'd you end up in the town?"

Mad Dog stepped back into Will's office and leaned against the door-frame.

"Nah. I grew up in Nebraska. Same difference, I suppose."

Will threw him the tennis ball.

"Moved here out of college. Got a teaching job at the high school back when Walter Dingman was the superintendent."

"Are you kidding? You were a teacher? How did I not know this?"

"I figured I'd work a few years, cut my teeth on small town stuff, then go find a gig in the city." He tossed the ball back and Will reached out to catch it with his right hand. He rolled the ball across his thigh with his palm.

"Charlie and Stu were teaching too. A few years later, the insurance company started picking us off one by one, seducing us out of the classroom with their big offices and bigger salaries. Probably ten guys left the district within a couple of years."

He reached up, inviting Will to throw the ball back. Will held it, squeezing it in his hand.

"By the time the insurance company was acquired by a bigger fish and swam away to the ocean, I'd married and divorced and pretty well settled here for good. I worked out a deal with them to be my first client as an independent adjuster. Next thing I knew, I needed a partner, you came along and look at us now. Such a happy couple."

"The happiest," Will said and threw the ball, aiming hard at Mad Dog's knees.

"Hey now." He jumped out of the way.

"So you came here for a job."

"Yep, guess so."

"Were you trying to get away from something?"

"Get away from something? Hell no. I was a twenty-two-year-old frat boy. What was there to get away from? I'd have stayed in school if I hadn't run out of cash. I didn't want to leave at all. But I needed a job and didn't want to have to move back home."

"So you were getting away from something."

"What? No."

"Yeah, you were. You were getting away from home. From your mommy."

"I don't think so. Came for the money. Stayed for the girls."

"Right. Lucky girls."

"What about you? You've never really said what brought you here."

"You brought me here, Mike. When you left the insurance company you asked me to go into business with you."

"Yeah, but seriously. Who leaves Chicago and moves to the middle of nowhere to be partners with a guy he met at a claims convention?"

Mad Dog sat down across Will's desk.

"I never pushed you about it, and pretended not to notice, because I didn't want you to get all touchy-feely with me. But man, you were a freaking mess when you got here."

"What?" Will sat up straight in his chair. "What are you talking about? I came and got the business set up while you drank coffee and golfed three days a week."

"You don't remember." Mad Dog shook his head. "Hell,

I was regretting ever proposing we be partners. I was afraid you were on your way to the loony bin."

Will stared at Mad Dog, not blinking, but remembering.

"You never slept. You wore the same clothes every day for a week at a time. You worked fourteen hours a day even when we had no claims. You always, always had a lit cigarette in your mouth. And you weighed like fifty pounds more than you do now. Don't tell me you weren't on the run from something in Chicago."

"Because now you are a psych expert."

"Listen, I know you think I don't know things. I like it better that way. But I was a psych major in college. I know a crapload about human behavior. I just don't like to listen to people talk about their problems so I don't say nothing about it. You, my friend, had run away. And if I was not mistaken, everything you ran away from in Chicago came along with you. Or at least you thought it had."

~

Mad Dog was right, of course. Just like Joe had been right. Hell, even Pearl was right, though Will couldn't for the life of him remember what it was she was right about. Maybe it was that the flowered apron made him look like her little sister, he thought, and kicked a rock from the sidewalk into the street.

After all his "I know everything about the human psyche, especially yours" bullshit, Mad Dog told Will he was taking himself too seriously and needed to come out for a drink with him and the other guys. Will resisted, turning down the invitation the customary Midwestern-three-times before he agreed to go along.

He left the bar before he finished his first beer, feeling restless as though the sounds of laughter and clinking glasses and country music on the jukebox were strips of cloth wrapping themselves around his body to entomb him.

Will took two dollar bills from his wallet and folded them under his bottle. "I'm out, fellas," he said, leaning to the side as he pushed his wallet back into his jeans pocket. "Have an early day at work tomorrow."

Mad Dog shouted behind him as he walked away. "Tomorrow's Saturday!"

27

Will waved a hand back at his friends without turning around and walked out the door. He turned left and kept walking, away from the bar and away from the office and toward nothing in particular.

It's no simple task wandering aimlessly in a small town. Every street leads to something, none of them go on for very long, and around every corner is a familiar site. Yet tonight, Will seemed to be managing *aimless* just fine. After what seemed like an hour walking darkened streets, he looked up to orient himself under a streetlight and saw a woman approaching. She'd just jogged across the street and her small dog was tugging on the leash toward a large maple in the boulevard. He stepped to the side and stopped, waiting for her to pass.

"Will?" she said as she approached the lit area.

Will looked up. "Huh? Oh, Cameron. Hi. What're you doing out so late on this side of town?"

"I'm just out for a run with Finn." Cameron was dressed in a black jogging suit with wide reflective stripes down the outside of the legs and sleeves and along the jacket's front zipper, which Will noticed was not completely straight. He looked back at his feet.

"But what do you mean 'this side of town'? We're just about home."

Will looked around and saw Judge Barkley's well-coiffed yard lit up by 200 tiny solar lights in a carefully engineered design around his garden, stone path and landscaping rocks.

"Oh. Yeah. And so we are." He rubbed the back of his

neck. "Looks like I lost track of things." As it turned out, for all his aimless wandering, he'd been walking ten minutes on a very direct route from downtown to Pearl's house.

Cameron was bouncing from one foot to the other, without lifting them from the ground to keep her body from cooling down before she continued her run. It reminded Will of the way Barbara would pace behind him when she thought he wasn't finishing something fast enough. He couldn't see her but could always sense her impatience with him. "Listen, don't let me keep you," he said, turning to go. "It was nice to see you."

Will walked away from his house, toward nothing in particular that he knew of. Cameron stood under the light, watching him walk, hands in his pockets, head down. She stopped her silent jogging in place.

"Will."

He didn't hear her and kept walking.

"Will," she called out.

Will turned and looked up, tipping his head sideways. "Yeah?"

"Pearl's house is this way." She motioned behind her with her thumb.

Will quickly scanned the street and saw the Methodist church at the end of the block ahead. "Oh shit. You're right."

Of course she was right. Everyone was right.

"Walk with us, Will."

"You sure? I don't want to—"

"Shut up and walk with us. We had a good run."

Will straightened and started back toward Cameron and Finn, for reasons he couldn't place almost feeling a slight happy skip in his step which turned as quickly to catching his toe on a high spot in the cement. Before he could get his hands out of his pockets to steady himself, he went to the ground, landing on his right shoulder and rolling over to his back. He could only see blackness and his head felt pinched. He heard Cameron shout and then felt Finn's tongue on his cheek as the Jack Russell earnestly tried to slobber him back into consciousness.

"Will, are you alright?" Cameron was on one knee next to him.

"I'm fine. Fine," Will mumbled. "But I can't see."

"Umm," Cameron said. "Maybe open your eyes, Will." She ran a hand gently against his forehead. Her skin was soft and warm.

Will realized he was holding his eyes shut, as though if he didn't look he might be able to convince himself—and Cameron—that he was not lying on the sidewalk in front of Judge Barkley's lawn.

Cameron was leaning over him, the streetlight glowing softly behind her head and her honey locks cascaded over her shoulder and onto his chest.

He pulled himself up on his left elbow and smiled weakly. "I should have thought to fall down a long time ago."

"You," Cameron laughed, and tossed her hair back. "Seriously, are you okay? Can I help you up?"

"Well, my shoulder feels like there's a little campfire burning in there. I should probably ice it when I get home." Finn jumped up onto Will's stomach and licked his mouth. He reached for the dog and dropped to his back again, wiping his mouth with his sleeve. "Maybe I should try to get up before

Finn here slobbers me to death."

"Come on, Finn, get down." Cameron gave the leash a light jerk and the dog jumped off Will's middle and onto the sidewalk. "Alright. Let's get you up."

Cameron held out an arm to steady him as he sat up and then got to his feet. His head buzzed when he stood upright and he leaned from side to side. "Maybe this wasn't a good idea yet. I'm going to sit."

He shuffled to the boulevard and slid down next to the maple. "I think I'll be fine if you need to get the dog home. I got up too fast. Just need to wait it out a few more minutes."

Cameron sat down next to him, leaning her back against the tree. "I'll wait with you."

"One of these times I'll get to make a good impression, right?" He tipped his head back against the silver gray bark.

"Maybe," Cameron said, chuckling. "We'll see how it goes."

Will rested his hand in the soft grass, playing with a small stone between his fingers. "Pearl would be very unhappy with my performance tonight, that's for sure."

"Pearl doesn't need to know anything about it," Cameron said. "Unless you're one of those guys who feels the need to tell his landlady everything."

Will tossed the stone into the lawn across the sidewalk.

"Something tells me you are not one of those guys," she said, scratching Finn's ears.

"Yeah, probably not."

Cameron sat quietly for a few minutes, then asked, "Whose beautiful lawn is this? I don't think I've noticed it before."

"It's really something at night with all the little lights.

Completely different look than daytime," Will said. "Belongs to Judge Barkley. Have you met him?"

"I don't think I have."

"The old judge is living proof that things are not always what they seem," Will said, as though every person alive walking around under their reshaped and painted-over selves were not such proof enough. But Judge Barkley was a perfect specimen. "He was famous for his gentility," he explained. "Always polite, never had a cross word for anyone. Never raised his voice to his four children, who walked to school every day holding hands. He'd employ just the right amount of calculated severity when delivering a hard verdict, and a kind of twinkling-eye sternness when he let a guy off easy."

"Is he still on the bench?" Cameron asked.

"Nah," Will said. "Been retired a year or so. Folks really miss him. Anyway, he's weaker than a son of a bitch. Stands about six feet tall and he's lucky if he weighs 150 pounds. Every year he gets a little more frail, but he's still out and about quite a bit. Pearl has him and his wife for dinner now and then."

Will reached for Finn and pulled him into his lap, holding the dog's front paws loosely until he laid down.

"So, one night last spring, he and his wife go for dinner to the Grainery. As he opens the door, a guy at one of the sidewalk tables who'd had a beer or two too many (and had been in Judge Barkley's courtroom a time or two) whistles at his wife—who really is quite stunning—and mumbles, 'I'd do her.'"

"Seriously?" Cameron asked.

"Yeah. Who says that to an octogenarian?" Will shook his

head. "Judge puts his hand on the small of his wife's back and follows her quietly in the door. Doesn't even flinch. Looks like he hadn't heard it, which everybody thinks was a good thing. But just before the door closes, he sticks his head out, looks the guy straight in the eye and says 'I'll thank you not to speak about my wife that way.'"

"Did you see this happen?"

"No, but I sure wished I had. Mad Dog was at the bar and told me about it the next day." Will rubbed his shoulder. "Old Judge Barkley walks in and lets the door close behind him and I guess the folks on the patio let loose in howls of laughter. When he and Mrs. Barkley left, the guy's still sitting there and raises his bottle of beer to them as they go by. 'Quiet everybody,' he says and pulls off his cap, 'The Duke of Barkley and his fair lady are passing by.' The judge nods lightly and they walk to their Lincoln Town Car without a word."

"That's crazy. What a jerk."

"Well, it gets good though. Ten minutes later, Judge Barkley pulls up to the curb again, but he's by himself. He dropped the missus off at home. As he gets out of the car, the jackwagon takes a swig of beer and laughs. He wipes his mouth with the back of his hand and looks around at all his buddies. 'Hey Judge. Beautiful night, ain't it?'"

"Judge walks up to him, rears back and punches the guy in the jaw. Now listen. This guy is huge, like 280 pounds, and he just tips over in his chair, all sprawled out on the patio."

Cameron laughed, covering her mouth with her hand.

"Everybody is on their feet and cheering. Judge Barkley shakes his hand a little in the air, turns around and walks to his car. Drives straight to the sheriff's office and asks to be arrested for assault. The guy was so embarrassed he refused to press charges, but Judge Barkley retired the very next day."

"He sounds like quite a character," Cameron said.

"Sure is," Will said, running a hand along Finn's back. "Not at all the guy you expect to find in that scrawny little body."

"Do you want me to knock on his door and get you some ice?"

"Hell no. I'll be fine." Will set the dog on the ground and rolled to the side to get on his knees and stand up. "See? Spry as ever. You ready to go, or do you need a little more rest?"

He held out a hand to Cameron. She smiled up at him, then took his hand and stood to her feet. "Yeah, I think I'm rested enough to walk another block, Mr. Spry Man Who Did Not Just Fall on the Sidewalk."

"Never happened," Will said. "I can ask Judge Barkley if he saw me fall outside his house, and he'll deny it. You have no witnesses to prove otherwise."

Cameron opened her mouth to argue, then thought better of it and just shook her head. "Alright. Let's go."

28

Cameron and Will stopped in front of Pearl's house. Finn sniffed at the sidewalk around Will's feet, weaving in and out between his legs until the leash had slipped around both ankles and he ran out of slack. Will stood with his hands in his pockets and looked into the coal of the sky.

"Well, this is the part where I should be walking you to your door," he said. "Pearl would give me hell for any less."

"Pearl Jenkins is not your mother, Will. And she's not your wife." Cameron looked up, trying to find the spot in the sky that held Will's gaze. "At least I don't think she's your wife. And if she is, then not walking me to the door is not the thing you'll catch hell for."

Will chuckled but didn't break his stare, focused on a star that was surely there, hidden behind the band of clouds, blocking his view like a cosmic child had found a use for a wad of dryer lint in his latest craft project.

"No, she's not my wife. And she's not my mother."

"So, what is it, then? Pearl has some hold on you."

"Rent control," Will said.

Cameron turned to look at him. Will lowered his eyes to meet Cameron's and smiled.

"Rent control," she said and looked away, wrapping her arms around herself against the evening chill.

"Pearl needs to feel like she has someone. I consider it part of the cost of living here. Took us a couple of years to find our rhythm, but since we did, my rent hasn't gone up."

"Son or boyfriend?"

"Well, I suppose it's some sort of combination of both."

Cameron turned back to him. "You know how creepy that sounds, right? And for money?"

"No, it's not for money. It's for no money. There's a difference. Call it nuance." Will looked at the house. "Damn," he said. "It does sound creepy when you put it that way. But it's not. I'm not an old lady's paramour."

"Oh, Will. I didn't mean —"

Will waved her off. "I know you didn't. I'd just never thought of it that way before. I'm not her son or her boyfriend. But somehow I'm the most important man in her life right now. I mean, she doesn't raise the rent because she doesn't need it. But she has to charge me something because it gives her the upper hand. And keeps people from talking."

Will fingered the tab on his jacket zipper. "You know how sometimes when you try to explain something that makes perfect sense in your head, but as soon as you attach words to it, it just sounds stupid, or small?"

"Yes, I know that feeling," Cameron said, raising one eyebrow.

"Well, that. Right now."

"Will, when I said it sounded creepy, I didn't mean—I mean—I don't know. You don't have to explain it, I think is what I mean. I get it. It's unusual, but it's not creepy to me. Anyone who has seen you together knows this."

They both turned back to the sky, watching the moon work its way out from between two patches of that dryer lint.

"Does Pearl know you climb on the roof?"

Will put his hands in his pockets. "Yeah, I sort of dropped that knowledge on her one day."

"What do you do up there?"

"Smoke. She won't let me in the house."

"Isn't it just easier to go out the back door?"

"Sure," Will said. "But there's something about a rooftop in the early morning." He turned to Cameron. "Ever been?"

"I haven't." She smiled. "Are you going to invite me?"

"A little forward, aren't we?" Will returned her smile. "Inviting yourself up to a man's roof on the first walk? I haven't even walked you to your door yet."

"I didn't invite myself onto your roof. I invited you to invite me. There's a difference. Call it nuance."

"Well, Pearl probably wouldn't mind if I had a little adult supervision up there." Will gestured toward the house. "Would you like to come up to my porch roof?"

"I'd love to." Cameron started toward the house. Will didn't move.

She turned back. "What's wrong? Cold feet already?"

Will pointed to his feet, now lashed tightly together at the ankles with Finn's leash. "Not cold, but a little tied up."

"Oh, right," she laughed. "We probably shouldn't bring Finn in the house."

"Pearl," Will said, nodding.

"Let me guess. Pearl doesn't like dogs." Cameron stood with her hands on her hips.

"She does, in fact. She likes them very much. Here's the thing. Finn would bark. Pearl would come rushing out of bed because there's a dog in the house and fawn all over him just because he's so cute she can't stand it and did you know that when she was just a girl in grammar school she had a little gray poodle that wore pink bows in her hair and one day she—the dog, not Pearl—ran away and never came home and Pearl never got another dog because she was so heartbroken and no one could ever replace Fifi anyway."

"Got it." Cameron bent down and untangled the leash. "And then Will and Cameron will never get to sit on the roof because Pearl the matchmaker will torpedo her own scheme."

"She did say you were pretty smart when she tried to sell you off to me."

"Sell me off?" Cameron squinted.

"Well, sure." Will stood stiff as her hands brushed against his ankles. "She had to do quite a sales job to get me to come to dinner with you that night."

Cameron stood, the leash in her hand. "No, she didn't."

"Okay, but she had to do a little coaxing."

"No, I'm pretty sure she didn't." Will saw the tiny white moon reflected in Cameron's brown eyes. He did not answer.

After a moment, Cameron touched Will's arm. "See?" she whispered. "Hang on. I'll be right back."

Cameron jogged easily across the street with Finn, his short furry legs scampering as fast as they could go to keep up. She opened her front door and nudged him inside, reaching down to unhook the leash. Cameron latched the screen door and jogged back across the street to Pearl's house. Will hadn't moved.

"Ready to show me the roof?"

"I hesitated," Will said, and looked into the sky.

"You hesitated? You don't want to go up?"

"I hesitated. When Pearl invited me to dinner with you, I didn't accept right away." He looked back at Cameron and slid his hands into his pockets. "I hesitated."

"Yes, of course you did." She motioned toward the porch. "The roof, Will?"

Will turned. "We should go up the back way. The front steps creak."

They walked around to the back of the house and climbed the tall wooden stairs to his door on the second floor. He wondered if Pearl had told Cameron about finding him there in his boxers. He stopped partway in the door. "I wasn't expecting company," he said. Of course, he was never expecting company. He'd never had a visitor to his apartment. "It might be a little messy."

"It's okay, Will. I live alone too, remember? If you stopped by my place unannounced you might discover how many nights I eat popcorn for dinner."

They passed through the kitchen. Will took the sole cereal bowl off the counter and put it in the cupboard. "There. That's better."

"This is where Pearl used to hustle me in pool," he said as they came into the den. "She's damn good."

"Used to? What happened? Did she get bored of beating you?"

"Nah, just too hard for her to get up the stairs anymore. Though I'd bet she'd find a way to get herself up here if she knew you were here. I wouldn't mind if she did come up now and then, actually. I miss being played. And she could attest to my hesitation, then, too."

"You don't have to round up witnesses, Will. I'll stipulate to the hesitation."

"Thank you." Will nodded firmly.

"All fifteen seconds of it."

"It was a solid thirty," Will said. "Not a second less."

"Of course it was." Cameron smiled. "You might have to have me up another day to shoot some pool. I used to be pretty good, but it's been years."

"You want to play right now?" Will reached for the rack.

"No, no. Your weeping when I beat you would surely wake Pearl."

"Alright. Another time." Will set the rack back on the green felt. "We were headed for the roof right?"

"We were."

"This way, then." Will crossed the room and waited by the door as he waved Cameron through. She stopped above the staircase and stared at the stained glass. It stretched from the landing at the base of the turn all the way to the second story ceiling, a pastoral scene in three panels. The streetlight threw a soft spray of colors at her feet on the brown carpet.

"Oh, my. I've wanted to see this glass from the inside since I moved here. It's really stunning."

"It is. It's beautiful," Will said, joining Cameron at the top of the dark cherry staircase. "I love to sleep in these colors. But some nights I stand up here and connect the lights with my feet."

"You do what?"

"Like this," Will said. He put his arms out slightly from his sides and tip-toed from one colored dot on the ground to another, stepping forward and back and pivoting until he'd touched each one.

"That looks a bit like dancing."

"Oh, but it's not dancing," Will said. "I don't dance." He kept moving, stepping back and forth between the lights.

"Barbara always said I was a terrible—"

"Barbara?" Cameron asked. "Who's Barbara?"

Will quickened his steps. "No one. No one important."

Cameron crossed her arms in front of her chest. Her mouth tightened.

Will didn't look up. "Really, she mattered once. A long time ago. She doesn't anymore." Will pointed to the lights on the ground. "Come on, race me. I bet I can step on all the colors before you."

Cameron didn't move.

Will kept moving his feet and cursing himself—and Barbara—silently.

"You wanted to beat me in pool. Beat me in colors instead," he said.

Cameron's face softened. "I'm hesitating."

"I can see that," Will smiled.

Cameron uncrossed her arms and stepped onto a blue circle on the carpet, then to a red.

"It's a little like chasing the lights from a disco ball except they don't move. It's a little more my speed," Will said.

"But how do you know when you've touched them all? They're so random on the ground."

"I have a certain order I always do them." Will held out a hand. "Here. Just follow me."

Cameron took his hand and followed a few steps left and right behind Will. "Wait a minute. How can I beat you if I am following your steps?" She pivoted and faced him, both of them still stepping around colors above the stairs.

"Note to self," Will said aloud. "The pretty girl might be a tad competitive."

"Says the funny boy who set up the contest."

"Well played." Will realized he was no longer stepping in his usual pattern but was mirroring Cameron's moves. They both stepped for the same yellow dot and their bodies came together and stopped.

"This Barbara person was wrong," Cameron said softly, looking up at Will. "You're a good dancer."

Will stepped back and raised his arm, bringing Cameron's hand into the air with his. She pivoted under the arch, then spun her way along his arm until she stood against his chest. Will held his arm around Cameron's shoulder and didn't move.

"Don't be too sure," he whispered. "Barbara tended to be right about a lot of things."

"I thought we decided Barbara wasn't important." Cameron took a small step backward. "Seems like she still gets to tell you what to think."

Will slipped his hand from Cameron's and put it in his jeans pocket. He rubbed the back of his neck with the other.

"Well," he said. "Yeah."

Cameron tilted her head and narrowed her eyes. "That's your answer?"

"Best I've got for the moment, I guess," Will said. "Some people get to keep asserting themselves even after they're gone, it seems."

"Is that right?" Cameron smiled lightly. She looked up at Will. "How long?" she asked.

"How long what?" Will asked, pushing his other hand into his pocket. His jaw clenched and he stared at the wall over Cameron's head.

"Since Barbara," Cameron said. "How long since Barbara?"

"Twelve years. Twelve years and a couple of months." He rolled his eyes. "Twelve years, two-and-a-half months."

Cameron giggled. "Do you know how many days?"

"I do, but it seemed a bit much." Will looked at Cameron. "It's been twelve years, two months, three weeks and five days since Barbara mattered."

"I don't think that's quite it yet," Cameron said, shaking her head.

"Okay. Twelve years, two months, three weeks and five days since I've been free from Barbara."

"Nope." Cameron smiled and touched Will's arm. "Try again."

He pulled away almost imperceptibly. "Twelve years, two months, three weeks and five days since I left. Happy?"

"Getting closer. It'll do for now." She ran a hand through her bangs. "We were on our way to the roof, remember?"

"We were." He motioned toward his room. "After you, Milady."

Cameron stepped inside the darkened room, Will just behind her. She felt along the wall inside. "Where's the switch?"

"Oh, yeah. Got it right here." Will flipped on the light and moved quickly to place himself between Cameron and the rest of the room. "You know how Pearl's house is really magnificent, right?"

"Of course. It's beautiful, and full of treasures at every turn." Cameron leaned to see around Will.

"Well this room is sort of the exception. Don't hold it against her." He stepped to the side and let Cameron in. She stood under the bare light bulb and turned around slowly, taking in the painted woodwork and peeling wallpaper.

"What in the world?" she said, still staring.

"I know. When I first moved in she didn't want me to stay. And she wanted me to feel like she was doing me a huge favor finding a space for me. Saw herself like the innkeeper in Bethlehem, you know? So she gave me the worst room hoping I'd move along quickly. This was the one room in the house nobody ever got around to refinishing."

"Does she still want you to go?"

"Oh, no. Hell no. She needs me here, though she'd never tell you that. Now she just doesn't want me to think I'm anything too special so she never had me move to one of the finished rooms. Either that or she's just long forgotten it. And I'd never embarrass her by saying anything."

"She'd never know if you used another room, Will."

"Oh, I know. And I should show you the others. The master bedroom has an antique four-poster bed and a fireplace with a fabulous granite mantle. But the truth is I really like my little bad boy room. I'm at home here."

"And you have a window to the roof." Cameron walked to the window.

"I do, yes. Out of bed and through the window in a snap."

"Really nice view of my house," she said and turned back to Will.

"I don't look, you know."

"What?" Cameron crossed her arms.

"I don't look. I don't watch you, even though I could. Being seen when a guy can't see who is doing the seeing is upsetting. So when you come outside, I look away."

"Isn't that your job? To watch people?"

"Oh, no. I couldn't," Will said. "Almost got fired from my

first job for it. I hire other guys if I need surveillance done. And I try not to need it."

"I see." Cameron ran a hand along the top of Will's television, mounted on the wall facing his small bed. "So my guys got you your cable alright?"

"I think so. Haven't had a chance to try it out."

"Well, I don't usually do home visits to check on my staff, but maybe we should check it out since I'm here." Cameron moved the bunched up quilt and sat down on the end of Will's bed and crossed her legs. "Where's the remote?"

Will felt warm. He rushed to the bookcase and rustled through the box left by the cable installer. He turned around in a circle and ran his hand through his hair. "I don't see it. Maybe they accidentally took it with them."

"I'm sure not," Cameron chuckled. "But look. My technicians offer top notch service. They even lose the remote for you, to give you the full man-gets-cable experience."

"We don't need to test it. I'm sure it's all good. Come on, maybe I should finish showing you around."

"Showing me around?" Cameron leaned back on her hands and tossed her head. Her soft curls fell around her shoulders and Will thought of all kinds of cliché things he might be able to say about them but his dry mouth prevented him from making a fool of himself with any of them. "Will, it's a room. What more is there to see?"

"Well, umm. It's a very interesting room, actually." He felt perspiration beading on his neck and he rolled his shoulders. "Look up here, for instance." He pointed at the ceiling. "You don't see exposed plaster and lathe just anywhere these days. It's a very authentic grunge look that not everyone has in their bedroom."

Cameron looked up and laughed. "Okay, now I think I have had the whole tour."

"Nope, not yet." Will bent down in front of his bookcase. "See, these are books. I keep them here. Sometimes I read them." His breathing quickened. He tried not to look at Cameron sitting contentedly on his bed.

"You have books. This is good."

"Uh, what else?" Will asked himself quietly as he got to his feet. "Oh, look." He walked back toward the doorway. "Here's something you should see." He waved a hand through the open space. "No door. Nope, none, nada. So anyone can come in at any time. Imagine that. Any old time they want."

"Yes, imagine all the scores of people wandering around on Pearl's nearly-empty second floor that might stumble in at any time of day or night."

Will took a deep breath, and then another. "Listen, I'm a terrible host. I'm not used to having people here. Can I get you something? Water? A beer? Bourbon?"

"I wouldn't mind a glass of wine, now that you mention it." Cameron stood and Will breathed a small sigh of relief, then realized he did not have wine.

"I, uh, I don't have any wine. I'm really sorry."

"That's fine. A glass of water would be fine." Cameron walked to the other side of the room. "What's this door go to?"

"The room has two closets. That one connects to the master bedroom. This room was actually the dressing room back in the day. Now Pearl just keeps stuff in that closet, tablecloths and such." Will thought a moment. "Hey, you know what?

Pearl likes a nice Pinot at night sometimes. I'll bet I could sneak you a glass from downstairs."

"Oh, gosh. Don't break into Pearl's. Water is really fine. Or tea if you have it."

"No, I think I could really use a beer and I don't know how I feel about drinking while you sip water. I'll just be a minute. Maybe you'll figure out where your guys stashed my remote while I'm gone."

Will hurried out of his room, through the kitchenette and tiptoed down the servant's staircase to Pearl's kitchen. He turned the knob without a sound and pushed the door open. It creaked and he held it still, listening for Pearl to stir. He pushed it open the rest of the way and crept down the last two steps.

"Good evening, Mr. Phillips."

"God! Pearl!" Will shouted and then clapped his hand over his own mouth, missing the last step and stumbling into the kitchen. He caught his balance holding the doorknob. "What in the hell—"

"Language, Mr. Phillips. It might be the middle of the night but we can still use our manners." Pearl was standing in her housecoat with her back to the sink, some sort of puffy sleeping cap on her head.

He gathered himself and stood straight, if not a bit winded. "What are you doing here at this time of night?"

"This is my kitchen, Mr. Phillips. I can come here anytime I like. The better question has to do with you and my kitchen and the middle of the night."

"But I thought you'd be sleeping."

"I thought I would be too. And I was, until all that racket

upstairs. Are you having some sort of dance party?"

"Racket? We were as quiet as mice."

"We? So it is a party. And you didn't invite me." Pearl raised a tall clear glass to her lips and took a sip of water to hide a smirk.

"Well, I didn't mean *we* so much as *I*. I was as quiet as a mouse."

"Then maybe the other mouse up there needs to learn some tricks from you if you're going to sneak around together in a creaky old house." Pearl set the glass on the counter. "At least tell me it's worth me being awake and you didn't drag one of your bar buddies home for a game of billiards on my table."

"Not a bar buddy, Pearl." Will wiped a hand across his face.

"Then who? Some floozy you picked up?"

"No! Pearl, stop," Will said. He felt his cheeks flush. "If you must know—and I know, you must—Cameron is upstairs."

Pearl clapped her hands together and smiled. "Cameron? She's upstairs? You got a second shot with her after that fiasco you made of our dinner?"

"Yes. And I'm trying not to screw it up. She'd like a glass of wine and I don't stock it."

Pearl cocked her head. "You want a girlfriend and you don't have any wine?"

"Who said I wanted a girlfriend?"

"You brought a girl home to your room, of all places. Only a girlfriend would put up with that. A hookup would be gone as soon as she saw your unmade bed. Tell me you at least hung up your towel today."

"Hookup? Pearl, where do you learn these words?"

"I know my way around. The towel, Mr. Phillips?"

"My towel was hung up. I hang it up every morning, just like you asked."

"But you don't keep wine for your new girlfriend."

"I don't have a girlfriend. Or wine. But if you could give me one, I might be able to manage the other."

Pearl leaned against the counter and took another drink of water.

"Come on, Pearl. If Mrs. Wilcox came over from next door to borrow an egg or cup of sugar, you wouldn't interrogate her about whether she was making a pie for old Mr. Waldner. So maybe you could let me borrow a little Pinot Grigio? And a glass?"

"You don't have a wine glass, either? Oh, Mr. Phillips. How could I not know by now how much work there is still to do with you?"

Will walked into Pearl's pantry looking for the wine bottles. "Well, we'll never get it all done tonight. Maybe you could tell me where to look so the woman waiting in my room doesn't give up and go home?"

"She won't go home, Mr. Phillips. I'm quite certain of that. She'll want the Pinot Grigio chilled. Take the bottle from the fridge."

Will opened the refrigerator and leaned down to peer into the bottom shelf. "If you have that glass, I'll just pour her some."

Pearl reached into the oak cupboard above the sink and lifted out two stemmed wine glasses. "Take the whole bottle. And two glasses. You'll drink wine with her tonight, not that pale ale you're always drinking that smells like deer piss."

"Language—"

"Don't want to hear it. There's too much at stake." She pushed the glasses into Will's free hand and opened a drawer. "You'll need one of these, I imagine."

Pearl held up a corkscrew and Will shrugged. "Here." She slipped it into his shirt pocket and patted him on the chest. She turned Will around by the shoulders and gave him a little push toward the stairway door.

"Thank you, Pearl," Will said. "I owe you for this."

"Yes, I imagine you do. Now let's get going."

Will started up the stairs and looked back as Pearl closed the door behind him.

"You're a lucky man, Will Phillips," she whispered. "A very lucky man."

29

"Hey, you're going to have to lighten up on the dance steps," Will said, doing awkward pirouettes into his room, wine bottle in one hand and two long-stemmed glasses in the other. He stopped in the middle of the floor. "Cameron?"

Will rushed back into the hallway. "Cameron?"

She was gone.

"Damn it," he said softly. "She didn't want wine. She wanted to go."

He set the bottle and glasses on the dresser and sat on the bed, dropping his face into his hands.

I tried too hard. Should've just gotten the glass of water like she asked, and I'd be sitting with her on the roof right now.

A loud creak make him jerk his head up, and Cameron stepped out from behind the door to the dressing closet. "Will?"

"Damn, you scared me."

"I'm sorry," Cameron laughed. "I didn't mean to startle you."

"Guess it's my night for it." Will shifted on the bed. "I see you've been off exploring. I suppose you're the sort who looks in people's medicine cabinets when you use their bathrooms, too?" he asked, a slight annoyance taking over his embarrassment. "You won't find much in mine though, just toothpaste, Listerine, and a shaving kit, though even at forty-five years old I can still go days before someone like Pearl thinks I need a shave." Will got up and walked over to the dresser.

"Aw," Cameron said. "Come on. A five o'clock shadow

would ruin your boyish charm."

"Boyish charm, my ass." He took the corkscrew out of his pocket and peeled the gold foil off the bottle.

"Well…"

In the mirror he could see Cameron leaning a shoulder against the closet door, her arms crossed over her chest, watching him. He quickly turned to position his back facing the dresser.

"Let's leave my boyish…charm… out of it for a second." He fumbled with the bottle and corkscrew. "You're an expert at this—maybe you could open this stubborn thing."

"You're not a wine drinker?" Cameron crossed the room. "Give me that."

"I know a beverage worth drinking by the sound of the *hwuut-clink* of the cap coming off. Wine? More of a *pop-thwunk*. Not the same."

"If that's so, how do you explain bourbon? And where's your beer?" Cameron took the bottle from Will's hands and set it on the dresser.

"I thought it would be nice to join you," he smiled.

In what looked like a single fluid move, she twisted the corkscrew into the top and pulled it out with a *pop-thwunk* that made Will jump.

"Goodness, you are jumpy tonight," she said.

"It was Pearl. Scared the hell out of me downstairs, and I'm still getting over it, I think."

"She was up?"

"Yes. Met me in the kitchen. She's like a cat. An old, arthritic cat. Anyway, she picked out the wine and insisted I drink it instead of the beer."

"So you're not just being sociable."

"Well, of course I am. It just wasn't my idea."

"I see."

"And then you popped out of the closet and gave my boyish heart another start."

Cameron poured the two glasses and handed one to Will. "Yeah, I'm really sorry about that." She raised her glass and took a sip. "Curiosity got to me. I wanted to see the other room. But I got caught up with the dresses. Have you seen them?"

"The dresses?" Will swished the wine around in his glass.

"Yes. There are old dresses in that closet. One looks like it could be a wedding gown."

"Dresses are … not really my thing."

"I'm not asking you to wear one. Just appreciate them. Come see." Cameron walked to the closet and opened the door. "Look at this," she said, handing Will her glass so she could pull Pearl's wedding dress down from the rod. It was covered in a lightweight plastic cover from the dry cleaner. "See this beautiful beadwork down the back?" She pulled the plastic cover up. "It's exquisite. Must be from around 1950. I can't believe she hasn't done more to preserve this. It's an heirloom."

"Probably that she kept it at all is a lot for Pearl. Her wedding is not likely one of those things she'd like to revisit."

"Oh?" Cameron let the plastic fall back down on the dress.

"She doesn't ever talk about it. But I hear things from time to time," Will said. "People talk."

"And what do these people say?"

"Pearl lost her husband when her kids were still pretty young. She raised them alone, which it sounds like she was doing even while he was alive. He married her for the Butler family fortune but never managed to hit it off with her father, so the father wouldn't let him into the lumber business. He made his way selling insurance on the road, and had women all over the state. When he did come home, he was pretty awful to her and the kids. Never laid a hand on them, I'm told, but they were just as happy to have him leave again."

"How did he die?" Cameron asked, her glass poised.

"Drove off a cliff."

"You're kidding." Her eyes widened.

"Nope. Had a 1954 Buick Skylark (cherry, I'm told) that was his pride and joy. Loved it more than his kids. Wouldn't let them ride in it unless he was trying to prove to someone he was a family man. And even then he made them sit on sheets of plastic. Anyway, he was making a sales call out in the Black Hills and lost it going around a curve. Went right off the side. Folks say the brake line had been cut."

"Was someone trying to kill him?"

"Seems not. The story is he cut it himself, trying to concoct himself a George Bailey moment and convince himself the world needed him. But Clarence the guardian angel apparently already had his wings and never showed, so the car went over the cliff and Ed Jenkins died in the arms of his first love, sheet metal and all, convinced the world would be better off without him, a notion some people around here consider very much to be true."

"And Pearl?"

"Oh, Pearl doesn't believe that. No. She despised him, of

course. He took her life away long before he took his own."
Will leaned his back against the wall and slid down to the
closet floor. "But Pearl would never wish someone over a cliff.
She always saw something in him, even if she couldn't ever
bring it to the surface. Even so, I don't think she has any interest in working to preserve that dress. It's an emblem of that
certain kind of death she experienced with him while he was
alive."

Cameron smoothed the plastic cover down the sides of
the dress and hung it back on the rod. "I knew she was a remarkable woman. I had no idea how she'd achieved that."

Will set Cameron's glass on the polished oak floor board
next to him. "Do you want to sit? I'm sorry I don't have much
for furniture up here."

Cameron turned and sat cross-legged next to him and
picked up her glass. "How'd we end up in the closet instead of
on the roof?"

"Someone went looking in an enchanted closet for Nar-
nia and discovered there were no fur coats at the back of the
wardrobe." Will smiled and stared into his glass.

Cameron laughed. "I guess I did sort of take us off course.
I'm sorry."

"It's okay. I have always loved closets. When I was a kid,
we had this long narrow coat closet in the front entry between
the den and the living room where my mother stored blankets
and sleeping bags. There was a light with a pull-string, and I
would go in there to read. Sometimes I got so comfortable on
all the blankets I'd fall asleep."

"In the closet? Why not just go to your room?"

"You're very practical, aren't you. My room was ..." Will

paused and looked up at the dresses. "At the time, I shared a room. Hard for a guy to get the kind of space to himself that he might get in a closet." He winked.

"Ah," Cameron said, taking a sip from her glass. "Are you going to drink your wine tonight or just swish it around?"

"I suppose I may as well drink it. I thought that maybe if this was really an enchanted closet it might turn into a cold lager."

Cameron laughed. "Enchanted closet, eh? I thought we already decided there were no snowy woods behind those fancy old dresses. Just another bedroom that you could get to through the regular door in the hall."

"Sure, but there are different kinds of enchantments. And a closet that has a secret passageway to another place—even if it's just another bedroom—feels enchanted to me."

He ran a finger around the top of his glass.

"Do you like fairy tales?"

Cameron wrinkled her nose. "You were right, that I am very practical. It doesn't seem like fairy tales do much for grown-ups. I don't quite believe in enchantments anymore."

"Ah," Will said, suddenly feeling like he was channeling Joe. "Maybe that's because you've never read the right fairy tales."

"Oh?" Cameron smiled and sipped her wine. "And what fairy tales am I missing?"

Will thought a moment. "Do you know 'The Wild Swans?'"

"'The Wild Swans.' Is that Grimm?"

"Well, it had a few dark spots, but overall I've always found it quite hopeful."

"What?" Cameron frowned, her face puzzled. "Wait. No.

I meant is it one by the Brothers Grimm."

Will laughed. "No. Hans Christian Andersen. 'The Silver Skates guy.'" He swished the wine around in his glass some more, still not convinced he would drink it. "I always find Andersen to have so much more nuance than the Grimm boys. They were all about warty witches in the woods and wolves with grandmothers in their bellies. A little ham-fisted if you ask me. But Andersen was more cerebral. Complicated family dynamics, that sort of thing. Fewer actual monsters, more regular folks with monstrous hearts."

"Is that right." Cameron smirked at Will over her glass.

"You're humoring me," Will said, lowering his eyes.

Cameron put a hand on his arm. "No, really I'm not. I've just never heard anybody break down the fairy tale guys like that. It's actually sort of interesting."

She noticed her hand on Will's arm and gently slipped it back to her glass, which didn't require two hands to hold but at the moment seemed like a good idea.

"You seem like a literature buff," she said. "Did you go to college for it?"

Will smiled and shook his head. "Nope. Studied the real trolls and monsters over in the political science department."

"Serious? You don't seem like a politician."

"I'm not. Just found it an interesting way to study people. 'By their politics ye shall know them,' as the Good Book says."

"For a guy who keeps so much to himself, you sure seem curious about people."

"Yeah?" Will raised his glass and took a sip of wine. His lips pursed as he swallowed. "What were we talking about before?"

"The wild swans. And how I'd never heard of them."

"Ah. That's right." He stood up. "Sit tight, I'll be right back."

Will walked across the room to his bookshelf and scanned the titles. He pulled a thick gray book from the case and blew the dust off the top. "Here we go," he said. "This is the one."

He sat back down across from Cameron and flipped through the pages. "I'll read it to you."

"You're going to read to me, in a closet."

"I can't think of a better place to read."

Will took his reading glasses from his shirt pocket and began.

"Far away in the land to which the swallows fly when it's winter, dwelt a king who had eleven sons, and one daughter named Eliza."

"Oh, gosh," Cameron interrupted. "The land to which the swallows fly when it's winter. That sounds so majestic."

Will chuckled. "Especially when you consider that a phrase like that could as easily refer to Broward County or Harlingen, since the birds around here all fly south to Florida or Texas in the winter. But Andersen makes it sound so ethereal."

"Sorry," Cameron said. "Go on."

"The eleven brothers were princes, and each went to school with a star on his breast, and a sword by his side. They wrote with diamond pencils on gold slates, and learned their lessons so quickly and read so easily that everyone might know they were princes. Their sister Eliza sat on a little stool of plate-glass and had a book of pictures, which had cost as much as half a kingdom."

"You know," Cameron interjected again, "it's really unfair that Eliza wasn't given the opportunity for more of an education like the boys—she just got a picture book."

"I don't know if that's a valid complaint or not," Will said, closing the book on his finger. "I mean, she's clearly valued. She has a book that cost as much as half the kingdom for Pete's sake. For just one book."

"But why not put even a fraction of that into teaching her to read? Who knows what she could do to expand her father's kingdom if he'd have been willing to invest in her brain and not just a fancy glass stool for her backside."

Will crossed his arms, tucking the book under one. "So, are you going to let me read you the story, or are you going to go all feminist *Princess Bride* grandson the whole time?"

Cameron put up her hand, then made a zipper gesture across her lips and motioned to Will to keep reading.

"Oh, these children were indeed happy, but it was not to remain so always."

"Ooh," Cameron said. "Foreshadowing."

Will looked at Cameron over his glasses, his eyebrows raised.

"Go on, sorry."

"Their father, who was king of the country, married a very wicked queen, who did not like the poor children at all."

"Okay, come on. What is it with the misogynistic fairy tale writers who always create these benevolent, if a little clueless, men and couple them with utterly evil women (except for the perfect and saintly first wives and mothers of their children who are mysteriously dead)?"

Will lay the book open in his lap.

"You seem to have some capacity for fairy tale analysis yourself." He smirked.

Cameron leaned forward. "I'm serious," she said. "They're all like this. Full of evil women."

She reached for the book and Will raised it up over his shoulder. "No, I'm reading it to you."

Cameron lunged forward and grabbed the book from his hand. "I'm going to show you." She started flipping through the pages. "Where were you reading from?"

Will reached out his hand for the book. "Let me have it. I'll show you."

Cameron kept flipping. She closed the old gray book and turned it.

"*Leviathan*," she said, running her finger along the spine. She looked up at Will, who cocked his head slightly. "Did Thomas Hobbes also write fairy tales?"

"In a manner of speaking," he said, easing the book from Cameron's hand.

"What gives, Phillips?" she asked. "Were you making the story up?"

"No, I'd tell a different tale if I were making one up. It's the real story but I don't have a book with it in."

"You were telling the story from memory?"

"It's sort of a favorite," Will said quietly, rubbing his fingertips against the embossed linen of the cover. "Pretending to read it felt less odd than reciting it."

Cameron looked into her wine glass, then looked up at Will. "Put the book down and tell me the rest?"

Will scooted next to Cameron and leaned his back against the wall. "Alright. Just never tell the guys downtown that I did."

"Our secret," Cameron said, making the zipper gesture again.

"Well, as things go, the king's evil new wife sends Eliza off to live with some peasant couple in the country, and then feeds the princes sand in their teacups. She tells the king all sorts of lies about them until finally he just doesn't care about any of his kids anymore."

"Those had to be some whopper lies, or the queen must have been some kind of beautiful," Cameron said.

"Yeah, Andersen didn't give the king much credit for thinking outside his pants, as best as I can tell." Will shifted, then slowly floated one hand upward as he continued, "Anyway, then she puts a curse on the brothers, trying to make them into ugly birds that will fly away from the palace. But she only manages to turn them into beautiful, voiceless swans."

Will leaned his head back against the wall. "So the swan brothers fly from the palace to the hovel where Eliza lives and see her playing with the only toy she had: a single green leaf. But because they can't speak, they can't do anything for her so they fly away."

"That's very sad," Cameron said softly.

"Yeah, and it gets worse. When Eliza turns fifteen, her father wants to see her so the queen summons her from the peasants. She enchants three toads and puts them in her bath. One is supposed to sit on Eliza's head and make her stupid, one is to sit on her forehead and make her ugly, and one is to sit on her heart and make her evil. Eliza gets in the bath and the toads do their thing, but because Eliza is so beautiful and pure, the curses don't work so all that happens is that the toads turn to red poppies on the bath water, instead of turning to roses, which is what would have happened to frogs in the bath with Eliza if they hadn't been enchanted."

"Red poppies, huh?" Cameron asked.

"Red poppies. Thinking that maybe Andersen and Neruda used to go out for beers after work." Will chuckled. "Since the magic wasn't working for the evil queen, she takes some walnut juice and smears it all over Eliza's face, and then messes up her hair pretty bad, and then presents her to the king, who doesn't even recognize her because she looks so awful, so Eliza runs away from the palace. She meets up with an old woman who tells her about seeing eleven swans and takes her to a place where she can find them. Well, around sunset, she sees the eleven swans flying toward her over the ocean, and when they land and it becomes dark, they turn back into her brothers."

"Wait. What? They suddenly are her brothers again?"

"Well, they are for a moment," Will explained. "But when the sun comes up, they turn into swans again. It's a day-night kind of curse."

"Oh, okay. Gotcha."

"Listen, I'm leaving big parts of it out. It's a pretty long story. She flies around with her brothers for a while and then she has a dream and a fairy in the dream tells her that she can save her brothers if she will take the stinging nettles—ones she can only find in a graveyard—and break them into pieces that will become flax, and then spin and weave eleven coats with long sleeves. And if she puts the coats on the swans, the spell will be broken. But if she speaks even one word, the whole deal is off and the brothers cannot be saved. So she sets off to make the coats, and this king finds her. Of course, the king falls in love with her—"

"Oh, gosh," Cameron said. "Is this going to get weird?"

"Well, the whole thing is already pretty weird, don't you think?"

"Point taken."

"The archbishop gets a little freaked out about the king's new sweetie and tells him she's a witch. Eliza gets thrown into the dungeon, and she keeps on making the coats for her brothers, thanks to some very helpful little mice. When the people haul her off to be burned as a witch, she's still wildly spinning these coats from nettles, and her brothers come swooping in and she throws the coats on them as they go by. But the problem is that one of the coats doesn't get quite done. As her youngest brother flies by, she throws the partial coat on him, and he turns back into a young man, but because the coat was missing a sleeve, one arm was left as the wing of the swan. And that's the story of 'The Wild Swans.'"

"That's it?" asked Cameron. "It ends there? What about Eliza? Is she killed? Do they burn her to death?"

"Oh, yeah. Eliza." Will took a drink. "No, no, she's fine. Once the brothers aren't swans anymore, she gets her voice back and says she's not a witch and everyone just believes her—which is wild since she just turned eleven swans into men which sounds totally like something a witch could do—and she marries the king."

"Why did you leave that part out? You were just going to leave me hanging?"

"Well, I didn't mean to. I just really like the part about the youngest brother and his swan wing. I figure, it's a fairy tale. It goes without saying that the beautiful girl is going to marry the king that was just about to have her killed."

"The girl saved everybody. She couldn't speak, she was sent to the dungeon, she knitted eleven coats with bloody hands and was on her way to be burned alive, the king is useless, and she's the one that saves them all."

"Yeah. Go figure, those damned misogynist fairy tale writers."

Cameron punched Will lightly on the arm.

"Easy there, you'll bruise my feathers."

"Oh?" Cameron raised her eyebrows. "You're hiding the wing of a swan under your shirt?"

"Why else do you suppose I always wear long sleeves?" Will asked. He stared back into his glass and twisted the button on his cuff.

Cameron leaned back and tipped her glass to finish her wine.

Will looked up at the ceiling above Pearl's old dresses. "Sometimes I come in here to think. Once—" Will paused, looking at his hands. He looked back up. "Once I imagined the ceiling opened to a starry sky and a white feather floated down into my hands."

Cameron tipped her head.

"I should say, I may also have been drunk at the time," Will chuckled.

Cameron punched him on the arm again. "I'll bet you bring all the pretty girls in here and tell them that story."

Will laughed with unease. "Well, I haven't told all the pretty girls." He took a drink. "Just one."

"Hmm." Cameron straightened.

"Of course, there was only one other pretty girl."

"And the not-so-pretty ones?" Cameron asked.

"There weren't any." Will ran a hand through his wavy hair.

"Oh." Cameron said, working a smudge on her glass with her thumb. "And did this pretty girl like the story?"

"She did not."

30

Will picked up the book and raised himself to his knee. "I should put this away."

Cameron watched Will walk across the room to the bookcase and went back to polishing her glass when he returned.

He held out a hand. "Let me help you up. I can walk you out."

Cameron looked up at Will, her eyes set but soft. "Pearl would be disappointed if you saw me out before you finished your wine."

Will tried to smile. "Wouldn't be the first time I disappointed Pearl."

"Hey, come on. We can talk about something else. But I like it in here. And I enjoy your company. Come sit again." Cameron patted the floor where Will had been sitting. He rolled his shoulders, which felt as though they were tightening into his skull. "Sit."

Will sat down, picked up his glass and chugged the rest of his wine in one gulp. He winced as he swallowed it down.

"We won't have to worry about Pearl now," he said, not looking at Cameron. "Emily Post would be proud, so now I can see you out if you like."

Cameron held her ground. "Damn, Will. You're like a wounded pup." She leaned her head against the wall and stared at a section of cracked plaster in the corner of the ceiling. "I'm not leaving while you're so grumpy. I think I'll just sit here and see if the ceiling might open to the night sky."

Will rubbed the back of his neck. "It won't open. It's an

ordinary ceiling in a turn-of-the-century constructed home. And there's a whole other story above us. Don't make fun."

Cameron stayed silent but held her gaze as though she really were wishing for the ceiling to dissolve into the stars.

"Telling you that was really the most ridiculous thing I've said in a long time. It would make me happy if you could just forget I did."

She didn't answer. Will grew silent as well, fidgeting with the button on his cuff.

Finally, without looking up, Will spoke again. "In the story, in a part I left out, before Eliza starts making the coats and gets thrown in the dungeon, the brothers take her with them from the peasant house and fly across the sea. It's very difficult because they are only swans while the sun is up, so they have to fly a certain distance every day to reach dry land before they turn into men again and drop into the sea and drown. The youngest brother takes special care of Eliza during this time, sheltering her with his wing from the harsh sun and wind."

"He loved her very much," Cameron said.

"He did."

"And his wing," she said. "It was very useful."

"It was."

Cameron took a deep breath. "I imagine that after they celebrated the breaking of the enchantment, they also mourned some that it was incomplete, at least as far as the youngest brother. That he still had his wing. But maybe they later came to be glad for that, knowing a wing could have some value."

"I thought you were too practical to appreciate a good fairy tale," Will said, his lips forming a thin smile.

"I am. This seems like more than a fairy tale."

Will pulled his knees up. "When I told Barbara that I had—" He stopped, wiping his hands across his thighs, his palms sticky against the soft fuzz of worn denim.

~

He saw Barbara puckering her lips and rubbing them together in the mirror.

"If you're just going to stand there, hand me a tissue."

Will pulled a tissue from the box and handed it to her, then went back to leaning on the counter. He pulled a pack of cigarettes from his shirt pocket.

"No, not here. I thought you were quitting," Barbara said. Will put the package back in his pocket.

"I am quitting."

"Usually when people say *quitting* what they actually mean is quitting," she said, blotting her lips.

"I have my own way of doing things," Will said, and pushed his hands into his pockets.

"Truer words have ne'er been spoken." Barbara leaned to the mirror and put her fingers in her hair. "Damn. Look here. Can you see my roots?"

Will didn't look. "Not a single one."

Barbara scowled at herself. "You know, people like you and all those girls who never get a gray hair—doesn't mean it's not a big deal to the rest of us."

Will stood straight and pushed his shoulders back, catching the softness of his profile in the mirror. He instinctively ran a hand over the scruff on his chin and pulled the cigarettes from his pocket again. As he walked away, he pressed a cigarette between his lips and pushed the back door open. He murmured, "Screw you, Barbara."

~

"What?"

Will heard Cameron's voice. He turned and shook his head lightly. "Oh, sorry. My mind went somewhere else, I guess."

"You were saying something about Barbara."

"Oh, yeah, right," Will said. He sat up. "The other pretty girl. When I told her—and shit, it's not like it should have been any surprise to her—when I told Barbara I was a man with the wing of a swan up my sleeve, she left. Looked me in the eye and walked away."

Cameron sucked in her breath. "Will—"

"Not everybody likes fairy tales, Cameron." Will pressed his thumb into his palm. "Not everyone likes them at all."

"No, I don't suppose everyone is ready to hear them. Some people even think they are too practical for fairy tales, in fact. Or so I've heard." Cameron smiled. "But people can learn. They can discover."

"I suppose. But just because they *can* doesn't mean they *will*." He turned to face Cameron. "I guess what I'm saying is people should be careful who they tell their stories to."

Cameron pulled her hair back from her eyes. "Do you think it's possible Barbara wasn't upset because of *your* swan wing, but because of her own?"

"Heh." Will leaned against the wall and saw Barbara taking herself in, facing every direction in the mirror. "I know you've never met the woman. But there wasn't a stray feather on her anywhere."

"For a guy who speaks in metaphor you are maddeningly literal," Cameron said.

"She had a metaphorical wing?"

"Sure she did. Doesn't everybody?"

Will started to roll his eyes and turned his head away quickly, hoping Cameron hadn't seen.

"Too late," she said. "I saw that."

"Et tu, Cameron? First Mad Dog, and now you're going to go all Oprah-psychobabbly on me now, too? I should have said goodnight early and not tried to lure you to the roof. Damn Finn and his leash."

"Oh, come on. You're just mad because someone is encroaching on your solitary pain." She cupped a hand to her mouth. "Come see Will Phillips, bearer of the Swan Wing, the only man who's ever known the disappointment of an ill-fitting life. The only man who's ever hidden his secret life. The only man who's ever—"

Will scooted away from Cameron without speaking.

"Am I right, is that what it is," Cameron asked.

"Stop," Will said quietly, staring at his hands.

"No, you stop," said Cameron, with a sharpness in her voice that was not unkind.

Will looked up.

"You want to think you have some corner on quiet despair. But everyone has a secret, Will." She looked up at the ceiling. "Everyone."

"You think so."

"I do."

Will thought of his secrets and pulled at his sleeve, wondering how feathers could give birds flight and yet weigh enough to keep a body pinned to the ground. He thought that if only he were winged on both sides, or neither, instead of subject to such imbalance, his life may have taken flight in ways he would find more satisfying. He could have used his wing to shield himself from Barbara's unrelenting assaults. But for Will it was as though the wing itself, otherwise a source of weightlessness and flight, were an actual albatross hung around his neck that he dragged along, keeping him close to the ground pecking in the dirt until it became his own sense of glory, like Nicholas Cage's Ronnie Cammareri after he cut off his hand, shouting inside his head, *I lost my hand! I lost my bride! Johnny has his hand! Johnny has his bride! You want me to take my heartache, put it away and forget?* Was this what Cameron was suggesting?

"Whatever it is, your secret's not that special, Will. Not when you consider everybody's got one. Or two or ten."

"Yeah?" Will asked, desperate to move the focus off himself. "Do you suppose Pearl has a secret? Or Joe?"

"Oh, I'm quite sure they do. You need to stop covering your eyes with your wing so you can see them."

He smiled, a slight hint of mischief at the corners of his mouth. "What do you think Pearl is hiding?"

"Gosh. I'd say money. Or maybe a secret lover."

"Money's too easy," Will said. "Everyone knows she has money tied up." His eyes brightened. "I think it's her husband."

"It's no secret she was married. You told me about it."

"No, no." Will became animated, gesturing with his hands. "I mean, what if he didn't drive himself off that cliff? What if there was a hit on him? An assassin cut the brake line?"

Cameron's face paled. "God, Will. You already said she couldn't have done it."

Will laughed. "Of course not. Not Pearl. Murder is too unseemly for her."

"That's good." Cameron sighed in relief.

"But local legend has it that after Ed Jenkins died, Pearl started seeing Orwell Hidgens, who owned the hatchery. Folks had suspected maybe there was a little something between them before Mr. Jenkins died and after a proper mourning period he started calling on her in the daytime. Maybe he put out the hit, and Pearl later found out about it and broke it off because she couldn't bring herself to be with a killer. Maybe that's her secret."

"Geez, you have an imagination. And I was just going to say maybe her secret is that she uses a box mix for her famous double fudge cake."

"For some folks around here, making a cake from a box mix would be a worse crime than having your husband murdered."

"You're kidding."

"I am not. You need to go to a few more small town potluck dinners and you'll see what I mean."

"Okay. Well, what about Joe, then?" Cameron asked.

"Joe? He's full of secrets."

"Why do you think that?"

"Why else does a guy leave the city and move to the middle of nowhere if he's not trying to bury secrets?"

"I don't know, Will," Cameron said. "Why else would a guy do that? Or a girl for that matter? At least Joe moved out here to retire. You and I left the city in the prime of our careers."

"You're saying you moved here to bury your secrets in the tall grass of the prairie?"

Cameron cocked her head. "What? No, wait. That's not what I was saying."

"Uh huh." Will smirked.

"Look, we were talking about Joe. What do you think he's hiding?"

"Right. Noted. Talking about Joe."

"I think it's embezzlement," Cameron said. "Joe embezzled money and ran away."

"Embezzled?" Will chuckled. "You haven't been to Joe's place. If he was hiding money, he'd have no idea where he put it. Nah, I think Joe is a spy."

"A spy?" Cameron laughed out loud. "Well, his cover is brilliant, if that's the case."

"It's perfect. He could have so many state secrets hidden in all his books, nobody could crack it."

Cameron picked up the wine bottle and held it to the light. "So, what was Barbara's secret, Will? What did being with you expose in her that made her leave?"

Will took the bottle from Cameron and twisted out the cork. "Barbara had no secrets, except that she colored her roots."

In fact, Barbara's biggest secret was Will. She had always understood this, and had always depended on him not to.

Will's phone buzzed and he felt instinctively for his hip,

then remembered he'd left the phone on the dresser with his wallet when he pulled *Leviathan* from the shelf.

"Hang on." He shifted to a knee and stood.

"You're one of those guys, huh?" Cameron said, not really asking.

"Those guys?"

"You know. Those guys who can't let their phones go to voicemail."

"Ah." He turned to Cameron with a wink as he reached for the phone. "You mean a claims guy. No, we can't ever let the phone roll."

This was, of course, another of Will's secrets: He cultivated the myth that claims calls were on par with 911 calls and had to be taken at any hour of the day. The benefit to him was that a well-timed call could save him from a chatty client or, as in this case, offer a needed change of subject. Earlier in their partnership, he and Mad Dog actually had an agreement to phone each other at odd intervals after hours in case one or the other was needing a diversion. And as much as he hoped it wasn't Mad Dog calling, he surely could use the diversion now.

Will tapped the phone. "I don't know the number. I should take it just in case." Cameron rolled her eyes.

"Phillips," he said, pressing the phone to his ear. Cameron started to get to her feet. Will motioned with his hand for her to wait. "Sure, I know Joe Murphy."

Cameron leaned toward Will, crinkling her eyebrows.

"His what? No, I think you're mistaken. No relation."

Will shrugged and held open his free hand toward Cameron. She crossed her arms over her chest.

"Oh, god. You're kidding me." Will's face went pale and he lowered his hand to the dresser. "Yeah. Of course, yes. I'll be there as soon as I can."

He tapped his phone and pushed it into his back pocket.

"What is it, Will? Did something happen to Joe?"

Will opened his mouth to speak. "I—"

"What happened? Who was it on the phone?" Cameron had stood up and her hand was on Will's shoulder now, her voice in a pitch Will hadn't heard from her before.

"I— He— That was the hospital in Colbyville. Joe has me listed as his next of kin."

"His what?" Cameron stepped back. "Wait— Why is the hospital calling in the first place? Is Joe okay?"

Will shook his head and ran his fingers through his hair. "No, he's not."

He sat down on the bed and stared at nothing in particular.

"Will." Cameron sat down beside him on the bed. "Is Joe—" Her voice disappeared.

"No, no," Will said quietly. "He's alive. Unconscious. Heart attack. I—" He looked at Cameron. "I need to go. I'll walk you out."

"No, you won't. I'll go with you." Cameron stood up.

He felt Cameron tugging at his sleeve but Will had already sunk below the surface, the weight of eleven feet deep pinning his outstretched arms and legs to the rough, speckled floor of the pool, his reddening eyes wide against the chlorine infused water holding him in place. Clouds eased their way across the surface until the sun was fully covered and the blue above him turned into an undefined mass of gray.

Through a blur, Will tried to speak, his words passing from his mouth as unformed sounds got lost in the thickness of the water. He breathed in deep, his lungs filling with water and pushing back out with long exhales and he wondered at the ease of breathing under water, not at all like he'd been taught at the city pool when he was a boy. He took in long draws, pushing water in and out and finding a comforting equilibrium with the immobilizing pressure of the water inside and outside his body. He saw a dark shape rise above the surface growing first smaller, then larger and larger before it crashed through, coming straight for him. He tried to roll left to avoid the collision but his body remained in place, pinned to the floor until the shape took hold of the front of his shirt and the sound, at first muffled in the enveloping water, became more defined and the tugging more urgent.

"Will— Will, come on. Let's go."

He turned and saw Cameron standing above him beside the bed, tugging at his shirt. "Hey. You're scaring me. Snap out of it. Let's go find Joe. I'll drive."

Will shook off the funk and stood. "Yeah, no. I'll be fine. Let me walk you out."

"I'm sure you'll be fine. I'm going anyway. If it makes you feel any better we can take your truck. But I'm driving."

Cameron picked up Will's keys and wallet from the dresser. "Now let's go." She pointed to the door.

Will looked at Cameron, his eyes red and his body feeling as though it had forgotten how to move.

"I'm not going to carry you, Will."

"No, I don't imagine you are." He pushed a foot forward and walked out the door, Cameron following closely behind.

31

Will sat quietly in the passenger seat the entire drive, only speaking to mention where to turn as they made their way to the hospital. As they pulled off the Interstate at the Veblen exit, Cameron asked Will how he met Joe.

"It's crazy," Will said. "I've only known the man a few weeks." He looked out the window, the twinkling of clustered and scattered farm lights as they drove down into the valley looking as much like the approach to a small city as to the open prairie. "There's no reason I should even care much. He's a customer, for crying out loud."

"And yet somehow in these last few weeks he's updated his records to include you." Cameron put on the blinker. "Interesting."

"You've met him, Cameron. He's not an ordinary old man."

"No indeed. Quite extraordinary."

Cameron pulled into the hospital lot and parked. "Let's go," she said, pulling the keys from the ignition.

Will slumped in his seat. "I'm not going in. I don't owe Joe anything." He held out his hand. "Give me the keys, please. I'll drive us back home."

Cameron closed her fist around the keys. "No. You're here. If I have to lose a night of sleep it's going to be for doing a good thing. Not driving here and back to watch you be afraid to find out why an old man cares about you."

Will's head drooped. Cameron got out of the truck and walked around the cab. She opened Will's door. "Out you go.

We're going in."

"Damn," Will murmured under his breath. "Woman's got backbone."

"What?"

"Nothing," he said. "Just hoping you can sleep when you get back home."

"Right." She put her hands on her hips. "Out of the truck, Phillips."

By the time the pair reached the nurse's station, Will had gathered most of his professional composure. He smiled at the gray-haired nurse in floral printed scrubs who was staring over silver framed glasses at a computer screen. She glanced up and raised her eyebrows. "Yes?"

"Will Phillips. I'm looking for Joe Murphy? He came in tonight."

The nurse picked up a chart from the counter and flipped it open. "Of course. Mark," she called to a young nurse across the U-shaped desk who was wearing navy scrubs and scuffed orange Crocs on his feet. "Mr. Murphy's son is here."

"Oh, no. I'm not—" Will started.

The nurse snapped the chart closed. "Take him to his room, please." She looked back at Will. "He's been asking for you."

"But I—"

"Come this way, Mr. Phillips." The young nurse turned to Cameron and pointed to a nook with three egg-shaped aqua fiberglass chairs and a small flat screen television where Rachel Ray was telling viewers how to prepare French onion baked potatoes. "You can wait in there," he said.

"She's with me," Will pointed out.

"Sorry, she'll have to wait. Family only." The nurse started down the hall.

"But I—"

"Will, it's okay," Cameron said, patting his arm. "Go see Joe. I've been wanting to learn something new with potatoes anyway."

"But I—" Will stopped, waiting for someone to interrupt him.

No one did, and he followed the orange-shoed nurse down the hall, his mouth still open with no words to speak.

The corridor narrowed to a fine point far ahead, seeming to stretch to infinity, or maybe just to Fargo. Will wasn't sure which was worse.

He knew the hall was really no longer than a few hundred feet and that his boots now seemed filled with sand, or buckshot or maybe even cement. He rubbed his eyes and shook his foot to the side, as though sifting out the sand, and kept walking.

The nurse stopped in front of room 352 and Will wondered why a twenty-bed hospital in a 1,000-bed town needed to pretend to be so cosmopolitan. He opened the door and stuck his head inside.

"Mr. Murphy? Your boy is here to see you."

"But I—" Will started, for what felt like the hundredth time.

"Look, Mr. Phillips. We all know you're not his son."

People had been saying that to Will about his own dad his entire life. It seemed strange to hear it from a nurse he'd just met, about a man he barely knew.

"We really don't care what kind of arrangement you have

with Mr. Murphy. He asked for you and we want to take care of him, so we called and here you are. The rest is none of our business."

"But I—"

"Don't make me say it again. Just go in, umm, Mr. Phillips. He's waiting for you."

Will bit his lip. "Thank you."

The nurse nodded slightly and walked away.

He heard the nurse's voice coming from halfway to Fargo while Will stood stood facing the closed door with his hands in his pockets.

"Well?"

He turned his head, shrugged, and pushed open the door. Joe lay on the bed, his head pressed into a starched white pillowcase on a pillow that was clearly too soft to support his neck. His face was white, stretched, the shadows under his eyes accentuated to a deeper hollow than Will knew to be true. A hospital gown with a navy blue print hung loose over one shoulder.

Will remembered visiting his grandmother in her hospital bed in the old red brick hospital in Delphi, Indiana, when he was eleven. She had turned sideways to reach a cup of water on the side table and her gown drooped open in the front, exposing a sagging, wrinkled breast. A child was not meant to see the nakedness of an elder, such frailty at its most-poignantly expressed, yet he'd been unable to look away or ever to unsee it, though in time he'd been able to alter the image, to superimpose her ribs, visible against the wrinkled skin which served to take his eyes from the unthinkable. It had come as a surprise to him that his grandmother had a woman's body, as though when a person reached a certain age, one retained the form but not the substance. He knew her slender, rounded shape to fill her traditional flowered dresses in way that was truly lovely. But it was better, it seemed, to see one's elders, particularly one's relations, in the abstract, something he could never again do after her breast tumbled out of her gown. Of course, such thoughts only made his aversion to hospitals grow, picturing his own body in the immodesty of the printed gown, wondering what parts might come tumbling out or come up just plain missing, should he not take care when reaching for a cup of water himself. *How might a man like him age*, he wondered, as the alternating meter of Joe's shallow breathing and a beeping monitor came slowly into focus.

"Joe."

He said his friend's name aloud, stepping the rest of the way into the room and letting the door close quietly behind him.

Joe lay still, eyes closed, chest rising and falling under the soft thermal blanket folded over as though he'd been slipped into a giant white envelope. Will had hoped to find him sitting up reading the *Argus Leader*, joking about his neighbors and doctors making a medical emergency out of a little heartburn. But Joe was not sitting up flirting with the nearest nurse. If in fact he waited for Will as they'd said, he waited in his sleep, for he was most certainly unmoved by Will's arrival.

He walked to the bed and put his hands on the side rail.

"How'd I ever get mixed up with you, old man?"

He counted the patches stuck on Joe's chest, wires leading out to whirring and beeping machines, counting things that should be impossible to measure from outside a body, yet there they were, showing up in flickering numbers, in zigzagging lines peaking and plummeting, defining the things that go on inside a man that no one can really see.

"Cameron came along, Joe," Will said quietly. "She's out in the lobby watching Rachel Ray make potatoes because they said only family could come back. And isn't that a little ridiculous because I'm here, Joe, not your son and they say they know it, yet here I am."

Will looked around the room. Two Mary Groth paintings hung on the far wall, the rich greens and golds and oranges of her prairie landscapes faded to insipid blues and violets and the matting burned yellow, subjected to the cold fluorescents buzzing overhead after years of overseeing patients living and dying in this room with the naugahyde recliner that smelled of Lysol and beef bouillon.

He looked back at Joe, still peaceful on his bed. "You look like hell under the lights too, my friend." He glanced at the door. "Wonder if there's a way to bust you out of here."

Will chuckled. "Who am I kidding? I can't even park the 16th minute in a 15-minute zone. I couldn't get us past the nurses here. Sorry, old man." He patted Joe's shoulder and then stepped back quickly, putting his hand into his back pocket in a fist.

"Listen. You wanna watch some TV? We can catch you up on the news." Will picked up the remote and pointed it at the television. He sat down in the brown chair and leaned back. "See here?" he asked, not waiting for an answer. "While you were sleeping, Obama struck a deal with Iran. Yep, Iran. Can you believe it? Made a whole lot of people froth at the mouth over that one." He pressed the remote to change the channel. "Sorry, man. I can't do Fox News. Not tonight." He laced his fingers behind his head. "What else... Oh, yeah. Donald Trump is still running for president because that's what the world has come to. But *Huffington Post* just said they'll cover his campaign in their Entertainment section instead of Politics." Will looked at Joe. "A guy who lives in a golden tower in New York is leading in Iowa. Can you believe *that*?"

The door opened and the older nurse came in.

"How's our patient doing?" she asked.

"Oh, he was just asking me if he could have a beer." Will winked. "Said something about feeling like he just carried a refrigerator across the room on his back."

The nurse chuckled. "That would sound about right." She lifted Joe's wrist and looked at her watch.

"Why do you still do that?" Will asked. "I mean, you take his pulse by hand when you have all these machines recording everything anyway."

"Human touch." She smiled. "People need to be touched, but we can't very well just come in here and randomly put our hands on patients. So this is a way we can still do that."

"Is that true?" Will said, leaning to read the nurse's nametag. "Myrna?"

"Well, it's true for me, even if it's not what the rulebooks say. I'm old school. Oh, I know the machines are helpful and all. But sometimes the body has things to say that patches and probes don't tell us. And a body needs to feel skin to remember it's alive."

"Why did you call me?" Will asked.

"Pardon?" Myrna looked up from her watch.

"Why did you call me when Joe came in? Why not a family member?"

"Well, you're listed in Mr. Murphy's chart as his next of kin. His paperwork says you're his son."

"Joe doesn't have any sons."

"I know. But when he was here last week after that thing with the baseball, he had us update it. So as far as we're concerned, you're his son."

"I've only known Joe a few weeks."

"He must feel like he's known you longer."

"Who was his next of kin before?"

"You know I can't tell you that."

"Why not? I'm his next of kin." Will smiled.

Myrna adjusted Joe's blanket, even though it hadn't moved since the envelope flap had first been folded back. "Anyway, it seemed a smart move on his part. At least you'd come see him. Hypothetically speaking, if his brother in Chicago were listed as his next of kin, for instance, he'd likely not show up unless Joe passed on."

Will looked at Joe, the shiner still visible and yellowing under his right eye. "Is that so." He looked back at the nurse. "He's a good man, Myrna. His brother is a fool. Hypothetically speaking, of course."

"I'll come back and check on you in a little while, Mr. Phillips."

"It's Will. Please."

"Alright, Will." Myrna smiled. "Would you like me to send in your fiancé?"

"My what?" Will looked up, puzzled.

"Your fiancé. In the waiting room. There's not much else for her to learn about potatoes."

"But she's not—"

"Joe told us you were engaged to a beautiful young woman. Looks like he was right."

"But she's not—"

"You must learn to hush, Will. We're doing this Mr. Murphy's way." She scrawled a note in Joe's chart and then snapped it shut and tucked it under her arm. "So. Shall I send her back?"

"Actually, yes," Will conceded. "I'd like it very much if you'd send Ms. Julian back. I'm sure Joe would be delighted to see her."

"She'll be right in, Mr. Phillips." Myrna dipped her head, turned and went out, leaving Will alone with the sleeping Joe Murphy.

He thrummed his fingers against the rail alongside Joe's motionless body. "Look, old man," he said softly. "I still don't know how you did it, squeezing your frustratingly charming self into my world that didn't really need the disruption. But you did it, and here we are, and so you sure as hell had better wake up." His hands wrapped around the bar and he found himself gently shaking the bed.

Joe didn't move. The rhythmic, shallow breaths went on and on, a slight rattle underneath them as though he'd like to start snoring. Will thought of Joe's wife listening to him snore night after night and wondered how often she got up and went to the kitchen for a glass of water, or maybe a sip of wine, to get herself back to sleep. He heard the soft creak of the door behind him and turned to see Cameron slip in. She held the door and muffled the sound of the latch with her body, then sidled up to Will at Joe's bedside.

"He looks like hell," she murmured.

"Remind me not to call you for the part where we put a good face on things, okay?"

"Oh, I'm sorry. I'm afraid I lose my signature nuance when I've been up most of the night. But listen, I have this new recipe for oven-roasted new potatoes and asparagus I'm dying to try out."

"It's okay," Will said. "He does look like hell." He pointed at Joe's right eye. "See that? He took a baseball to the face getting out of the car the other night after our dinner with Pearl."

"Holy..." Cameron said. "Guy's had a terrible week."

"Yeah. You know I'm not just his next of kin, right? He told them I'm his son."

"His son?" Cameron laughed. "And how did he do that?"

"He updated his records when he was in the ER for his shiner."

"Joe never had a son."

"I know."

"He could have just made you his emergency contact. He didn't have to make up a story."

"I know."

"What's he up to?"

"I don't know. But I'll tell you what—" Will jabbed Joe softly in the arm with his finger. "You'd better listen to this part, Joe. If I'm somebody's son for all of ten minutes, he sure as hell better stick around for a while."

Cameron put a hand on Will's arm. "Easy there. Looks like someone else loses their nuance when they're tired. Don't be poking the old guy. You'll wake him."

"That would be bad? He's unconscious after a heart attack. It's not like he's napping on a Sunday afternoon."

Cameron slipped her hand into Will's and gave it a light squeeze. The two stood at Joe's side, neither speaking.

After several minutes, Will broke the silence. "I think he wants to give you away."

"He what?" Cameron asked, looking at Will. Will kept his eyes on Joe.

"He wants to give you away. At the wedding."

"What wedding?" Cameron pulled her hand away. "Do you need more coffee? Or less coffee? What is your sleep-deprived mind yammering about?"

"They didn't tell you when they brought you back?"

"Tell me what?"

"It's family-only back here. They didn't tell you how you got in?"

Cameron looked at Joe, back at Will, then at Joe again. "He didn't," she said.

Will turned to face Cameron.

"Sneaky old rascal."

32

"Joe doesn't waste any time," Will said.

"No, I suppose he figures we're not getting any younger." Cameron smiled and smoothed Joe's blanket at his chest.

"Hey, did you see that?" Will asked.

"See what?"

Will pointed to Joe's hand. Joe's thumb twitched. "He's waking up. Look."

"Oh, Will, you watch too much television. People's fingers and toes move involuntarily all the time. It doesn't mean he's waking up. I'm sorry."

Will put his hands on the rail and set his jaw. "I've owned a television for just slightly longer than I've been Joe's son. This isn't me watching too much TV."

"Right," Cameron said. "I'm just a sleepy killjoy. Sorry about that."

Will turned and leaned his back against the bed rail. He crossed his ankles and put his hands in his jeans pockets. "You're probably right, though."

Joe's hands balled into fists.

"Will, look." Cameron pointed at Joe's hands.

"What, is it real as long as you're the one who sees it?"

"No, seriously." She tugged on his sleeve. "I'm sorry, okay? But look—"

Will turned. Joe's eyelids fluttered and his lips pursed, then relaxed. Will leaned over the bed.

"Joe?" he said. "Hey, Joe. Is that you in there?"

Will turned to Cameron and grinned. "See? It's not just

wishful thinking. He's waking up. He's really waking up."

"He is, Will. He is." Cameron returned Will's smile and rested a hand between his shoulders as he leaned down.

"I'm going to go get a nurse," he said, rushing for the door. "Stay here and keep him awake."

"Oh, right. I'll just use my secret magical powers to keep a man alert."

"Umm. You have them. You might as well use them," Will said and ducked out the door.

When Will came back into the room with Myrna, Joe's eyes were open and Cameron was leaning sideways with her hip against the rail talking to him cheerfully with her hands. She turned her head when the door opened.

"Look who decided to join us," she said.

Will hurried to the bedside. "Hey Joe. Nice of you to wake up for your party."

"Is it time for the party already?" Joe asked, his face shadowed with confusion. His voice was raspy. He turned to Cameron and said, "Millie, could you get me a drink of water?" He cleared his throat and winced in pain. "I feel parched."

"Millie?"

Will reached behind her for the water pitcher and cup. "Yes, the water's right here, Millie." He filled the cup and handed it to Cameron. "Mind the straw so you don't poke out his good eye."

She took the cup and turned back to Joe, holding it so he could sip from the straw while Myrna held one hand on his forehead and the other on his wrist.

"It's good to see you're waking up from your nap, Mr. Murphy," she said. "How are you feeling?"

"Feel like hell," Joe said, then turned to Cameron. "Sorry, my Love. I know you don't like me to curse."

Cameron looked at Will and mouthed, "My love?"

"It's okay, Joe," Will said. "Millie will forgive you a little cursing after the scare you gave us all. I think I heard her use a word or two herself. I'm sure she's just happy like the rest of us to see you up and at 'em."

He took Cameron's arm and stepped back from the bed. "Millie was his wife. I guess we'll have to rethink our engagement since you're already married."

She put a hand to her mouth to cover a laugh. From across the bed, Myrna said, "Listen, Will. Why don't you take Millie down for a cup of coffee? Maybe your mother would like a cookie too. We called the doctor and he'll be in to see Joe shortly."

Cameron gasped audibly. Myrna winked. Will smiled and took Cameron by her elbow toward the door.

"Yes, that sounds nice. Let's go, Ma," he said.

Cameron's mouth dropped open.

"But I—"

Will guided Cameron through the door and let it close behind them.

"I can't believe you are going along with this whole Millie thing," Cameron said as she and Will walked into the small hospital cafeteria. The overhead lights were off, and the room was lit by just the sickly glow of an assortment of vending machines and the hanging lights over the food service area, lined with clean scrubbed stainless steel warming pans. A stack of colorful melamine trays sat at the start of the line. Will drummed his fingers across the top one, in 1960s pink.

"Hey, you ever take these out sledding in the winter where you came from?" he asked, an impish grin on his face.

"We weren't allowed to take them out at my school," Cameron said, still annoyed.

"Yeah, I never did," Will said quickly. "I knew some people though." He scanned the machines and reached into his pocket. "Coffee? It'll be terrible, but maybe you'd have some?"

Cameron walked over to the line of machines. "Good heavens. This is a hospital. How can they feed people this garbage? Flaming Hot Triple Spice Tortilla Chipsters, Double Cheese Dipped Cheezy Balls, Super Frosted Sugar Dipped Toaster Pops, White Chocolate Covered Gummy Bears? Do they have a conveyor from these machines straight to the ER? I wonder if they dispense cigarettes somewhere here too."

Will put his hand to his shirt pocket and found it was empty. "Shoot. Did you want one? I can run out to the truck."

Cameron turned to face Will. Her look was in keeping with the cold stainless steel in which he now found himself enclosed. "You're kidding, right?"

"Right. I would imagine I'm kidding. That's exactly what I am doing."

"You're going to let those go one of these days, I hope."

He felt the chill of the last time he was asked not to smoke. He turned in a circle scanning the room. "Coffee. Weren't we looking for coffee?"

Cameron wiped her hands on her joggers and stepped away from the vending machine. "Yes. Coffee. And yes, it's going to be terrible." She pointed to the last vending machine. "Over there."

Will rubbed two quarters between his index and thumb

and jingled two more in his pocket. "But look. It's gourmet." The machine boasted fresh brewed coffee drinks featuring Tommy's House Blend, a mellow cinnamon roast and a dark New Orleans roast, all of which could be whipped into a frothy cappuccino in a paper cup right before your eyes.

"How can they claim to be mixing a fresh brewed cappuccino with instant coffee granules and powdered milk? Nobody believes there's a tiny barista trapped in that machine running on a caffeinated hamster wheel. Do they make the executives at these companies actually drink this swill?"

"Does *who* make them? There's a reason they're called the company executives, Cameron."

"I think I might just like a glass of water." She walked away toward a fountain in the corner.

"I want to watch the machine whip my coffee." Will grinned and pushed his quarters into the coin slot and pushed the backlit square buttons for New Orleans Roast, Extra Dark, Whipped Milk.

As the cup dropped into the compartment he thought of his trips to the airport to pick up his father after his monthly business trips. Before the 9-11 attacks, parties could meet arrivals at the gate and he and Molly became familiar with the concourses at O'Hare, running up and down the wide corridors on plush carpet patterned with brightly-colored geometric shapes in the greens, golds and oranges of the 1970s. Molly took the left side and Will took the right, sticking his fingers into the coin return of a hundred pay phones, usually making at least a couple of dimes a night that would net him a packet of Hot Tamales at the corner Tom Thumb superette the next day. One night as they hopscotched over the colored squares on their way back to the gate, he pushed the Coke button on a soda machine and felt the small lurch of the dispenser activating. A cup dropped into place and the fizzy brown sugar syrup flushed out on top of a deposit of crushed ice. Will stood frozen in place and Molly clapped her hand over her mouth. They looked at each other, turned and ran for their lives back to the gate, abandoning the ice cold Coke in the machine to a traveler with more courage to claim the spoils.

"Why didn't you take the Coke," his mother asked, looking up from *Better Homes and Gardens*, amused at their hasty return to the black vinyl seats in the waiting area of Gate E107.

"We didn't pay for it!" Will had exclaimed, certain he would have been arrested and charged with petty theft had he made off with someone else's drink. If only they'd pressed the coin return instead, they'd have been 25 cents richer and far less out of breath. Will dared to press a drink button on every soda machine he saw for the next seven years, seeking to redeem his cowardice, never seeing another drink drop for free from the cosmic testing center he often credited with so many of his unexplained circumstances.

Will pulled his cup from the coffee machine and held it under his nose. He shrugged and motioned to a table in the corner off the end of the serving area that was reasonably well lit. Cameron lifted her water glass to her lips and walked ahead of him. He slid a chair out from under the table for her and sat down on the opposite side.

"Nobody believes you're old enough to be Joe's wife, Cameron. But who's going to argue with an old man who just regained consciousness?"

"You were ready to argue about not being his son."

"Well, yeah. But that was different. And I got over it as soon as he woke up."

"You mean as soon as he woke up and took the attention off his good-for-nothing son and put it on his old lady? Is that what you mean by as soon as he woke up?"

Will took a sip of his coffee and winced hard, trying not to spit it out.

Cameron laughed. "It's as bad as I thought, yes?"

He swallowed and grabbed Cameron's glass, gulping down half her water.

"No, no. Not at all," he said, wiping his mouth. "Much worse."

Cameron picked up the coffee cup and sniffed it, turning away quickly. "I'm not kidding. This hospital is in the business of patient creation."

Will chuckled and pushed out his chair. "Let me get you another cup of water."

"Yes, please. Backwash, you know?"

Will smiled. "I know."

Cameron looked up at Will as he came back with the water. "So really, when are you going to quit?"

"What?" he asked, sitting down.

"Smoking. When are you going to quit for real?"

"I can quit whenever I want," Will said, taking a long drink from the ribbed plastic cafeteria cup.

Cameron burst out laughing. "Can you, now."

Will smiled. "Of course I can't. Otherwise I would have already. I've cut back, over time. Used to smoke a helluva lot more, but then I had reason to. But it's kind of like the last five pounds people can't ever quite lose. I have my five cigarettes a day I can't quite break myself of."

"What's that about?" Cameron wrapped her hands around her cup, rubbing her thumb along the nicked plastic rim. "What's the hurdle?"

"Equal parts nicotine and Barbara, I imagine."

"Barbara? The Barbara that doesn't matter anymore?" Cameron's brow wrinkled.

"Mr. Phillips?" The young nurse stuck his head in the cafeteria door. "Mr. Murphy is asking if you're still here."

"It's Mark, right?" Will asked. "Remind me to commend you to your boss for an impeccable sense of timing."

Will smiled at Cameron and stood. He swung a hand toward the door. "Well, Millie. We should go see how Dad's doing."

"You're terrible," Cameron said, pushing on her chair. "I'll see about having him ground you."

Will and Cameron walked into the hall outside the cafeteria. The nurse was already out of sight.

"Damn," Will said. "Do you remember how we got here?"

"Some day I'll teach you to read the sun and shadows and moss on trees. For now, just go left."

"Umm. Those things are unhelpful in the middle of the night and indoors."

"Sure, but then we can always read the actual signs." Cameron pointed across the hall to a sign that said "ROOMS 200-298" with a right arrow and "ROOMS 300-398" with an arrow to the left.

Will looked at the back of his hands, then put them in his pockets and walked to the left, Cameron snickering behind him.

When they reached Joe's room, Will walked in and smiled to see Joe propped upright on his bed, a tray in front of him with a cup of juice.

"Hey, Pop," he said. "You look like hell."

Cameron punched him in the arm.

"Will!" Joe said, and smiled weakly. "Oh, and look. You brought Cameron. Your Mrs. Jenkins will be quite pleased to see the two of you still getting along."

Cameron slipped past Will and leaned over the rail to kiss Joe softly on the cheek.

"You gave us a quite a scare. But you're looking better already."

"Say, Cameron," Joe whispered. "Did you see my wife here earlier? She's quite a looker. Gotta watch out for Will here. I think he has a little something for her." He winked at Cameron.

"You," she said, and smirked.

Joe dozed off after nibbling on a slice of white toast with peach jelly and a few sips of his apple juice. After some assurances from Myrna that they would take good care of him for the night, and not feed him anything from the vending machines, Will and Cameron left the hospital at 3:00 and drove home.

Cameron leaned her head against the window glass and slept most of the way. Will turned the radio on low and listened to classic 70s rock, the rhythm he tapped out on the steering wheel always a beat or two off. He fought the urge to dig in the glove box for a cigarette.

33

Will had no sooner laid back on his pillow, shirt unbuttoned and belt unbuckled but otherwise fully dressed when his wakeup alarm sounded on his phone. Joe or no Joe, Will needed to get to the office and work on the Schmidt fire. Nina needed a place for her kids and at least for now that meant getting a place for Justin to come home and bed her. *It's just another kind of work*, Will reasoned; not the kind of job Nina trained for but the job she had, all the same. She surely knew it and this was, she saw, her best hope for caring for her children and making sure they were fed and clothed. But if Justin could get what he wanted without needing to come home, then he didn't need to put his house back up and Nina would have nowhere to go.

This was why, among other reasons, he avoided coffee at the café with Mad Dog, Stu and Charlie. They rolled dice for the coffee buy and analyzed people's lives like they were no more than that, not real people. The few times Will tried to stand up to them about people like Nina he was derided as a hippie liberal who wanted nothing but to throw other people's money at a problem.

Which was true, Will knew. To throw money after a problem doesn't often solve it, at least not without creating new ones, but throwing dice and not throwing money doesn't exactly do much either.

Even Robin's Maid Marian wept, at least according to Keats: the wild bees weren't singing to her for "honey can't be got without hard money."

Will dropped his toothbrush into the cup and stared at

himself in the mirror. A half-moon of toothpaste foam sat at the corner of his mouth. His eyes were shot red. He bent over the sink and filled his hands with cold water, splashing his face again and again and finally held it in the stiff terry of a towel that had been hanging on the rack a few days too many.

Coffee. That much he knew he needed. But Charlie and Stu would have no time for Keats and Robin Hood this morning. After he showered and dressed and ran his fingers through his damp hair without looking in the mirror again, he drove to the Coffee Bean on Main Street. He rarely went into the little coffee shop unless he needed neutral public space to meet with a claimant. He felt uncomfortable about coffee shop coffee and besides, it was one of those places where the baristas tried to force a familiarity that did not exist in fact and just created needless awkwardness Will rarely had time for.

He pulled open the heavy glass door and was instantly reminded that, more than a coffee shop, the Coffee Bean was an experiment in sensory overload, as voices of customers talking and laughing mixed with the eclectic Indie stylings of the Staff Picks weekly playlist to form virtual bricks in an acoustic wall held together by the mortar of the espresso machine's roar over clanging cups. The oily scent of roasted coffee beans piled in burlap sacks was oddly soothing while at the same time overwhelming.

"Good morning!" The smiling girl at the register crooned. Her blonde hair was shaved on the right, and straight bangs fading from a cherry red to black fell across her left eye under her official red Coffee Beanie, complete with propeller. A fine gold ring rested obediently under her nose, bobbing up and down when she spoke, in rhythm with her plump lips, painted a smooth purple.

You know where you live, right? Will wanted to ask her. But he refrained. He stood with his hands in his pockets, looking up to scan the three enormous chalkboards suspended over the happy girl's head, straining to read the names of drinks he'd never heard of in the dim light of the currant painted walls and heavy mahogany furniture.

"What can I get started for you? The usual?" she asked.

"The usual?" Will was still scanning the boards for a regular coffee.

"Yeah. You know, like you usually order."

Will hadn't been in the Coffee Bean more than two or three times in the three years since the owner had purchased the old Exchange building and refurbished it for upscale boutique shops. Somehow the coffee shop met a need and survived while the parade of gift shops and apothecaries that had occupied the adjacent space marched on as casualty after casualty of the rural economy.

"The usual. Um, sure. Why not," Will said.

The rainbow-haired girl tapped a couple of keys on her register . "Okay! That's a triple low fat soy macchiato, right?"

"Um, no. I was thinking just coffee. You have that here, right?"

The barista let out a laugh that reverberated off all the metal of the place and stopped as abruptly as it started. "Of course we have coffee."

"Alright then. Coffee. Black. As tall as you have."

"Sure!" She turned to a coworker. "One enorme café ordinario, blanco, two percent!" She shouted, though he stood within arm's reach and had observed the entire conversation.

"No, not blanco. Black. No milk," Will said.

"Oh, right! I always forget you take yours black!"

"No problem." Will pulled his wallet from his back pocket.

The barista took a paper cup from the top of the stack and opened a Sharpie marker. "What's your name again?"

"Will."

"Sorry, your name?"

"Will."

"Oh, okay! Spell that?"

"Will. $W - I - L - L$."

"Oh, right!" She scrawled across the back of the cup and handed it to her coworker at the prep station.

Will paid for his coffee and hesitated before he dropped two quarters into the tip jar decorated with green tulle and ribbon and small, bright-colored foam flower stickers. "TIPS NOT EXPECTED—BUT APPRECIATED" read the yellow index card with bent corners taped to the jar and accentuated with a smiley face complete with dimples and a small tongue. These were the burdens of expectations Will could never remove from his shoulders, those that masqueraded as appreciation, but appreciation that as soon turned to resentment when such non-expectations failed to be met.

He turned from the counter and stepped back to peruse the postings held to a slate framed corkboard with small, gold-headed thumbtacks and advertising everything from farm equipment auctions and the Knights of Columbus pancake supper to a cooking class at the courthouse and a used stationary bike for sale. Handcrafted wreaths made from recycled red plastic drink cups were clearly less popular than six-week-old kittens, judging by only two tear-off phone number strips left on the photo of adorable calicos next to the intact page for the wreaths for sale.

"Enorme café ordinario for Walt!"

Will continued reading.

"Walt! We have your café ordinario!"

He wondered if there was a place that gave them permission to make up the names of coffee drinks as though they meant something real.

"Hey Walt!" Will turned to look for the missing customer and caught the barista's eye. She was standing at the counter staring at him, tall paper cup in hand. "I've got your coffee here. Have a great day!" She set the cup down and walked away.

Will glanced left and right and saw no other customers waiting. He felt his hands ball into fists and he looked at his boots. He glanced back up and forced a smile. "Thanks," he said, and walked to pick up his coffee. He pushed the door open with his hip, opening the top of the cup as he did so, only to see steam rising off a light brown foam. He stopped and looked back inside where the Coffee Bean staff stood alongside the espresso machine, their beanie propellers spinning along with their animated conversation. He kicked the door the rest of the way open with his boot and walked out, pressing the cap back on. Inside his cab he slipped the cup into the holder in his center console and saw the name "Walt" written in thick, loopy black letters across the top.

You got the usual, Phillips. Just like you ordered.

34

Will set his coffee cup on the desk and let the strap of his brown leather satchel slip off his shoulder, catching it at his elbow. He slumped into his chair, bag lying across his lap, and let his head rest against the chair back.

He couldn't remember a single day in his career in which he had not felt eager to work. Work filled Will. It grounded him, rooted him to his place in the world unlike anything else could. But today was beginning to look like that day.

Nina needed a place to live. Pearl needed company. Joe needed a family. Cameron . . . Cameron didn't seem to need anything, which seemed unfortunate. And Mad Dog—

A green tennis ball skimmed across Will's desk and he jumped as it bounced off the wall behind his chair.

Mad Dog.

Mad Dog needed child care.

"What the hell, Mike?"

Mad Dog whistled the Rolling Stones' "You Can't Always Get What You Want," the song he always said should be the claim adjuster's official theme song, as he went into his office across the hall. "Morning, Willie!" he called, then went on whistling.

"Good to know I can count on you, at least," Will said, picking up the ball and squeezing it in and out in his left palm. "What are you working on today, Mike?"

"Gotta finish up that pipe burst at the Fitz place. What a freakin' mess. Have to drive up and meet the contractor this morning. Don't know why. Half the thing won't be covered anyway."

Will plugged his laptop into the docking station on his desk. The Windows startup song from Mad Dog's computer sounded the mournful end of a peaceful hour.

The chorus from Will's machine chimed in a few bars later. He pulled Nina's file from his bag and stared at the pages thinking about all the ways his work, even if performed impeccably, would always come up short. Nina needed what he could never write enough insurance checks to provide, and as long as she stayed with a guy like Justin, she'd never have the chance to find. He'd seen it happen before. The woman worked day after day trying to get the house rebuilt, too exhausted from juggling kids and fixing meals in a residence hotel, fighting contractors and insurance companies, she'd have nothing for her man on the few occasions when he did come looking for a little ass, so he'd find a little somewhere else. Oh, he'd keep her around long enough to get things put back together and just when she'd let out a sigh of relief that the house was ready and they could all go back home, he'd tell her he'd pay for the hotel a few more days but then she was on her own, that his new girl would be moving into the house with him.

He could see it coming with Nina. But there was no way to warn her. And maybe no need. Deep down, Will knew that she knew this, that it was just the transactional life she lived, and thanks to the fire she'd managed to purchase a few more months with Justin, which wasn't so much a life with Justin as much as a place to live and food on the table for the kids. She would already know this and before long would begin to notice the single guy working for the contractor and would make sure Lucy Mae felt comfortable around him. Nina was a smart woman, savvy, resourceful, fierce about her kids. She would do fine, Will told himself, as he reviewed the emergency living expense provisions in the policy for the twelfth time, making sure he'd found all the possible allowances for her.

Not that it matters. He hit the Save to Upload button on his report. *Claim checks make terrible bandages for flesh wounds.*

He leaned back in his chair and put his feet on the desk as the report left his screen to embark on its instantaneous journey through cyberspace to the insurance company rep's desktop 726 miles away. He picked up the tennis ball and tossed it toward the suspended ceiling panels, trying to hit an old water stain directly above his head. He pondered his next project for the day.

Instinctively, he picked up his phone. It rang a second later.

"Phillips," he answered as he tapped the green phone icon.

He sat up. "You're releasing him today? Isn't that a little soon?"

Will switched the phone to his other ear. "Well, yeah, sure. Medicare. But still."

He paused. "But he can't take care of himself. He lives alone for crying out loud."

Will's face reddened and he stood up from his chair. "Look. I don't care what his paperwork says. I barely know the man. I am not his legal guardian."

Fists clenched, Will listened a while longer, mumbled "Very well," and hung up.

He walked to his office door, closed it softly and let his forehead fall against it, standing still for several minutes. Mad

Dog was still whistling in his office.

Will finally turned, facing into his office, leaning his shoulders on the door. With a heavy sigh, he dialed Pearl's number.

"Oh, good, you're home. Mind if I stop by for a minute? I have a big favor to ask of you."

The phone call would give Pearl a few minutes to imagine the most outlandish thing Will might ask her to do, which would in turn make the favor he would in fact ask seem small, even trivial in comparison.

When he got to the house, he tapped lightly on the screen door and stepped into the back entry without waiting for her to answer. "Pearl?" he called into the kitchen, peering around the corner.

Pearl was at the sink, drying her hands on a colorful towel. "What's your big favor? If you need to be late on your rent again—"

"No, no. My rent will be on time," Will said. "And I've never been late a single month, by the way." He pointed at the table. "Listen, can we sit a minute?"

"You look very serious, Mr. Phillips. Yes, let's sit."

Will pulled a chair for Pearl and sat across the table from her. "You remember my friend Joe?"

"Do I remember? I'm old, Mr. Phillips, but I can remember a man you brought to dinner three nights ago."

"Great. Well, he's doing alright now—"

"Were we worried he wasn't doing well after dinner? If there's anyone we should have been worried about after that fiasco I think it would be me—"

"No, no. Dinner was fine. Of course. Listen, he had a slight heart attack—"

"Oh dear. Is he—"

"He's okay, like I said. His neighbor Midge found him. Spent the night in the hospital. "

"That Midge sure seems to keep an eye on him," Pearl said. "I think she's a little sweet on him."

Will opened his mouth to answer and closed it, tipping his head slightly. "Um, okay. Anyway. Cameron and I were at the hospital with him most of the night. Now they want to release him."

"That's wonderful he's doing so well so quickly."

"Sure. Wonderful," Will said, rubbing the back of his neck. "They're releasing him to me. He needs home care. He can't stay alone."

"Releasing him to you?" Pearl's eyebrows nearly reached her silver hairline. "Why on earth would they release him to you? You barely know him. And you couldn't take care of a goldfish. I'm sure Midge will be sore."

"It's a long story."

"You'll tell it to me? I do love your stories."

"Yeah, I'll tell you. You'll especially love this one. Could think of it as payback for the dinner guest stunt."

"Payback stories. Better yet."

"The best. Anyway. About the favor. Can I bring Joe here?"

"Here? To my house? Why in the world would you think to bring him here?"

"Well, I can't move up there. I have a business to run. You have plenty of rooms upstairs. I thought if I could bring him here, well, you could kind of keep an eye on him during the day."

Pearl pushed her chair back slightly. "You would like me to keep an eye on your new friend all day while you go to work?"

"It would only be a couple of days, Pearl. Until he gets his legs back under him. He's a good guy. You enjoyed his company. You could reminisce about all those summers you didn't know you were together."

"It isn't enough that you get yourself into these predicaments, but you have to drag me into them as well."

"Gosh, Pearl. You make it sound like I do this all the time."

"Remember those chickens you 'rescued' from the side of the road and I had to babysit while you tried to find a farm to take them?"

"Comparing a grown man to chicken-sitting?" Will asked with his impish grin. "I'm surprised at you."

"And how about the time you volunteered to bring sandwiches for the Rotary Club fundraiser and then had to leave town all of a sudden because of some cyclone somewhere and I had to make fifty sandwiches in two hours?"

"We don't have cyclones around here, Pearl. It was a flash flood and a very nice family whose house washed out. I had to go."

"Cyclone. Flash flood. Same difference."

"And I didn't even ask you. You volunteered. And you had two days notice but made the sandwiches all in two hours because you are just that good."

"Why thank you, Mr. Phillips." Pearl smiled and sipped from her teacup. "But flattery won't help you this time. After that stray kitten, I am immune to your emergencies. I will not be conscripted into your old man project."

"Can you promise not to tell anyone these stories? I have a reputation, you know," Will said.

"Of course I would never tell them. I have my own reputation to take care of."

"Good. Let's seal that pact with this one last favor," Will smiled, putting out his hand. "For Joe's sake."

Pearl held her teacup to her lips and stared at Will over the top.

"Fine." Pearl set her cup back on the saucer, nudging it into the saucer's depression with the bend of her middle finger. Arthritis had extracted a high price from Pearl's hands, wide knuckles loudly punctuating otherwise slender, delicate hands. Will wondered how long since the fingers of a tender lover had laced between hers and when her skin, despite its loosening and translucent thinning had been touched beyond the requisite poking and palpating of the physician or the accidental brushing up against of the embarrassed sixteen-year-old bag boy at the grocery. To live in measure with one's age must surely not mean one day out of nowhere casting off its innate desire for the feel of another's skin.

"It's settled, then." Will returned Pearl's steely glare with his boyish smile and squeezed her hand gently. "I'll get his room ready."

Pearl didn't move. It was possible she hadn't blinked in a full three minutes.

"It'll be fun. You'll see."

From Pearl, nothing.

Will pushed back his chair and stood. He smoothed the front of his jeans and slid his hands into his pockets.

"Okay then. I'll be going, I guess."

He headed toward the stairway and reached for the door knob.

"Go up the front stairs, Mr. Phillips. You'll need fresh sheets for the bed from the closet in the hall."

Pivoting on one foot, Will leaned over and gave the still motionless Pearl Jenkins a light kiss on the cheek and called out a quick "Thank you!" as he hurried through the butler's pantry toward the front of the house.

Pearl had enough sets of sheets, crisply folded and neatly stacked in the hall closet, to supply an army barracks. Dishes clanked together in the kitchen and the sound of Pearl's whistling carried through the dining room into the hall.

"Damn, she's good," Will said as he clicked the closet door closed, faded green linens tucked under his arm.

She'd done it, that Pearl. By making him fight to bring Joe home and letting him think he'd beat her in the game, Pearl made him unwittingly eager to take on this challenge and care for his guest.

So damn good.

35

Upstairs, Will felt along the top of the cherry door frame of the adjacent bedroom for a slender skeleton key and played it into the lock. The antique crystal knob turned easily and the door creaked open.

Sunlight poured in through the bay window, laying softly across the furnishings, which were covered in white sheets. The doors, windows and wainscot paneling were finished with a light birds-eye maple. A brass chandelier hung from the ceiling, which was covered in embossed tin painted a faded rose. The plush burgundy carpet showed little sign of wear. The room was exquisite, with fine art hanging on the walls and an antique phonograph in the corner.

Arms folded across his chest, Will stood in the doorway and took in the richness, only once glancing toward his own room which now felt like the Addams Family in black and white on an old console television with rabbit ears antennae next to an Imax 3-D movie tour of Buckingham Palace.

"Pearl?" he called, without realizing he'd meant to speak.

"Yes, Mr. Phillips?"

Pearl's voice was soft, and Will could have sworn it came from just behind him, not from the kitchen where he'd left Pearl sipping self-satisfaction from her teacup. Her voice didn't even sound like it came from the base of the stairs, the closest Pearl had come to Will's second floor existence in a couple of years.

"Pearl?" Will said again, this time realizing it. He didn't move.

"What is it?" Pearl asked, still softly.

Will turned around slowly. Pearl stood on the landing, holding the railing while red and blue and green light circles from the stained glass surrounded her tan orthopedic shoes laced up over compression hose.

"Holy hell, Pearl—"

"Language, Mr. Phillips." Pearl smiled.

"I think I'm entitled."

"I think you're not. Do you have a chair for a lady?"

Will threw the sheets into the room toward the bed.

"Yes, I do. Hang on." He darted into his room, then put his head back into the doorway. "Don't go anywhere."

"Nowhere to go."

"Do I need to get two rooms ready so you can stay up here now?" He came out carrying a small wooden side chair. "Or were you thinking I would carry you back down the stairs when you're done checking my hospital corners on Joe's bed?"

Pearl held Will's arm as she sat down. "I think I surprised us both, Mr. Phillips. I just have to take my time."

Will leaned against the cast-iron radiator on the landing outside his room.

"So. What are you doing up here?"

"I wanted to make sure the room was okay."

"You don't think I could handle that?"

Pearl looked towards Will's room. "Well, it's not that…"

Will chuckled. "Alright. Point taken. In my defense, I don't have a lot to work with in there."

Her eyes went to the floor, then up to the room Will had opened. Pushing against the chair, she raised herself to her feet. Will stepped quickly and offered an arm, letting Pearl lead them into the vacant bedroom.

She stood silent just inside the door a moment, then lifted the cloth from the dresser, rubbing her palm over the smooth top. She pushed the fabric further back and traced her index finger along the shape of a heart carved into the wood, the letters *P.B.* and *D.J.* on either side. She tugged at Will's arm and pointed at the blemish of teenage romance. "I caught heck from my daddy for that one."

Will whistled low and shook his head. "Look at that, will you. He took you out behind the woodshed for it, so to speak?"

"No, he didn't lay a finger on me. Didn't even raise his voice. Daddy took me to the mill and showed me slices of trees. He taught me how to count the dark rings to figure the age, and then he showed me how the rings tell the tree's story —how you could tell if there had been a drought because the rings got thinner and closer together for a few years. And sometimes, if the rings were thicker on one side than the other, he called it *reaction wood*, when a tree would balance itself out if something was pushing on one side, growing thicker on the other side to support it."

Pearl pulled the dusty cloth toward herself to cover the carving back up. "He showed me a dark lesion between the rings of one and said, 'Look here. This is where the tree was wounded in a forest fire.' The tree grew back over the scar, but it was still there, part of the tree where nobody saw it." She patted the dresser with an open palm. "I told him the wood on the dresser was dead, that it would never grow back over the carving. 'That's right,' he said and drove me back home and told me to help my mother fix dinner."

She smiled. "I only went out with that damned Dickie Jacobs—"

"Language," Will said.

"I'm entitled. I only went out with him twice before he dumped me for that perky little Bridgette. I'm still stuck with him and his scars."

"So why haven't you ever refinished the dresser now that it's yours?"

"Mine?" Pearl looked up at Will. "Oh, no. It's not mine. It's still my daddy's. And my daddy taught long lessons."

She pointed at the sheets piled on the floor. "Let's get the bed made for your friend."

36

"Take a drive with me?"

Cameron fitted her Bluetooth into her ear. "Do we not say 'Hello, this is so-and-so' when we call anymore?"

"I'm not so-and-so. And we have caller ID. You knew it was me when you picked up."

"Try again," Cameron said, and tapped the red End button on her phone.

Will sat at one of the two stoplights in town staring at his phone in his palm.

Cameron Julian
0 minutes 17 seconds
Call ended

The screen went dark, leaving him with his mouth hanging open.

The light changed and Will didn't move. After a few moments a tap to his side window jarred him and he turned.

"Mind moving along, Phillips?" Rick Weigel stood at his window, laughing. "Light changed two minutes ago."

Will smiled and put up his hands apologetically, then pulled ahead. He'd never gotten used to this part of the small town way, how drivers only used their horns to say hello to a pedestrian or passing motorist, not to express anger or warnings or motivate another driver to action like on the streets of Chicago when honking was like breathing. He figured he'd lost days of his life to the cumulative minutes spent at an uncontrolled intersection, each driver waving the other on and nobody driving forward.

Rick Weigel was visible in the rearview mirror as he got back into his pickup as Will cleared the intersection. He tapped his phone to redial Cameron.

"Cameron Julian."

"May I speak to Cameron Julian, please?"

"Hi, Will. It's me."

"Ms. Julian, this is William Phillips speaking."

"I know. What's up?"

"I wonder if I might enjoy the pleasure of your company for a drive this evening."

"Enough now. Stop."

"As you wish."

"Go for a drive? Tell me you aren't wanting me to go look at crops with you."

"Crops? Of course not," Will said. "It's only May. There's not much to look at. But we can go out and do that some Sunday in July."

"Oh, great. I can't wait."

"Listen, go with me to pick up Joe? Pearl says he can stay with us."

"Wait. Pick him up? He's staying with you? What's going on?"

"Yeah, they want to release him but he has to be in my care. This next of kin stuff is total bullshit."

"You're moving him in with you and Pearl? She's okay with this?"

"She'll never say it out loud, but she loved the idea. Part of her mission to civilize me. And part of her little crush on Joe."

"So I'm supposed to spend another night at the hospital

with you and Joe? I'm exhausted, Will."

"Oh. Yeah. Of course you are. I just ... uh ... thought."
Will was silent. "Hey, never mind. I'm sorry. I'll go get him,
but maybe you'd stop over sometime while he's with us? I'm
sure he'll get a little bored with us and away from his house."

"I'm sorry, Will. I didn't mean—"

"No big deal, Cameron. This isn't your thing anyway.
I shouldn't be dragging you into it."

"Stop talking, would you? I wasn't saying I wouldn't go.
You just surprised me that he's getting out already and that
he's coming here."

"Yeah, I'm still a little surprised myself... at all of it."

"Pick me up in an hour?"

~

Cameron pulled her laptop from a sleek black leather bag lying
on the seat between her and Will. She waved the cord playfully
in the air. "Surely a claims guy has a truck equipped with AC
power?"

"Yep. But I'm old school. There's a power inverter in the
glove box."

"Pretty sure I don't even know what that is," Cameron
said, dropping open the lid. The Barbie head rolled onto its
side. "Oh, look who's still here."

Will reached in past Cameron's hand and pulled a small
yellow and black box with two power outlets from under the
manual. "Here you go. Just plug it into the lighter."

"Well, isn't that a fun little gadget. I'll bet you could power
a small refrigerator off that."

"Probably true. But I can't fit one in the glove box."

"Sorry about working. But I've got reports due to Corporate by the end of the week and I'm backed up."

"Not a problem. I'll try not to prove too big a distraction."

Cameron shifted in her seat, arranging the computer comfortably on her lap and tapped at the keys as they pulled onto the interstate. Will drove the now-familiar route to Colbyville in silence, only occasionally turning to the right for a glance at his companion, regretting his promise to let her work in peace.

It could be argued that Will didn't need anyone to accompany him to the hospital to retrieve Joe. More likely than not, Joe would tell a story or two about one of the nurses he took a shining to and then nod off to sleep the rest of the trip. But considering that no part of his relationship with Joe to date had gone according to expectations, he had no reason to think this part would either. Joe would have him following some billboard advertising to the historic straw bale museum or some such thing as they traveled home. And Joe's vast and eclectic interests and knowledge of things most people didn't realize even existed made the idea of transporting even an infirm and mildly-sedated Joe, without incident, seem somehow out of reach. It wasn't all Joe's fault, of course. Will seemed to lose his footing in the ordinary world of ordinary things and ordinary obligations in the face of Joe's extraordinary interests and, Will would admit, his charm.

But at the moment, Will also faced the extraordinary obligation of collecting and caring for Joe, and wisely sensed the need for fortification against the old man's otherwise easy disarmament. Cameron Julian could be just the sort of reinforcement—

"Hey, is that Joe?" Cameron jabbed Will's arm and pointed out her side of the windshield.

Will leaned over as though it would help him see more clearly through an already unobstructed, wide open sheet of glass, or maybe he meant to erase from view the image of a man, about Joe's age and size, stepping off the curb from the hospital parking lot into the street about a half block ahead.

"What the hell—"

"Pull up there, Will. And be careful."

"What the hell—"

"You already said that."

"What the hell—"

The man looked both ways before walking across the street, pulling along a tall silver wheeled pole with a bag of clear fluid hanging from it. When he reached the other side, he pivoted and began walking in the same direction as Will and Cameron were traveling.

"What the hell—" Cameron shielded her eyes as Joe turned his back to them, the sides of his hospital gown flowing widely and freely in the brisk South Dakota breeze.

"You see?" Will asked, pulling up to the curb opposite Joe and hastily putting the truck into park. "The right words for this are few."

He yanked off his seatbelt and threw open his door. "Hey, Joe," he called, as he jumped out of the truck. Cameron hurried out and met him coming around the front of the truck.

Joe turned around.

"Will! Look at you. And Cameron! Well." Joe smiled and clapped his hands together. "Imagine seeing the two of you here." He looked around, his eyes first sparkling, then graying over. "Of course, by 'here' I mean, umm, where exactly are we?"

The two moved gently, one to each side and guided Joe across the street toward the truck.

"Colbyville, Joe," said Will. "We're right here in Colbyville. You've had a little stay in the hospital."

Joe snapped his fingers. "Of course. That explains a lot." He shuffled along, his untied laces wrapping around each other between his feet.

"You left in a bit of a hurry, eh Joe?" Will asked, opening the passenger door.

"Funny, about that," Joe said, resting a hand on the side of the cab. "They said I could go home. So I started getting dressed. Couldn't get my shirt on over this contraption." He shook the IV line hanging out of his forearm. "And I never did find my pants. I don't know what they were thinking, but if I learned anything while I was in there, it's that you don't argue with the nurses. So when they said I was supposed to go home, I did my best. I got my shoes and socks on and off I went. Midge said if you don't show you can handle yourself independently, then they don't let you go home. They just trick you into sitting in a wheelchair like they're going to let us race in the hall and then they wheel you across the street." He pointed over his shoulder toward the old brick care center behind the hospital with his thumb. "Nobody gets out of there."

"You did great, Joe," Cameron said, holding the door.

"Yeah, you did," added Will. "But maybe we should go back and find your pants. I know from experience the lack of them is hard to explain to some people." He started to help Joe into the cab when the breeze caught the gown again, laying a fold across Will's arm and giving him a fresh and un-welcome view of the old man's backside. He pushed the fab-ric off his arm and glanced at his leather seat. "Hold on a sec there, buddy." He put a hand on Joe's arm. "Cameron, there's a blanket behind my seat. Can you grab it?"

Cameron jogged around the front of the truck and came back with it, then turned to look away from the men toward the street. Will spread it open on the seat, then helped Joe step up, folding the blanket over his lap. He patted him on the leg. "There you go. All snug."

He swung the door shut. The IV tubing, still running from Joe's arm to the bag, was now neatly pinched in the door. Cameron laughed and pointed to the IV stand.

"Well," Will said, and ran his hand through his hair. "Huh."

"Back to that are we, Mr. Man of Few Words?"

"It's all I've got."

He took the bag off the stand, opened the door, then threaded the bag and the tubing back out the open window to-wards the stand. Once the bag was safely hooked in place, he closed the door.

"Managed," he said, smiling. "Joe, think you can hold onto the pole out the window if I drive real slow?"

"I can sure try. Just don't try any of those fancy 4-wheel stunts.

Cameron stared at the men with her arms crossed. "Re-ally?"

Will was certain she rolled her eyes under the soft curl of her honey bangs.

"What? I can drive slow. It's just across the parking lot.

It's perfect."

"Right," Cameron said, walking to the door. She nudged Will out of the way with the back of her hand and lifted the IV bag off the stand hook, handing it in the window to Joe.

"Can you hold on to this?" she asked.

"Well, I do believe I can," he answered, setting the bag on his lap.

She picked up the pole, turned it on its side and laid it in the pickup bed. "Managed." Cameron looked sharply at Will, walked around the truck, got in and slid across the seat next to Joe. Will stood on the curb with his hands in his pockets.

"Sure. That's another way. It should work."

He slapped his hand on the hood twice as if to prove the truck were solid enough. "Okay then, let's go." He got back behind the wheel and drove to the hospital entrance. Cameron snapped her gum. Joe hummed quietly. Will did not speak.

"Wait here."

Will jumped out of the truck and jogged through the automatic double doors. Inside, he looked both directions down the wide hospital hallway. It was deserted. He spotted a wheelchair sitting idle outside a room and made a move for it. As the automatic doors dragged open again, he heard a voice behind him.

"Hey. You can't take that. I'm going to use it for Mr. Wicks."

He hesitated. His shoulders slacked and he turned, ready to bring back the wheelchair so nurse Myrna could take Elvin Wicks, a seeming full-time resident at the hospital, for better than a sponge bath.

Myrna stood in the hall scowling, hands on her hips and a large purple stain on the front of her floral scrubs that said she was in no mood for it today. In that moment Will decided he wasn't either. He faced her, wheelchair between them, fingers wrapped firmly around the handles. His annoyance and exhaustion collided with her patronizing defiance and he gripped the handles tighter.

"You can have the wheelchair and take Elvin for the bath he doesn't want any more than the one you gave him last week, or you can hold on a freaking minute and let me bring in the runaway patient none of you apparently even know is gone yet."

Myrna's hands fell, as did her face.

"That's what I thought." He spun on one foot and wheeled the chair out the door.

By the time he lined the chair up next to the cab, Cameron was already easing Joe out of his seat and Myrna was running down the walk.

"What in the world is going on here?"

"Oh, hello Myrna." Joe smiled up from his chair. "Seems we had a little misunderstanding. The kids here don't believe you sent me home."

Will draped the blanket across Joe's lap and Myrna got behind the chair and started pushing. "They're right, you old jackass." She leaned hard into the chair as she pushed it up the sidewalk ramp. "A guy as well-read as you surely ought to know the difference between 'You get to go home today' and 'Get the hell out of here.'"

She stopped to wait for the door and Will started to feel sorry for her. He put a hand on her shoulder. "Don't be too hard on him, Myrna. He's fine. No harm done."

"Will."

Cameron was still standing at the curb. "What?" he asked. "I'm a little busy right now."

"No, come here."

The doors opened and Myrna pushed Joe inside.

"Right now?" He threw up his hands.

"Yes."

Will shoved his hands in his pockets and walked toward Cameron, hoping she would notice the extra emphasis he added to each footfall.

"What is so important." He looked back at the doors as they closed behind Joe and his nurse. "I need to get inside."

"No, you don't." Cameron slipped a hand under her hair at the back of her neck and pulled it out of her jacket collar. "Let Joe and Myrna take care of things. We'll go in when they've settled down a little."

"But I'm —"

"No, you're not his son. You're a name he wrote on a form. You're not in charge of him."

"But he—" It occurred to Will that since meeting Cameron it was possible he'd started far more sentences than he'd finished.

"He doesn't need you right this second. He needs Myrna to get him back in his bed and for the doctor to make sure he's really ready to go."

Will's eyes narrowed. Was this how it was for every man? Were other men surrounded by women who were right? The Barbaras, who made themselves right because that's how they knew to get through the day. But the Pearls and Camerons too, who maybe didn't need to be right but found themselves that way all the same. Or was this just the story of a man like him, a man who as much as he wanted to be right didn't believe most days he actually was.

He started for the door. "I'm going in. You can stay out here and be all boundaried if you want."

"At least move your truck first. You're blocking the entrance."

How did she do that? He dropped his head and walked back to the truck. As he turned the key in the ignition, he looked out the window at Cameron, who was standing quietly on the sidewalk.

"Riding or waiting?"

She smiled, her head tilted slightly. "Waiting, I think."

He put the truck in drive and lurched forward, spraying a little gravel from behind the rear tires.

~

When Will came back up the sidewalk, his striped cap was pulled over his ears and the collar of his jacket turned up against the chill wind.

"Now can I go in?" he asked, not pausing as he passed Cameron.

"Don't be mad."

"I'm not." He waited to the side of the open doors for Cameron to walk through, then followed behind.

"Right."

They walked, together, without speaking, down the corridor to Joe's room.

Myrna folded back the blanket over Joe's chest as Will and Cameron walked into the stark hospital room.

"Wait," Will said, pointing at Joe. "Why is he back in bed? I thought you were cutting him loose."

"He cut himself loose." The monitor clicked into a hum and a row of lights flitted across the screen as she pressed a button on the side. "Actually," she said, jiggling the IV tube, "he didn't cut himself loose at all. He walked out with all his connections intact."

Joe beamed from the bed and folded his hands on his lap.

"Look at this. Three of my favorite people all in the same room. I should have a heart attack more often."

"Or you could just have a dinner party, Joe." Cameron stepped up to the edge of the bed and put a hand on Joe's arm. "Much less work. For everyone."

"Because you haven't seen Joe's house yet," Will muttered from just inside the door where he was still standing, leaned against the wall with hands balled in fists in his jacket pockets.

Cameron shot a glare at Will. "Anyway, Joe. We're glad we found you."

"Were you looking for me?"

"Well, not looking, exactly, no. But—"

"Listen, Myrna," Will cut in. "Are you guys still letting the man go or did you revoke his parole over the attempted jail-break?"

The nurse crossed her arms over her chest and narrowed her eyes at Will. "Doc wants a minute with him, but I imagine he's still on the street today. Medicare won't let us extend his stay since he was healthy enough to go for that walk."

"Disorientation doesn't count for anything these days?" Cameron asked, her eyes wide.

"For this guy? Nah. Just another day in the neighborhood." Myrna looked at Will. "Figured his son would know that."

She looked at Joe. "Stay put for five minutes, alright? I'll track down Dr. Wagner and see if we can't officially make you somebody else's problem." Myrna stopped at the door and looked at Will. "Go get a cup of coffee. I'll let you know when it's your turn."

In the cafeteria, Will handed Cameron a paper cup of bad coffee from the machine, feeling an unwelcome bit of déjà vu. "Thank you." She looked out the window and held the cup between her hands.

"I didn't know I was taking in a runaway." Will pulled out a chair.

"Maybe it's not like that. Maybe he is just one of those guys who only hears what he hears—they told him he was going home today, so he went home. Just super literal, you know?"

"Yeah, probably that." Will raised his cup to his lips, pretended to drink. Cameron could be right, if it weren't Joe she was talking about. Joe's nuance was masterful. Of all the possible explanations for his bizarre breakout from the hospital this morning, being too literal would not be one. Not for a man who could sense some of Will's deepest longings in a random reading of Archibald MacLeish.

"Look, once you get him home, you won't have to worry. Pearl will watch his every move. And she'll fill him with so much cherry pie he'll never leave anyway."

Will laughed, for the first time all day, and raised his cup toward Cameron. "Now on that, I'm quite sure you're right."

The two sat quietly looking out the window for the next

half hour, sometimes lifting their cups but never actually drinking; sometimes starting to speak and then saying nothing. Will felt strangely at ease beneath the silence. Cameron seemed tired, but otherwise content, which helped ease the nagging bit of guilt about insinuating her yet again into his misadventures with Joe Murphy.

"You kids ready to get your old man out of my hair for real this time?" Myrna stood in the doorway and tapped her watch with two fingers. "Let's go. I have other patients to bathe." She winked at Will.

"Be there in a minute." He pushed out his chair and reached for Cameron's cup. "Should we go do this?"

Cameron laughed. "Is that a real question? I think we are already doing it."

Doc Wagner was just coming out of Joe's room when Will and Cameron arrived. Will reached to shake his hand. "You're sure he's okay to go? This confusion isn't something we need to worry about?"

"He should be fine. Looks like he just got a little eager to get out of here." He opened the chart in his hand. "You can expect a little confusion going forward. He's had some trauma, coupled with medication and going to a strange place. So watch for that. But he's in no danger."

"Alright. Well, thanks for taking care of him."

"That's what we do. Now go take your dad home."

"But he's not—" Will stopped himself this time. "Yeah, okay. Thanks. I will."

Cameron pushed the door open and walked in, Will following behind.

"Okay Joe, let's try this again, alright?"

Will strode to the bed. "Let's get you dressed and out to the truck. Maybe we'll be home in time for Pearl to feed us dinner."

"Pearl? She's coming for dinner?" Joe's eyes brightened.

"Nope, better than that. You're coming for dinner. For a few dinners, actually. Doc wants you to stay with us for a little while until you get your feet back under you for good."

"Is that right." Joe yanked off the covers and sat up. "Sounds wonderful. Let's go."

"Whoa, slow down, my friend. You need clothes this time."

Cameron handed Will a stack of folded clothing. "I'll wait in the hall."

Will set the stack on the bed as Cameron left the room and turned to face the window with his back toward Joe. "Let me know if you need help."

"All set." Will turned back after a few minutes to find Joe dressed to the waist, shoes untied and his hairy round belly hanging over a unbuckled belt.

"You can get that, right?" Will pointed awkwardly to Joe's belt.

"Of course. But I was waiting for my shirt. Do you have it?"

Will knelt to tie Joe's shoes. "I don't. It wasn't in the stack?"

"Nope. No trace of it." Joe turned in a circle, arms spread out. "One of my favorite flannels, too. Gray with a warm fleece lining. Pretty sure the doc nipped it. I hear they do that in these places, pretend they had to cut it off in the ER, like they didn't learn how to work buttons in medical school."

"Umm, right." Will stood. "Or it might have been misplaced. You said you had it before you went out before." He opened the door into the hall and asked Cameron to check with the nurses.

"I'll be glad to get out of this place, though the innkeepers are certainly friendly enough. And they make the most exquisite Jell-O. Have you tried it?"

Will studied Joe, trying to decide if was playing him. "Haven't had the pleasure of hospital Jell-O since I was a boy getting my tonsils out."

"It's to die for." He grinned and buckled his belt as Cameron came in the room.

"Nobody's seen his shirt. They think he hid it to make them look bad."

Joe let out a hearty laugh, his loose flesh shaking. "They love me here."

"Will, maybe you could give Joe your shirt," Cameron said, looking away from Joe.

"Well… I… but I'm wearing my shirt." He stiffened.

"Handy. That way you don't have to go to the truck to get it. Take it off."

Will moved toward Cameron and spoke mostly between his teeth as though Joe wouldn't notice. "I don't know what's to be gained by having me go shirtless instead of Joe. He can throw on the gown. We have to pick up clothes at his house anyway."

"Oh, come on. You have a T-shirt under. Give the man your button-down and let's get out of here."

"It's a short drive to my house," Joe said. "I'm fine, really. And I think Myrna would enjoy getting one last look at this carnal wonder." Joe posed in a faux flex, curling a fist up near his forehead and pivoting on one foot.

"Joe!" Cameron laughed. She looked at Will, a look he had no answer for but to go quietly to the corner of the room and slip off his tan canvas jacket. He folded it in half and laid it neatly over the arm of the chair.

He heard Cameron and Joe talking by the bed, Cameron writing down a list of things Joe needed to pick up at his house before his sleepover with Will and Pearl. Their voices faded into what sounded like a great rushing wind around his ears as he unbuttoned his red plaid. He felt cool perspiration on his neck even as goosebumps pricked the skin of his arms and legs. He slipped his right arm out of the long sleeve, leaving it hang over half his upper body as he pulled his jacket over the exposed arm. Then he stood—shirt half on and half off under the jacket—unable to keep moving, to keep removing what he'd been asked to forfeit. The sound of rushing wind now seemed to come from both inside his mind and all around him in the room. He pleaded with himself. *Just be a man. Can't you just be a man? It's not so hard, is it, Will Phillips?*

He breathed deeply and looked up at the flecked ceiling tiles before he finally let the red plaid fall from his left arm to the floor, then he quickly twisted his arm behind to slip it into the waiting jacket sleeve, which became a cover for a webbed, dark rose pattern, almost fractal-like, that began about mid-forearm and crept up under his white T-shirt sleeve. Now the coolness gave over to a burning sensation that felt seated in memory as much as in this moment. He shrugged the jacket into place and bent to pick up the flannel shirt from the floor. When he turned back he saw Cameron's eyes fixed on him.

"Did you get that last one, young lady? I said we should be sure to get my toothbrush. The one they gave me here has hard bristles." Cameron turned to Joe. "What? Toothbrush? Got it." She scribbled on the notepad in her palm. Will's jaw tightened and he felt warmth in his cheeks as his faced flushed.

He yanked his cap from his jacket pocket and pulled it down over his ears, handing Cameron the shirt.

"I'll go get the truck. Meet me out front."

37

The cold wind struck Will's face like the flat side of a grain shovel as he stepped out of the double doors of the hospital. He staggered forward, hands in his pockets and shoulders hunched down into his jacket, noticing the absence of the soft shield of his shirt collar folded against his neck.

In his head, he cursed at Joe for not being able to keep track of his shirt in a clinically immaculate hospital room. He cursed at Cameron for thinking a shirt under his jacket mattered to an old man who would walk down the street pulling an IV pole while his resplendent white ass blared Blue Moon to the whole neighborhood. A full string of curse words about the nursing staff chased around inside his brain that he wanted to usher out into the gaping expanse of the parking lot but his jaw was clenched so tight he couldn't peel his lips apart.

The slam of the door shook the cab so hard the GPS fell off the dashboard onto the passenger floor. Will leaned over with a grunt, almost falling off the seat himself and picked it up. He wrapped the cord around it, his chilled fingers yanking each loop around with a snap. The cord was stiff from the cold and kept slipping off the corners until he let out an inarticulate yell, wadded the cord into a ball and crammed the jumbled mess into the glove box. He slapped it shut.

The door popped open.

He slammed it again, and then again. Each time, the door dropped open, the unhooked latch looking back at him with a gap-toothed grin.

"Damn you, Barbara."

He said it softly, almost kindly, then turned in his seat, planting his back against the door and kicked at the glove box with his foot, ramming it into place.

It held for a moment, then fell open.

Will pulled up his knee and planted his boot into the glove box door one last time. A skid mark went across the front from his black rubber sole. He heard plastic snap and the door dropped open and crashed to the floor, the GPS and tangled cords on top of it.

He looked at the mess and kicked at it, pounding his fists on the steering wheel.

"Damn you, Barbara!" He was crying now. "Damn you." Will leaned his head against the backrest with his eyes closed and slid down in the seat. A tear moved slowly over his cheekbone and dropped onto his jacket.

"Damn. You." He rubbed his arms.

His phone buzzed in his pocket. He pulled it out and slammed it against the dashboard once for each buzz until it stopped, then tossed it onto the seat beside him and rested his head on the wheel.

The phone buzzed again. He left it laying on the seat and didn't move.

When it rang a third time, he picked it up and pressed Answer without looking.

"Damn you, Barbara," he said into it, then dropped it between his feet. A woman's voice was speaking from the floor. "Will? Will, where are you?"

He kicked the phone under his seat and remained hunched over the steering wheel.

The voice stopped and a few minutes later there was a

tapping at the window. He didn't move.

The tapping went away, but then the passenger door opened.

"Will?" Cameron's voice was quiet, but mildly anxious. At the least, uncertain.

He lifted himself from the steering wheel slightly and faced her, feeling as foolish as he'd ever felt with her.

"I'm ah—just—I was going to pick up guys up."

"I know. Joe's at the door. Waiting. You didn't come and you didn't answer your phone." Cameron picked up the glove box cover and climbed onto the seat. "You okay? Something happen out here?"

"I'm fine. Had a little problem getting the GPS put away, is all. And I must have lost my phone."

Cameron picked up the GPS and wrapped the cord snugly around it, then set it back inside the compartment before she eased the door back onto its hinges and pressed it shut. It wouldn't latch.

"See? Damn thing's broken," Will said.

She reached up to the topside of the latch and the Barbie head dropped into her palm, a gash in the back of her head where the catch had been jammed in. "That explains a lot." She smoothed the doll's hair over the wound with her thumb.

Will held out his hand and Cameron set the doll head into it. He brushed hair out of her eyes with his index finger, opened the the glove box and dropped her gently back inside.

"Sorry," Will said, as much to the doll as to Cameron.

She patted his knee lightly and put her hands in her pockets. "Let's go get Joe before he comes looking."

The hospital's big double doors pulled apart to reveal

Myrna standing behind Joe in his wheelchair in theatrical fashion, as though opening on a scene from a medical drama. Joe tried to stand, only to have Myrna quietly clamp a firm hand onto his shoulder. He slumped in his chair under her grip as though she had been trained by Mr. Spock while Cameron hopped out of the cab. Will leaned over and dug around under his seat, reaching for his phone. Cameron put her head back in the truck.

"Can you go grab Joe's bag?"

Will looked blankly out the window. "Joe doesn't have a bag. His visit wasn't exactly planned. That's why he doesn't have a shirt, remember?" He wiped off the screen of his phone with the side of his fist.

Cameron shifted her feet and looked at the seat, then back at Will.

"Look, whatever this is"—she made a spiraling gesture toward Will with her hand—"I'm sorry. But we need to get Joe loaded up. Come out and help."

Will set his phone on the dash and got out, without looking at Cameron. As he came around the front of the truck, he stuck his hands in his pockets, straightened his shoulders and smiled.

"They're really cutting you loose, eh?" he said as he took the wheelchair from Myrna's place behind and pushed Joe toward his pickup. Cameron stepped aside and held out a hand to Joe as he got up from the chair and climbed into the passenger seat. She laid a blanket over his lap and closed the door.

"Thank you," she said to Will, walking past him. She slid across the driver's seat next to Joe.

"Can I get my chair back, Mr. Phillips?" Myrna stood in

front of the entrance, arms crossed. Will wheeled the chair back up the easy slope of the sidewalk.

"Here you go. Thanks for taking care of him."

"Tell him to stay away for a while now. We don't like when people keep coming around."

Will smiled from one side of his mouth. "I'll tell him."

He climbed into the cab next to Cameron, who was pushing buttons on the radio.

"Joe is talking about Rebroff again. Says maybe Public Radio might be playing him."

"Right at this moment? Because they only play Rebroff? Then that would be called Rebroff Radio. We don't have that station here."

Cameron adjusted her jacket and managed to throw an elbow into Will's side.

"Oh, gosh. I'm so sorry," she said, turning to scowl at him.

Will moved away, putting more space between him and Cameron. "No, no. My fault." Pushing a button on the radio, he said, "Here, this is Public Radio. But I think it'll just be news this time of day, no Russian opera."

Cameron turned the radio off and they rode in silence to Joe's house. When they pulled up, Archie ran over to the side of the truck. Midge, Joe's neighbor, was just coming out the front door and called for him to come back.

"Oh, no. Joe, I totally forgot about Archie and the cats. I'm so sorry."

"Not to worry. Midge stopped up to see me at the hospital and said she would check in on them and feed them. She and Archie are good friends."

Will got out and jogged around to open Joe's door. Joe was halfway out before he got there.

"Easy there, Joe," Cameron said with a hand on his back. "You've not been on your feet much the last few days."

"Nonsense. Nothing like being home and petting one's dog to bring a fellow back to good health." He reached down to scratch Archie's ears. "They should have brought him up to my room. Would have cut my stay in half and saved Medicare wads of money."

Will laughed. "Might have, Joe. But if you'd cut your stay in half, you'd not have had a stay at all."

Cameron closed the cab door as she got out. "I don't mean to break up the party, Dog Lovers of America," she said. "But, umm. Pearl."

"What's that?" Joe looked up.

"Pearl," Cameron repeated. "She'll never stand for bringing Archie into her house."

"She's right, Joe." Will crouched to look Archie in the eye. "I'd forgotten the animals. I don't think Pearl will go for a menagerie."

"You don't think she can be persuaded?" Joe smiled. "Archie can be quite charming."

"I see that," Cameron said, putting her hands in her jacket pockets as Archie nuzzled at them. "But it might take some time. Do you think Midge could watch them a little longer?"

"She's a good sort. We could see. I would hate to over-step Pearl's hospitality." Joe started toward the house. "Hello, neighbor," he called to Midge.

"Joe!" Midge waved from the doorway. "It's so good to see you up and around." Pulling her housecoat closed around her, she opened the door for Joe. "Did you pick up hitchhikers on the way home?"

"No, I'm the hitchhiker, I'm afraid. Midge, meet Will Phillips and Cameron Julian, my makeshift family until the doctors are convinced I can take care of myself again."

"You kids moving in?" Midge asked, staying by the door with her hand on the knob.

"Oh, no. Your neighborhood is quite safe, Ma'am," Will chuckled. "Joe will be staying with me a few days until the doctor clears him to resume his wild bachelor living."

"I see." Midge shifted her weight onto one foot, eyeing Cameron. "You all live together?"

Cameron looked up, realizing Midge was addressing her. "No, no. Gosh, no. I'm along for the ride." She waved her hands in front of her. "Promise. Just the ride."

"Alright then." Midge closed the door and walked into the dining room.

Cameron stood in the entry, where the kneeler still partially blocked the way into the dining room. Will leaned in next to her and whispered under his breath. "It's okay. He's happy here. But you might like to keep your hands in your pockets."

"Emily seems a little less herself, Joe," Midge said. "Hasn't come out of your room since you left. And I'm not sure that she's eaten at all."

"Oh?" Joe started toward his bedroom. "Not a thing?"

"Nope. I even tried setting a basket of baked goods out for her by the window. I know she likes sweet people-food. Not a bite."

Joe slipped in and closed the bedroom door behind him.

"Umm, Midge," Will said, "I don't suppose you could

keep looking after Joe's pets a little a few more days, until he can come home? I don't think it will be much longer."

"Well, I don't mind it so much. Archie is a good companion. And Eliot is no trouble. But I'm afraid for Miss Emily. Don't want her dying on my watch."

"You don't think she could be sneaking food somewhere and you just didn't notice? I mean, you can't really know which of them is eating what, right?"

Midge glared at Will. "You can know if you care to know. She's not eating. Not leaving anything in the litter, either."

"Well, I guess that'd be another way to know," Cameron said.

Will tapped on the bedroom door. "You doing okay in there, Joe?"

Joe didn't answer. Will leaned his ear against the door and tapped again. "Joe?"

Cameron stepped over a pile of newspapers. "Is he okay? Maybe you should go in."

"I don't want to walk in on anything."

"Walk in on anything?" Cameron asked. "We just brought a sick man home from the hospital and he's alone in his room with a hyper-introverted cat. What are you going to walk in on?"

She nudged Will out of the way and opened the door. "Joe? Can we help you get your things?"

Will followed her into the room. "Joe?"

"This room. What in the world—" Cameron turned around in the immaculate room. The bed was made, a bright white duvet cover laid over it. An antique chair with wide-striped red and blue upholstery sat in the corner. Joe's shirts and pants hung neatly in the closet, evenly spaced and organized by color. A row of old books sat between pewter bookends on the dresser next to a shallow dish full of loose change. A black and white photo of a couple in a thin gold frame rested on a crocheted doily, overseeing the room. The man was much younger, but from the eyes, clearly it was Joe. The woman, slight, with dark pin curls falling just above her shoulder, must have been Millie.

Joe was nowhere in sight. Cameron looked at Will, who walked to the window and pulled back the drapes.

"Where is he?" Cameron pushed the clothes inside, peering into the deep closet.

Will heard rustling under the bed and got down on all fours and lifted the bedskirt gingerly.

"Shhhh," Joe lay flat on his back and smiled, a gray cat tucked firmly under his arm. He gently stroked her fur. "She's a little anxious over the commotion."

Will sat back on his knees and motioned to Cameron, pointing straight down to the bed. Cameron got down on the floor on the other side and lifted the bed skirt. Joe turned his head in her direction, with barely enough room to clear his belly and the cat under the springs of the old bed. He smiled.

"Am I allowed to laugh?" Cameron asked, rolling back onto her heels and dropping the skirt. She pulled her hair away from her face and stood. "Out, Joe. Let's go."

Joe inched his way out from under the bed, pushing with one hand against the floor and the other hand holding onto Emily, until he was out past his waist. "She knows I'm not suited for this sort of nonsense anymore." He gently lifted the cat off his chest and held her out to Will. "Here, hold her a minute so I can get up. If I let her go, we'll never find her."

"I uhh—" Will stepped back.

"Now, she may be unfriendly, Will. But that's just the enigmatic legacy she's trying to live up to. She's not unkind." Joe held her out again. "Please. Just for a minute."

Will reached down slowly and took the cat, holding her under the arms out in front of him, legs dangling and gray eyes looking mournful.

Joe pulled himself the rest of the way out from under the bed and rolled to his side, then pushed up on an elbow, eventually getting to his knees, where he braced himself on the footboard and eased himself to his feet.

He reached for Emily. "Goodness, Will. She's a cat. Not a child with a smelly diaper." He held Emily close and soothed her with soft strokes along her back. She looked toward Will and opened her mouth, showing her small teeth. Will was certain he heard a hissing sound and jumped back, bumping into Cameron.

"Whoa, there," she said, pushing against him with her hands to regain her balance. "Like Joe said. It's a cat. And a scrawny one at that."

"But it just—" Will started. Joe leaned his head down and kissed Emily's fur. "Never mind."

"We should get going, Joe." Cameron looked around the room. "Do you have a suitcase so I can pack up the things we put on your list?"

Joe pointed to the closet. "Should find one in there." He sat on the bed, still scratching the cat's ears.

Cameron stepped inside the closet and came out with a battered brown hard-sided suitcase that looked like it came from a 1950s movie. She opened it across the bed. "Will, grab some T-shirts and things from the dresser."

He opened dresser drawers and found boxers and T-shirts. Picking them up in a single pile, he plopped them into the suitcase while Cameron pulled several hanging shirts and jeans from the closet. Joe watched his friends moving around his room from the side of the bed, a contented look on his face.

"Can you move things so I can get his hanging clothes in?" Cameron folded the clothes over her arm.

"Just lay them on top," Will said.

"They'll wrinkle."

"Works the same way if you put them in front and I pile the boxers on top." Will smiled at his packing logic, well-practiced after years of traveling with a stuffed duffle bag.

"Pile is kind of the problem," Cameron said, lifting the underwear out with one hand and laying the shirts into the suitcase with the other.

"It's a short trip. And I'm pretty sure Pearl will be happy to iron for him. She's always offering to show me how her ironing board works."

Cameron folded a T-shirt and slid it into an opening in the side of the suitcase without looking up at Will. "Not sure I'd recommend following that logic with Pearl."

"What else was on your list, Joe?" Will rubbed his hands together. "Books maybe?"

"Well, we didn't put her on the list, but it looks like we'll be needing to bring Emily along. I'm afraid she'll stop eating altogether if I disappear again. She's skin and bones since I left. And look—" He turned the cat toward them. "She's peaked."

"Peaked?" Will tried to hold in a snicker. "Joe. She's covered in fur. How do you see peaked?"

"She does look a little gaunt, Joe." Cameron leaned down and caressed Emily's face in her hand. She glared at Will at the same time the cat opened its mouth and hissed at him again.

"I'm just not sure how it will go over with Pearl, bringing a cat into the house." Will put his hands in his pockets and stepped farther back. "She was pretty adamant about no pets when I moved in."

"Well, who says we have to tell her?" Joe asked.

"What?" Cameron said. "You think we can sneak a cat into Pearl's house?"

"There is no sneaking anything where Pearl Jenkins is involved," Will tugged at his boxer hem with his hand in his pocket. "Trust me on this."

"Well, let's think about this," Cameron said. "It's not like she would be chasing around the place. Would she stay put in your room, Joe?"

"Of course she would. And she's very quiet. We could just bring her carrier and litter box and Pearl would never have to know."

"Yeah. A cat and a litter box in Pearl Jenkins's house. What could possibly go wrong?" Will shook his head. "Listen, if the cat gets made, I'm denying everything."

"Right." Cameron closed the suitcase with a laugh. She put a knee on top and snapped the latches shut with a hard click. "Now I almost want Pearl to find the cat just to watch you try to pretend you didn't know a thing about how a poor old invalid got a cat and her litter box upstairs next to your bedroom without you noticing."

"Hey now with the invalid stuff. I'm right here."

"Sorry, Joe, it's an expression. Was just using it for effect." Cameron patted his shoulder. "It was for Will's benefit anyway. I'm expecting you to go with me and Finn on our walks in the morning." She set the suitcase on the floor. "What else do we need?"

"It's just for a couple of days, right?" Joe asked.

"Right," Cameron and Will blurted out at the same time.

"Clean clothes, a couple of books, and sweet Emily. I shouldn't need anything else."

Will picked up the suitcase and motioned the others to the door with a sweep of his hand. "Shall we?"

38

"You should take Joe to the front door," Cameron said, as Will turned down the alley behind Pearl's house. "I'll get him inside, and you can go around back and get the cat upstairs."

"Emily hates me."

"Will." Cameron narrowed her eyes.

"If I'm the one who takes her into a strange place, she'll remember and always associate me with that trauma. She'll hate me more."

"Will."

"I know. I'll drive around front." He drove past the house and went around the corner, pulling up to the front sidewalk. The drape in the living room window fell closed and Pearl opened the front door momentarily.

"Bring his suitcase, too," Cameron said.

"But I'm bringing the cat."

"And I'm telling Pearl you went around back to bring Joe's suitcase up." She opened her hands. "So bring Joe's suitcase up."

"I'll bring the suitcase up."

Joe sat silently in his seat, smiling out the window as Will put the truck in park. "Here you go, old man. Your new home away from home."

"You two are still bantering, just like when you were small."

"Joe?" Cameron put a hand on Joe's knee.

He looked at Cameron, eyes moist and gray. "Your mother's place looks different than I remember. Bigger."

She gave Joe's leg a little squeeze. "Let's get you upstairs.

You could probably use a little rest after all the excitement today."

"Rest. Of course." Joe stared out the front window, but didn't move. Will returned Cameron's glance with a shrug.

"Let's do this." He got out and jogged around to open Joe's door. "Out you go, my friend. Cameron will get you inside while Emily and I sneak up the back."

Joe stared ahead. Will reached and turned Joe's face. "Hey. Look at me." Joe smiled lightly. "Whatever you do, remember: We did not bring a cat to Pearl's house."

"We didn't bring the cat? I thought we were bringing her along. I didn't ask Midge—"

"No, we brought the cat. She's in the back. But if Pearl finds out, it's curtains for all of us."

"Oh!" Joe laughed and slapped his leg. "Of course. I know that." He pushed Will out of the way and got out of the truck. Ducking his head back into the cab, he grinned at Cameron. "You coming with me, or shall I advance on Mrs. Jenkins unsupervised?"

"Coming." Cameron scooted across the seat and hopped out of the cab. "You will not be making any advances on anyone at the moment, thank you."

"Of course, you're right. More nuance. Timing is everything. I'll work on it." Joe started up the walk.

"You'd better keep an eye on him." Will shook his head at Cameron. "I'll meet you inside."

"No diversions, Will. I need you inside."

"Coming," he said, and started the truck.

Will parked in the back and pulled the cat carrier from behind the seat. He took it by its black plastic handle and tucked the bag of litter under his other arm and hurried up the back stairs. He set the carrier in the bathtub, as though the cat could use one more layer of captivity, and as though the sides of a bathtub would be fortress enough even if she were free of her carrier.

"Okay, cat. Sit tight. We're in this together." Emily sat with her back to the carrier window, but he heard her hiss as he patted the top of the crate. He strode out of the bathroom, down the hall, and descended the staircase where he found Cameron, Joe and Pearl huddled inside the front door. Pearl had on her best Sunday dress and if Will were not mistaken, had just had her hair done.

"Mrs. Jenkins, do you have a big event today?" he asked. "We're so sorry if we disrupted your schedule."

Pearl pressed her hands against the hair pulled up at the back of her neck, fussing as though there were errant strands, which there were not. "Why, no. I'm not off anywhere. Just an ordinary day greeting visitors at the humble Jenkins mansion."

Cameron gave Will a pleading look, but he was too pre-occupied to notice, and walked past her on his way to Pearl. "Well, you look simply radiant. Is this flowered dress new?"

Pearl's cheeks looked suddenly rosy. "Mr. Phillips, since when do you notice what I'm wearing?"

"Will, let's get Joe upstairs and settled in, okay?" Cameron put her hand on his shoulder and pushed him lightly toward the stairs. "You brought his suitcase up?"

"Oh, umm. No. I guess I should go do that." Will darted toward the dining room.

"I swear, that boy." Pearl ran her hands over the front of her skirt.

"Pearl," Cameron said, "I'll get Joe upstairs and show him his room, and then I'll stop back down before I go."

"It's the one on the right, dear," Pearl motioned with her hand up the stairs. "Oh, silly me. Of course, you've been upstairs and already know what's what."

Cameron blushed and turned quickly toward the stairs.

"Did you and Mr. Phillips have a nice time?"

"A nice time?" Cameron looked back at Pearl.

"Yes. On your date the other night."

Cameron's brow furrowed. "Date? I'm not sure—"

"My dear girl. You don't have to play coy with me. Didn't Mr. Phillips tell you I was in the kitchen when he came down to scavenge from my wine cabinet?"

"Oh! Right. With all this other business I'd totally forgotten." She turned back to the stairs. "Hey, Joe, take it easy there. We're not racing to the top, okay?"

"So it was a nice date then?" Pearl started up the stairs behind Cameron, holding firmly to the handrail.

"Yes, of course, It was nice." She stopped on the landing and waved her hands in front of her. "But no, wait. It wasn't a date. I ran into Will on my run. And then he fell and got a little woozy so I came back with him to make sure he was okay and we decided to go up onto the roof. I mean—"

"My roof?" Pearl reached the landing and rested her hand on the window sill. "And I thought he'd stopped doing that. You fall off my porch roof and I'll have myself a nice lawsuit and you won't be able to keep dating him."

"We are *not* dating."

"Yes, Dear." She patted Cameron's arm. "Of course you're not. I don't know what else to make of wine on the rooftop outside a man's bedroom, but you go on calling it what you like."

"We never even got on the roof," Cameron protested.

"Oh?" Pearl's eyes widened.

"No, that's not—we were reading."

"Oh, now it's reading? I do like the sound of that."

"You girls coming up?" Joe leaned over the top rail outside his room. "I think you're supposed to be keeping me out of trouble."

"Coming," Pearl and Cameron said at once.

Pearl put her hand on Cameron's shoulder. "We'll talk more later."

Cameron pointed a finger at Pearl. "No, there's nothing more to talk about. We were reading. *The Wild Swans*, in fact. By Hans Christian Andersen."

"Of course you were. Reading. Now go on up." She smiled her most Pearl Jenkins-ish smile.

Cameron pursed her lips and turned back, calling up the stairs. "Did you find your room, Joe? It's the one—"

"—on the right. Gotcha. I found it just fine."

"Everybody all set up here?" Will came around the corner carrying Joe's suitcase under his arm.

"Hey, is that a billiards table in there?" Joe pointed toward the den where Will had just come from.

Will looked behind himself. "Sure is. Do you play?"

"It's been a long time. So maybe it's fairer to say 'I played.'" Joe folded his hands over his belly. "But boy, did I play." He smiled and nodded his head, proud of his past accomplishment.

"Is that right? Cameron says she used to be pretty good

too. We should have a game sometime."

"Well I've never quite gotten the hang of that billiards business," said Pearl. "But Mr. Phillips used to try to teach me a thing or two." She had made her way to the top of the stairs and was holding tightly to the newel cap.

"Oh, here Pearl, let's come away from the steps." Will set down Joe's suitcase and took Pearl's elbow in his hand. "Yes, sure. I taught you everything you know."

"We could play right now." Pearl clapped her hands.

"Right now?" Cameron, who had been leaning absent-mindedly against the wall, jumped. "I might have to take a raincheck on that. I was thinking to go home for a bite to eat and a nap. It's been a long day already, you know?"

"Oh, no dear. I have a little lunch ready downstairs. But we could play one teensy game of pool first. Then you'll have your lunch and you can go home for your nap."

"Pearl, Cameron's got a point. I'm sure Joe could use a little rest too."

"Just one little game. What do you think, Mr. Murphy?"

"Well, remember, I'm a bit rusty. So maybe it wouldn't take too long to clear me out."

"Go rack 'em up, Mr. Phillips." Pearl pushed through the others and made her way to the den. "Let's play that Oddball game you tried to teach me."

Cameron looked at Will. He shrugged and mumbled. "Don't look at me. What I say doesn't count for much around here." He walked behind Joe into the room. "It's 8-Ball, Pearl."

"Oh, of course. Eight Balls. I'm always forgetting that."

Joe looked back at Cameron, arms crossed, still at the top of the stairs. "You said you were pretty good, right? May as well give in. Come be my partner."

"Should we make a little wager, then?" Pearl slid a cue stick off the wall.

Will rolled the rack across the table, rearranging the balls so the black 8-ball was in the top corner. "We don't need a bet, Pearl. This is just a nice little game between friends."

"But I always wanted to be able to bet on a game of pool. My daddy never let me play."

"Pearl, you know—"

She tapped her cue stick lightly on Will's shoulder. "Just you never mind. Our friends would love to play for stakes."

Cameron turned to Joe and whispered. "How good are you?"

"Been a while." He laced his fingers and cracked his knuckles. "But I used to do alright. Men's League Champ three years running at Gin's Pub in Chicago."

"We can take them. She sounds like she's barely played."

"Twenty dollars then?" Joe asked.

"Well," Pearl looked back at Will and smiled. "That's seems a little steep. And I'm short on cash. But I do have a gift card from Back Ribs Brewery. Would that work?"

"I do have a certain weakness where barbecued ribs are concerned." Joe rubbed his hands together. "Combine that with a clean game of Solids and Stripes, and I can't resist."

Pearl pressed a small chalk square against the tip of her cue stick. "Are we playing Alabama style or Misery?"

All three stared at her. "I thought you didn't play," Cameron said, with a hand on her hip.

"Oh, well," Pearl waved them off. "They play those pool tournaments on the cable TV all the time. What else is a lonely old lady supposed to do in her big old empty house at night but watch?"

Will passed behind Cameron and whispered, "You'd better hope Joe's still got it, or you've been had."

She turned back. "I should hope Joe's still got it? You do realize how ridiculous that sounds when you're counting on a woman to win this for you, right?" She rested the bottom of her stick on top of Will's foot and pressed down. "Maybe Joe and I both still have it."

He winced and wiggled his foot free. "Of course, that's what I meant. It'll take both of you to outplay Pearl."

Stepping away from Cameron, Will rapped his knuckles on the edge of the table. "Alright then. Who gets the break shot?"

"Let's let Susan B. Anthony decide." Joe pulled his hand out of his pocket and poked a finger through the coins in his palm, pulling out a gold dollar. He returned the rest to his pocket and flipped the dollar into the air with his other hand. "You call it, Pearl."

"Heads," Pearl said. "No, wait. Tails."

Joe caught the coin and slapped it to his forearm. "You're sure now?"

"Yes. No. Oh, dear." Pearl put a hand to her mouth. "Mr. Phillips?"

"What do you want to do, flip a coin to see what you should call in the coin toss?" Will chuckled. "Call heads, Pearl. Go with your first instinct."

"Heads. Okay." She smoothed the front of her skirt. "Yes. No. Tails, Mr. Murphy."

Joe barely lifted his hand off the coin and peeked in. "Well, you kids aren't going to believe this."

"Don't keep us in suspense, Mr. Murphy. I'm so excited to be able to play I can barely stand it."

Joe covered the coin and called Cameron over. "Take a looky here."

Cameron pumped a fist in the air.

Pearl's eyes dropped and she turned to Will. "Looks like we don't get to break."

"Tails!" Joe bellowed, and he and Cameron laughed out loud.

"Oh, my stars!" Pearl punched Joe in the arm. "I thought you'd say heads for sure."

"Nope. It's all yours."

"Well, what are you waiting for, Mr. Phillips?"

Will straightened. "Oh, sorry. I thought after all that you'd want to break."

"Oh, no. I'm too nervous. And I don't know the first thing about how to break. You do it."

"Umm, okay." He picked up the white cue ball and tossed it in the air, catching it backhanded as he walked to the kitchen end of the table. Will set the ball down and crouched to look at the line. He picked the ball up and moved it to the other side, repeating the crouched view. Standing back up, he pointed the cue stick in a line from the cue ball to the blue striped 12-ball at the side of the pyramid. Then he put the cue stick behind his neck, arms draped over the ends, and did a couple of deep squats and twisted his torso from side to side.

Cameron crossed her arms. "Really?"

"I need to get in the zone, you know? There's a rack of ribs on the line here. Not to mention my dignity."

"Your dignity. Over a game of pool."

"Some of us get it wherever we can find it."

"Mr. Phillips, stop fooling around now," Pearl pressed. "Our lunch will spoil waiting for your zone to find you. Break already."

"Alright, alright." Will shot, sending the balls clacking against each other and scattering across the table. The red 3-ball crept to a stop near the far side pocket.

"Oh, rats. None of them dropped. I knew I should have been the one to break," Pearl lamented.

"Of course you should have. That's why you insisted I do it." Will leaned back against the wall, holding his stick in front of him like a door he could close on himself.

"Do you want first shot, Joe?" Cameron asked, looking sidelong at Will.

"You take it. I have a hunch you girls are going to have the advantage today."

Cameron walked around the table, stopping here and there, leaning sideways to analyze her shot. She stopped in front of Will, lined up and shot the cue ball between the blue 2-ball and the purple striped 12-ball, skimming the side of the orange 5-ball and sending it slowly along the side, bumping the red 3-ball and sinking it.

"Okay then!" Joe clapped. "We will be solids."

Cameron stayed along the table, eyeing her next shot. Half the balls were clustered together and none had a clear shot toward a pocket. She set up and banked a soft shot off the side wall to nestle the cue ball in the middle of the cluster.

"Your shot, Pearl." She gave Will a smug smile and stepped back from the table.

"My word, Mr. Phillips." Pearl picked up the chalk again and twisted it against the tip of her cue stick. "I don't know how I'll ever be able to do anything with that white ball surrounded by all those colored balls."

Will leaned over the table and pointed. "Well, I think if you hit it just right, from this angle, you could knock things loose and—"

The clack of balls interrupted his thoughts as Pearl reached across from the other side, spraying the cluster of balls outward and driving the red striped 11-ball into the side pocket.

"Or, you know—"

Pearl came around the corner of the table and poked Will in the belly, leaving a perfect blue dot on his shirt. "Yes, I do know. I'm playing, Mr. Phillips. Try to pay attention."

Will stepped back and sat down on an antique wooden chair in the corner, watching Pearl in silence as she cleared all but one of the striped balls off the table, the cue stick standing upright between his knees.

Pearl's 9-ball rolled to a stop just shy of a corner pocket and she tapped the bottom of her cue stick against the floor in protest. "Darn it. So close, too."

Joe laughed a big belly laugh. "You're a hustler!" he said. "You should have told us she was this good, Will." He unbuttoned his sleeves and folded them up to his elbows.

Will tugged on his jacket cuff, slipping it over his hand to the knuckles. "I figured you'd see for yourself soon enough."

"Well, it's a good thing it's only a $20 bet, though I sure was looking forward to those ribs."

Pearl beamed from the end of the table.

"I wouldn't write off those ribs just yet, Joe," Cameron

said. "We're just getting started."

"I don't know if I can outshoot that performance." He crouched and scanned the table. "Though it looks like you left me a gift at the side pocket." Joe lined up a shot and dropped the 2-ball. He worked his way around the table, not missing a shot until all that was left was his 5-ball, Pearl's 12-ball and the black 8-ball staring with its white eye at Will from across the table.

"Everything hinges on you now, Mr. Phillips," Pearl said. "No pressure though, of course. I can always get another gift card."

"Thanks for the confidence, Pearl." Will stayed in his chair, studying the table.

"I think you could make a nice easy shot from over here." Pearl held her stick out, drawing a line in the air from the cue ball to the purple striped 12-ball. "Bank it off the back side and she'll go right in."

Will stood without speaking, walked behind Pearl and lined up an unlikely shot from the other side of the table.

"No, Mr. Phillips. Didn't you hear me?" Pearl said. "Over here."

"I heard you." Will did not look up.

He rested a hand on the felt, laying the cue stick across his knuckles and sliding it back and forth.

"That will never work."

"You're probably right."

Time seemed suspended as the blue tip of his cue stick struck the white cue ball and for a split second Will saw Pearl's tiny, perfectly round head rolling across the table toward the side, banking at just the right angle and knocking into the 12-

ball, which rolled dutifully into the corner pocket.

He stood upright and felt the cue stick slide through his hand, the rubber tip bouncing against the floor.

Pearl threw both hands in the air and turned in a circle. "You did it! That was a ridiculous shot, but you made it."

"Quite impressive, my friend," Joe said, his head shaking.

Cameron watched Will from across the room without saying anything.

"Anyway, you got lucky there. I see no reason for you to have taken such a shot when I showed you a guaranteed winner."

"Every reason in the world," Will said softly, eyeing the 8-ball sitting safely behind Joe's 5-ball.

"You'll take the sure shot this time, of course," Pearl said. "Look over here now. I'll be taking that rib dinner out of your rent if we lose."

Will kept his eye on the 8-ball. "There are no sure shots Pearl. I know you know this."

"And I know you understand the value of the surest-shot, Mr. Phillips. Come look." She pointed with her stick.

Will walked slowly around, stopping where Pearl was tracing a line from the cue ball to the side wall to the 8-ball. "It would work, surely better than any idea you have."

He looked up at the ceiling, watching the fan blades circle. As he lowered his eyes, he saw Cameron under the window opposite him. She looked at the floor. Will turned to Joe, who smiled and nodded slightly.

"Mr. Phillips? You'll take the shot. It's a good one."

"It is a good one, Pearl. Maybe even damn close to sure." He leaned down and looked across the table again.

Pearl let out a deep breath and stepped back to the wall out of the way, a hand to her mouth, and watched.

Will rested the cue stick on his hand and pulled back, then straightened again and went around the corner of the table.

"Mr. Phillips." Pearl dropped her hand to her waist. "We agreed that was a good shot."

"We did agree."

He set up at the table again and without thinking pulled back his cue stick and let it smack into the cue ball, sending it sailing across the table in a nearly opposite path as Pearl had pointed, taking an extra bounce off the sidewall before finally knocking into Joe's ball which rolled toward the 8-ball, tapping it into the side pocket.

"No way." Cameron stood with her hands on her hips. "That shouldn't have worked."

"Probably not," Will said.

Joe was laughing. Will stiffened, bracing for Pearl.

"Shouldn't have worked at all." She slid her stick into the rack on the wall. "That's quite enough of this. We should go get our lunch."

"We've been hustled," Joe said to Cameron as he motioned her toward the door.

Cameron smiled. "Not the only ones, I think."

Will came around the table, pausing behind Pearl to let her go through the door ahead of him.

"There was no reason for that." Her glare softened. "But I do have to admit it was a damn good shot."

39

Pearl had prepared a light lunch with sandwiches, her famous macaroni salad, and a fresh rhubarb pie.

"This is fantastic," Joe said, licking both sides of his fork after his last bite of pie. "They told me at the hospital I couldn't eat stuff like this anymore, and look, here I am!"

"Well, the hospital was right," Pearl said, looking at her lap. "I just wasn't quite ready."

Cameron put her hand lightly on Pearl's arm. "We should talk about that sometime. I can help you out with some ideas for what you can feed this fella."

While they were eating, Pearl relived with great dramatic flourishes her favorite shots at the pool table, telling how her sometimes-boyfriend Jack had taught her to play since her father had forbade it, sneaking her into the billiard hall after school. She shushed Will when he tried to remind her that Joe and Cameron had made a good showing, whittling the table down to just one ball each before he took the final two shots to win the game for her. "They just got lucky," she said, "the same as you did when you took those fool risky shots at the end and nearly blew away all my hard, skillful work."

When Cameron let escape a yawn and began to stretch her neck and shoulders, Will jumped out of his chair. "Well, it has certainly been a long day already. I'm sure you're wanting to get home."

Cameron nodded ever so slightly, glancing at Pearl from the corner of her eye.

"Let me see you out," he said.

"I know my way to the door. I'm good," she said.

"No, really. I'll walk you."

Cameron shrugged and excused herself, thanking Pearl for the lunch and telling Joe to let her know if there was anything at all he needed.

"Practice up while you're here, Joe. We're going to have a rematch soon."

"Absolutely," Joe said, scraping his fork across his plate for any last tastes of pie. "You were always so good at checkers. Not sure why you choked there at the end and let her take you."

"Checkers?" Cameron turned back at the pantry door.

Will cupped her elbow in his hand, guiding her back to the door. "Leave it," he said softly.

"Of course. Checkers."

"I do love checkers myself," added Pearl, not missing a beat. "I'll find my board and we'll play this afternoon. I might even teach you a few things."

"I'm quite sure you will," Joe said, "but I'll warn you, I played a lot of checkers during all those long hours at the station. I might actually be able to take *you*."

"Looks like they're going to do just fine together," Cameron chuckled and she and Will walked through the dining room toward the front door

"They are. She'll keep him in line, that's for sure." Will rubbed his neck. "I'm a little worried about Joe though. First he's breaking out of the hospital and then forgetting who we are and now the checkers thing…"

"It's probably nothing, Will. He's been through a lot. Between the trauma and the meds and moving to Pearl's house, he's asking his mind to process quite a load. He's just having trouble keeping up."

"Maybe. Let's hope you're right."

Cameron gave Will's arm a little squeeze and slipped out the door. "Call me later." She turned back at the bottom of the porch steps. "To let me know how things are going, I mean."

"I will." He leaned his shoulder against the door frame and watched his friend walk across the street, trying to remember when was the last time he'd had someone he'd consider to simply be a friend. Not someone he had to take care of, not someone he worked with. Just a normal person who would be a friend. He couldn't remember anyone, with Barbara having eclipsed all his relationships when they were together, and the ghost of Barbara eclipsing them all now.

Finn was jumping up at the screen door and barking a small dog *yip-bark*. When Cameron opened the door and reached in to hook up his leash, Will turned back into the entry to find Pearl standing behind him.

"I'm just going to stop jumping when you make your mysterious appearances, okay? It will save us some time."

"I sent Joe up the back way to his room to lie down. You must keep an eye on him."

Will sighed. "You're afraid he'll try to make off with your silver candlestick holders?"

"Don't be ridiculous." Pearl waved him off with the back of her hand. "The silver is locked up in the chest. I mean he's not thinking clearly. He's completely forgotten my brilliance at billiards and thinks we played checkers."

"Oh, that." Will pushed his hands into his pockets. "I know. Cameron thinks he'll get back to himself once he's had some rest and a chance to acclimate."

"She might be right." Pearl crossed her arms, rubbing a hand along her sleeve as though she were chilled. "She might be wrong."

"Well, so you see why he needed a place to stay."

"Oh, I didn't doubt he needed that." She tugged at an errant curl behind her ear. "I'll deny it if you ever repeat me saying this, but I'm glad you brought him home."

"I won't test you on that."

"No, don't," Pearl said. "Anyway. You should get up there and get him settled. Tell him he should be good and take a rest and he can come down later and we'll have tea."

"You'll spoil him, Pearl."

"Spoil him nothing. If he's going to be here he's going to at least keep me company."

Will smiled and leaned in to give Pearl a light kiss on the cheek. "Thank you." He turned and jogged up the stairs two at a time, the steps creaking mournfully every time he put his weight into them.

When he poked his head into Joe's room, the old man had his back to the door. Will knocked lightly on the maple casing and Joe turned around, buttoning a striped Oxford shirt. "Figured you'd be wanting your shirt back. I noticed you were a little reluctant to give it up."

"Nah, it wasn't that. It was just a little chilly in your hospital room, you know?"

"It was a little snug around my middle, anyway," Joe laughed, patting his belly. He picked up Will's plaid flannel from the bed and held it out to him. "Here you go. Many thanks for saving me the embarrassment of having to go out in public in a hospital gown."

"Uh…"

"Well, more than once, anyway." Joe chuckled, shaking his head. "Some strong medicine they've been giving me. I think it was that Myrna woman slipping me Roofies in my orange juice, hoping to take advantage of me later."

"Myrna the nurse. I'm pretty sure that's not her game."

"Well, you can say that because you weren't her love prisoner. I've seen things no man should have to. And a few more sponge baths than were needed, if you ask me."

"Right. Well. I didn't ask you, now that you mention it. And I think I don't need any more visuals I can't unsee, so thanks."

"Gotcha." Joe looked around the room. "Say, where's Emily?"

"Oh, yeah." Will pointed out the door with a thumb over his shoulder. "She's down the hall. Come on and I'll show you where the bathroom is. You can bring her back."

Joe followed Will down the hall. "So what's really up your sleeve, Will?"

"What?"

"Your sleeve. What are you hiding up there?"

Will turned into the bathroom without answering and picked up Emily's carrier, holding it out to Joe. "Here you go. Back together again."

Joe put his face up to the window grate. "Well, hello there. 'Who are you? Are you nobody too?'" Emily purred inside her cage. "I'll have you out of there in no time. And you can go prowl around looking for some hope with feathers."

"Are you sure she won't go downstairs?"

"She's a good cat, Will. But who can be sure of anything?"

"Great. Well, maybe at least close your door when you go out and let's hope she stays close when you're here."

"She'll be fine. And didn't you say Pearl was fond of Emily Dickinson?"

"Moreso than John Keats, anyway."

Back in his room, Will slipped off his jacket and pulled his boots from his feet, letting them fall to the floor as he flopped over on his bed and pulled the blanket up to his chin. He rubbed a hand along his arm, feeling every pink and purple ridge of the scars under his fingertips as his eyes closed, hearing Barbara's voice in the foggy background.

Be a man for once, little Will.

40

Will sat up in bed, turning his head to hear a light bass thumping through the wall between his room and Joe's.

"What the—"

He tossed his pillow to the side and threw off the blankets, padding to the hall in his stocking feet and listening at Joe's door. He rapped on the wood lightly with his knuckles at the same time as he turned the knob and opened the door to find Joe with one arm extended, the other wrapped around his imaginary dance partner. Joe's eyes were closed as he soft-shoed into a twirl with Nina Simone crooning about where a guy shouldn't smoke.

Apt, Will thought, and pulled the door closed.

"Will? Is that you?"

The door opened and Will stood face to face with a grinning Joe Murphy. "I had no idea Pearl would have this room so well appointed. Have you seen the old phonograph in here?"

"Uh, before you came along I'd never been in the room."

"I see. Come look." Joe waved Will into the room. "It's a Grundig Majestic. Suitably named, really. Look at the smooth mahogany finish." Joe lowered the cover over the turntable where the *Little Girl Blue* LP was spinning, an old diamond needle scratching out her sultry voice. He ran his hand over the top of the lowboy chest and then pulled open the front to reveal a radio console.

"AM/FM. This has to be vintage 1958, if I'm not mistaken. Model 7028." Joe folded his hands. "Perfect. That's when the album came out."

"I don't remember packing any records for you, Joe. "

"No need. Pearl has the place stocked with all the best." He pointed to a rack of records on a small table next to the Majestic console. "Absolute treasures here." He flipped through the jackets. "Ah, yes. Here we go." Joe slid out a black record and stopped the turntable. He set the record on the spindle and cued up the arm, handing the red cardboard sleeve to Will.

Will turned it over to see a smiling black haired woman in a white blouse and bright red scarf and slacks, with sparkly gold ankle-high boots.

"Patsy Cline."

"Sure. 'I Fall to Pieces'?"

Will looked up and scowled at the implication. "Oh, nice."

"You're telling me. It was one of her number one hits. Woman was a powerhouse. Don't tell me you've never heard."

"Of course I've heard. I remember she was a big part of that Loretta Lynn movie when I was a kid. *Coal Miner's Daughter*. Hated that movie because I was too young to know better, but it was the early days of cable and it played over and over for a month. Sometimes it was the only thing on TV so I watched it probably a dozen times. The scenes with Patsy Cline made it watchable. Drop dead gorgeous, that woman. Sang that song, 'Crazy'." Will whistled and turned the jacket over.

Just then, his phone buzzed. He held up a finger to Joe and put his phone to his ear. "Phillips."

Will rolled his eyes.

"Yes, Mike. I still work here. Had some personal things to take care of today." He smiled at Joe, who had turned back to flipping through Pearl's record collection.

"Yeah. That's fine. I can take it. Just send the details and I'll head right out."

Will pocketed his phone. "Hey, listen. I've got to out. Nasty accident on Highway 26. Insurance company wants someone on-scene."

"Oh, sorry to hear it, Will. Anybody hurt?"

"I think so. Overturned tractor trailer. And a ditch full of cargo."

Joe sat on the bed, Patsy Cline resting on his lap. "Well, Emily and I will find something to amuse ourselves for the rest of the afternoon, I imagine. Won't we, Emily?" Joe scratched behind the cat's ears.

"Thanks, Joe. Don't forget Pearl said she'd play checkers. I'll check in with you as soon as I get back into town."

Will hurried back to his room and grabbed his bag. He turned back just before he took to the stairs to see Joe still sitting on the bed. He hadn't moved. Letting out a sigh, he looked at the ceiling. "You'll regret this," he said softly to himself. Then, to Joe, he said aloud, "Think you can stay put in the truck?"

Joe's face lit up. "I can do anything you tell me to."

"Put your shoes on. Let's go."

Joe was still zipping up a beige Harrington jacket, collar turned up at his ears, as he climbed into Will's truck parked behind Pearl's house.

"What are we going to do, Will?" he asked as he pulled his door shut. "This is all quite exciting."

"I don't know about exciting. But we are going to the scene and then the *I* part of *we* is going to get out and do my job and the *you* part of *we* is going to sit in the cab and wait. You should be able to get NPR on the radio." Will turned around to check the rear window and backed into the alley. "Maybe they'll be playing your buddy Rebroff."

"You got his name right." Joe beamed.

"Of course I did. Just wouldn't want anybody else to know I paid enough attention."

"What a remarkably structured illusion you live." Joe's expression hung suspended somewhere between wonder and pity. "I imagine you think it's working, too."

"It does work. It works just fine, thank you very much."

"Of course." Joe folded his hands on his lap, and Will drove in silence to eight miles north of town on Highway 26 —an old, winding, two-lane stretch of road that still served as the primary connection for haulers between Dennison and its next largest neighbor, Simmons. As they approached the scene, the southbound lane was closed off with orange cones just before Flick's Twist, a sharp S-curve named for the notorious dairy farmer who took it a little too fast and rolled his truck back in 1954. The town lost old Malcomb Flick and a whole load of milk that day.

Deputy Roundleg stood as flagman in the lane, holding off traffic to allow the line of southbound cars to pass. Will lowered his window. "Hey Jeremy. How's it looking?"

"It's a mess, Will. You here to work?"

"Yep. Tractor trailer is mine."

"You can drive up a little ways, and park on the approach. You'll have to walk the rest of the way in."

The deputy looked up and stepped back from the truck, waving through the ambulance coming toward him in the northbound lane, lights flashing but siren off.

After it passed, Will asked, "Is that my guy?"

"I think so. Other guy didn't appear to be hurt." Jeremy took off his hat and wiped his forearm over his close-cropped hair. "Nothing serious though. He should be alright."

"What are we hauling?"

"I don't want to spoil it for you. Go on up and check it out." Roundleg grinned. "You'll know before you get there."

"Shit." Will put the truck back into drive.

"Oh, no. Nothing like that fertilizer spill." The deputy laughed. "You might even like it." He slapped his hand on top of the cab to send them on their way. Will gave him a short wave and drove ahead.

"Did you read about that ship that lost a load of rubber ducks on the ocean?"

Will looked at Joe. "Is there a punchline?"

"No joke. That was the actual cargo. Ship on its way from China to the U.S. lost a few hundred containers during a typhoon. Set almost 30,000 little yellow ducks adrift. There's a book about it: *Moby Duck*."

"No kidding."

"None. You can't make this stuff up, Will. Those ducks went everywhere. The guy that wrote the book found one in Alaska."

"Huh. And I usually just get to deal with corn or the occasional misfortune of a rendering truck overturn."

"Nasty."

"There aren't enough showers in the world after dealing with a pumper truck full of liquid waste from some Rocket Burger franchise." Will shuddered involuntarily at the memory of a highway and a half dozen sedans coated with thick, greasy sludge like they'd been freshly stuccoed.

"So what do you think this one is?" Joe unbuckled his seatbelt and leaned forward to see around the curve as Will pulled off onto the approach and parked.

"You're staying here, remember?"

Joe put his hands back in his lap. "Of course. Of course. I'm just getting comfortable."

"I'll tell you all about it when I get back."

"Yes. I'll be sitting right here."

"Turn on the radio. Don't make me regret bringing you any more than I already do."

"No regrets. I don't have them. I don't cause them."

Will pulled his bag from the back seat and straightened his cap. "Right." He slammed the cab door and started up the highway, leaving Joe to play with the radio dial.

As he started around the curve, a sweaty, yeast-like smell confronted him like he'd just walked into a frat house on a Friday night.

"Oh, no." Ahead, he saw the semi trailer on its side, rear gate open and several silver kegs rolled out, along with dozens of cases of beer strewn across the roadway, rivulets of malt liquor running down the asphalt and pooling at his feet.

"'Bout time you got out here, Phillips."

A bearded man six inches and 100 pounds Will's senior emerged from the ditch alongside the overturned trailer, thinning silver hair hanging limp down to his shoulders from under a greasy blue cap with a bright yellow TOW GUY logo emblazoned on the front.

Karl Wainwright's Tow Guy operation was not the only

tow company in Dennison. In fact, he didn't even have a shop in Dennison but had his base thirty miles away at the junction of two interstate highways where he had ready access to six different towns, each with their own tow guys, all run by locally born and raised moms and pops. He also wasn't the cheapest and he surely wasn't the best at what he did. But somehow, every trucking fleet manager in the region seemed to be enamored of him, and they had his number in their speed dial, calling him first, and their insurance companies second, when one of their rigs went down.

"Happy to see I'm not going to be asking you to scrape chicken parts off the road this time, Karl," Will said, remembering another of his more distasteful misadventures with Karl and his Tow Guys. "Your boys should enjoy this one a lot more."

"You saying something about one of my boys, Phillips? Like they might be more fond of beer than of chicken?"

"Nah, I'd never say such a thing like that about any of your boys. I've seen them at Wings Night at Baby Backs Brewery and it's really a toss up which they like more." Will pulled a pen from his shirt pocket and propped his clipboard against his belly, writing in the margins as though there were something important he needed to take down. "I was actually just saying that you still don't have a sense of humor."

Wainwright took off his cap and rubbed the top of his bald head. Will stifled a laugh.

"What the hell is wrong with you now?" The mechanic put his cap back on and slid it back on his head.

"Nothing wrong at all. Just had never noticed how much of that Founding Fathers thing you have going on." He gestured in a half circle around his head. "You know. The Ben Franklin hair and all."

Wainwright's nostrils flared. "Ain't nothing wrong with my humor, Phillips. Or my hair. You just be sure to let me know ahead of time if you're fixin' to say something funny so I know when I should laugh."

"Easy, Karl." Will folded the paper over the top of the clipboard and started sketching a diagram of the roadway and truck. "I'll buy you a beer when we're done."

"Har har. They teach you these jokes in your fancy adjuster school?"

Will motioned toward the trailer. "You move anything yet?"

"Nah, they just got the driver out a couple of minutes ago."

"How is he?"

"He was conscious. Jabbering a mile a minute. Looked like a few cuts on his face but otherwise he seemed fine to me."

"And the other guy?"

"Other guy's fine. Not a scratch."

"What about his car?"

"That's what I'm talkin' about, dumbass." Wainwright shook his head. "Not a scratch on the car. He didn't hit nothing."

"There was no collision?"

"Nope. Guy in the Mitsubishi veered into the beer truck's lane going around the curve. Trucker swerved to avoid him." Wainwright twirled the toothpick in the corner of his mouth with his tongue. "Over-corrected and turned himself over like a pretty girl in the back of your pickup."

"Do you charge extra for being disgusting?"

"Nope. All part of my basic service package."

Will put his pen back in his pocket and walked toward the crash, stepping between beer cases and broken glass. "I need your guys to clean this up," he called over his shoulder.

"Way ahead of you, as usual. I have a couple of skid steers coming in and we'll just shove it all into a dumpster container to get it out of here."

Will turned back. "You can't just chuck it all, Karl. I need you to preserve the unbroken bottles."

"The hell we will. That's way too much work. Easier to cut your losses and just destroy it all."

Karl Wainwright was still standing in the middle of the highway, arms folded over his chest. Will walked back, broken glass crunching under his boots. He winced and kept walking.

"Did you go to a fancy adjuster school, Karl?"

"I went to the School of Hard Knocks. We didn't need no pencil-pushing classes for namby pambies."

"Congratulations on your achievement." Will pointed to the disaster on the roadway. "That is the insurance company's cargo." He pointed to his own chest. "That makes this *my* crash scene. And that means, even though you forget it every damn time, you work for me today."

Wainwright closed his mouth around the toothpick and clenched his jaw, jamming his hands in his pockets.

"Your guys are going to sort the cargo. You've got three guys plus yourself. I don't care how long it takes you, but I'll only accept a bill for an hour each to pull and load the unbroken bottles and cases and another man hour plus equipment to clear the road and haul out the rest. If you can't do it, then take your guys back to your castle on the hill and I'll call Tibbets Wrecking. They'd love to finally get a job away from you. It would be good for Global Alliance to see that there are folks that will work faster, better and for less money than the Tow Guy they've got such a crush on."

Wainwright's lip curled almost imperceptibly, but not enough that Will didn't see it. "You done?"

"Maybe. Are you? Or are you going to get to work?"

The Tow Guy kicked a loose pebble. "Just as soon tell you to go pound sand. I suppose we'll make it worth our while since we're already here." He pulled his cap down. "But I'm taking a case home with me."

"And I'm citing you the appropriate insurance code." Will took his pen out of his pocket and wrote the time on his claim log. "Get to work or get off my crash scene, Karl."

Will walked away. Wainwright stood watching him. About a hundred yards out, he shouted, "Get a safety vest on or get off the highway."

Without turning around, Will raised his right hand up to his shoulder and extended his middle finger.

He completed a walk around the overturned tractor trailer, taking photos from all the corners. He slipped a gauge from his jeans pocket and checked the tread depth on the tires, making notes on his clipboard as he went along. In the background, Karl Wainwright screamed orders at his crew, telling them they could work all night but he was only paying them for an hour because goddamned insurance company penny pinchers wouldn't pay a guy for an honest day's work.

"It's just that they see so few of those honest days, Karl," he muttered under his breath as he crouched down to examine the identification plates on the red Kenworth cab. He often marveled at the way a relationship that was supposed to be predicated on trust between the parties—the insurance company and a policyholder and all the many vendors who might be involved—was so perennially marked by disdain and mistrust from the outset.

Will wanted to believe them. He really did. But he also knew that even the best of them, even the sweet silver haired lady who offered him tea and invited him to watch *The Price is Right* with her after he got off her roof—even she was convinced the company was determined to cheat her in some way. This certain skepticism would, in many a policyholder's mind, permit them to think of a way to cheat back. A little padding in the estimate, adding in a little damage from a totally unrelated incident, an extra item or two in the inventory that they never actually owned but sure would be nice to have. Insurance companies have so much money, they tell themselves, most of it swindled from hard working folks. What's a little extra on one little claim? Will was certain that when his appointed time came, the coroner would stamp "Nickeled and Dimed" as the official cause of death on his certificate.

By the time the Tow Guys had the unit hooked up on the wrecker, Will had what he needed from the scene. He leaned on the hood of Deputy Roundleg's black Durango and discussed the investigation while overseeing the crew picking through broken beer cases.

"You know you'll be lucky to salvage less than half a dozen cases, right?"

Will tipped his hat back. "Yep."

Roundleg chuckled. "Then why?"

"Because Karl Wainwright owes me a few. Last time I was on a scene with him was a grain truck overturn. Ditch was full of corn. I told him to pick up the clean corn with the grain vac so they could haul it to the elevator and scrape the ditch with his skid steer to clean up the rest."

"Was that the wreck on old 57 last month?"

"That's the one," Will said. "Wainwright made a lot of noise about how long that would take but finally said he'd take care of it. I figured it wasn't that complicated and went home. They sucked up the clean corn and swept off the roadway into the ditch and threw a little dirt on it. Billed me for twelve man-hours and equipment, telling me he had six guys there for two hours just cleaning up corn." He shook his head. "You know what happened."

"Yeah. I know."

"I told him you have to clean the ditch or the deer come to feed. It's just too close to the road."

"For what it's worth, Mrs. Wiggins had a .09 blood alcohol, Will. She shouldn't have been on the road."

"Maybe so. But if Karl Wainwright would have cleaned up the ditch like he was told and paid to do, those three deer wouldn't have popped up out of the ditch and Francie Wiggins wouldn't have banged up her new Buick Lucerne on the American Family Insurance billboard, either."

"A little irony, eh?"

"A lot. Especially since she's with Allstate."

"She came out of it okay."

"She did. Lucky. For all of us. I'd be looking at a helluva lawsuit." Will cracked his knuckles. "Anyway, I don't leave Karl

Wainwright alone at a scene anymore. That's for sure."

"Speaking of, you figure they'll be done soon? My shift's almost up."

Will stood and called out, "Getting close, Karl?"

"Just fifteen minutes more, Mister Boss Man Sir." Karl made a mock pleading gesture with his hands folded in front of his chest.

"Scumbag," the deputy mumbled.

"Yeah." Will looked back toward his truck, suddenly remembering Joe. "Hey, keep an eye on our scumbag for a minute? I need to go check on something."

He made his way back down the highway thinking it would have been better to have let the Tow Guys clean the debris the easy way. Karl's crew clearly had more than fifteen minutes left. They hadn't yet collected the errant kegs nor sprayed off the pavement. "No," he decided. "It's the principal of the thing."

As he rounded the curve, he saw his cab was empty. *Dammit, Joe. Why can't you ever listen?* He looked across the ditch and the adjacent field, frantically scanning for his friend, hoping he hadn't wandered far.

"Will!" Joe shouted from the shoulder across the highway. "Over here!"

There sat Joe on a stool he'd fashioned from a keg turned upright, an open bottle of beer in his hand.

"I can see why you love this job so much."

Will's jaw clenched.

The mistake, of course, was his. He didn't put the beer in Joe's hand, but he did bring an old man who'd just had a heart attack and had been released too early from the hospital out to a crash scene. A crash scene with beer. Joe had merely done what any other guy in his shoes would do left alone in a pickup for two hours on a highway littered with full, unopened bottles of beer.

Joe had listened to *All Things Considered* on the radio for as long as he could. He explored Will's glove box, organizing his maintenance records, registration and insurance cards by date. He found the Barbie head and spoke to the girl briefly about her plight. He braided her hair and tucked her back inside, then looked over the back seat to see if Will had left a newspaper or magazine behind. Finally, he opened the door to let in a little fresh air. From there, it was all but decided that he would, little by little, make his way out of the truck (just to stretch his legs), around the curve (only to see how things were coming) and plop himself down for a little refreshment (it would go to waste otherwise, after all).

Will relaxed his jaw and rolled a keg up beside Joe to sit down. He held out his hand.

"The beer, Joe. Let's have it."

"Oh, I think not," Joe said, and raised the bottle for another drink.

"Look. You are hours out of the hospital—a hospital you have no business being out of, I might add—and I'm pretty sure beer is not on your orders."

"Well, it should be. Does a world of good for a man's soul."

"But not for his heart." Will's hand was still extended. "The beer."

"Get your own. There's plenty." Joe motioned across the highway with his bottle.

"I don't want a beer, Joe." Will leaned his head back and looked at the sky. "I want you to give up yours."

Joe tipped the bottle and chugged the last few swallows. "Sorry, Will."

"You know what's going to happen when Pearl picks up the smell of beer?"

"We don't have to check in with our house mother, do we?"

"You have no idea, Joe. She has a way of knowing things. She probably already knows."

"Look at me, Will." Joe slid his pinky finger into the bottle and pulled it out with a *thwonk*. "I'm in reasonably good health. Well, except for some back pain and this little heart thingy. Otherwise, good." He put the tip of his finger to his lips. "But I'm seventy-five years old. I don't get out a lot. And my clarity of mind is not what it once was."

Will looked up and met Joe's eyes.

"What." Joe said. "You suppose I didn't know this? We know. Our minds have ways of telling us even as we slip every little bit away from ourselves, giving us time to come to terms. But there are few, if any, more difficult things to relinquish than our minds. So we go on as though we didn't look it in the eye, as though it cannot see us." Joe shook his head. "Listen. If the thrill of sitting on a beer keg in the middle of the highway drinking a bottle of Coors that rolled right up to my foot and invited me to open it somehow speeds my ultimate demise by a few days, then so be it. I've lived a rich, full, happy life."

He handed Will the empty bottle. "Here you go. It was fun. You really should have joined me."

"Probably right. But it's too late now. I really don't want you to have another."

"You know what they say about snoozing."

"Yep." Will stood to his feet. "Always losing."

Joe put his hand on his knees. "Time to go?"

"It's time." Will held out a hand.

"I'm fine." Joe stood on his own and smoothed his khakis. "Where do we get to go tomorrow?"

"Probably to the doctor." Will smiled. "I think you have an appointment with the cardiologist."

"You won't mention—"

"Of course not." He checked the time on his phone. "But first we need to go home and not tell Pearl."

"You don't happen to have an onion, do you?"

"An onion?"

"Sure. Onion and garlic are great masks for liquor breath. If nothing else they keep people at a good distance."

"Right. No. I don't usually keep them with me."

"Well, I thought I'd ask. You keep other unusual things in your truck."

"Oh? Like?"

"I noticed a cute blonde with a clean neck cut."

Will rolled his eyes. "Sometime I need to get rid of that thing."

"But why would you do that? I'm sure it makes a great conversation piece."

"Exactly." Will opened the passenger door and waved Joe inside. "Up you go."

"Maybe you have a stick of gum?"

"What are you, a teenager? Gum doesn't work."

Will slammed the door and walked around the front of the truck. He threw his bag and clipboard behind the seat and climbed in. "We'll swing by the grocery store and I'll get you an onion."

"And I'll eat it like an apple?"

"You want it dipped in caramel?"

"I think I'd rather you grounded me. Just get me some scallions. I can nibble on the greens."

"All part of the thrill of the day, eh?"

"Best day ever."

~

"Now listen." Will turned onto the gravel parking pad behind Pearl's house. "Go up the back way. Wash up in the John. Put on clean clothes."

"I've only worn these today. And I haven't spilled a thing," Joe protested.

"Change clothes. I'll have a hard enough time explaining to Pearl why you smell like sun and wind and sweat. Sun and wind and beer sweat is not a conversation I'm going to have with her."

"Right. Not sure how a change of clothes will change that. But you're in charge." Joe unbuckled his seat belt. The strap let go from his hand, the buckle slapping against the side glass. "Have I complicated your life very greatly?"

Will sat with his hands on the wheel at ten and two. "As a matter of fact," he said, looking straight ahead, "you have."

Joe's head drooped just slightly.

"You have also added something that I'll one day understand as *good,* even if today I can't for the life of me figure it out."

Joe beamed and opened his door. "That's the spirit. You're learning to wait out the arrival of good things."

"I think they are on backorder."

"Not everything ships from the same warehouse, Will. You might get several packages."

"Just what I need. More packages like this one."

Joe climbed out of the cab and reached back inside to open the glove box. "I'm going to take her inside with me."

"Need to practice your nylon hair braiding?" Will pointed to the doll head, noting the braids Joe set had come loose.

"Well, that. I just didn't tie it off. I need some of those little bitty rubber bands. You happen to have a neighbor kid with braces?" Joe made a stretching motion between his fingers and thumbs, the doll head pressed against his palm. "While we wait for your packages to arrive, we might try to get to the bottom of the Barbie head."

"There's no bottom, Joe. Just a pretty face."

"Unfortunate for us," Joe said with a grin.

"Go upstairs and clean up." Will's voice grew sharp. "I'll check in with Pearl about supper."

41

Will slammed his door shut and left Joe standing behind him as he jogged up Pearl's back porch steps and opened the door to the kitchen. "Pearl?"

"No need to shout, Mr. Phillips. Just come in." Pearl stood at the center island chopping onions with a large silver chef's knife. A pile of golden Klondike potatoes sat next to the cutting board.

"Oh, look at you. Hard at work."

"Indeed I am. Thank you for noticing."

"I always notice how hard you work."

"Oh?" Pearl asked. "It wouldn't hurt you so much to notice out loud now and then."

"Everything okay with you?" Will asked, reaching for a chunk of potato.

Pearl slapped the flat of the blade against the top of the pile. He jerked away.

"Holy—You could have cut my hand right off." He put his hands safely into his pockets. "I think I like you better with a towel than a knife."

"You were in no danger. Don't carry on so."

"Okay then. Like I said. Everything okay with you?"

"Just fine. And you? You sounded a little short with Joe just now."

"I what?"

"You were a little curt with your friend when you sent him upstairs to clean up. And I'm not at all sure why someone who moved into my home to convalesce would need to 'clean up' as though he'd been, oh, I don't know, outside my home doing something more strenuous than, say, a game of checkers like he promised." Pearl chopped through another small onion without looking up. "But maybe that's just me."

"Okay. It was foolish of me. I let him do a ride-along with me this afternoon. He was supposed to stay in the truck but he ... um ... got out and walked around."

"That's it?" Pearl put her hands on her hips. "He's supposed to get a little walking in each day. So that's perfect."

"Perfect?"

"Yes. I'm pleased you got him out so I don't have to make an issue with him about it later."

"Of course." Will leaned against the counter and stretched his legs out in front of him. "That's what I was thinking too."

"Now, I've been reading up. He also needs a better diet. No more of that greasy restaurant food. And no meat."

"No—meat?"

"That's right. We don't want him having another heart attack. Especially while he's here. We can work on his diet and exercise and turn back some of the damage. So, no more meat."

"What's gotten into you?"

"Cameron showed me some articles on the Internet." Pearl always pronounced Internet as though it were three words. *In-ter-net*. "I've been reading all afternoon. And I found this wonderful 30 Day Food Blog with the most beautiful photographs. The writer says that vegetarians eat more than lettuce. Did you know this?"

"Well, yes, I—"

"I did not. You should have told me. I thought they just

ate lettuce. And carrots. And chicken."

"Vegetarians don't eat chick—"

"Of course they don't!" Pearl slammed the knife through another onion. "Need you remind me of that embarrassment all over again?"

"You are the one who said chick—"

"Never mind what I said. And never mind the chicken. We are having potato and broccoli casserole tonight. It has fennel seed so you will think it tastes like sausage."

"I will?"

"Yes. You will." Pearl scooped the onion into a skillet of hot olive oil on the stove. "And so will Joe. Cameron told me I could put a little liquid smoke in things too, and no matter what I fix it will taste like I just brought it in from the grill."

"I'm not sure that's exactly how it works—"

"Don't be such a Debbie Downer, Mr. Phillips. If you're not here to be supportive in this major change then you can just fix your own meals." She stirred the onions with a wooden spatula. "And don't you dare tell Mr. Murphy our little secret about the fennel seeds. I want him to think he's eating meat so we can break this to him gently."

Will stared at Pearl, wondering if she and Joe were on the same path of gradual confusion together.

"By the time he moves back home to Colbyville he'll be a new man. Like he's twenty years old again."

"Because of fennel seeds?"

"Not just because of fennel seeds. Don't be ridiculous. We'll need the liquid smoke, too."

"Well, there's always dessert, I suppose." Will ran his finger along the pointed edge of the key in his pocket. "You aren't putting fennel seed in the dessert, are you?"

"Fennel seed in the dessert? Goodness, you are being ridiculous. We'll have an apple for dessert. Fresh, sweet, and light."

"Apple pie?" Will stood. "I can't wait."

"My Lord, Mr. Phillips! Have you lost your mind? There will be no more pie. I could have killed that man at lunch, serving him the rhubarb pie. And with ice cream! Why did no one stop me? The man just had a HEART ATTACK." She wiped her hands on her apron. "No, I mean an apple. Not an apple pie."

"Oh."

"You know, this will be good for you, too. You're a little soft around the middle." Pearl giggled into her hand. "I just saw a meme about that on the Internet today. They call it Daddy Body."

"That's Dad Bod."

"Oh, of course. Memes like fewer syllables."

"Are you going to be using the Internet a lot now?"

"Well, I'll need to for a while. I need to find heart healthy makeovers for all my delicious recipes."

"I see."

"I had no idea there was actually so much information on the Internet. You should have told me about it."

"Should I have?"

"Yes. I've so much to catch up on. Do you know this Kim Karla—no, Karma Kimmy—Oh, dear. I forgot her name—Did you know there is a person who makes millions of dollars just posting self portraits on the Internet?"

"You mean selfies? You have a whole new vocabulary in

just one day. It's Kardashian."

"Of course. That's it. Kim Kardashian." Pearl moved the onions around in the skillet.

"Tell me. If I had come to you last week and shown you a 30-day food blog and said you should buy stock in liquid smoke, what would you have said?"

"I would have listened and weighed your ideas carefully. You know me, Mr. Phillips. I am very open minded."

"No, you wouldn't have. You'd have whipped me with a towel and sent me upstairs with an extra slice of pie hoping I'd come to my senses." Will crossed his arms over his chest. "This is Cameron's doings."

"Cameron? Don't be ridiculous. Have I ever refused to listen when you tried to show me the benefits of a vegetarian diet—I mean, *lifestyle?* That's what it is, you know, a lifestyle. I read that. Anyway, have I ever?"

"Well, no. But that's because I never—"

"Then you have no reason to believe I wouldn't have listened. Shame on you for always thinking the worst, Mr. Phillips." Pearl dropped the potatoes into a casserole dish. "Best get with the program, young man. Big changes are afoot."

"How long are you expecting Joe to stay, Pearl?" Will popped a potato chunk into his mouth and bit into it with a crunch.

"As long as he needs to, of course." Pearl tapped the side of the casserole dish with her wooden spoon. "Don't snitch the potatoes, Mr. Phillips."

"You've diced enough for an army."

"Of course, there are plenty. But they're bad for you raw."

"Oh, that old wives' tale?" Will winced as he swallowed. "Uncooked potatoes don't give you worms."

"Don't be disgusting. Of course they don't. But they do have a dangerous toxin if you eat too much raw. And you don't get the nutritional benefit until a potato has been cooked."

"We're going to have to start calling you Encyclopedia Jenkins. One day on the Internet and you're like a walking web portal." Will reached for a glass from the cupboard and filled it at the sink. "If I could figure out how to sell ads on you, I'd make myself—I mean, us—a fortune."

"Hardly a fortune, Mr. Phillips. The ad model for funding on the Internet has collapsed." She sprinkled salt and pepper and a generous dash of fennel seed over the dish. "Terribly oversaturated, you know."

"I don't think I know you anymore." Will took a drink. "When did you become able to take in so much information in such a short time?"

"I've always been able. I just didn't know there was so much information to be had. A girl can only read the weekly paper so many times. And I've been through all the books at the library."

"The library." Will nodded. "I got a book there once. Not many to choose from."

"Yes, I imagine Mr. Carnegie's grave is a busy place, what with all the spinning he's doing in there right now. Think of what he could have done with Mr. Gore's Internet."

"Al Gore doesn't own the Internet, Pearl."

"Of course not. But he did invent it. Good thing he wasn't all tied up being the President. He'd never have had the time."

"I—He—" Will set his glass down. "Oh, never mind. But

I don't think Mr. Carnegie would have preferred the Internet to his libraries."

"He wouldn't?"

"Nah. Look at his buildings. He wanted the physicality of *place*. He wanted people to be present and connect with things and each other. Community."

"Maybe. But if Mr. Gore would have been inventing the Internet at the time Mr. Carnegie was building libraries, I think it would be a different world."

"I'm not sure what it means, Pearl, but I think you're right."

"Of course I am." She slid the pan into the oven and turned the dial on her timer to forty-five minutes. "What time will you and Mr. Murphy be down for dinner?"

"What time would you like us?"

"Six o'clock. Sharp."

Will looked at his watch. "Then we'll be down at six o'clock. Sharp."

"Well, alright." Pearl sighed. "You won't be coming down early to help me finish getting ready?"

Will looked at Pearl. The timer ticked in the background reminding him that his conversations would always, inevitably, go this way, just waiting for him to catch the trip wire with his foot and set off some sort of hidden explosive device.

"But, I—You said—"

"There's no need to tell me what I said, Mr. Phillips. We just established how good I am at remembering what I hear."

"Well, I'm sure that what I meant was that Joe will be down at six o'clock sharp. But I will be down at five-thirty to help you finish up."

"Oh, that's very sweet of you. You don't have to help."

"But—" He cocked his head. "But I… insist. I'll see you at five-thirty."

"That will be nice, Dear." Pearl turned back to the sink and washed her hands.

Will watched her for a moment before pushing his hands into his pockets and walking out through the butler's pantry and into the dining room. He stopped at the bottom of the staircase and rested his hands atop the giant mahogany newel post, staring up at the stained glass.

"You do it to yourself, Phillips. Every damn time." He spoke softly, as to a sleepy child being tucked into bed. "Barbara was no aberration. She was just more clear about her intentions. Make no mistake. Everyone wants the same thing from you. Stop believing better of them."

42

Will walked up the stairs to his room. As he passed Joe's door he stopped and tapped his watch. "Pearl says six o'clock sharp. So don't be late."

Joe lowered his *Sports Illustrated* magazine as Will walked away. "Got it. Hey, have you seen the new prospect the Cubbies are bringing up from Triple A?"

"Not now, Joe."

Will stepped into his closet and turned on the stereo. A black LP dropped onto the turntable as he lay back on his bed. Dylan growled out from the speakers about who exactly a person might be looking for.

He rubbed his temples and held his eyes closed.

"Josh Douglass."

"No, Bob Dylan." Will answered Joe without opening his eyes.

"Not the music. The prospect. The Cubs." Joe held up his *Sports Illustrated* magazine from the doorway.

"Joe, please. I said not now."

"I think he may be able to help them turn things around. He reminds me of Ernie Banks. That's the last time they had a good first baseman as far as I'm concerned. Could make all the difference, you know." He rolled the magazine and slapped it into his open palm. "'Course, I don't know so much about sports. But I thought you might be interested."

"Another time maybe I would be." Will rolled toward the wall. "I'm a little tired right now, Joe."

"Yes. Tired. Of course." Joe turned to go, then stopped.

"You are a man given to brooding, Will. You've noticed this?"

"Have I noticed this?" Will sat up in his bed. "Joe, how did we go from 'Not now' to exploring whether I am given to brooding?"

"Oh, I don't know that we're exploring anything, really. I just asked if you'd noticed." Joe rubbed the light silvery scruff at his chin. "But of course you've noticed. How could you not?"

"We aren't doing this, Joe."

"'This'? Heavens, no. We're not doing 'this'. I just stopped by your room to talk to you about the Cubs (the door was open, after all). And you declined. And I made a simple observation. There is no 'this' in that."

Will closed his eyes and leaned his head against the bare plaster wall behind his bed. "The door is not open, Joe. The door is just... not. And I am not brooding. I've had a few late nights this week. You know?"

"Late nights. Indeed. Brooding can be useful though. Some of the greatest works of literature came from a man's brooding. Women writers brood far less, you know. They don't have time."

"You don't know that."

"No, you're right. I don't. But I know women. They wouldn't have time to brood. It's a luxury generally reserved for men."

"Virginia Woolf."

"Yes, what about her?"

"She had plenty of time to brood, as I recall."

"That's different. She had a room of her own. Most women don't. And you'll also recall that her brooding ended badly."

"Some fine literature, though."

"My point exactly. So what are you writing?"

"Writing?"

"Yes. For all this brooding, I'd expect to see you writing something."

"I'm not a writer, Joe."

"Yes." Joe slid the magazine under his arm and folded his hands behind his back. "So you should stop. Splash some water on your face and tuck in your shirt. Brooding does not become a man who is not a writer."

"How can you come off as a feminist and be so sexist at the same time?"

"I contain multitudes, Will."

Will let out a loud laugh and swung his feet to the floor. "Don't we all."

"We do. Some of those multitudes are larger than others."

"How do you do it, Joe?"

"Do?"

"How do you win people—me—over all the time?"

"Oh, I don't know. I gather one of the personalities in that throng must be quite charming."

"Quite." Will looked at his watch. "Damn. It's almost 5:30 already. I need to go help Pearl finish dinner."

"I'll go. Haven't cooked since we grilled together."

"Gosh, that feels like ages ago. But no, if I don't show up Pearl will be upset."

"I'll say I volunteered. It'll be true."

"Nah. She was in a strange mood. She'd blame me for tricking you into volunteering."

"So, I'll just tag along. Then it won't be about you."

"You don't know Pearl. If I were old enough she could make the first World War about me. But sure. She was in a strange mood before and if you are along perhaps she'll stick to her brighter side."

"Goodie. I was getting bored up here in my room."

Will buttoned his shirt. "Joe, we've only been back from the beer spill for an hour."

"An hour? In some cultures that's the same as a week."

"You just made that up."

"We don't know that it isn't true."

"Is this what you do? Make unfounded statements that people can't disprove?"

"Disproving a negative thing is quite difficult."

"Yeah. Let's go."

"You should call Cameron tonight."

"Where did that come from?"

"She likes you."

"Uh, there you go again."

"So prove I'm wrong."

"Doesn't matter. I think Cameron has had enough of me this week."

"Maybe. And maybe she could use to see you without having to go the hospital and such."

"You're pushing, Joe. Don't push."

"Maybe you're right. We could always ask Pearl what she thinks."

"Ask Pearl." Will laughed. "And why would we do that?"

"Well, if I can get the testimony of two witnesses I could prove my point. You seem interested in proof."

"Pearl is biased. She thinks she orchestrated me and Cameron. She'd want you to be right."

"You and Cameron. Are you a couple?"

Will's eyes widened. "I—no. I didn't say we are a couple."

"But you said Pearl orchestrated you and Cameron. Like you and Cameron are a thing."

"We are friends. We do things together. Like a team. You could call us Team Murphy. That's what we are."

"You should call her tonight. Say you will, or I'll ask Pearl to weigh in."

"For Cameron's sake, let's not do that."

"Just for Cameron's sake?"

"Well, mine too. But my sake is sort of tied up in Cameron's. If I put her in an awkward position I put myself in an awkward position by extension."

"The more you talk the more you sound like a thing."

"You should stop now."

"We'll see what Pearl thinks."

"We already know what Pearl thinks. Get your shoes."

43

"Did you go to work with Mr. Phillips today, Mr. Murphy?"

"That I did." Joe slid Pearl's chair out and waited for her to sit and scoot forward before taking his own seat at the dining room table. "Did we not get rid of that pesky Mister business the last time I was here?"

Pearl dipped her head and blinked, unfolding her linen napkin and laying it across her lap. "Of course we did. These old habits, you know."

"They are harder to lick the older we get." Joe shook out his napkin and tucked it under his chin. Pearl's eyes widened and she opened her mouth to protest when Will gently set his hand on top of hers.

"He's not me," he murmured.

Pearl closed her mouth into a tight smile. "Yes. Yes they are."

Will lifted his hand and laid his own napkin across his lap. "Joe was a great help today, in fact."

"Is that right? Do tell me what you did, Joe. And promise me you weren't following Mr. Phillips around on some high roof." Pearl spooned a serving of hotdish and reached for Joe's plate. "I might just have my own little heart attack."

Joe laughed and held out his plate. "There's a reason I retired from the fire department. I like to stay on the ground these days." He stirred his fork around the steaming casserole on his plate. "You could say going to work with Will is a little like going to Happy Hour at the bar."

"Oh?" Pearl raised an eyebrow.

"Not every day is like that, Joe." Will handed Pearl his plate. "I had to go take care of a semi load of beer that overturned on the highway."

"You were there?" Pearl tapped the serving spoon against Will's plate to empty it. "Enid Blomgren told us about it at coffee this afternoon. We thought it would be fun to bring out our patio chairs with some pretzels and peanuts."

"That's what was missing!" Joe pulled up his napkin and wiped his mouth. "Pretzels."

Will shot a look at Joe.

"You don't mean—" Pearl held the serving spoon over her own plate.

"I just mean if a guy—or lady—is going to go out to a big beer spill, he—or she—should have some pretzels."

"But you didn't— "

"Oh, my stars. Can you imagine someone who just got out of the hospital sitting on a keg in the middle of the highway drinking a beer? Without pretzels?" Joe grinned and reached for the green beans.

Pearl stared at Joe. "No, of course not. I cannot imagine anything quite so foolish." Her eyes narrowed. "And of course, Mr. Phillips would never have allowed something like that on his watch."

"Yes. Your Mr. Phillips takes his responsibilities very seriously."

Will straightened in his chair. "Pass me the beans, Joe?"

Pearl looked back and forth between the two men at her table. Will wondered if the whiff of mischief she'd picked up was tainted with barley and hops.

"I am going to be outnumbered here for a while, am I

not?" she said.

"You could always invite that nice Ms. Julian over to balance things out."

Will glared at Joe. Pearl turned and gestured toward Joe with her fork. "You're exactly right about that."

"I don't think you need to worry about being outnumbered, Pearl. Joe looks to be a free agent."

"Come on, Will. You're the only one who doesn't want to see what there is to see. Even Midge could see it when we went to pick up Emily."

"Emily?" Pearl cocked her head. "Who is Emily?"

Will leaned his head back and closed his eyes, quietly wishing for a return to the less complicated life of just days ago when his biggest concern was whether Mad Dog would sit at his desk and write on his tablet.

"Emily Dickinson, of course," Joe answered, not missing a beat. "We stopped at my house for a few things—especially for my toothbrush. I just did not like the one they gave me at the hospital. And I grabbed my copy of *The Poems of Emily Dickinson*."

"I love Emily Dickinson. You will bring it to read after checkers tonight?"

"I'd be delighted." Joe pulled his napkin from his shirt and wiped his lips. "I'll read the one about the wing with feathers."

Will looked up from his plate where he'd been studying the scattering of fennel seeds in the hotdish. "Wing with feathers?"

"*Thing*. The thing with feathers." Joe wiggled his finger in his ear and pointed at Will with an impish grin.

"Seems I'm going to need Cameron here after all," Will said under his breath.

"What was that, Mr. Phillips?"

"Oh, nothing. Just remembering I need to make a call."

"Well, if you mean you need to call Ms. Julian, there's no need."

Will's fork froze midway to his mouth. He looked from Pearl to Joe and back again to Pearl.

"No…need? What does that mean?"

"I already called her. Mr. Murph—I mean, Joe—thought it would be nice if she came by tonight."

"And when exactly did we find time for this conversation?"

"When you boys came down to help me with dinner, of course. Don't you remember?" Pearl reached for the pitcher, condensation droplets trickling down the narrow grooves of the hand-cut lily design in the crystal. Will studied her small mouth as she formed words, and watched as she pressed her lips into a small smile. He saw less of the petty smirk he wanted to convince himself was there and more of a sincerity, even kindness, than he'd been able to easily attribute to Pearl as of late. It felt like ages since she'd caught him on the back stairs in his boxers and invited him in for coffee and a good story. But how long had it really been since his life complicated itself—no, since Joe complicated it, and since Cameron. Just days? Maybe weeks? He'd invited none of this upon himself and yet here it was. And now here was Pearl, not whisking towels or brandishing knives, but just being kind, even if her kindness further complicated his life.

"I don't remember that conversation, no," he said, finally,

lifting the pitcher from Pearl's hands and tipping it to fill her glass with ice water.

"Oh, that's right. You had to step out for a few minutes."

"You sent me to the store for a head of lettuce. Which I see you didn't use."

"Well, by the time you got back everything was ready to go on the table so I skipped the salad."

Joe cleared his throat and tapped his sternum with his knuckles. "Maybe I should have a little of that water over here."

Pearl had no plans for a salad, of course. Her kitchen protocols were far more orderly than would allow for a last-minute salad, even with her new-found dreams of plant-based eating grandeur. He'd been played, again, by Pearl's unending, meddling kindness.

"You sent me to the store so you could talk about Cameron and me?"

"Oh, heavens no, Mr. Phillips. Everything needn't always be about you, you know." She fanned her fingers to wave him off and took a sip from her glass. The ice cubes clinked as she set the glass back down. "Mr. Murph—Joe—one day I am going to get that right. Joe wanted a moment alone."

"Exactly. He'd been dogging me to call Cameron before we came downstairs and he convinced you to get me out of the way so he could tell you to call her."

"Joe," Pearl turned to Murphy, who was quietly shoveling forkfuls of casserole into his mouth. "Do you have a cell phone?"

Joe wiped his mouth and reached around to his back pocket. "Sure do." He held up a thick vintage Nokia phone with worn silver buttons and a small gray LED display. A patch of duct tape held the battery cover in place.

"You see? If Mr. Murphy wanted to call Cameron, he surely could do it himself."

"Then what? Why did you two need a special little moment alone?"

Pearl looked at Joe and raised an eyebrow. Her eyes were soft. Joe put his phone back in his pocket and nodded. "Go ahead."

"Mr. Murphy wanted to know if I could set him up with a poker game."

Will pushed his chair back slightly from the table. "Wha— A poker game?"

"He didn't think you would approve."

Will picked up his napkin and twisted it between his hands. "But he thought *you* would?" He pointed at Pearl. "And wait. He thought you'd be able to set him up?" Will laughed and scooted his chair back up to the table. "That's a good one," he said, picking up his fork and poking around in his hotdish. "That is a good one."

"I did, though," Pearl said softly.

"Did what?" Will chewed and swallowed, still chuckling.

"Set him up for the back room game at Marvelle's."

"Wait. How do you know about that game? I can't even get in. Mad Dog can't even get in."

Pearl smiled her most demure smile. "Because all of you are tinhorn gamblers. They want serious players."

"Tinhorn. And you know this because …"

"Surely you don't think pool and checkers are my only hustle, Mr. Phillips."

"You've been in the back room at Marvelle's? For poker?

I don't even know who you are any more." Will smiled and leaned on his elbow, resting his chin in his hand.

"Oh, of course you do. Don't be silly. You know exactly what you want to know." Pearl picked up her fork. "Now get your elbow off the table and stop staring. It's impolite."

"Can you get me in?"

"No." She pointed with her fork. "Elbow."

Will sat up straight. "Come on. I have money."

"I should hope so, seeing you pay so little for rent. But no. You're too young to lose it. And you might need it for a nest egg, you know, if things work out with you and Cameron."

"Ah, and so we come full circle. Joe asked you about the poker game and then asked you to call Cameron."

"No."

"But you called her while I was gone."

"Yes."

"Then?"

"It was Pearl's idea to call. She wanted to get more of these here—" Joe waved his hand around the table "—veggie recipes." Joe reached for another serving of broccoli potato casserole.

"You two have it all figured out, don't you."

"Come now, Mr. Phillips. Do you really believe we have so little going on that we want to spend our time plotting for you?" Pearl spread butter over a warm slice of wheat bread. "And do you really think the potluck mavens I coffee with have any idea how to prepare healthy vegetarian meals for you two? Enid Blomgren's specialty is beefy noodle hotdish and Francis Oberholdt's repertoire is limited to eight different varieties of six-layer Jell-O Pudding dessert. Having Cameron

Julian across the street is like having my own personal Rachael Ray right in the kitchen."

"Rachael Ray is not a vegetarian."

"Don't deflect. It would be like that if she were. Besides. Rachael Ray is really good with potatoes, and vegetarians love potatoes."

"And fennel seed."

"Yes, I imagine Rachael Ray knows what to do with fennel seeds too."

"So Cameron isn't coming to see me."

"I am so sorry, Mr. Phillips. She is, in fact, not."

"So I could go to my room after dinner and no one would protest."

"Would you protest, Mr. Murphy?"

"Well, I would say it's a damn shame for you to miss her visit." He turned to Pearl. "Pardon my French. But I do figure a man ought to do what he thinks he ought to do." He put his knife through the butter and picked up a slice of bread. "Almost forgot this," he said, tapping the crust. "What about you, Pearl. Would you protest?"

"Goodness, no. It's been an exhausting week and I completely understand if you want to go upstairs early and rest." Pearl smiled. "Ms. Julian would understand too, I'm sure."

Will wiped his mouth and set down his fork. "Well then. That's all settled."

Joe folded his arms across his chest and sat back in his chair with a wide grin, his joy at being in the company of his new friends spilling over.

"Joe," Pearl said touching the left side of her chin with two middle fingers. "You have a little butter."

He dabbed at his chin with his napkin and raised his eyebrows for Pearl's approval.

"No, other side." Pearl cocked her head and moved her mouth to mirror Joe. "A little higher. There you go."

"I don't know the last time someone told me I had food on my face."

"I'm so sorry to embarrass you, Joe." Pearl patted his hand.

"Embarrass? Are you kidding? When you eat alone at Denny's Café every night, there's no one to tell you when you squirt catsup on your cheek or dribble Western dressing down your shirt. The waitress won't tell you because she's afraid for her tip. Too bad, too. I'd double it just for the attention."

Will's irritation softened, reflecting that the isolation of his friends was not a solitude they chose in the same way he had, but an imposition life had delivered to their respective doorsteps, a package of not at all what they had ordered.

"I'm glad you're here, Joe," Will said.

Joe's eyes glistened and he looked away quickly, reaching for the water pitcher. Pearl reorganized the bread basket and pulled the breadscarf over the top. Will looked at his hands in his lap, rubbing a small blue ink mark off his first knuckle with the opposite thumb. No one spoke for what felt to him like a full ten minutes while he rubbed the knuckle red, when it was more likely just five seconds or so before the doorbell rang.

"Cameron! Thank goodness!" Pearl let go of the bread basket and all three pushed their chairs back and stood, announcing in unison, "I'll get it!"

Pearl bumped into Joe on her way to the dining room door and he stopped to motion her by.

"Wait," Will said. "We shouldn't all go. Let me."

"No, no," Pearl said. "She might not be expecting you. I invited her; I should go."

"I never get to answer the door any more. Can I go?" Joe's eyes looked watery like Archie's.

"Umm, yeah. I think you just outdid Pearl and me. You go."

Joe walked to the front door smiling. He turned back to see Will and Pearl in the dining room doorway, Will's hands behind him tucking in his shirt and Pearl smoothing the front of her skirt. Joe gave them a thumbs-up signal and continued to the door.

"Lord have mercy. You'd think we all wanted to go out with her."

"I do not want—" Will bit off his words when Pearl gave his hand a hard squeeze.

"Don't say that unless you really mean it." She spoke quietly through her teeth. Will knew without looking that Pearl's smile was unflinched by her words and made a mental note to ask sometime when they were all in better moods why she didn't find herself a good ventriloquist gig. The kids in the hospital's children's wing, at the very least, would be enchanted.

"Come in, come in," Joe was saying as Cameron came in and stamped her feet lightly on the rug as though shaking off snow, though the clear, late spring evening was completely dry. She leaned and gave Joe a light air kiss at his cheek. He turned to Will as she passed by him, grinning widely and giving him another thumbs-up. Will looked at the ground and made another mental note to remind Cameron that she now lived among the reserved Swedes and Germans and such displays of affection were unexpected, discomfiting to some, even, and a firm handshake would do just fine.

Pearl rushed forward grasping Cameron by the shoulders and giving her an air kiss of her own—something he had never seen her do with even her closest friends—as though she had read Will's thoughts and felt compelled to silently rebuke his reservations. "Cameron dear, it's so good to see you."

"Oh, and you too, Pearl," Cameron said as she *muah'd* into the air on Pearl's other cheek.

"So glad to see the Italian *famiglia* reunited," Will said, putting his hands in his pockets and pulling his shoulders in, simultaneously feeling ignored and wishing to squeeze himself through one of the tiny knots in the birds-eye maple.

"Hi, Will." Cameron smiled at him. He dipped his head in reply. "Pearl, I brought you something." She held out a bright floral gift bag with fuchsia tissue poking out the top.

"Dear, you shouldn't have." Pearl blushed the culturally-prescribed degree, waving Cameron off with one hand and reaching for the bag's soft cord handles with the other, demonstrating the smooth, practiced *no-no-yes* of this same stoic Swedish-German community.

"Oh, it's nothing, really," Cameron said, fully fluent in this unwritten code herself. "It's a starter cookbook for vegetarian dishes. I've been using it so long I have them all memorized. So I'm passing it along to you."

Pearl slid the dog-eared book out of the bag and flipped through, stopping occasionally to exclaim about the beautiful photography and exotic colors, here and there inquiring about an unfamiliar piece of produce.

"This will be so much fun," she said, finally slipping the

book back into the bag. "Let me clear the dishes and then we'll sit and you can show me your favorites."

Will stepped aside from the doorway to let the women through. They walked past him into the dining room as though he weren't there, leaning their heads together and laughing. He stood straight. "Go ahead and sit. I'll clean up the dishes."

Pearl turned. "Oh, no, Mr. Phillips. You needn't do that. You were on your way upstairs for the night."

"You're not staying?" Cameron stopped at the pantry door and looked back.

"Well, I—"

"He had a full day. Big beer catastrophe on the highway." Joe had come up behind Will and clapped a hand on his shoulder. "Our friend is pretty well tuckered out and was just telling us how he thought he'd retire early tonight."

"Is that right," Cameron said. Will detected the slightest smirk and thought she could use some tutoring from Pearl on facial expression management.

"Well, I was going to. But it would be rude of me to come down and enjoy Pearl's fine cooking and not help with the dishes. So I can manage to stay up just a little longer." He picked up Joe's plate and scraped bits of hotdish onto Pearl's plate, then slipped it underneath and reached for his own.

"You're a dear, Mr. Phillips. Such a good help." Pearl smiled and he wanted to believe she meant it. "Do be careful with the plates. They chip so easily. And you'll want to wipe the glasses by hand. The dishwasher spots them too badly." She slipped her arm through Cameron's and pushed open the door. "Let's go to the kitchen."

Will poured the water glasses back into the pitcher with a sigh, watching as the pantry door swung closed behind them.

Joe watched from the other doorway. "Caught your second wind?"

"Just don't want to leave Pearl with all the cleanup."

"I can do them so you can go rest."

"No, thanks. I'm good."

"A pretty girl can do that, you know. Replenish a man's stamina. There's certainly no shame in admitting that."

"I'm still plenty tired, Joe. As you should be. I just want to help with the dishes. There's no shame in that, either."

"Oh, sure. I'm flagging a bit. But as I said, there's nothing quite like the revitalizing power of a beautiful woman."

"She's too young for you, Joe."

"Thus vainly thinking that she thinks me young, although she knows my days are past the best, simply I credit her false-speaking tongue: On both sides thus is simple truth suppressed."

"What?" Will leaned on his palms on the table.

"Shakespeare. Sonnet 138."

"Oh, okay." He gathered the silverware and piled it loosely on top of the stacked plates, narrowly avoiding the cold casserole sauce on his hand. "But, *what?*"

Joe smiled softly. "Shakespeare wrote 138 about aging and lies."

"You're going to recite it to me even though I have no idea what you're talking about, right?"

"No, I won't recite it to you. Not all of it, anyway. You can look it up later."

"And is there a point you'd like to make with it?" Will was

exhausted, beautiful women or not. He could feel impatience taking shape in his words and working their way out of his mouth before he could re-form them.

"Oh, love's best habit is in seeming trust, and age in love loves not to have years old. Therefore I lie with her and she with me, and in our faults by lies we flattered be."

Shakespeare's double entendre sunk in and the idea of Joe lying with anyone now made Will uneasy. "You weren't going to recite the whole thing."

"I didn't. A sonnet has fourteen lines."

"Great. Fifty-seven percent is close enough."

"That's pretty good math."

"Occupational hazard." His weariness had now shifted well beyond impatience and was letting even improbable jealousy toward Joe creep in. "Even with a poetic lie she's too young for you."

"Do you really think so? I didn't think we were so terribly far off."

Will banged the spoon against the casserole dish. "Way off, Joe."

"Gosh." Joe's face fell. "Will, I don't mean to sound untoward, but how old is Pearl?"

"Pearl? Oh, man. Like seventy-six, maybe seventy-seven?" He set the plates inside the empty dish and looked up at Joe, feeling his face flush. "Wait. Pearl?"

Joe looked toward the kitchen and laughed. He pointed with his thumb through the wall as though they could see Pearl and Cameron poring over the cookbook and pulling ingredients off the pantry shelf. "You thought I meant—"

"Cameron. Yes." Will looked up from the table and put his

hands in his pockets. "I feel like an ass, Joe. I'm sorry."

"Well, we have established that you're tired, right?" Joe laughed. "She's a lovely woman, Will. Beautiful, intelligent, self-possessed."

"All true."

"Wonderful cook."

"Best in the county."

"If I thought I might like to, um…" Joe cleared his throat but didn't continue.

Will pulled out a chair and motioned to Joe to sit, then sat across the table himself. Joe remained standing, hands folded in front of him, looking every bit the nervous seventeen-year-old boy that he must have felt inside at that moment.

"What I mean is, um, would you mind it terribly if I were to, um…" Joe shuffled his feet.

"What, Joe? Do you need a glass of water?"

"No, I'm fine. I would like to court Pearl." He steadied himself with a hand on the chair. "There. I said it."

Will suppressed a laugh, trying to respect the gravity Joe had brought to the matter, conveyed by his uncharacteristic fit of nerves. "Are you asking me for permission?"

"Well, yes. I believe I am. You are the closest thing to her father I know, after all."

"Her *father*?" Will put his hand over his mouth and leaned back in his chair. Joe stood straight, hands still folded over his belly where the bottom button on his shirt strained against the tug of the two sides of fabric, his otherwise tall stature dwarfed by the high ceilings and stately cherry wainscot behind him. "I know you've been having a little trouble putting things together these past few days, Joe. But nobody would ever mistake me for a guy who could fill old Pete Butler's shoes." He shifted forward in his seat, placing his hands on the table. "And how is it I can possibly be both Pearl's father and your son? We still need to talk about how that works."

"Well, it is a bit of an interesting dynamic, don't you think?" Joe smiled and his hands relaxed. "Would make for an interesting story if a brooding sort of fellow ever wanted to write it."

"Cut it out. We're talking about *you* now." Will stood and extended his hand to Joe. "No matter, anyway. If you need someone's blessing to woo Pearl Jenkins, I'm happy to give it."

Joe clasped Will's hand. "You won't regret this," he said, shaking Will's hand vigorously with both of his.

"I won't? But are you sure you won't? Are you really feeling up to this?"

"I've no right to be feeling up to anything, Will. In the last week I've been beaned between the eyes by a baseball out of nowhere and had a heart attack. But I've felt better since you checked me into Hotel Jenkins than I've felt in ten years. Might be Pearl's cooking. But I'm betting it's just Pearl."

"Well, the cooking can go a long way…"

"And if I may be so bold, I think maybe I'm good for her, too."

"Is that right."

Joe straightened his shoulders, pushing out his chest as he slid his hands into his pockets. "It is. She softens when I'm around."

"She softens?"

"Yes. I see how she is with you when she thinks you're alone. She softens when she knows I'm here."

"Maybe she's just being polite until she gets to know you better."

"I don't think so. I think it's more than that." Joe rubbed his chin. "Is she harder on you lately?"

"Well, now that you mention it."

"That's me."

"That's you. The Joe Effect. I never read you as a guy who thought so much of himself."

"Oh, I don't know that I do. Could be Cameron, too. Or maybe a combination. But she softens around me. And if she's harder on you lately then that means she's feeling anxious around me and she's saving up for you when I'm not around."

"Pearl Jenkins, the great Economist of Aggravation," Will said. "You really think you've got her figured out?"

Joe laughed. "Heavens, no. If I should be so lucky as to spend the rest of my life with Pearl I sincerely hope not to have figured her out. Where would be the joy in such a thing?"

"Well, maybe if I give you my blessing, you could give me a few pointers in exchange."

"Too late for an exchange. You already gave it. And I've given you pointers. Like when I told you to call Cameron."

"Right. That's not what I meant."

A laugh carried through the butler's pantry door from the kitchen.

"Listen," Will said, handing a stack of plates to Joe. "Take these to the kitchen. Dish soap is in the cabinet under the sink, left side. There are dishtowels in the center drawer of the island. Or, Pearl probably has one in her hand you could relieve her of."

"And?" Joe took the plates.

"And washing the dishes will go a long way toward that…softening…you think is going on."

"Where will you be?"

"In bed. I'm going up for the night."

"But I thought that was just to prove something to me and Pearl about Cameron."

"Maybe it was. And maybe now it's to prove something to me." He clapped Joe on the back. "Congratulations, old man. Don't blow it." Will stopped at the dining room door. "Make sure Cameron gets home alright."

"You mean, all the way across the street."

"Well, yeah. It's farther than it looks."

"You could stay and walk her out yourself, you know. Even walk her across the big scary street." Something lit in Joe's eyes, as though he apprehended something Will did not yet know. "That was your plan, wasn't it?"

"I didn't have a plan." Will did a poor job of masking his annoyance. "Just make sure she gets home alright. I'm going to bed."

An hour later, Will was still awake, lying flat on his back staring at the plaster and lathe on the ceiling when he heard Cameron and Joe talking and laughing on their way to the front door. Joe offered to walk her to her door, and of course she refused, insisting it was only a few steps across the street and she was just fine. As soon as he heard the latch of the front door click, he sat up in bed and leaned toward the window to watch Cameron walk across the street, simultaneously counting the creaks on the stairs as Joe climbed up to his room. Cameron was not quite to her door when he heard Joe hit the third step to the top which, thanks to a loose board, had a certain clunk in addition to the sorrowful creak, signaling the end of his watch. He laid back down quietly and held his eyes shut, the rumpled quilt pulled up to his chin, covering that he still had on his plaid cotton shirt over his T-shirt, cuffs still buttoned. Had he sat up for one more step, Joe would know he was awake and it would be another half hour of conversation.

And had he sat up for one more step, he wouldn't have missed Cameron turning to look up at his window above the porch roof as she reached for her front door handle.

Joe stood in the doorway, silhouetted by the colorful glow of the streetlights through Pearl's stained glass.

"Will," Joe whispered.

Will didn't answer.

"Cameron got home just fine. You should call her tomorrow."

He didn't move.

Joe stood a little longer, then turned and padded down the hall to the bathroom to get ready for bed.

Will rolled onto his side, holding the quilt to his chest and facing the wall. He smiled to no one in particular. He might call Cameron tomorrow. He might not. Such a small thing, really. But it was a small thing he would decide for himself.

44

Will had no sooner settled into his desk the next day when Nina called.

"Justin should have the insurance check by now," he told her.

"I know. He does. And they've started tearing out the kitchen." Nina's voice shook. "But I need to tell you something."

"Okay," Will said, and pulled out his yellow legal pad, tapping his pen against the top margin. "What's up?"

"I can't—I can't talk about it over the phone. Can you come?"

"You need me to come to Fergus?" Will needed a day in the office. A day without travel, without a hospital, without adventure. Without Nina or Joe. He opened his drawer and took out his calendar, flipping open the pages "How's Friday sound? I'm pretty booked this week."

Nina sniffled. Will closed his eyes and put his hand into a fist against his forehead. "Can you—" She stopped. "Can you come sooner? Today?"

"Nina. There's really not much more for me to do on your case until the work is done. What is it you need?"

"It's not about the work. Please. Can you come?"

Will closed the calendar with a sigh and shoved the drawer shut. "Yeah. I can. I'll be there after lunch."

"You live!" Mad Dog threw his keys onto his desk from the doorway and smiled at Will. "I was thinking to call the Mounties to find you."

"We don't have Mounties, Mike."

"No, but I thought maybe you'd run away to Canada. Happens a lot in election years."

"Right." Will pushed back in his chair. "Doesn't look like the place collapsed while I was not here. Pretty sure I even took care of a beer spill for you."

"For *me*? Sounded more like you took care of the beer spill for your grandpa." He snickered, never able to be patient enough for his own punchlines. "Or should I say your grandpa took care of the beer spill for you?"

"Hey." Will sat up straight and pointed a finger at Mad Dog. "He only drank one—Wait." He sat back. "How'd you know about that?"

Mike laughed and shook his head. "Roundleg came into Marvelle's after his shift. Like a guy would even want a beer after that."

"I owe him one for his loose lips, then."

"Don't blame Roundleg. He's not the one who brought an old civilian to a crash scene."

"Civilian?" Will stood up, ignoring the beeper going off in his brain telling him to stay sitting, reminding him he was no pre-pubescent needing to defend his father's virility against charges of who could beat up whom from the playground bully. "You have no idea who you're talking about. The guy is old Chicago fire. He'd be better at any crash scene than you or me or even Jeremy Roundleg." He pressed his hands into his desk. "So, yeah. Just—watch yourself."

Will's voice trailed off and the stricken look on Mad Dog's face turned to glee. His eyebrows shot up and his mouth curved into a wide grin. Mad Dog's shoulder's shook as he began to laugh.

"Oh, little Willie." He looked at Will a bit longer, shook his head and walked away singing, "Willie, Willie."

Will's cheeks burned and he felt lightheaded. He sat down and held his head in his hands, wishing for his old life—his normal life—back. Then feeling perspiration prick at his neck he realized he didn't know what that meant, his old life. "What was my old life?" he mumbled in to his fingers. "What did my normal life look like?"

His phone vibrated on the desk, jarring him back to the four walls of his office and to the sound of Mad Dog whistling across the hall.

He picked up the phone and put it to his ear without looking at the display.

"Claims. Phillips."

Will tapped his pen against his desk.

"Nina, I'll be up after lunch. We can talk then, okay?"

He stopped tapping.

"The police station? Why the police station?"

Will's head dropped into his hand again. "Nina, I'm an adjuster. Not a lawyer. You need a lawyer."

He listened for a moment, then set the phone screen-up on his desk and stared at it, frozen. Nina's inarticulate sobs, packaged and shipped across the eighty-seven miles between Will's downtown Dennison office and an interview room at the police station at 7th and Main in Fergus. The tiny particles of her despair crowded together and screamed out of his phone.

Did this woman have no friends? Come to think of it, did anyone Will knew—besides Mad Dog, who didn't deserve them—have friends? Could she call no one in her town to help her? Could she not call a family member?

The phone quieted and Will picked it up. "Nina. Can't you call your mother?"

The sobs started again and Will held the phone away from his ear. "Okay. Okay. I'm on my way. But you need to understand there's nothing I can do. You need to call a lawyer. Call a lawyer for Robbie right now."

Nina's son Robbie was twelve years old. Will remembered him sitting in the lawn chairs with Lucy Mae and their sister the first night he was at Nina's house after the fire. He looked more like he was nine, the way adolescent boys when they hit a certain age can look like small men with full beards or like tiny children, clear skin and round faces and happy eyes until they turn sixteen. Or eighteen. Or some of them twenty-two. There was no way from looking at a twelve year old boy to know what you were really seeing. Robbie was one of those with the baby face. Like he should be on a playground. Not someone who needed a lawyer. Will had made out from Nina's mangled sobbing that the police thought Robbie had something to do with the fire. Nina's fire? Or another fire? He couldn't be sure. At this point, he wasn't sure he even wanted to know. But he told Nina he would come.

Will pulled Justin's file from his drawer, locked the drawer and shoved the file in his bag. He slammed his laptop shut and unplugged the cord with a yank. Bag over his shoulder and laptop under his arm, he stopped at Mad Dog's door.

"On my way back to Fergus. Some kind of development."

"A development."

"Yes."

"Does this mean your girlfriend wants you to take her to lunch before, you know—" Mad Dog made a lewd gesture with his hands.

"You're an ass." Will walked out.

"I'll take that as a *yes* then, Willie." Will heard Mad Dog's laughter as the door closed behind him on the street.

Crazy.

"Maybe it's not your old life you really need, Phillips," Will chided himself as he climbed into his truck. His arm tingled under the scarred skin and he tugged at his sleeve, undoing the cuff and tucking it in to button it up tighter against his wrist.

He drove back to the house to check on Joe before he left town. Nina would have to wait while he tended to his other client in need of a best friend. He couldn't imagine what she needed from him anyway. Even if the kid had something to do with the fire, he'd get a copy of the report and send it to the insurance company and it wouldn't make a lick of difference as far as he was concerned. Unless he could say that Justin somehow put him up to it, all he had was a firestarter kid belonging to a woman with no assets to go after. Anyway, that made no sense and no way would the kid say it. Justin hadn't even been able to tell Will the names of Nina's kids when he gave his statement. He'd hardly be the kind of guy to collude with a twelve-year-old he pretended didn't exist, to burn down a house he rarely stayed in.

But then what kind of guy *would* be the sort to collude with a twelve-year-old to start a fire? Will's arm tingled again and he shook it off into the air as he turned into the gravel behind Pearl's house. He thought he smelled Barbara's perfume as he opened the door. Ever so faintly. Ever so briefly.

He jogged up the back steps without checking in with Pearl. Joe was not in his room and Will heard her soft laugh from downstairs.

He stood at the landing and called down. "You kids playing checkers already?"

"Are you home so soon, Mr. Phillips? Seems like you just left."

"Got that right," Will said, ambling down the steps. He found Joe and Pearl at the dining room table, breakfast dishes pushed aside and the checkerboard between them. Most of Pearl's black checkers were still on the board, a few stacked with crowns. Joe was down to three.

"Not going so well for you, Joe," Will said, pointing at the board.

Joe chuckled. "Don't tell her, but I'm letting her win. I know a few things about hustling myself."

"No, Joe. I'm pretty sure you do not." Pearl laughed and captured another of his red pieces.

"Listen, I just wanted to check on you. I got called back to Fergus on a thing and I'm not sure when I'll get back today."

"Another claim over there? You were just there a few weeks ago." Pearl frowned.

"Same case. Something's come up with the fire."

"A fire?" Joe lit up. "I have some expertise, you know."

"Well, I think this is mostly a hand-holding mission."

"Is that right?" Pearl raised her eyebrows. "And just whose hand do you propose to hold?"

"It's not like that." Will scowled. "Something about the homeowner's kid. Or stepkid. Girlfriend's kid. Anyway, they've got him at the police station and she wants me to come over like there's anything I can do about it."

"You must think there's something you can do," Joe said. "Or you wouldn't be going."

"When I grow up I want the world to be as simple for me as it is for you, Joe."

"Heh. The whole world isn't so simple. But sometimes you are."

"Thanks."

"Anyway. I could maybe offer some assistance. As it turns out, I have some expertise at hand-holding, too." Joe glanced across the table at Pearl. She blushed and dipped her head.

"You should take him along, Mr. Phillips. He might be helpful, you never know. And how much more trouble could he be than he was yesterday?"

"Good point. Alright. I could probably use the company. Go get your jacket."

45

"So, what if the kid started the fire?" Joe broke the silence as they drove down Old Highway 48, a narrow and tattered black ribbon of asphalt that curved and cut its way through flat, empty fields where farmers were just starting to get out in their tractors to disc through the crusty soil and detritus of last year's corn harvest to begin planting again.

"What if he did?" Will repeated the question, looking off across one of those fields on the left. "Well, then he'll probably go to jail. Juvie, anyway. Which is really too bad, too. Besides the whole pyromaniac thing, he's probably a sweet, intelligent kid looking for a means of self-expression."

"Listen to the pop psychologist-philosopher go." Joe smiled. "So. Okay. He is all those things and goes to jail. What does it have to do with you?"

"If it's an intentional fire, of course the insurance company would want to know."

"But you said before that it didn't matter."

"It doesn't," Will said. "I mean, it does. But it doesn't."

"And you wonder why nobody understands insurance."

"No, we never wonder that." Will smirked. "We know why. It's like this. It doesn't matter because unless Justin did it, or was in on it, the insurance company still has to pay out. So in that sense, it doesn't matter. But if somebody else started it, then the insurance company could go after them to pay them back. So then it does matter."

"So young Robbie could have one heck of an IOU."

"He could. Probably won't though. He's a minor, so the

IOU would be Nina's. The state caps parental liability at a couple grand. And Nina doesn't even have the assets to collect that from. So we're back to it not mattering. Insurance company isn't going to want to spend thousands of dollars just to collect a couple."

"That's good news for Nina, anyway."

"Yeah, but a guy in an office in a Chicago skyscraper is going to want to paper his file, so he'll act like it matters, at least for a while."

"All that to say, why are we going to Fergus, Will? This could all have been handled with a few phone calls, I would think."

"I told Nina I would come."

"But Nina is not your client. The insurance company is. There's no investigative reason for you to go."

"Nina asked me."

"Yes. But you could have told her *No*. This isn't part of your job."

"Do I look to you like a guy who says *No* a lot, Joe?"

Joe chuckled. "Well, now that you mention it, you sort of have me there. No, you don't."

"I mean, it wasn't part of my job to visit you at the hospital or move you to the house with me, either."

Joe's grin faded and he shifted in his seat. He stared out the side window as the rows of freshly tilled soil rolled by.

"Joe, I didn't mean— Look, I'm sorry, man. It's different, you know?"

"Is it? Seems to be an easy enough explanation for befriending me, too."

"Except I came to your place uninvited with dinner, once."

Joe's head turned slightly. "But you came at first to get your thermos."

"And," Will grew animated in his efforts to convince Joe he was not another case of not saying *No*. "And I invited you to Pearl's matchmaker dinner party. You didn't even know anything about that. It was all on my own."

"True," Joe said softly. "You didn't say *No* to coming to the hospital though."

"How could I? And you've never even given me a chance to say *No* about you calling me your son."

"Perhaps I sensed that would be the bright line for you, the thing you would finally have the courage to refuse." Joe relaxed in his seat and turned toward Will. "Would you have said *No* to that?"

"To posing as your son?" Will raised his eyebrows. "Of course I would have said *No*. But you've still not given me a chance to."

"I don't plan to, either." Joe smiled, as though only to himself. "At least not for now."

"Later?" Will asked. "I can say *No* later?"

"We'll see. You need more time, more information to make an informed response."

"I see. I'm not your son, Joe."

"Of course you're not. That's why I won't ask you to say *Yes* or *No* yet. You need more time."

"Right. Just last night you were not giving me a chance to say *No* to being Pearl's father. Just how much more time and information do you think I need? Or how many more family members do I need to masquerade as before you think I am ready to give an answer?"

Will took a deep breath, wanting to be careful not to speak so carelessly again. Even if these things were true, surely he could find a way to express them that wouldn't poke into Joe's tender spots. He knew this, Joe was his friend. Even if he made himself an exasperating one. And he knew that he was traveling to meet Nina at the police station in Fergus not because he counted himself her friend, but because he truly was incapable of saying *No* at key moments. Joe was riding with him because he wanted the company. And he was living in his house and sharing meals with Pearl and getting away with telling people he was his son and probing into his psyche with seeming immunity because he was his friend. Not a customer, not an assignment, but a friend.

"I'm not sure how much time you need, Will," Joe said. "But it'll be a little longer at least."

"A little longer." Will shook his head. "Okay. I'll be anxiously waiting over here."

"No need to be anxious. You will know when it's time, even if I don't."

"Right."

"Meanwhile, tell me about Nina and Robbie. Why are we going to Fergus?"

"I told you already. Nina asked and I can't say *No*."

"It's more than that, Will."

Will felt heat travel from his wrist to his elbow as though hot water had just been injected into a vein. He rolled his shoulder inside his jacket.

"You do that every time I say her name. Have you noticed?"

"Do what?"

"Writhe."

"I writhe? Of course. I writhe every time you say Nina's name."

"You do."

"I do not."

"It's true. I ask about Nina or her fire and your whole body reacts."

Will's shoulder went up toward his ear and he froze. "That is not true." He eased his shoulder down, mentally ordering each muscle in his upper body to relax, one at a time.

"Okay," Joe chuckled. "As you wish. It's not true then."

Will clenched his jaw shut, resisting the urge to answer.

"So let's talk about Robbie."

"Robbie?"

"That's his name, right? If there's nothing special about Nina, let's talk about Robbie instead. Did he start the fire?"

"Did he start it? I have no idea. The fire marshal chalked it up to an unspecified cause."

"Well, that could mean anything."

"Yes, that's what I gathered from unspecified."

"No, I mean it doesn't mean the fire was started or not started. Just that there was no obvious cause. So Robbie could have started it."

"I suppose I could have hired a forensics guy to come in and give me a cause and origin. But a bunch of money later we'd all know exactly what we do right now: the fire started under the deck next to the house. No accelerant, no electrical, no witnesses, no suspects, no nothing. Nina's cigarette probably wasn't out when she dropped it and it probably fell into a pile of leaves instead of the can, and that probably ignited the cedar decking and then it's off you go. Accidental fire. Not much else to say."

"Makes sense. Could have been a kid with a book of matches the same way though."

Will pulled his arm tight to his ribcage.

"Not right there on the deck. Kids don't play with matches where they could get caught."

Joe turned to look at Will.

"Is that so?"

"Well," Will cleared his throat and tapped the GPS. "At least in my experience. I mean, you've probably seen way more of these than I have. You ever have a fire from a kid playing with matches right out in front of everybody?"

"A kid who's never had fire in his hands wouldn't know the difference. So, he's fiddling with the matches, gets a flame and it startles him. He drops it, gets afraid he'll be in trouble, and he runs, not realizing the match is still lit and there's a leaf pile there, and *Boom!* There goes the house."

"I suppose. But Robbie's pretty old for that. A twelve-year-old has lit a few matches, don't you think?"

"Maybe. Maybe not. Did Nina say they think he started Justin's house on fire?"

"I don't honestly know what she said. She was pretty upset."

"I remember this case we had once. Sixteen-year-old kid was home when the house went up. It was electrical. Totally accidental. They lost everything. The kid was having night-mares and was just absolutely petrified of fire. They said this one time they were at a birthday party for a little cousin and when they lit the candles, he freaked out a little like Franken-stein around a flame, and he ran off and hid for the rest of the afternoon. So his dad wanted to get him over this fear and took him out one day with a box of big wooden kitchen matches and told him to light up."

Joe shifted to face Will as he told the story, adjusting the shoulder strap away from his neck. "As a matter of course, I really despise most forms of therapy that compel exposure to the very thing that causes distress." He waved a hand. "Anyway. The kid won't light them so finally the dad does, to show him how simple it is. He lights a match and holds it up between his thumb and index finger and watches it start to burn down. Then he tosses the box to the kid and tells him to light one before flame burns his fingers. The kid refuses and is starting to cry. The match is burning down farther, getting closer to his dad's skin. 'I'm not putting it out until you light one!' his dad yells."

Joe raised his voice here, like he was the father. Will's neck felt hot. "Still, the kid won't do it so the dad screams, 'You're going to get me burned, you little sissy! Light a goddamn match!' "

Will couldn't hold his body back and kept his grip on the wheel while his entire being twisted in the seat. He hoped Joe was enough involved in his story not to notice.

"Well, the kid got it done," Joe said. "He fumbled and finally slid the box open but the matches spilled out on the ground. He grabbed one and broke it against the strike pad. It took a couple more but he got one lit while his dad screamed in pain."

"The dad didn't blow the match out?" Will was incredulous.

"Not until the kid did it. Third degree burns on his fingertips. Which he blames the kid for to this day for being such a panty waist."

"And the kid?"

"Well, once he finally got a match stick to light, he was so startled he threw it out of his hand. It landed on the pile of matches he'd spilled and the whole thing went up in one huge poof. The kid was mesmerized."

"Mesmerized? I'd have thought traumatized."

"Both, actually. Of course he was traumatized. First by the house fire, then by his father. But he was fascinated with the fire once he'd seen it up close. Ended up starting his garage on fire one day. And turned out before that happened he'd been out behind the garage every day for months, lighting different things on fire to see how quickly they'd go up."

"Nice going, Dad. At least the kid isn't afraid of fire anymore." Will held his body stiff and gazed out the window.

"All that to say, maybe this has nothing to do with Nina's fire. Maybe the kid took the trauma of their house burning and turned it into his own fascination with trying to control the wildness of the flame."

"You think he started a different fire?"

"You said you didn't really understand what Nina said. Maybe the kid started a fire somewhere else."

"Great. Who's the pop psychologist now, with a little conspiracy theorist for good measure."

"You don't even know the kid started any fire. And that doesn't make me a conspiracy theorist. People, especially kids, have all kinds of reactions to trauma."

"You think I don't know this?" Will unconsciously reached and massaged his forearm.

"Oh, no. I do think you are quite intimately aware."

~

The truck turned off the highway and Will parked at the curb in front of the Fergus Police Station, a sprawling gray brick building on the outskirts of town between a convenience store and tack and Western shop, built just a few years prior in an effort to modernize the city's decaying facilities. A dark bronze statue of a smiling man in uniform tipping his hat with one hand and resting the other on a holstered sidearm towered at the entrance in homage of Jerry Martell who famously served as local police chief from 1967 to 2001. The chief's welcoming presence was poor cover for the sobering fact that most people do not visit the police station of their own volition, and those who do come voluntarily generally still do so because of some manner of misfortune.

Will was still standing under Chief Martell's shadow, staring past the portly belly that pulled against the buttons of his bronze starched shirt and rested on his duty belt, when Nina burst through the double glass station doors. She rushed him, throwing thick arms around his neck and sobbing into his shoulder. Will staggered backward, grabbing the chief's bent knee for balance. He held his other arm awkwardly out from his side, avoiding contact with the contractions of Nina's convulsing body. He knew neither how to console the unstrung woman clinging to him nor how to extricate himself from her grasp.

Where the hell was Joe? He turned his head back toward the truck where Joe had just shut the passenger side door. "Hey, a little help over here?"

Joe ambled up the curb and made his way to the Nina-Will jumble, with his right hand held out. "You must be Nina," he said.

Will twisted himself free, turning Nina by her shoulders to face Joe. "Yes, yes. Nina, meet my good friend Joe Murphy." He wiped his hands on the front of his jeans. Nina brushed her hair away from wet cheeks and meekly held out a hand to Joe. "Joe knows a thing or two about fires and I thought it might be good to bring him along."

Joe looked at Will. Will shrugged. He let him come along. He might as well give him his street creds.

Nina sniffled. Joe reached into his pocket and held out a folded white handkerchief. She took it and turned away to blow her nose and wipe her face. Will mouthed "Thank you" to Joe. He smiled and nodded.

"Nina, what in the world is going on with Robbie?"

She turned back and offered the hanky to Joe. "No, no." He waved her off. "Keep it, please." She wrung it between her hands as she tried to relate the events of the last few days.

"They say he started the hardware store fire."

"Hardware store fire?"

"You didn't hear about it?" Nina frowned.

"I live in Dennison. We don't hear everything that happens over here right away."

"Oh, well. There was a big fire at the hardware store on Thursday night. They say it was Robbie."

"Why do they say that?"

"I don't know. It's ridiculous. Robbie would never do something like that."

"Where was he Thursday night?" Will asked. "Was he at home?"

"Well, no. He stayed at a friend's house."

"Do you know what friend?"

"Yeah, that Kerber kid. Wesley."

"Did you talk to his parents?"

"He lives with his dad and his dad was out. And that kid is nothing but trouble. Robbie didn't do this."

"Why did you let him stay there?"

"Am I supposed to watch him every minute? He's twelve years old. He is supposed to be able to be on his own sometimes."

"But if you knew—"

Nina's eyes welled again and her tightened lips began to quiver.

Joe moved closer to Nina, creating a buffer with his body between her and Will. "Let's think about that later," he said softly. "Nina, why do they think it was Robbie?"

Nina was still glaring at Will. He took a step back and leaned a shoulder against the statue, staring at his feet as he recalled his first encounter with Nina and stepping between her and Mad Dog in much the same way as Joe had just done. What had just happened here? He felt shame over not being callous enough to refuse to come when Nina called. And now that he was here, he felt shame at being so callous as to suggest this distraught woman was to blame for her son torching a hardware store. As though he even knew whether any of this was true. He watched Joe and Nina, seeing their mouths move but unable to make his brain form the sounds he heard into actual words from either of them.

The old man is doing my job, he thought, rubbing his arm. *Except this isn't even my job. Nina has some nerve looking at me like that when I don't have to be here at all.*

He caught Nina's eye again and she looked away.

God. I am Mad Dog.

Will straightened and stepped back to Joe and Nina. Joe stopped talking in mid-sentence and they both turned to him. "Look, Nina." He scratched the side of his face. "I'm sorry. I had no business —"

"It's okay." Nina sniffled and wiped her nose with Joe's handkerchief. "I asked myself the same thing."

"Still. I should have kept my mouth shut," Will said, sliding his hands into his pockets. "Anyway, I thought the older kids were at your mom's."

"She could only keep them a couple of days. Once we got settled in the hotel suite, she brought them back. It's been so cramped in there. You can't turn around without bumping into one of the kids. They fight over everything. Who gets the chair. Who gets the remote. How many days they've been eating pizza." She wiped her eyes with the back of her hand. "I thought having one less kid for the night might be good for everybody. I shouldn't have let him go."

"But you don't think he had anything to do with it, do you?"

"I don't know what to think, Will." Nina wrung her hands and looked up at the sky, forcing back more tears. "I don't know what to think. They aren't telling me anything."

"Have you seen Robbie?" Will asked.

"No. That's what I was just telling Joe. They won't let me see him."

"Did you call a lawyer?"

"I can't afford a lawyer."

"Alright. We need to start there. No way should they have a twelve-year-old without you or a lawyer. I've got a friend who owes me a favor."

Will pulled his phone from his pocket and took a few steps away from the others. Joe motioned to a granite bench behind Chief Martell. Nina sat down and dropped her face into her hands while Joe patted her shoulder. As Will waited for Christina Sharp to pick up he wondered if Joe was consoling Nina with poetry.

So many poems arise from tragedy, he thought, wondering why it wasn't more common for adjusters to write. Sure, plenty of famous poets had a hand in the insurance business—Stevens, Eliot, Collins, Kooser. But they were execs or worked on the banking or sales side. The ones who experienced real poem-fodder up close every single day were the claims folks.

Come on, Chris. Pick up. Just look at Nina. Tell me there's no poem there.

> *She eats fear with morning coffee—*
> *chunks of ash black in her mouth,*
> *worries cinders*
> *between delicate fingers*
> *mixed with a trickle*
> *from her cheek*
> *to spread on burnt toast*

"Christina Sharp." The woman's voice in his phone startled him and he jumped.

"Chris, hey. It's Will Phillips."

"William J. Phillips as I live and breathe."

"That's not my middle initial."

Christina laughed. "How the hell are you?"

"I'm good, good," he said, rubbing his forehead. "Listen—"

"To what do I owe the pleasure?"

"Listen, we should catch up. But right now I need to call in that favor."

Will tapped the red End Call button and pocketed his phone with a sigh. Not the tired sigh he'd been letting out all day, but a sigh of relief. He straightened his shoulders and felt it for a moment before walking back to Nina and Joe.

"Help is on the way, Nina. Chris Sharp is the best there is. She'll get Robbie out of there tonight. And then we can figure out what to do next."

~

Will and Joe were still sitting on the granite bench behind Chief Martell when the double doors of the station swung open and Christina Sharp emerged smiling with an arm over a shaken Robbie Miller's shoulder. Nina followed close behind, wiping her reddened eyes with Joe's borrowed hanky.

They hopped up from the bench and hurried over to the others. Will tousled Robbie's sandy hair. "Hey, big man. Nobody can hold you, right?" He dug in his pocket and pulled out a pair of dollar bills. He handed them to Nina and motioned to a soda machine at the end of the sidewalk.

Nina took the money and turned to Robbie. "Come on."

Will watched them walk away, then looked back to

Christina. "Well?"

Christina slid purple framed glasses to the top of her head, pulling back straight dark hair. "They aren't charging him. Not now, anyway."

"What'd they have him for?"

She adjusted the strap on her briefcase on her shoulder. "He was bragging at recess about starting a fire. Thanks to this see-something-say-something business they are drilling into kids' heads, some girl went to the teacher, who went to the principal, and you know how it went from there."

"Did he start a fire?" Will asked. "I mean, did he start *that* fire?" He wasn't sure if he meant the hardware store or Nina's house. They had taken him in for the hardware store fire, but maybe they wanted him for both. Robbie looked like a kid who spent most of his time switching between an Xbox controller in his hand and a book. But he knew his was also the kind of kid who could surprise you.

"I don't know. He's pretty shook up," Christina said. "Hard to say if he was playing around and something went wrong or if he was just bragging and had nothing to do with anything."

"Are they going to charge him later?" Will asked.

"Doubt it. Pretty obvious they had nothing to work with and they were hoping he'd give them something."

Joe got a peculiar look on his face. "Do you know what he *did* give them?"

Christina smiled. "I'm pretty sure he gave them nothing. I mean *nothing*." She gestured with her hands in front of her. "Considering how frustrated they were, if he said anything at all, it wasn't helpful. And he told me he didn't say a word the whole time."

"Not a word?" Will frowned. "A twelve-year-old kid says nothing at all? Didn't spill the beans about pulling his sister's hair or taking the heads off all her Barbie dolls?"

Joe looked at Will.

"It could happen."

"Not a thing. Or so he says." Christina shook her head. "Said his stepdad—Justin?—told him if the cops ever talk to him not to say a single word. So he didn't."

"Justin has a history with the police?" Will asked.

"If it's who I'm thinking of. I've seen him around the courthouse some."

"You'd think if he was going to coach him he'd tell the kid to ask for a lawyer."

"Yeah, well, if he's who I think he is, he's also not the brightest light in the chandelier."

Nina and Robbie rejoined them, Robbie guzzling a green bottle of lemon lime soda as he walked.

"So we can go home now?" Nina asked. "Or, I guess I mean to the hotel? The little kids are there with a friend."

"Yes, " Christina said, rummaging in her bag. "Here's my card. I think they're done with him. But if they reach out to you again, you call me." She snapped her bag shut and put a hand on Robbie's shoulder. "And you, young man. You do just what you did this time. Don't say anything—Well, say one thing. Say you want to talk to your lawyer."

"I'll call you tomorrow, Nina, " Will said. "Go get Robbie something to eat."

Nina shook Christina's hand and thanked her another three or four times before she and Robbie turned and walked toward the Colony Suites a few blocks away.

Christina crossed her arms over her chest. "So, Will Phillips. What have you been up to?"

"Oh, you know."

"Do I?"

"Just the usual things. Climbing roofs. Counting beans. Comforting single mothers."

"How'd you get in the middle of this mess?" She cocked her head. "You're still soft, aren't you?"

Joe snickered and put his hands in his pockets, pretending to whistle and look at the sky.

"Listen—" Will started, and then looked at the ground.

"Say, " Christina said, "since we're evened up now on favors, maybe you should buy me a cup of coffee. Bring me up to date. And maybe your dad can tell me a few stories."

Joe beamed.

"Joe is not—" He stopped again. "Yeah, sure. Where do you want to go?"

"Meet me at Woodburn's downtown. You'll like it."

46

Joe picked up *The New York Times* from the leather sofa in the back corner of the dark coffee shop, slap-tongue saxophone sounds punctuating an impassioned conversation between two college students at a table behind him. He set the paper on a wood block coffee table and motioned to Christina to sit down. She dropped her briefcase on the middle cushion and sat back into the sofa with a sigh. Joe sat down in the side chair and smiled.

"So how do you know our boy Will?" he asked, folding his hands over his belly.

"Will? We met in Chicago."

"You're from Chicago?" Joe's face lit up.

"No, no. I did my undergrad at Northwestern. I'm a hometown girl. Grew up just down the street from here."

"I see." Joe's shoulders drooped, and then he brightened again. "You two dated in college?"

"Dated Will?" She shook her head and laughed, pulling her hair behind her neck. "Does he date people now? Because nobody dated Will in college."

Joe slumped again and glanced toward the counter where Will was showing the barista his receipt and lightly tapping his boot rhythmically into the toe-kick under the counter.

"It's not that nobody wanted to, " Christina added, seeing Joe's disappointment. "It's that he wasn't exactly … available."

"What do you mean? If he wasn't dating anyone else he would be available, wouldn't he?"

"Has he ever told you about Barbara?"

"Barbara?" The corners of Joe's mouth turned down as he thought, and he shook his head. "No, I don't believe he's mentioned anyone by that name."

"Well, that's probably his to tell, not mine. But she was my roommate. Will didn't date anyone because of Barbara."

"They were—a thing?" Joe looked up to see Will again. He was walking across the café holding three coffees in an awkward sort of paper cup pyramid in front of him.

"They were not. Not a dating thing, anyway. A different kind of thing I guess. Let's say it didn't go well for anyone who showed an interest in him."

Joe stood and took a coffee from Will and handed it to Christina. "There you are. I thought maybe the barista was trying to hire you, it took so long."

"Don't get me started. It is so hard to get a simple cup of coffee in these places. They shouldn't call them coffee shops." He set the other cups on the table and sat on the far end of the sofa.

"Christina was just telling me you met in college." Joe smiled.

"Was she?" Will looked at Christina. She lifted the cup to her mouth, breathing in but not drinking the steaming coffee. She shrugged. "It took them long enough that you were able to tell Joe all my secrets?"

"Pretty much." Christina tucked one leg under her and pulled the hem of her skirt over her knees.

"This is what I get for being the nice guy and buying the coffee."

"It's what you've always gotten for being the nice guy. You just haven't learned yet."

"Did she tell you how I wrote her senior paper in Con Law, Joe?" Will took the lid off his cup and set it on the table. "She'd have flunked out and never made it to law school without me."

"It's true, " Christina laughed. "I sure did miss you when it came to the Bar exams, buddy."

"Did you, now."

"I did. Missed you after school too. I still don't understand how you live an hour and a half away and I never see you."

"You don't keep in touch?" Joe's eyes widened. "What is it with you and beautiful women?"

Will and Christina both blushed. "In his defense, Joe, it does turn out I'm married."

Joe turned the paper sleeve on his cup. "Do you keep in touch with other friends from college, Christina? Like, your roommate?"

Will stiffened and looked at Joe, then at Christina. "Damn. You weren't kidding."

"Oh, relax, Will. This is why you should never play poker." She sat upright and put a hand on Will's knee. "He asked how we met. I told him my roommate was a friend of yours. All your so-called secrets are safe, my friend." Christina tore open a sugar packet and poured it into her coffee. "Barbara and I exchange Christmas cards. That's about the long and short of it."

"What's her zip code these days?" Will looked over the top of his cup, hoping for nonchalant but knowing he sounded too interested. He set his coffee on the table and leaned back in his chair, crossing his hands over his belly in a gigantic overcorrection.

Joe stifled a snicker and gulped his coffee in an overcorrection of his own, wincing at the scalding he'd just given his unsuspecting esophagus.

Christina laughed at them both. "You two should really take this on the road. You're great together. I'd pay to see the full performance."

Swishing the coffee in his cup, Will half rolled his eyes. "Okay then. So where is she?"

"Highland Park, of course. You would expect any less?"

"No, I suppose not. That's what she always wanted. And I couldn't deliver."

"Did she want to be kept by you, Will?" Joe's eyes widened.

"Not... exactly." Will shifted in his chair, staring into his cup. "Barbara Roberts was not exactly the kept woman type."

"What you mean is that she was not a typical kept woman," Christina corrected, stirring a slim brown straw in her cup. "She absolutely wanted to be kept. But she had her own way of keeping, too."

"Who is keeping her in Hyde Park?"

"Nick Sartell."

"Still? I thought he was a rebound."

"He was. And we all thought she was going to cut him loose. But she changed her mind. No one ever knew why."

Will thought back to that last phone call he'd had with Barbara, then said, "You know he's gay, right?"

"Everyone knows. But then, no one knows. She has deniability."

"Plausible." Will nodded.

"Exactly."

Joe listened intently, turning his head back and forth with

each volley of the conversation between two old friends, like he was sitting in the stands at Wimbledon.

"Are they married?" Will asked.

"No, " Christina said with a small smile. "She would never agree to it. Being able to walk tomorrow without legal obstacles gave her the leverage she needed with Nick."

"She's still cold."

"Ice."

"They deserve each other."

"It's true."

"Let's talk about something else," he said.

"Are you seeing anyone?" Christina asked.

Will broke the cadence of their back-and-forth with a long pause. Joe interjected on his behalf. "He's working on it."

He scowled at Joe.

"Working on it, eh? What does that look like?" Christina sipped her coffee and raised an eyebrow at Joe. "I may as well ask you, because he won't tell me anything."

"I'm not working on anything."

"He's very modest, you know, " Joe smiled. "A lovely woman moved in across the street from us and he is a little sweet on her."

"Will is sweet on a lovely young woman? That *is* sweet— And wait a second." Christina pointed between the two men. "Do you two live together?"

"Well..." Will started.

"That's sort of a long story. The short version is I am a temporary guest of his landlady." Joe tapped his chest. "Recovering from a little scare with the old ticker. But speaking of sweet, his landlady is a very sweet piece of—"

"Joe!"

Joe turned to Will. "What? I was just going to say that Pearl bakes a very sweet piece of pie."

"That is not—"

"Well, it's true. She does."

"Of course she does. But—"

Christina laughed. "Seems like you two were made for each other." She looked at her watch. "Listen, I need to get going. Big case coming up for a paying client."

"Look," Will said. "Send me a bill for Nina."

Christina punched him lightly on the arm as she stood. "I'm kidding, Willie. Glad I could help out. And clear our account."

"Thanks so much for coming on such short notice. You're a lifesaver." Will stood and gave Christina a light embrace.

"Don't be such a stranger, okay? Bring your lovely young lady with you next time." She grinned at Joe. "And the sweet piece of pie."

Joe let out a belly laugh and shook Christina's hand. "I do hope to have her on my arm the next time I go anywhere."

The two men stood at the table, coffee cups in hand, watching as Christina Sharp made her way between crowded tables to the exit.

Without turning, Joe said softly, "You have some stories it might be time to tell, Will Phillips."

47

"It is possible, Joe, that some stories are best not told." Will twisted the white cap on his cup back and forth in his hand. He stayed standing, hung in the chill air between sitting back down and telling Joe everything and bolting for the door to get home and back to work without another word.

"It is something of a tragedy, then, don't you think, that we are here in a coffee shop instead of a bar?" Joe dropped into his chair with a grunt and motioned Will back to his own.

"A bar?"

"Sure. Coffee is not as effective for eliciting the reluctant story. Homer said so." Joe tipped his head back and closed his eyes, reciting a little too loudly for Will's comfort, even amidst the clanging of dishes and the continual roar of the espresso pumps.

> *It is the wine that leads me on,*
> *the wild wine*
> *that sets the wisest man to sing*
> *at the top of his lungs,*
> *laugh like a fool—it drives the*
> *man to dancing…it even*
> *tempts him to blurt out stories*
> *better never told.*

"So you would ply me with wine until I blurt out the story you think you want to hear."

"I thought it might work, yes."

Will remembered the night in his closet with Cameron. And wine.

"It is not impossible."

"It might also be good to remember that it is one thing for a person to wish to hear a story. It is another altogether that a man's story wishes telling."

"Why are you so sure there is a story that wishes to be told?"

"I'm an old man, Will. We just know things." Joe raised his cup to his lips, then set it back down. "So maybe just tell me this, and you can make it the short version: What happened to your arm?"

Will instinctively reached for his arm, massaging a hand over his scarred bicep. He grit his teeth against the buzzing in his ears. *Who is this man, this Joe Murphy, who feels so free to insinuate himself into a guy's life, to demand stories as though he's owed them? What had Joe ever done for Will besides cause him one headache after another, and if it were possible there were some miniscule debt owed, for something—but what?—surely it had been satisfied by now between dinner, the hospital, the bringing him to his house, the making believe to be his kin. Who is this man? Who does he believe himself to be?*

~

He rubbed his fingers over the bumps and grooves on his arm, reminding himself to inhale, and to do so deeply. In the fog of his brain, behind the insipid acoustic Inde music twinging out of the overhead speakers of the coffee shop, he heard Barbara cajoling. Always, she was cajoling.

"You light one now, Willie. Come on, I want to see yours

blow up."

Will was crouched in the tall grass behind the old water tower. The bluff overlooking the river was a favorite place for the neighborhood boys to launch bottle rockets and hot air balloons made from birthday candles and the lightweight plastic sacks from the one-hour Martinizing shop. That day, they had met up to engage in their own air strike of sorts, each of them having gathered their collection of model airplanes. David Kingsley had a pack of firecrackers they were plugging into the planes and lighting, then launching them off the bluff with slingshots where they blew to tiny bits of shattered plastic airplane parts over the river.

After a couple of rounds, the boys had grown bored. The explosions were not dramatic enough. Sure, the planes blew apart, but they wanted to see a burst of flame and imagine they were watching John Wayne and the boys in the *Sands of Iwo Jima.*

David had just the thing, he said, and had ridden home on his bike and returned with a can of gasoline and an old shirt of his dad's. They drew straws, and Will lost, which always happened when they drew for long straw instead of short. Barbara would hold the sticks and they would each make their choice. Then the other boys would snap theirs in half between their fingers behind their back before holding it out to compare to the others. Will couldn't—wouldn't—do it, so he always had the long straw no matter which one he drew.

The other boys would be the pilots. Will would be munitions. He crouched down on one knee in the grass tearing off small strips of the checked cotton shirt, then soaking them in gasoline and stuffing them into the belly of the plane before plugging it with a firecracker.

It worked. Sort of. The explosions now had a brief, but dramatic, poof of flame before they dropped into the river below. If a guy laid on his belly and looked over the bluff, he could pretend to be right there on the beach watching enemy planes go down one after another. Absent the screaming and blood, of course.

The boys cheered with each round of explosions and subsequently jeered Will for his meticulous preparation. His caution with the gasoline was slowing down their assault, they complained, and surely they would lose territory if he didn't hustle. He would be remembered for all history as the one who let Omega Beach fall into enemy hands, all because he was a scaredy cat about a little gasoline.

Will tried to move faster. He did not want to be remembered for anything, much less for being that guy, the one that would give the enemy Omega Beach. He tore off strips of fabric as fast as he could, dipped them into the fuel can and stuffed the long row of planes. Where did they keep coming from? He couldn't imagine his friends having so many airplanes in their collections. And their dads were going to be furious when they saw the whole collections were destroyed.

Barbara knelt down beside him to help. Of course, the thing with Barbara was that she wasn't much help. She should have been back by the fence with all the other girls, but she was here beside him making him even more nervous than the boys did. She was mostly suggesting and correcting and saying a lot of why-don't-yous that only got a guy more rattled. She thought it would save some time if Will would soak a larger piece of cloth first, then tear strips. "It's that many fewer times you'll have to dip into the can. Think of the time you'll save," she said.

Will protested, but Barbara pouted, and Will gave in. It was their way. Now he had a large patch of cotton cloth, soaked and dripping with gasoline. He held it to tear the strips, which was harder now that it was wet. He felt a trickle run down his wrist and arm and reached with his other hand, wet with gasoline, to wipe his sleeve on it and keep his arm from getting wetter. The smell of gas, which he had always strangely enjoyed when he helped his father pump gas and wash the windows of the old brown Monaco was now making him lightheaded and a little ill.

"You should really do one too, Will. It's just not fair that you are only munitions. Tell David you want to be a pilot too."

"But I don't," Will told her. "I was just getting good at packing the planes just right. Did you see how that last Mustang fighter jet went off?"

"Oh, I don't even know what these are, " Barbara said, standing and smoothing her skirt. "I just think you should get to do one too. Stand up to those boys."

"I don't need to. I like my job here."

"I wonder if you are afraid of the boys or afraid of the fire." Barbara held a finger to her pursed lips, looking off over the river as if she were thinking very hard.

"Neither. I'm not afraid. I just don't want to." Will wiped his nose with the back of his hand. He thought the gasoline fumes might have burned all of his nose hair away. He shook his head. "Now let me work so they don't run out of fire power again."

Will reached for another plane and realized he had armed

them all and their assault on Omega Beach would soon be done, once they blew up the last six planes in their fleet.

David and the others came and grabbed their choices, leaving the last Marauder jet sitting next to Will's blue sneaker. "There you go, Will. There's one left for you," Barbara said.

"Nah, they can have it." Will stood and wiped his hands on his jeans.

"You *are* afraid, Will. I was kidding, but you really are. You're afraid of a little fire." Barbara ran a finger along his hairline at the neck.

"I am *not* afraid." Will rolled his neck, shaking her off.

~

"Not afraid of what?" Joe smiled his bemused smile at Will. "Not afraid of a little story?"

Will jumped in his chair and looked at Joe.

Joe felt his own face and wore an expression of mock horror. "Am I a ghost? Am I really here?"

"Cut it out." Will looked into his coffee.

"Easy there." Joe chuckled. "Somebody was a little lost in his thoughts."

"Yeah, I guess I was."

"So, is it true? Are you afraid of a little story?"

"Not of a little story, no."

"Perhaps you should be."

"I should?"

"Sure. Many a man has been undone by a little story." Joe sipped from his cup.

"So then, all the more reason not to tell it."

"Oh, I don't think I said anything of the kind. The thing people don't always want to realize is that stories have great power whether they get told or not. Those men I mentioned? I was thinking they were brought to ruin by their *failure* to tell the story. People do fret so much about the stories like the monster that ate New York City. But they forget it's possible for a man to be eaten alive from the inside out."

"Yeah, yeah. Turn the spotlight on old Will's demons, Joe. The oh-so-scary monsters within."

"I need remind you of nothing at all. You are fully aware of your own man-eating monster. Or monsters. All day long. You just find it convenient to blame *me* for bringing it up. And if that helps you get to the point of telling the story, then sure. I'm happy to keep letting you play target practice with my head." Joe wadded up his napkin and balanced it on the top of his head with a mischievous grin.

"It might be easier if you didn't find so much amusement in it, you know." Will didn't try to conceal the annoyance in his voice.

"Oh, Will. It isn't amusement so much. What I most enjoy is seeing you win this argument with yourself. You could have gone to the truck a half hour ago when Christina left." Joe rocked his cup softly back and forth against the table with the beat of the Mumford song playing in the background. "You are the one who wants to tell the story. I don't need to hear it. I have many books with many stories that I could read if I just wanted a story."

"Speaking of going to the truck, we should go. I have a desk teeming with actual casework I need to do."

Joe stood and threw back the last of his coffee in a single

gulp and motioned with a thumb toward the door. "Ready when you are."

Will reached for Joe's cup and dropped both in the trash as he went by on his way to the door. Joe followed close behind.

"You can finish the story you were remembering on the drive."

"Is it not apparent what happened next?" Will glanced at Joe over his shoulder.

"Painfully so, in the mechanics, at least." Joe passed through the door as Will held it open with his foot. "A little gasoline, a little gunpowder, a little match, that's all quite apparent."

"Then you don't need me to say more." Will rubbed his arm.

"No, I don't. We already decided I don't need any of it, remember?" Joe stopped on the sidewalk beside the truck and put his hands in his pockets. "The question is what story do you need to tell, in order to give notice to that thing with fangs that keeps chewing through your insides."

Will held Joe's gaze for a moment. He spoke softly. "I should have told you to keep the thermos." He shook his head and walked to the cab to get in.

Joe stood his ground on the sidewalk until he heard Will's door slam shut behind him. "You're getting very close," he whispered, and erased the smile from his face before he turned and climbed into the pickup.

By the time Will turned into the gravel driveway behind Pearl's house, the two men had not spoken a word during the hour and a half trip from Fergus. He put the truck in park but left it running. Joe opened his door.

"You are not coming in?"

"Going back to the office." Will patted his briefcase, laying on the seat between them.

"Ah. Very well then." Joe slid off the seat onto his feet outside the cab. "I'll see what my little sweetie pie is up to then."

Will watched Joe ease himself up the back steps of Pearl's porch. At the top, Joe turned back with a kind smile and waved. Will couldn't help but smile back, shaking his head in mild bemusement at the way Joe, even at his most incisive—and persistent—could still be so disarming.

He was looking over his shoulder to back out into the alley when Pearl opened the screen door to let Joe in and so didn't see the way she blushed when he leaned in to give her a light peck on the cheek.

Will drove down Main Street, slowing as he passed Cameron's office. He scanned the large plate-glass windows from his side of the street, hoping she would happen to be in the lobby so he could catch a glimpse of her. She did not happen to be, of course, and he drove on, chiding himself for spooking around at the same time as he wondered what he'd have done if she would have been out front in the lobby and seen him gaping from his cab.

Would he park and go inside to say hello? Or would he accelerate even harder, nearly mowing down Mrs. Bilger, who was now shuffling through the crosswalk in front of him, tugging her pull cart full of grocery sacks behind her. He rolled to a stop and waved. Mrs. Bilger stopped in the middle of the road to sling her oversized handbag back over her slumped shoulder before giving Will a wide, partly toothless grin and waving back.

A horn sounded behind him. Startled, Will realized Mrs. Bilger was already on the sidewalk and he pulled ahead.

Back at the office, he stumbled over Mad Dog's boots as he came in the door. They left fresh imprints of soot on the carpet and the smoky smell hit his nostrils. "Damn it, Mike. Why can't you leave your work boots outside so they don't make a mess and smell the place up in here?"

"Good afternoon to you, too, Willie." Mad Dog stuck his head out of Will's office. "Lady told me this morning while I was looking at her garage—well, what was left of her garage, anyway—and she was all weepy and sniffly, you know, and she said 'I used to love the smell of campfire.' How do you like that?"

"On a different day I might say it sounded downright poignant."

"You're in another fine mood, I see." Mad Dog padded across the hall in his stocking feet. "Well, I still love the smell of campfire."

"I never did."

"Really never? Not even a single happy weiner-roast memory?"

"Really never. I only smelled campfire as a kid one time, actually. Went on a class camping trip with my 5th grade teacher." Will went into his office and dropped his briefcase on the chair and straightened the stapler and tablet Mad Dog had rearranged. "Out in the god-forsaken woods somewhere. We had nothing to do all day, then sat up all night after some clown scared the shit out of us with ghost stories. I sat by the fire freezing my ass off because it was too cold to sleep in my tent. And I wondered why people with warm houses would ever go to so much trouble to spend the night like homeless people just for fun."

"Always great to have you in the office, Sgt. Killjoy."

"Seriously. People think about romantic nights under the stars or fishing with their dads or even just toasting marshmallows around the fire. I only remember the feeling of freezing cold and no sleep and a whimpering tent-mate who was homesick an hour after we got off the bus. And now I can't even think of any of those things as pleasant by comparison."

"How do you do this job? It's kind of campfire-y half the time."

Will snapped his laptop open with more force than was needed, and caught it before it tipped over on his desk. "Because I'm a goddamn grown-up, Mike. Sometimes you just have to do things no matter what happened when you were twelve."

Mad Dog snickered. "You were kind of an old 5th grader."

"Shut up, Mike."

Mad Dog made a mock saluting gesture and turned back to his own desk.

Will dialed into his voicemail and let the messages play back without his awareness as his mind drifted to Barbara and all the Friday nights she'd beg him to take her to the bonfire at Theresa Lynn's farm, knowing full well his aversion to campfire smell had little to do with sitting out in the cold in his Batman pajamas when he was twelve. He rolled his neck as he felt her tease the curl behind his ear.

She leaned in and crooned. "Sometimes you just have to do things."

48

If anyone had asked, Will couldn't have recalled how he found himself standing in the street in front of Cameron's house later that evening.

He had, in fact, come home from work planning to warm up a plate of mashed potatoes and beef tips from the freezer, then turn on his new television for the first time and fall asleep early. It occurred to him that now that he was paying for cable, he ought to at least discover what channels he had available besides Major League Baseball.

When he rolled into the driveway, Joe was out the door and on the back porch before he even got the truck turned off. The door creaked as he pushed it open with his foot, leaning sideways to reach his briefcase from the passenger side.

"Will!" Joe was waving his arms as though he were trying to flag him down in a crowded airport, not the only person standing on an open porch Will would have had to walk right past to get to the stairs to his apartment. "Over here, Will!"

"Hey, Joe." Will smiled and shook his head, pushing the door shut behind him. "I see you there."

"Oh, good. I wanted to catch you before you went up." Joe thumbed over his shoulder toward the door. "Pearl found a delightful recipe for butternut squash we're trying out. We set a place for you. "

The man lives here now. It's like he's an extension of Pearl, Will thought.

"Did you, now." Will motioned toward the stairs with the briefcase in his hand. "Listen, I'll be down in a minute. Let me run upstairs first."

Will didn't run up the stairs. He didn't even jog. It would be fair to say he trudged, thinking he was finally going to get a quiet night all by himself and, now, he was not. *These people...* he started to think, and then stopped, not knowing what exactly it was he wanted to think about these people.

He dropped the briefcase on the counter in the kitchenette and went into the bathroom. He bent over the sink and splashed water on his face, then reached for a towel, refusing to even look at himself in the mirror. *I already know I need a haircut.*

In his bedroom, Will filed through the plaid shirts hanging in the closet in dutiful rows, knowing Pearl would expect him to put on a clean shirt. And what was it about a clean shirt, anyway? He was in his office all day. He didn't dribble soup down the front at lunch, and he wasn't steeped in beer smell or covered in dirt from crawling under a house. Why should he have to change?

Clean shirts, he decided, were sorely overrated.

He unbuttoned his red plaid and eyed a blue plaid before opening his dresser drawer and pulling out a soft, if mildly tattered, gray sweatshirt, cracked white emblazoned across the front spelling HARVARD, the front leg of the H peeled off. He put the sweatshirt to his face and took a deep breath, then pulled it on over his T-shirt.

Unsure if it was defiance or the old sweatshirt's comfort he was feeling, Will kicked off his boots, unbuckled his jeans and let them fall, stepping into another pair of Levis, faded to near white in spots and worn through in some inopportune others. He sat on his bed, feeling oddly content, and reached down to put his boots back on. Bent over with the laces in his hand, he saw the white toe of his Chuck Taylors poking out from under a rumpled T-shirt that hung over the side of his laundry basket in the closet. He let his boot drop to the floor and went to the closet for his black low-tops and sat down on the wood floor to put them on.

Will mused that he felt almost spry when he got himself up from the floor. He reached under his sweatshirt to tuck the T-shirt into the top of his jeans. It is possible that at least one of his steps out of his room toward the stairs had a skip in it. "No one will ever know for sure without surveillance video," he answered the creaking step as he passed by the high stained glass.

Turning the corner to the dining room, he met the smell of Pearl's butternut squash coming from the kitchen. "What kind of people eat butternut squash this time of year anyway?"

"Usually the best kind."

Will jumped, thinking Pearl and Joe were in the kitchen. He looked up and saw her reflection across the table in the buffet mirror.

"Cameron."

"Hello, Will." Cameron stood. "We're looking casual tonight."

"I, uh. Well." He smoothed the front of his jeans, which were not wrinkled and in need of smoothing. He ran a hand through his hair. "I don't think I knew you would be here."

"Clearly you did not." The door swung open from the butler's pantry and Pearl walked in carrying a casserole dish between two flowered oven mitts. "You came down for dinner? I can't quite tell if you're here to join us or if you're on your way to one of those old man little league games."

"Pearl." Will hurried across the room. "Let me get that for you." He grabbed for the dish and Pearl yanked it away.

"Be careful, young man. This is hot. We don't want you burning yourself."

Will let his arm fall to his side. "Of course. We don't want that." He slipped his hands into his back pockets so his elbows stuck out behind him like a chicken.

Pearl tipped her head toward the table. "Do you think I could put this down now?"

Will was flushed now, and stepped back. "Yeah. Yes, let me get out of the way." He stepped around Pearl and into the kitchen. "Let me see if Joe needs anything else."

The door swung behind him and he found Joe wiping down the counter with a dish towel.

"Thanks for the heads-up, Joe."

"Heads up?" Joe turned around. He looked at Will from head to toe and started to laugh. "Pearl has her expectations about decorum for a reason, you know. Come ready and you'll be ready. No advance notice needed."

"Yeah, well, the one time . . ."

"It's been just this one time, eh?"

"Actually, yes. Believe it or not."

"I believe it." Joe set the towel next to the sink. "I have seen you and rules." He pointed to the pitcher on the counter, condensation dripping down the side. "Grab that, would you?"

Will picked up the pitcher and turned to go back into the dining room.

"Uh, Will."

He leaned into the door with his shoulder. "Yeah?"

"Word to the wise." He pointed a finger. "Don't turn your back to Pearl tonight."

Will froze, suddenly unable to remember which boxers he was wearing and whether the plaid of his shorts showing through the back of his jeans would either clash with his sweatshirt and offend Pearl's fashion sensibilities or would be a nice matchup and make him look like some sort of obsessive who coordinated his underwear with his outerwear.

Does it matter? he asked himself as he stood, shoulder still to the door, and Joe waiting patiently for him to finish processing this information so they could go into the dining room.

He concluded the coordination of his shorts and shirt would not matter to Pearl nearly as much as if she saw there was something to coordinate at all and decided his best course of action would be to follow Joe's advice and keep his back to the wall or his ass in the chair, literally as much as proverbially. He would deal later with whatever it was that compelled him to assert this defiance in the first place, jotting a mental note to remind himself it is surely more simple to just keep playing by other people's rules. Maybe he even liked it.

"Ready?" He smiled at Joe.

"Ready." Joe followed him out to the dining room where Pearl was already serving the hotdish onto everyone's plates. Cameron was telling her about a vegetarian café in Uptown Minneapolis that she was sure Pearl would love.

"But I hear the parking is atrocious in the city, dear," Pearl said, shaking her head. "Probably best that I just learn to cook these dishes myself so I don't have to go all that way."

"I could drive you. We could go on tour." Joe leaned over and kissed the top of Pearl's head as he walked around the table to his chair. "We could make signs to hang on the truck: PEARL AND JOE DO VEGETABLES. And when we see those billboards with the cows saying EAT MOR CHIKIN, we could roll down the windows and yell 'Not even that!' as we go by." Joe scooted his chair up to the table and waved a hand at Will. "Sit, man. You're making us all nervous standing there like the butler. Maybe even the butler that did it."

Will stood to the side of the table, holding the water pitcher in front of himself in both hands, mentally navigating the maneuver to his chair which involved either turning his back to Pearl or to the buffet mirror, which was in Pearl's line of sight. He stayed to the side of the mirror. "Who wants water?"

"Just pour some for everyone and sit down, Dear." Pearl held up her glass. "Joe is right. You're making us all nervous."

He leaned across the table to fill Pearl's outstretched glass. Then he turned to Cameron, still not moving from his position at the corner. "Do you feel nervous?"

Cameron lifted her glass and wrinkled her brow. "I don't know if I would say nervous exactly. It's more like—" she turned to Joe. "Joe, what's the word for when you feel embarrassed or uncomfortable about a situation but it's for someone else?"

Will closed his eyes so Pearl would not see them roll halfway into the back of his head.

"Oh, yes. I know what you're thinking of but I can't put my finger on the word. It's not *chagrin*. Maybe *shame*?"

"No, *shame* isn't it. That's too strong. It's like *awkward*, but not really."

"Yes, yes. I know just what you—"

"Will!" Cameron startled him with a shout and Will jumped,

splashing water on the table. "My glass is full. You really need to pour with your eyes open."

Will set down the pitcher and grabbed the napkin from his plate and mopped up the spill. Pearl, strangely, was silent, watching the chaos unfold and having nothing to say to Will about his obvious buffoonery. He took the opportunity to slip to his chair, hoping Pearl was more focused on the spill than the back of his Levis.

"*Empathy*," she said quietly.

"What?" Will said.

"*Empathy*. That's the word you're looking for."

"Yes!" Cameron dabbed the last bit of water from above her plate. "I like that a lot better."

~

"So maybe now you are ready to tell us why you've come to dinner dressed so inappropriately, Mr. Phillips." Pearl waved Will to his chair with one hand and passed a spare linen napkin to Cameron with the other. "It's as though everything I've ever told you about dressing for success has fallen on deaf ears."

Will unfolded his own napkin and laid it across one thigh. "Come on now, dinner with friends isn't exactly a job interview, is it?"

"Who said anything about a job? I would think your friendships would call for even more care, anyway."

"I had a heck of a day on the job," Joe blurted.

All three turned to Joe. "You did?" Pearl frowned. "But I thought you were home all day."

"Oh, you don't know all I was doing. I had more fun at work than I've had in years."

"What did you do, Joe?" Cameron asked. "Tell us about your day."

"Well, Bud and I got called out to an accident. We took the old red fire truck out, sirens blaring and everything. Tractor trailer full of beer overturned on the highway. Can you believe the luck?"

"But that wasn't—" Will started, then stopped when he felt Pearl's pointed shoe against his shin.

"Oh, everybody was fine. They didn't even really need us out there. So we just pulled up and had us a couple of beers while they got the road cleared off."

Will shifted in his chair. "But Joe, that's not—"

"That's a funny story, Dear," Pearl interrupted. "What happened next?"

"Well the tow truck driver was being a pain in the ass." Joe caught himself and put his hand to his mouth. "Oh, I'm sorry about that." He smiled, proud. "He was giving us a hard time. But I let him have it right back."

"But you weren't the one—" Will felt Pearl's shoe again and turned to her with a glare.

"You should go refill the water pitcher that you spilled, Mr. Phillips." She pushed the pitcher into Will's hands and pointed to the door. "Go on."

Will looked at Pearl, then Joe, then Cameron, who shrugged, and finally scooted his chair out and went into the kitchen, mumbling the whole way. "He didn't give the tow truck driver jack. That was me." He turned on the cold water and held the pitcher under it. "It wasn't even today. And we weren't out there with a fire truck."

"Of course you didn't have the fire truck."

Will jumped, nearly dropping the pitcher against the stainless steel sink.

"Pearl. Seriously. He's just making up stories and you and Cameron are eating it up like, oh, I don't know. What sort of food is like eating up stories?"

"I've no idea anymore. This new diet—sorry, lifestyle— Cameron has us on has my food brain all in a dither." Pearl reached around Will and turned off the faucet. "Probably squash. We're eating up Joe's wild stories like butternut squash."

"Whatever. That doesn't really sound like it. Eating them up like candy—even popcorn—would sound much more appealing."

"Right, but I think 'kale chips' would be about as far as Cameron would let us go."

"She's really not all that forceful, you know. She'll let you eat what you want. She's just responding to your interest."

"I know. I just find it easier to have someone to pin it on. And she's very accommodating that way."

Will blinked and decided not to take it any further than that. "Okay. Well, why are you letting Joe go on about a story you know is untrue?"

"Oh, Will." Pearl's eyes turned sad and she looked at the floor. Looking back up, she said, "Don't tell me you haven't seen it. You have to have seen it. I'd sooner believe Joe's malarkey than that."

"Seen what?"

"Joe. He seems to get…confused. Just sometimes. Not always."

"I thought it was the meds coming out of his hospital stay."

"I'd hoped so too, but it seems more persistent than that."

"You think he's—"

"Maybe. And anyway, I was reading up—"

"How do you have time to read up on anything besides fennel and liquid smoke?"

"I am an efficient woman, Will Phillips. We all are." She put her hands on her hips. "I know how to do my Googles."

"Googles?" Will winced. "That's a plural noun now?"

"And I can read about more than one thing at a time. There are people who say dementia should be treated like improv. So, instead of rebutting the person you do just like you would on an improv stage and walk into their reality with them. And instead of saying 'That's wrong!' you say something like you would to an improv partner, like 'Yes, and...'"

Will scowled. "But then he'll think his reality is correct."

"Don't be so self-righteous. It's not like his reality is saying he can fly off the roof with his papier-mâché wings and you need to keep him from killing himself. He's just telling us a story."

"Did he try to do that?"

"Do what?"

"Fly off the roof?"

"Heavens, how would I know? The roof is your territory." She smirked. "I've not been up there since this was my granddaddy's house."

Will opened his mouth to protest.

"Don't." Pearl put a hand on his arm. "Just think of it as exaggeration. A little hyperbole from a lonely old man never killed anybody." Pearl walked to the door and turned back as she pushed it open. "And maybe don't take him out onto the roof while he's here."

49

Joe went through the rest of the evening's meal with no further lapses in his grasp of details, no more tall tales or turning himself into a story's protagonist that he hadn't actually lived. Will wondered if it was still related to his medications and thought about calling Joe's doctor. Odds were good he'd be willing to talk to him, being Joe's son and all.

He decided to wait. Pearl was already keeping an eye on Joe and would surely let Will know if something needed attention. And besides. Who was Will to be pointing fingers, seeing as he was just now standing in the middle of the street between Pearl's house and Cameron's, Finn's leash in his hand, and having no earthly idea of how he got there, or why.

Aliens were always an option, of course, and probably at least as plausible as any other explanation at this point. He would like to go home and go to bed, maybe wake up to realize he had not been standing bewildered in the middle of the street after all. But he had Finn with him, and taking the dog up to his room was impractical. He'd have to explain to Cameron why he'd absconded with her dog (when he didn't have an answer to that yet). And bringing a dog into territory now, covertly, claimed by Emily could prove disastrous.

He had only one real option: take Finn home and maybe, in the process, Cameron would fill in enough gaps in his synapses that he'd remember what happened.

Finn had waited patiently for Will to finish his protracted mental processing and start walking again. The black Chevy pickup that had just turned off the highway onto their street, not so much.

Will jumped at the sound of the horn and screeching brakes, snatched Finn up from the ground and half trotted across the pavement to the curb. He scratched Finn behind the ears. "That was a close one, eh?" He looked the dog in the eyes. "How did we get here, little guy? Did I take you out for a walk, or was it the other way around?"

The dog stared back at Will, blinking slowly. He curled his tongue around and licked Will's hand.

"Okay then. We're done here." Will put Finn on the ground and stepped back, shaking his hand in the air like it had just touched a hot stove. He held it away from his body. "Pretty sure it must have been the other way around. I never volunteer for licking."

As they walked up the steps to Cameron's front door, Will looked down at Finn. Finn didn't look back up. "Not personal, you know. Licking is licking."

Finn let out a series of short barks as Will rapped on the screen door. "You're standing right here with me, Mutt. The whole bark-like-you're-standing-on-the-back-of-the-couch-looking-out-the-window thing is a little off."

Cameron opened the door, grinning. "There you two boys are!" She took the leash from Will's hand and reached down to rub Finn's head as he ran into the house. "You must have found all sorts of fun. You've been gone for ages."

"Ages?" Will raised his eyebrows.

"Well, in dog walking time, sure. Finn's little legs really only go so far, so fast you know."

"Oh, right. He's actually a little bit hard to keep up with."

"You're kidding."

"Well, no. He had us cruising around so fast I don't even know where all we went."

Cameron narrowed her eyes. "That might be more you than Finn."

"Possibly true." Will noticed his hand was still sticking out awkwardly from his side and held it up. "Hey, listen, can I borrow a little soapy water? Dog walking hazard."

Cameron snickered and opened the door wider. "Of course. It's the least I can do." She motioned down the hall and Will slipped into the bathroom and turned on the light with his elbow.

"Hey, do you want a beer or something?" Cameron called, when he had turned the water off.

"Do you have one?"

"Well, not exactly. You know me, just wine. But we could go to your place and get one."

Will looked at himself in the mirror, wondering if the dark circles under his eyes were always there or if it was the lighting in Cameron's bathroom. "Um, taking you up to my place right now, with Joe next door, is probably not the best plan. I'd really be good with a cold glass of water." For all he knew, he'd already had a few drinks.

He dried his hands and walked out to Cameron's living room. The walls were covered in dark oak paneling and the room was sparse, but tastefully furnished. There was a single painting on the wall, an abstract in deep reds and yellows, and this surprised him. Cameron seemed too practical, too ordered, to appreciate the mystery of an abstract piece of art.

"Who's the artist?" Will asked, stepping opposite the leather sofa to take it in.

"An old college friend." Cameron handed him a glass. "No one you would know." She looked away. "No one anyone would know."

"I see." Will took her evasion as a cue not to ask another question about the painting or the artist. "So," he said, clearing his throat and settling in at the end of the sofa. "Pretty good story how Finn got me to take him out for a walk, yeah?" He smiled, looking a little bit goofy, hoping Cameron would pick up where he left off. "Bet you never saw that coming."

Cameron sat down at the other end of the sofa and pulled a leg up under her seat. "No, I can't say I was expecting you to take Finn out. But after that dinner it was pretty much anybody's guess what might happen next."

Will looked around the room. "Whoo, boy. Yeah. Quite the mealtime. Pearl's going to stop inviting us all over, one of these days."

"She seemed happy enough."

"Did she?"

"You don't see it? It's all over her. Her face, her hands, her step. I think it's Joe."

Will looked at Cameron, then let his eyes fall to the floor.

"What is it?" she asked.

"It's just—" Will held up his hands and pulled one up to rub his neck. "I have to be honest with you. I don't really remember much about dinner."

"You don't remember dinner?" Cameron turned on the couch. "None of it?"

"I remember being in the kitchen with Pearl filling the water pitcher that was still mostly full." Will poked a finger into the threadbare spot on the knee of his Levis. "I remember I wasn't dressed to her standards. I don't recall what we ate, what we talked about, or how I ended up taking your dog for a walk."

Cameron tilted her head and looked hard at Will but didn't say anything.

Will looked at the floor between his feet, imagining the winding curves of the wood grain to be a small river on which he could float away.

"I think you need some sleep."

He let out a low chuckle.

"I'm serious," Cameron said. "If it were someone else, someone just going along, merrily enough in their normal little life, and all of a sudden couldn't remember a whole evening that happened less than an hour ago, I might think there was something to be concerned about with a sudden memory blackout. Even Joe, I'm a little concerned about. But you?" She clasped her hands together in front of her and brought her index fingers together into a point toward Will. "No. Not you."

Will looked up. "You have a strange way of offering comfort, you know?"

Cameron laughed. "I'm sorry. That wasn't really meant to be comforting. Not in the way you think, anyway." She lifted her glass. "I just mean that in your case I think there's a simple explanation and it's not particularly worrisome." She took a sip of water and set her glass back on the coffee table. "At least not long term."

"But we should worry short term?"

"No." She shook her head. "Not unless you don't take care of it." Cameron took a deep breath. "Look. You've had a heck of a couple of weeks. You just met Joe and started spending time with him. You just met a pretty girl and started spending time with her." She winked. Will blushed and looked away. "You've had to deal with Joe's crisis and trips in the middle of the night and then this Nina person running you ragged. You don't sleep. I just think you're exhausted. That has a way of catching up to a person."

"I'm just tired, you think." Will looked toward Cameron, his eyes not meeting hers but seeming to search the space behind her.

"I do think. Hell, I've just been along for a tiny bit of this carnival ride and I'm exhausted."

"I just need some sleep."

"Well, that and you need to resolve whatever it is with this Barbara person."

Will stiffened and tilted his glass back and forth. "Is that a thing with you?" He didn't look up.

"A thing?"

"This Nina person. This Barbara person. Is that another way of saying 'those people'? Or do you always refer to other women like that?"

"Other women? Like, besides myself?"

"What?" Will scowled. "What does that even mean?"

"It means if they are 'the other women' then you've made some sort of assumption about who I am."

Will paused and looked at the hole in his knee. "I didn't say 'the' other women." He brushed his palm against the soft wear of his jeans and his voice dropped, nearly inaudible. "I would never make that kind of assumption."

Cameron turned in her seat again and leaned forward.

"I'm sorry, Will. I didn't mean—"

Will's shoulder rolled up against his neck, sort of a one-sided shrug. His arm felt cold.

"You might be right, though," Cameron said in a near whisper. "Maybe they do feel like the other women."

50

"Did we just have a fight?"

Will pressed his palms into his knees and turned to look at Cameron, his eyes shadowed.

"Our first one, I think, if you don't count the hospital." Cameron smiled slightly and held his gaze. Will knew this look, her eyes darting back and forth searching, working so hard to find that tiny opening into his thoughts. He closed his eyes and held them that way.

He and Barbara did not fight. To fight assumes two independent actors in opposing positions, even when one is severely outmatched for skill or wit or prowess. With Barbara, there was no opposing position, only Barbara's. There might be an occasional disagreement, but even that would be brief, lasting only long enough to determine which point of view (Barbara's) would be of most benefit to Barbara. There was, at bottom, nothing to fight for, much less about.

Will did not know how this worked. The only time he fought with Barbara was the day she left. The day he did not follow her. The same day she called Nick Sartell and told him he should take her out to dinner.

As far as he understood, to fight meant only to lose. Never mind he had nothing of his own at stake anymore. Loss was gain, even if he didn't know it at the time.

His first and last fight with Barbara hadn't taken long. She'd made a rare visit to his apartment in Chicago. They usually only went to her loft. She even had a room for him to stay in there so he didn't have to go home late at night. She liked for him to take her to breakfast at the diner downstairs. That afternoon she barged in unannounced, not even knocking but using the key she'd insisted he make for her years ago, "just in case." She spent little time at his studio and complained from the minute she walked in the door until she left about everything from traffic (his place was on the same street as hers, just five blocks down) to the noisy neighbors (an elderly couple, one of them on oxygen, who sat in recliners and read books most of the day, never went out and baked him a loaf of bread once a week).

Will was lying on the sofa in jeans and rumpled white T-shirt reading Grisham's *The Pelican Brief* that had just come out. He jumped up when she came in, straightening his hair that was bent funny on one side from resting on the pillow. He brushed off the cushion where he'd been resting his feet.

"Barbara! I wasn't expecting—"

"Of course you weren't." She dropped her purse on a chair and raised her elbows in a gesture meaning he was to help her off with her coat. He hurried over and slipped the black wool with faux mink collar off her shoulders and folded it gently over a chair in the kitchenette. He paid five times as much for this one-room apartment in Chicago as he paid for the whole second floor in Pearl's house. Barbara often made a point to tell people that she could stand in the middle of the living room and touch every wall in the place. Even then, she'd say, he still needed to hire a housekeeper. It wasn't true, of course. There were at least two arm's lengths from the middle of the room to the walls. And he kept an immaculate space, a fact Barbara never accepted in small part because it bothered her that he kept his boots on indoors and in larger part because it made a better story to have people believing more in her graciousness to endure his slovenly existence.

"I was in the neighborhood and thought I'd pop in."

"In the neighborhood? We live in the same neighborhood."

"No, we don't." She put both hands up to shape her coif. "That's nothing but the propaganda of the wannabes who live on this side of the square."

"It's literally five blocks —"

Barbara held up her hand, making a single open and closing gesture like a duck's bill, holding her fingers together in the air, and Will stopped talking like he was supposed to. She crossed her arms over her chest and took a slow walk around the perimeter of the apartment. Will half braced for her to pull out a white glove.

"Aren't you going to ask why I came over?"

"You said you were in the neigh—"

She waved the back of her hand at him. "There's no talking to you some days. Typical man. I have to spell everything out."

Will rubbed his neck. "So—what brings you here?"

"I wanted to tell you some wonderful news!" Barbara stopped walking and turned toward Will, then grimaced slightly and turned back toward the bookshelf where there was a photo of her and Will and a half dozen high school friends taken at their last class reunion. "Do you have to be dressed like that?" She motioned over her shoulder.

Will spread his arms and looked down at himself, then up at Barbara's back. "Like what? I'm just sitting at home, by myself. I don't need a suit and tie for that, do I?"

Barbara turned around but kept her eyes fixed on the wall above his left shoulder. She made a quick, cutting motion toward him. "That, there. It makes me uncomfortable. Don't you have some long sleeves or something?"

He held out his scarred arm and looked at it, dark pink against the white of his T-shirt. It was strange to him how his face could feel so hot and his arm so cold and both so prickly at the same time. He rolled his shoulder back, feeling like it might detach from his neck, and walked silently behind the accordion partition that separated his sleeping area from the rest of the studio. He sat down on the bed, his whole body rigid and his eyes wide.

In all the years since he started himself on fire, Barbara had never mentioned it. Not once. She visited Will in the hospital every single day after it happened. She was at his side (or rather, let him be at hers) at every event through high school and college. Even now, as working professionals in the city, they went everywhere together. Most people considered them a couple. Others thought they were best of friends, almost like siblings. Those who were closest knew that wasn't quite it, though they didn't know quite what it was. In that moment on the side of his bed, Will wondered, for the first time, how they could be any of those things. How, when a person was standing right there when it happened, the person refused for years to ever talk about the trauma in which he could have lost his arm. How could they never talk about the day he thought he had died, or the awful days afterward when he had so deeply wished he did?

Now, suddenly, years later, Barbara is so uncomfortable with his scarred and misshapen arm that he has to put on long sleeves in his own house?

He reached up and loosened a blue plaid shirt from its hanger. He slipped his good arm in, opposite the way he usually got dressed, always wanting the scar side covered first. He stood in front of his mirror, staring at his upper body, T-shirt half tucked into his belt, shirt hanging off his left shoulder, mangled arm hanging limp on the right. He crossed the bare arm over his chest and flexed his bicep. He heard her teenage voice crooning in his ear. *You're afraid of a little fire.*

"Damn you, Barbara."

"Did you say something?" Barbara called from the living room. "Get your shirt on and come out here already. I have such good news to tell you."

Will realized that while Barbara had never said anything about the accident, neither had he. They had never talked about what happened. And why it did.

He left the shirt hanging off his left side and walked back into the living room, jaw tight. He caught Barbara's eyes and did not let go.

She waved her fingers at him like children running. "Come on, get that covered up."

"I'm working on it. But I didn't think you would be bothered by seeing it."

"Well, I most certainly would. What is wrong with you that you would think that?"

"You've never seen my arm, have you?"

"Don't be ridiculous. I've seen it a million times. I was there, remember? Before, during—and after."

"Yeah."

"Especially after. When nobody else wanted to be with

you. With *that*." She waved at his arm again and turned away.

Will stood still, making no effort to finish putting his shirt on. He wanted her to take a long look. He wanted to ask her, "Have you ever really looked? Up close? Ever felt the bumps and ridges and pits?"

He didn't ask. He never asked. He knew the answer even before Barbara rushed to the kitchen, heels clicking hard against the wood floor. She grabbed her coat. "I don't know what's the matter with you but you need to stop it. Stop coming at me with that thing."

Will remained still.

"Do you remember what you said right before my sleeve started on fire? Do you?"

She stared at him.

"Why can't you just be a man?" Will pushed his arm into the sleeve and began to button the front. "Do you remember that? Why I'm like this? Who made me this way?"

"Boys doing dumb boy things, that's what made you that way. You wanted to be just like them. Now get out of my way." She pushed past Will and threw open the door. She turned back in the hallway, her eyes fierce. "Don't call me later."

Barbara disappeared from the doorway and Will stood unmoving in the light shaft from the hall. His face didn't feel prickly any more. His shoulder relaxed. His arm felt warm.

Will opened his eyes. Barbara was gone.

Cameron, on the other hand, was still there, eyes still searching. He felt perspiration wicking into his T-shirt, which was now sticking to his skin on his back. His shoulder rolled and he closed his eyes again.

"Hey now," Cameron said, nudging his arm. "Don't go

away again. You're scaring me a little here."

He opened his eyes again, but kept his gaze toward the floor, certain that they had turned a cold gray. If Cameron were already disturbed at his affect, seeing his eyes drained of color would only alarm her further. He rubbed his neck.

"I, uh, need to use your bathroom."

"Didn't you just do that?"

Whether she asked as a matter of concern or curiosity hardly mattered to Will, who was feeling too overwhelmed in his own thoughts to be able to make such distinctions, or even care about them

"I drank a lot of water at Pearl's, okay?" he snapped, wishing he hadn't.

Cameron leaned away. This, Will noticed.

"Damn. I'm sorry, Cameron." He stood and wiped his palms, now clammy, on the side of his Levis. "I think you're right. I need to get some sleep." He walked slowly down the hall to her bathroom. He murmured, "Couple of weeks? It's been an unusual *month*."

Will closed the door behind him and ran cold water on his hands, staring at himself in the mirror. The dark circles were still there, maybe even darker than a half hour ago. He splashed water on his face and held a soft, golden yellow towel from the rack against his skin. He couldn't place the fragrance, a vaguely familiar one, but it enlivened him somehow. He dried his hands and peeled his now drenched T-shirt away from his body, flapping it and the plaid button-down over it in the air to try to dry it and his skin.

After a few minutes—or was it an hour?—he tucked his shirt back in and buckled his belt. He leaned on his hands against the sink and looked at himself one more time. "Go home, Phillips. Before you break something."

Cameron was gone when Will got back to the living room. His shoulders sagged as he started toward the front door. He heard water running in the kitchen and stopped. "Slip out quietly or go say goodnight?" he mumbled to himself. "What's the best option when a guy's been an ass? You should get out of here now, Phillips. You'll only make things worse." He clenched his jaw. "Probably," he argued back at himself. "But I can make them worse or let them get worse on their own." He turned, slowly, and walked to the kitchen, rubbing his neck and hoping Cameron had a soft spot for sheepish.

Will stopped in the doorway and put his hands in his pockets. Cameron looked up from the sink and turned off the water. She picked up a towel and dried her hands. Her face was inscrutable. "Feeling better?"

"Not exactly." He rubbed a toe against the tile floor. "Look, I'm sorry. Really. I don't know what happened."

She set down the towel and stepped toward Will. "You don't like to fight."

Will scowled. "Does anyone?"

"Well, some people like it, I suppose, when it gets them what they want. And there are others of us who, even if we don't actually like to fight, can at least appreciate the good parts."

"Good parts?" Will shook his head and stared at the floor. Barbara's voice echoed in his head.

Don't call me.

Cameron leaned forward and stood on her toes, her lips touching his. Will pulled back, covering his bottom lip with the top and rubbing a finger just below his mouth. He looked over Cameron's head toward the window under the sink.

"The good parts," she said softly. "Sometimes if a fight ends the right way, there are good parts."

He lowered his gaze to meet Cameron's eyes. She was smiling, seemingly more amused than put off by his reaction. "I'm not...familiar...with the good parts."

"Maybe you just need the opportunity to make the discovery, then."

"Good parts," he whispered, drawing in a deep breath and hoping to catch the scent of Cameron's skin again, just now connecting it with the fragrance of the yellow towel. "Is it required to fight first, to get to the good parts?"

Cameron squeezed his hand and stepped back, laughing. "Am I supposed to believe that you don't know how this works?" She looked up at him. "That I'm Dennison's most eligible bachelor's first?"

"Pearl hasn't told you?"

"Does Pearl know?"

"I figure everyone knows. My past relationships—or should we say relationship—was strictly look but don't touch."

"But that's been over for a long time, right?"

"It has. But smoke's got a way of sticking to your clothes."

"I *do* know." Cameron tipped her head and looked up at him again. "I've heard, though, that sometimes people get new clothes."

51

It was late when Will crossed the street to Pearl's house. He put his finger to his lip as he walked, as though needing to be sure it hadn't been taken from him. The porch light was on, but he didn't think he had the capacity for any more conversation so he walked around back to slip in through the kitchen.

As he turned back from quietly pressing the latch closed, he saw Pearl and Joe sitting in the breakfast nook playing checkers. He jumped.

"Damn."

"Language, Mr. Phillips?" Pearl smirked. "You left dinner so abruptly. Did my dessert not agree with you?"

Will opened his mouth to answer but Joe interjected. "You remember that Emily Dickinson line, Will? That one about how 'saying nothing . . . sometimes says the most.'" Joe rubbed his finger against his bottom lip.

"I know the one." He put his hands in his pockets. "I, uh, took Cameron's terrier for a walk."

"That's nice of you, dear." Pearl jumped a checker over Joe's and removed it from the board, adding it to the stack of black discs in front of her with a triumphant click. "Still, abrupt."

"Say nothing, Will. It's better," Joe said, looking over his remaining checkers and tapping a finger on his much smaller red stack.

Saying nothing, in this case, was indeed the simplest, whether it said little or much. The truth, not even told slant, was that he had nothing to say. He knew from his conversation on Cameron's sofa that right after Pearl served dessert, he'd excused himself, and Cameron, saying he had promised to take Finn for a walk, waving off Pearl's insistence that Finn was a dog without a wristwatch and wouldn't know the difference if he lingered a tiny bit longer. But wouldn't she want him to be the sort of man who keeps his commitments? He'd pressed her, maybe for the first time being able to turn Pearl against herself. Cameron, though she had no idea what he was doing, played along and told Pearl that she might be surprised at how perceptive to small slights Finn could be at times. So they left together and she sent Will off, leash in hand, with the dog for a walk.

None of it made any sense, and Will figured everyone knew it, especially Joe, who was kindly offering Dickinson's advice to plead the Fifth.

"It's been a long month—erm, day—and I'm going to turn in." Will motioned toward the stairs with his thumb. "Thank you again for supper, Pearl. Forgive me for being abrupt."

"Of course, dear." Pearl didn't look up from the board, her chin resting in her hand. "It's still your move, Joe."

Upstairs, Will went into Joe's room and took the Patsy Cline album off the turntable. He slid it onto the spindle of the player in his own room, then collapsed backwards onto his bed, boots still on, and tossed a tennis ball two-handed up and down from his chest toward the ceiling.

~

"I have a doctor's appointment in the morning."

Will turned his head to find Joe leaning against his door

frame. The tennis ball dropped and bounced away, rolling under the dresser. He slid his hands into his pockets and looked back at the ceiling.

"That's good, right?" he asked.

"Well I don't know if it's anything, except required." Joe smiled. "Condition of my release."

"Small wonder they didn't fit you with a GPS anklet."

"Maybe you're the one who needs that, after your disappearance tonight."

"I went for a walk." Will's jaw clenched. "With Finn."

"Yes. I know. But Cameron called after you didn't come back and wondered if you came here instead."

"With Finn?" Will grunted. "I hardly think so."

"Of course not. But you'd been gone a long while, it seems. Long enough to concern people."

Will closed his eyes.

"What's the doc want with you?"

"Recheck. See if I can stay out on parole." Joe straightened. "Hoping to get my driving privileges back."

Will thought for a moment about not being able to drive and his tone softened. "Think he'll let you?"

"Hoping so." Joe chuckled. "Really not the same to have to ask a girl on a date and then ask her to drive, too. Especially awkward if you have to tell her how to get to Inspiration Point. So to speak."

Will smiled. "Pretty sure she knows where that is. So to speak."

"Quite sure you're right. Even so. Kind of wipes out all the romantic nuance if you have to tell her to drive out there, instead of just easing your way while you talk, and just conveniently pulling into a little tree grove. You know what I mean?"

Will stretched his neck. "I'm really trying not to know what you mean, Joe."

"Anyway. Wondered if you might be able to drive me up to Colbyville. If the doc says I can drive, I'll just need a ride back to my place."

"Your place?" Will's voice rose and he looked at Joe. "You'd not need to come back here then, I guess, huh?" He looked back at the ceiling, swallowing hard against the lump that arrived altogether unexpectedly in his throat.

"Oh, I'll have to come back here. I'm pretty sure of that. Doc Wagner owes me one." Will turned his head just in time to catch Joe's wink. "I just need to get my truck and a few changes of clothes, maybe a book or two. And check on Archie."

"Sure. I can take you. What time is the appointment?"

"Eleven thirty."

"I'll pick you up at ten."

52

"Myrna, my dear." Joe tipped his head lightly as he and Will passed through the double doors to the hospital. "You're looking as lovely as ever."

The nurse turned back from the empty green wheelchair she was pushing down the hall. "Mr. Murphy. How nice to see you." She scowled at Will. "I see you brought your son with you again."

"My son?"

"Yes, Walt over there." She gestured in Will's direction.

"I'm not—"

Joe turned toward Will. "Oh, yes!" He smiled. "My son Will. He drove me in but I'm hoping the old man will give me my keys back today so I can get around without a chaperone." He grinned at Myrna. "If you know what I mean."

"I'm quite sure I do not." She tossed her head stiffly and started back down the hall with her wheelchair. "Doctor Wagner's office is to your left, down the clinic wing."

"Am I really such a burden to you, Joe?" Will asked.

"You? No. It's like I said, just having to ask for a ride everywhere."

"Well, hopefully Pearl and I don't have to take you around too much longer."

Joe lowered his voice. "If I'm honest, I'm not really sure a guy can feel safe riding with Pearl. After that whole thing with her ex, you know."

"Geez, Joe. She wasn't even in the car that day." Will stopped. "Wait. She told you about that?"

"Sure." Joe beamed. "We're open about everything."

"Everything? But—" Will poked Joe in the shoulder. "Does that mean you've told her how you pretend that I'm your son?"

"Oh, come on," Joe chuckled. "You think I would tell her about that?"

"You said everything."

"I did. All the skeletons. All our deep, dark secrets. Vices. Regrets. That stuff."

"Yeah. So why not about this next-of-kin charade?"

"That's not a deep dark secret from my past. That's just a present time legal practicality. And no one, including the hospital staff, actually believes it." Joe nudged him with his elbow as they walked down the hall. "Lighten up, Walt."

Will flinched as Joe picked up his pace. "I'm going to be late for my appointment."

~

"Had good Doc Wagner eating out of my hand back there, don't you think?" Joe held his head up as he turned the key in the lock and pushed open his back door.

"Right out of your hand. I'm surprised you didn't write out the prescriptions you wanted and just ask him to sign them."

"I thought about it. But it seemed like a bit too much. I got what I wanted..." His voice trailed off as he stopped at the top of the short steps into the kitchen, hands at his sides.

"Oh? And what was that?" Will stopped behind him, still on the stairs. He looked up. "Hey, you going in?"

"Uh, yeah. Sure." Joe stayed put.

Will took another step. "And by that you mean today sometime, right?"

"Sure. Yeah."

Still, Joe didn't move.

Will approached from behind and gently put a hand on his shoulder. "All the way, Buddy." He whispered in Joe's ear. Joe shuffled over a step, just enough for Will to slip in behind him.

He stopped, hands at his side, right next to Joe.

"What the—"

"Language," Joe mustered.

"Right."

The kitchen was clean. *Clean* clean. Trash bags gone, sinks and countertops emptied. Walls, floor, cabinets scrubbed to a sparkle.

"I uh—" Will stopped. "I uh—had no idea the cabinets were white."

"I uh—" Joe started. "I uh—sort of forgot that. But I guess they are."

"How did this hap—"

"Well, hello boys!" The kitchen door burst the rest of the way open and Archie nearly knocked Will off his feet. Midge stood midway up the steps behind them. "I saw your truck in the drive. Had no idea you were coming back today, but it's great to see you!"

The men snapped out of their stupor and Joe crouched down to greet Archie, scratching his ears. "There's my boy! Who's a good boy?"

Will stepped to the side and extended a hand to Midge to help her into the kitchen. "What happened here?"

Midge beamed. "I had a little spare time this week. Thought it'd be nice if things were tidied up a little before Joe got back." She glanced toward the dining room and her smile dropped just slightly. "I didn't get to all of it, 'course."

"Oh my heavens, Midge. This is amazing. Just this room." Joe stood to his feet and swallowed. "I don't even know what—"

"You don't need to say anything." She slipped her hands in her back pockets and thrust out her chest, proud of her work. "It was my pleasure."

"It hasn't looked like this since … "

"I know." Midge's eyes misted and she rested her hand on Joe's shoulder. "I know."

Will looked around the kitchen to avoid Joe's eyes, then turned and walked through to the dining room, which, as Midge had hinted, hadn't been touched since Joe had last been in his house. Years before that, more likely. Archie bounded through after him, nearly knocking him into the wooden table covered with Joe's flea market and liquidation sale treasures. Archie stopped short in the living room, in front of the sofa. He sniffed around, letting out some low murmurs before looking up at Will, eyebrows raised as only a dog can do.

The fur pile Will had seen before was gone and Midge had thrown a clean blanket over the cushions. There were a couple of rag rugs covering the bare floorboards and the bookcases had been dusted. Will remembered his first time in the house, Emily pacing back and forth, stepping around morsels of cat food scattered across the black and white keys. Even that had been cleared off, paw smudges wiped clean. Archie slumped to the floor with a grunt, dropping his head between his massive paws.

Will reached down and scratched behind his ears. "Hey, old boy," he said. "Change can be hard. But you'll grow into it." He stood up and straightened the blanket, pulling a corner over the sofa arm. "Never know. You might even start to like it."

Joe shuffled in behind Will and the dog, letting out a whistle. "Guess I'd been gone longer than I thought. Midge has been working hard."

"She has, Joe." Will hesitated, then sat down on the edge of the sofa, hands awkwardly resting on his knees. He tipped his head toward Joe's recliner. "Take a load off."

Joe eased himself into the chair with a deep sigh of contentment as his body leaned into the familiar spacious fit. He folded his hands over his belly and smiled at Will.

"It's good to be home."

"Is it?" Will raised his eyebrows.

"Well, yes. Of course," Joe said. "It's also good not to be home."

"What do you mean?"

"The comforts of home can be had in places that aren't home, Will." He strummed his fingers. "A guy just has to be open to new things. New places. New ways."

"Are you looking forward to getting back here?"

"I could be. I don't know that I need to be."

"Back here or looking forward to being back here?"

"Yes."

Will rolled his eyes, then looked away quickly.

"I saw that."

"I suppose you did," Will said. "Just once I'd like to talk

to you about something that could be straightforward."

"Would you?" Joe smiled. "I mean, you talk like you do. But it's pretty clear to anyone paying an ounce of attention that you favor anything but."

Will's eyes rolled again and he straightened. This time he didn't bother to look away.

"What do you want to do, Joe? Really."

"I want to finish the work Midge started. I want to build a library and get my books from Chicago. I want to sell the house. I want to take Archie for a walk."

Will stood up. "You want to *what*?"

"Take Archie for a walk." Joe smirked. "Or did you mean the part about the books?"

"The walk, Joe. Definitely I'm talking about the walk." Will paced the room, rubbing his neck.

"Okay. Let me get his leash. We can go right now." Joe pushed up out of the chair. "If you don't think you'll... get lost."

"Um, sure. I guess. I suppose Archie knows his way back."

~

The two men walked outside together, taking their time, with Archie just happy to be at Joe's side again. At the end of the sidewalk, Will paused and looked back at the house. "How long you been thinking to sell the place?"

"Oh, about ten minutes or so. Since right around the same time I saw my kitchen countertop." Joe bent over and snapped the leash onto Archie's collar. "Had forgotten what the house could be like with the right person—any person, really—caring for it."

"You don't think that person is you?"

"Clearly not," Joe said. "Look what's become of it under my care." He looked up at the clouds. "Millie was that person. It's time to let the house go back to her. Or someone like her."

"This is pretty sudden, Joe. And, um, big."

"Sure it is." Joe chuckled. "Some of us don't need years."

Will shot Joe a glance. "I'm sure you're not thinking of anything in particular."

"Oh, but I am."

They walked in silence for several blocks, except for the occasional encouragement for Archie to pull his nose out of someone's flowerbeds.

"What do you want to do, Will?"

Will kept walking.

"What do you want to do?" Joe's voice was patient, kind. But steady. Unrelenting.

"I guess I'll be helping you get the house ready to sell. Good timing. We're heading into our quiet season. Should have some extra time on my hands."

"Nice of you to offer. But that sounds like something *I* might want you to do." Joe tugged gently on Archie's leash. "But what is it *you* want to do?"

Will pushed his hands into his pockets and picked up his pace. "Don't know, Joe."

"You know this is untrue, yes?"

"Do I?"

"I believe you do."

"Why do I need to tell you what you already know?"

"Remember that whole thing about poets and naming,

Will. There's a lot of power in it." Joe stopped walking and brought Archie in close, bending to scratch his ears. "I want you to know the power of saying out loud what you want. You're terrified of it, so you refuse to say what you know."

"It's tiring, being with you."

"Imagine being me."

"I'd prefer not."

"Very well." Joe started walking again. Will stayed put under the shade of a tall oak on the boulevard.

You won't get what you want, Will. Not until you can just be a man.

Will balled his hands, still in his pockets. His jaw tightened. Joe was a good block ahead, walking on as though he wasn't even there.

He pulled his phone out of his pocket and tapped on his contacts, scrolling through. He stopped at Julian, Cameron, his thumb hovering over the green phone icon. His hand dropped to his side and he looked down the street again, Joe and Archie blurring against the trees.

Will looked back at his phone and scrolled on, his thumb stopping at Roberts, Barbara. He tapped open the contact and stared at the photo, a blonde glamour shot looking through him with an intensity that nearly folded him in half. He raised his thumb and hovered. The street was quiet, and the constant South Dakotan breeze had let up. With a deep breath, he tapped the tiny trash can in the upper right.

Are you sure you want to delete Roberts, Barbara?

Will stared at the question.

Are you sure...

The breeze picked back up, lifting his hair off his forehead… *you want to...*

He touched his finger to the screen.

Yes.

YES YES YES.

He tapped his phone again and again as if to remove any lingering traces of code that might bring her ice blue eyes back out of the device's storage.

Will slid the phone into his back pocket and wiped his hand on his jeans.

"Hey, Joe!" He called out, starting to jog toward his friend, a fading figure walking ahead with a dog.

"Hold up, old man," he shouted again. "Are you ready to head back to Dennison? There's something I want to do."

This book includes various references from or to the following companies, brands, and sources:

Double Indemnity, a film (1944) produced by Paramount Pictures; Tootsie Roll, a trademark of Tootsie Roll Industries; Wrangler, a trademark of Wrangler Apparel Corp.; Silverado, a trademark of General Motors LLC; Levis, a trademark of Levi Strauss & Co.; Hammond, a trademark of Suzuki Musical Instrument Manufacturing Co., Ltd.; "Hit the Road Jack" is a song written by Percy Mayfield; KMART, a subsidiary of Sears Brands LLC; Formica, a trademark of The Diller Corporation; Hamilton Beach; Toyota, a trademark of Toyota Jidosha Kabushiki Kaisha; F350, a trademark of Ford Motor Company; Chevy, a trademark of General Motors LLC; Dodge, a trademark of Chrysler LLC; John Deere, a trademark of Deere & Company; International, a short form of International Harvester, a trademark of MTD Products Inc.; Tahoe, a trademark of General Motors LLC; Dakota, a trademark of Chrysler LLC; Superbowl; Ranger, a trademark of Polaris Industries, Inc.; Twinkies, a trademark of Hostess Brands, Inc.; Styrofoam, a trademark of The Dow Chemical Company; *The Twilight Zone*, a television show (1959-1964) produced by Cayuga Productions in association with CBS Television Network; *The Price is Right*, a television show (1956-1965) produced by Mark Goodson-Bill Todman Productions, National Broadcasting Company (NBC), and American Broadcasting Company (ABC), (1972-present) (originally titled *The New Price is Right*) produced by Price Productions, Fremantle, Cinema Vehicle Services, Mark Goodson Productions LLC, Mark Goodson Television Productions and Mark Goodson-Bill Todman Productions; Barbie is a registered trademark of Mattel; Buick LeSabre is a car model (1959-2005) produced by General Motors; Hefty is a brand of household products owned by Reynolds Consumer Products, Inc; Eggo is a registered trademark of the Kellogg Company; Fisher-Price is a subsidiary of Mattel; *Dragnet* (1951-1959) a television show produced by Mark VII Ltd., (1967-1970) a television show produced by *Dragnet* Productions, Mark VII Ltd., and Universal Television (2003-2004) a television show produced by Wolf Films in association with Universal Network Television; Chicago Cubs an American professional baseball team based in Chicago, Illinois; ESPN Inc., a subsidiary of Disney Media Networks (a division of The Walt Disney Company) also owned by Hearst Communications; Bubs Daddy a registered trademark of the Hershey Company; Thermos a registered trademark of Thermos L.L.C. owned by Taiyo Nippon Sanso Corporation; Crocs a trademark of Crocs, Inc.; Pepsi is a carbonated soft drink manufactured by PepsiCo; The American Red Cross (ARC); Super 8 a registered trademark of WHG TM Corp; Ford Ranger (1983-present) a series of models produced by Ford; *Moonstruck* (1987) produced by Metro-Goldwyn-Mayer in association with Star Partners; *The Towering Inferno* (1974) produced by Twentieth Century Fox, Warner Bros., Irwin Allen Productions, and United Films; *Airport* (1970) produced by Universal Pictures, and Ross Hunter Productions; *Airport 1975* (1975) produced by Universal Pictures; *Airport '77* (1977) produced by Universal Pictures; *The Concorde... Airport '79* (1979) produced by Universal Pictures; *The Poseidon Adventure* (1972) produced by Twentieth Century Fox, Irwin Allan Productions, A Ronald Neame Film, Kent Productions, Inc.; *Jaws* (1975) produced by Zanuck/Brown Productions, and Universal Pictures; Chrysler a registered trademark of Chrysler LLC; *Sports Illustrated* an American sports Magazine owned by Authentic Brands Group; Brylcreem manufactured by Unilever; General Electric Company (GE) is an American multinational comglomerate; Emily Litella a fictional character created and performed by Gilda Radner; Denny's, a registered trademark of DFO, LLC; Random House, part of Penguin Random House, owned by Bertelsmann, also owned by Pearson LLC.; *Young Frankenstein* (1974) produced by Gruskoff/Venture Films, Crossbow Productions, and Jouer Limited; Toyota, a registered trademark of Toyota Judosha Kabushiki Kaisha; Hertz, a registered trademark of Hertz System, INC.; Motel 6, a registered trademark of Motel 6 Operating L.P.; CNN, a registered trademark of Cable News Network, Inc.; Folgers a registered trademark of The Folger Coffee Company; Mr. Coffee a registered trademark of Sunbeam Products, Inc.; Dickey, a registered trademark of Szerszen, and Czeslaw; Roper, a registered trademark of Whirlpool Properties, Inc.; Durango, a registered trademark of Chrysler LLC; Stetson, a registered trademark of John B. Stetson Company; Carhartt, a registered trademark of Carhartt, Inc.; Oprah's Book Club, a registered trademark of Harop, Inc.; Oreo, a registered trademark of Kraft Foods Global Brands LLC; Sam Adams, a registered trademark of BBC Brands, LLC; Bic, a registered trademark of Bic Corporation; Weber, a registered trademark of Weber-Stephen Products Co.; WD-40, a registered trademark of WD-40 Manufacturing Company; Fred Flintstone is a fictional character in *The*

Flintstones (1960-1966) produced by Hanna-Barbera Productions, and Screen Gems Television (a subsidiary of Columbia Pictures Corporation); Scotch, a trademark of 3M Company; McDonald's, a registered trademark of McDonald Corporation; Guess Jeans, a registered trademark of Guess? Inc.; Yiruma is a pianist; Pinterest, a registered trademark of Pinterest, INC.; Comic Sans MS, a typeface designed by Vincent Connare and released in 1994 by the Microsoft Corporation; Sharpie, a registered trademark of Sanford, L.P.; Volkswagen is a German automaker; New York Mets are a Major league baseball team based in New York City; Red Man a registered trademark of Pinkerton Tobacco Co. LP; Copenhagen a registered trademark of U.S. Smokeless Tobacco Company LLC; "The Wreck of the Hesperus" (1842) a poem by Henry Wadsworth Longfellow; Fiestaware a registered trademark of the Homer Lauglin China Company; Francie a registered trademark of Mattel, Inc.; Skipper a registered trademark of Mattel, Inc.; Stacie a registered trademark of Mattel, Inc.; Todd a registered trademark of Mattel, Inc.; *The National Enquirer* an American supermarket newspaper published by American Media, Inc. Lucky Charms is a registered trademark of General Mills IP Holdings I, LLC; Botox a registered trademark of Allergan Inc.; Camel a registered trademark of R. J. Reynolds Tobacco Company; Grand Prix a registered trademark of General Motors LLC; Lincoln Town Car a registered trademark of Ford Motor Company; Listerine a registered trademark of Johnson & Johnson; Buick Skylark a passenger car produced by Buick; Buick Lucerne a car produced by Buick; Buick a registered trademark of General Motors LLC; *The Princess Bride* (1987) a movie produced by Act III Communications, Buttercup Films Ltd., and The Princess Bride Ltd.; Rachael Ray a registered trademark of Ray Marks Co. LLC; Mary Groth a South Dakotan artist; Lysol a registered trademark of Reckitt Benckiser LLC; Fox News a registered trademark of Twentieth Century Fox Film Corporation; *The Huffington Post* a registered trademark of thehuffingtonpost.com, Inc.; Gummy Bears a registered trademark of Ferrara Candy Company; Hot Tamales a registered trademark of Just Born, Inc.; Coke a registered trademark of The Coca-Cola Company; *Better Homes and Gardens* a registered trademark of Meredith Corporation; "You Can't Always Get What You Want" a song by The Rolling Stones on their 1969 album *Let It Bleed*, Decca Records, and London Records; Windows a registered trademark of Microsoft Corporation; Bluetooth a registered trademark of Bluetooth SIG, Inc.; Jell-O a registered

Also from T. S. Poetry Press

The Joy of Poetry: How to Keep, Save & Make Your Life With Poems, by Megan Willome

An unpretentious, funny, and poignant memoir. A defense of poetry and a response to literature that has touched her life. I loved this book. As soon as I finished, I began reading it again.

—David Lee Garrison, author of *Playing Bach in the D. C. Metro*

On Being a Writer: 12 Simple Habits for a Writing Life that Lasts, by Ann Kroeker and Charity Singleton Craig

A genial marriage of practice and theory. For writers new and seasoned. This book is a winner.

—Philip Gulley, author of *Front Porch Tales*

Poetry at Work, by Glynn Young

We don't give ourselves enough time for poetry—at work or at home. If we did, our business life might be less stressful and more satisfying. We might find our work more rewarding. We might, as Young suggests, find the poetry at work.

—Scott Edward Anderson, Global Marketing Director, Cleantech at Ernst & Young, author of *Fallow Field: Poems*

Made in the USA
Monee, IL
11 November 2019

16646209R00307